PRAISE FOR *TIME AND REGRET*

"With fluid prose and a keen eye for detail, M.K. Tod takes readers on a decades-spanning journey of wartime loss, family secrets, and ultimately, redemption."

—Holly Smith, managing editor,
Washington Independent Review of Books

"Spiced with mystery and a spark of romance, *Time and Regret* is an immersive journey into one man's brave but terrifying slog through the killing fields of France and Flanders during World War I. Tod's prose brims with exquisite atmospheric detail, drawing the reader into an unforgettable story."

—Juliet Grey, author of the
Marie Antoinette trilogy

"*Time and Regret*, equally captivating and suspenseful, presents well-drawn characters who strive to resolve past mysteries and overcome present obstacles. M.K. Tod is an impressively gifted storyteller who creates relatable conflicts and believable dangers. Highly recommended!"

—Margaret Porter, author of
A Pledge of Better Times

"*Time and Regret* is something as rare as a treasure hunt with heart. Between the gritty trenches of World War I, the romantic allure of present-day France, and the cut-throat New York arts scene, M.K. Tod has spun a gripping family drama that delves deeply into the effects of war on the human soul and takes us on an intriguing journey of self-discovery. It is a book rich in hard-won wisdom and crucial historical insights, and Tod's perceptive voice leads us unfalteringly through some of the darkest chapters in human history to a very satisfying conclusion."

—Anne Fortier, author of *Juliet*

TIME
and
REGRET

TIME

and

REGRET

M.K. TOD

Text copyright © 2016 by M.K. Tod

Published by Lake Union Publishing, Seattle
www.apub.com

Amazon, the Amazon logo, and Lake Union Publishing are trademarks of Amazon.com, Inc., or its affiliates.

ISBN-13: 9781503938403
ISBN-10: 1503938409

Cover design by Laura Klynstra

Printed in the United States of America

To my children—Lesley and Greg, and Brian and Julia.

CHAPTER 1

March 1991

Divorce is a process, not an event. It takes months to unfold, a barrage of emotional ups and downs as denial is replaced by grief, grief by anger, and anger gradually eases into acceptance. To complete the process, Jim's possessions had to go, so every Sunday since early February, I had tackled a different room in the house.

At first, removing his things made me cry—the rainbow trout he caught at Medstone Lake, a baseball autographed by Mickey Mantle, a tennis racket from when he captained our college team, his collection of antique maps. But now the process felt more like scraping off successive layers of skin, raw and painful, a necessary prelude to life beyond marriage.

Jim had requested the divorce—*demanded* would be a better word—saying our marriage no longer worked. According to him, we had lost the magic—whatever that phrase meant—along with a host of other well-worn platitudes, like I would thank him for it in the future and he would always cherish what we once had. To say I had been shocked is a massive understatement.

Weeks of tears and pleading had achieved nothing, and finally, in an exhausted, robotic state, I had acquiesced. Lawyers and paperwork followed, and I'd turned my attention to reassuring our sons, Paul and Michael, that Jim and I loved them very much and would continue to be friends. Friends? Even being civil was a challenge, but I had become an expert pretender.

That morning I was in the attic surrounded by boxes, dressed in my comfort clothes—faded jeans, sneakers, and a baggy sweatshirt that said "GO THE DISTANCE." Jammed with discarded toys and furniture and objects that might someday prove useful, my attic is like many others, a space rarely visited, with dim lighting and cobwebs screaming "dust me" from the corners. I had been sifting through boxes since seven a.m., and now five garbage bags stood by the stairwell, making me think of doomed prisoners awaiting a last-minute reprieve.

The attic was the last room to clear. Once it was done, I could begin to look forward, but at that moment, sitting amid so much shared history, my feelings flip-flopped between numbness and nostalgia.

Get a grip, Grace. Finish these boxes. Then you're done, done, done.

The box in front of me contained a jumble of mementos, and I picked up a college yearbook dated 1970, idly turning the pages full of smiling faces. Beneath the yearbooks, two shoe boxes contained photos and I looked through a few, pausing first at one with Jim and me in a field of sunflowers and another on a beach at Mykonos. In both scenes, he stood behind me, arms wrapped around my waist. I put these two photos in a pile designated for further consideration.

In an accordion-style folder, I found cards congratulating us on Paul's and Michael's births, my graduation program, school reports, ticket stubs, a slim book of poems, and two bunches of letters held together by rubber bands. Frowning, I pulled out a twenty-year-old letter and began to read. *He did love me,* I thought, tears slipping down my cheeks. Releasing both rubber bands, I read them one by one, sighing over remembered incidents and pausing to wipe my eyes before gently placing each letter into a garbage bag as though laying a corpse to rest.

I got up and looked out a tiny window at the street below, where my neighbor was walking her dog in the rain, the dachshund waddling along, chest barely clearing the puddles gathered on the sidewalk. I wasn't the first person to experience divorce, and I wouldn't be the last, but I had never imagined *being* divorced, the pain of starting over, the feeling of rejection, the twist of shame when I glanced at my ringless finger, and a still-bruised soul. Thunder rumbled in the distance, followed by lightning that flickered across the sky. A god-awful day for a god-awful task.

Cross-legged on the floor once again, I lifted a metal tackle box onto my lap. A rusty clasp held it closed, the kind that required a strong thumb to release the catch. I pressed hard to no effect, then pressed again with both thumbs. "Stupid thing," I muttered. I shook the box. *Doesn't sound like tackle gear.*

Grumbling, I traipsed down two flights of stairs to the kitchen, where I kept a few tools in what was referred to as the junk drawer. No sign of my boys, which wasn't surprising for a Sunday. Back in the attic, with a hammer in one hand and a screwdriver held against the clasp with the other, I banged hard. The lid popped open.

"What on earth . . . ?" I said.

The smell made me wrinkle my nose, reminding me of the time our basement flooded while we were on vacation and the weeks required for the odor to disappear. On top was a gray belt with a silver buckle. The items beneath were equally strange: two brass buttons adhering to bits of gray cloth; a picture of four soldiers; a tattered envelope marked *JANE*; a hand-drawn map; a letter with a return address in London; a magazine dated 1980; and four small notebooks tied together with a ribbon. At the very bottom were three bullets. Astonishing.

A memory surfaced: a summer day when my grandparents had come for dinner and my grandfather had brought along a battered tackle box. Must have been eight or nine years ago. I remember wondering why he wanted to store something like that at our house, but Grandpa had not explained and the boys had been running around causing havoc, so the moment to ask had passed. Jim must have put it in the attic, but why had Grandpa left these particular items at our house? How very strange.

The envelope marked *JANE* contained a series of letters written from a place called Longuenesse, the first dated January 12, 1918. Given some of the details described, Jane must have been a nurse, but was she a friend of my grandfather's or someone more significant? The other envelope contained a letter from a man named Alan Butler, and referred to healing wounds and dreadful English weather. It closed with the words "get as many of those bastards as you can."

On the back of the photograph were the names Pete, Martin, Bill, Michel, and the date, May 1915. Four young soldiers looking keen and energetic, arms around one another's shoulders as if huddling to hear the quarterback call the next play. Martin was my grandfather. There was no mistaking his angular face and the shape of his eyebrows, asking a question even in repose.

The map, full of squiggles, arrows, and strange notations like *FB4* and *3.C.1*, revealed nothing, and the magazine was in French, an art magazine of some sort. After removing the ribbon from the notebooks, I opened the one on top, and a piece of paper slipped out.

I rocked back on my heels. A box full of curious mementos and a strange note from my grandfather—the man who raised me and who died almost ten years ago.

> *4/3/72*
> *To my dearest Grace, read carefully. I never should have taken them.*
>
> *Love always, Grandpa*

CHAPTER 2

May 1991

My grandfather's baffling note and the contents of the tackle box pursued me everywhere: to the grocery store and the dentist; to meetings at work and rush-hour trips home; while standing in the shower and washing dishes after dinner. Everywhere.

Grandpa's war diaries—the notebooks he left behind—were both fascinating and disturbing. At the outset, he was keen and ready to serve, but soon the details became gruesome as men under his command died or suffered wounds so terrible he thought they should have died. As the months and years unfolded, he wrote about the senselessness of it all, furious that military leaders treated soldiers as little more than ammunition. He wrote about meeting my grandmother and the deaths of everyone he cared for. In the end, he was crushed by despair.

I went to the library and researched World War I. To understand the experience of those on the front lines, I read accounts of that war's appalling reality and the physical and mental trauma soldiers suffered. I found military maps and looked in vain for markings such as those my grandfather left on his map. I studied uniforms of German, English, and Canadian soldiers, peering at belts and buttons. Yet nothing brought me any closer to answering the question that plagued me: What had Grandpa taken that was so important he left a secret box of clues behind?

Read carefully. I never should have taken them. As Grandpa directed, I had read them carefully, not once or twice, but three times. The diaries revealed no overt clues to suggest a secret message. And what might he have taken? Surely not the belt and buttons or the bullets. I couldn't see how such items would have prompted deep regret. Could Grandpa have been referring to taking the lives of German soldiers? In over three years he must have killed many Germans, but that was in the line of duty. Regret? Yes. But not the kind of regret his note implied.

One evening, Paul found me poring over a map of France, marking locations mentioned in the diaries.

"You're obsessed, Mom. Why don't you just go to France and visit those places?"

I would have hugged him right there and then, but he was fifteen and at that stage where his mother's affection was decidedly uncool, so I simply smiled. "You're absolutely right, sweetheart. That's exactly what I should do."

The next day, I called a travel agent, and the following Saturday, I went to see my grandmother.

After my father died and my mother fell apart, I lived with Grandmama and Grandpa from the age of five to twenty-three. Perhaps I was a contrary child, or perhaps looking after a child in your fifties and sixties was too taxing; either way, Grandmama and I were often at odds, and now that she was ninety-two, grumpiness was her daily companion. I tried not to take it personally.

"I cannot comprehend why you're going, Grace," she said now. "What on earth do you expect to find over there?" Grandmama waved one hand as though banishing a servant, a gesture that had become increasingly imperious as she aged. Despite the promises of expensive cosmetics, age spots dotted her hands and face.

We were sipping tea in the living room of her Upper East Side apartment, a room filled with traditional furniture and a collection of art featured on more than one occasion in *ARTnews*. Although New York had been her home for seventy years, my grandmother retained a distinct English accent. I kept my voice calm.

"I just told you, Grandmama. I obtained a copy of Grandpa's war record, and I want to visit the places where he served. And besides, I need a break."

"Why do *you* need a break?" She tapped her cane on the Persian rug for emphasis.

I took a slow breath and lifted the Wedgwood teapot, which always reminded me of the year my grandmother insisted on new chinaware. Nothing but Wedgwood would do, and Grandpa had complained about the cost for months. "More tea?" Grandmama shook her head. "Divorcing Jim has been hard on me. With the boys and my job and everything else, I'm worn out. I need a break. Simple as that."

"And at the drop of a hat, you're going off. Who will look after the boys? You cannot possibly leave them for four or five weeks."

When I first hatched this plan, the boys had been my primary concern. However, their reactions were enthusiastic, Paul's in particular; my sensitive child seemed to know the trip would be good for me. Michael had called it awesome, his favorite word for anything significant.

"The boys are fine with the idea, and I've spoken to Jim. He's pleased to have them until school ends, and then they'll be at camp for two weeks. Afterward, they'll stay with him another week or so until I return."

"Well, your mother and I need you."

Was that her usual grousing or was something else implied? I decided to ignore the edge in her voice. Grandmama often brought up my mother, who had lived in an institution since the year after my father died in a plane crash.

"Mother hardly knows me anymore."

"But I need you. You're being selfish. It's not becoming."

My uncle had died when he was two years old, and Grandmama had had no other children. I was an only child. In the past, such an accusation might have caused me to waver, but I held firm. Grandpa's puzzle was an unexpected gift, one that deserved close attention. I chose not to mention the contents of the tackle box, particularly the diaries, or ask if she knew what my grandfather had taken. If Grandpa had wanted her to know, he wouldn't have left the box at my house.

France shone like a distant beacon. Following Grandpa's path would lead me in the right direction.

Emotional health was the other reason for an extended vacation. Beyond the grief of losing my marriage, I felt burdened by people and chores: my mother and grandmother, Paul and Michael, work responsibilities, financial matters, and the myriad details of running a household. I was tired of putting the needs of others ahead of mine. If that was selfish, so be it.

My best friend, Joan Patterson, called the trip a divorce honeymoon. My boss at Colonial Insurance had been apoplectic.

"You can't possibly leave now," he'd said when I'd asked for time off. "You're in charge of marketing. The merger is almost finalized, and your role is critical. If we don't get enough synergies in marketing and sales, the board will be down my throat."

"But you know nothing much will happen in July, Rick. Too many people on vacation. Charlotte and Larry have everything under control and I'll return well before August. You know I've never taken more than a week at a time in all the years I've been here." I'd handed him a copy of my itinerary. "If you really need me, you can leave a message at one of these hotels."

And now I gave a similar response to my grandmother. "You'll be fine for a few weeks. Philomena comes every day, and she'll do your errands if you need help. You have my itinerary, and I've written out the exact numbers you need to dial plus the time difference. You can call me whenever you want, and I'll call you once a week."

My grandmother harrumphed, which I counted as a small win, then cleared her throat in an exaggerated fashion.

"Well, I suppose I'll just have to manage on my own."

PERSONAL DIARY

MARTIN DEVLIN—19th BATTALION,

4th BRIGADE, 2nd DIVISION

February 5, 1915

Enlisted today. A whole mess of forms to fill out. Looks like I'm signing my life away. Guess I shouldn't joke about that. Went down with Bill Jackson, who's been chomping at the bit to get in the fight. Last September, everyone thought the war would be over in a few short months. Reality is somewhat different. Mother won't be happy to hear the news, but I feel duty bound. If we don't stop the Hun, who will?

March 1, 1915

My battalion has gone to the exhibition grounds for training. I'm all kitted out with uniform and insignia but won't get my 2nd lieutenant stripes until I'm officially commissioned. Must be more than two thousand men here. I share a tent with three cadet officers. Michel Diotte speaks French and

English and is a good sort, Pete Van Leuven is second-generation Canadian of Dutch heritage, and then there's Bill. We're all fast becoming friends. Mornings are regular training, and afternoons are officer training. I prefer the practical stuff of mapping, communications, artillery, and rifle practice. Drills and marches are a necessary evil. The army emphasizes order, and this applies to all things, from the precise angle of a salute to the fold of a blanket. Mother would be proud.

March 22, 1915

We've just heard the news about action near Neuve Chapelle. A win but one with horrible casualties. Can't help thinking that I will soon be there. I wonder if I will distinguish myself, or perhaps merely getting through it will be enough. My friends don't talk about this sort of thing much, though I sense more intensity than before.

May 23, 1915

After two days of unexplained delays, we are finally on board the RMS Royal Edward. She used to be a passenger ship but seems sturdy enough, powered by three steam turbines that shudder and bellow like a caged beast. Captain Butler says our ship is also carrying ammo and small arms in addition to more than 1,000 men. Conditions are very crowded.

May 26, 1915

The fleet has assembled. It's a massive thing with more than 21 ships plus battle cruisers to offer protection as we cross the Atlantic. Communication between ships is prohibited, only orders from the flagship, which points to the seriousness of our endeavor. Portholes are darkened at night. We travel at the speed of the slowest vessel, rarely more than ten knots. Bill and I were on deck as we left Newfoundland behind in the setting sun while up ahead a full moon rose. Rather beautiful except when you consider our purpose.

May 31, 1915

Rough days at sea and drenching rain. Many down with seasickness. Waves are high and occasionally shoot our ship forward like a canoe riding the rapids, so we are making good time. I never realized the enormity of the ocean. Captain says we will soon be in the danger zone where German subs patrol. Today the guns are fully manned on deck just in case. Everyone is on alert.

CHAPTER 3

June 1915

The ship's siren jerked him awake. Bells began to clang, sharp and insistent. Beyond the porthole, all was black, water indistinct from sky. Martin Devlin tossed aside his blanket and rolled off the bunk.

"What do you think's up?" he said as he grabbed his shirt and began fastening every other button.

"Another drill, no doubt," said Bill Jackson.

"At two a.m.?"

"Keeping us on our toes, Dev. Keeping us on our toes." Dev was the nickname Bill had used since they were ten years old. "You know the saying—never be caught below when there's danger at sea."

Martin pulled on khaki pants, thrust his feet into his boots, and grabbed a life jacket. "See you up top," he called over his shoulder before rushing along the corridor and down to the lower deck where his platoon slept. Time was critical.

"Shake a leg, Murphy. Finnegan, where's your life jacket? C'mon, men. Hurry up. Muster stations in less than ten minutes."

"Jeezus, Lieutenant. It's the middle of the night."

"No point in complaining, Private. You'll have your beauty sleep later. Get a move on, boys. Anyone missing?"

A straggly line of men stood in front of Martin, some with uniforms in disarray, others yawning, tufts of hair protruding from beneath their caps. Bells continued to clang. Beyond the cabin came the rumble of boots and muffled voices.

"Where's Burton?"

"Here, sir." A baby-faced soldier straightened up. "Adjusting my puttees, sir."

After daily drills, organizing men to muster stations was a well-ordered process. Almost routine. Martin checked his watch. Three minutes left. He signaled his platoon forward.

As soon as they reached C deck, he knew it was no ordinary drill. Instead of carefree comments and easy smiles, senior officers looked grim, and Butler waved his arm like a policeman herding unruly hooligans. More alarming was the sight of men loading the big guns.

"Is everyone in position, Devlin?"

"Yes, sir." Martin raised his eyebrows.

Captain Butler motioned his lieutenants, Martin, Pete, Michel, and Bill, forward. "The *Scandinavian* is under fire. If you look to starboard you might see the flash of an explosion. Ship's commander is in touch with control. He expects to take evasive action, so all men will remain at muster stations until further orders. No smoking. Keep your platoons quiet and calm."

"Captain, will—"

"That's all I know." Butler turned on his heel, crossed the deck to an open doorway, and thumped down the stairwell.

Martin rejoined his men. He could almost taste their fear. A flash erupted in the distance. Cool night air slipped down his neck.

He took a breath and exhaled slowly. "Captain says we're to remain quiet and calm. Absolutely no smoking. Everything's under control, and I'm depending on you to follow orders. Keep your life jackets on and fastened at all times. As soon as I know anything else, I'll tell you."

Sirens and bells ceased, the ensuing quiet full of sound: waves splashing against the hull, pennants snapping in the breeze, engines growling, men breathing. Martin crouched low like the rest of his platoon. Nearby, Michel placed a hand on someone's shoulder, and Pete tucked a cigarette behind his ear. Bill stood at the railing. The ship veered left, rocking like a bobbing cork.

Oil mingled with the tang of sea air. A machine gun locked into place with a distinctive snap. The ship turned right.

For more than three hours, RMS *Royal Edward* zigzagged, randomly changing direction and speed, and it was almost five a.m. before they were dismissed, bleary-eyed with fatigue.

At breakfast, Butler reported that all other ships in the convoy were safe. "Brigadier says the *Scandinavian* suffered minor damage. They think it was a U-boat caught off guard."

"Was anyone else attacked?" Martin asked.

Butler shook his head. "They launched a few torpedoes and disappeared. Very strange. Good thing our escort will soon be here."

After a further four jittery days on board, Martin was eager to disembark for a few hours in Southampton before crossing the channel to France. All that morning, soldiers crowded the exit ramp, jostling one another, shouting cheerful greetings or times to rendezvous. Officers remained on board until all others were accounted for, so it was not until eleven that Martin left the ship with Bill Jackson, Michel Diotte, and Pete Van Leuven. For six hours, they were free from responsibility.

"What shall we do, fellows?" said Michel as they stepped on shore.

"That's easy," Martin said, "food, beer, and women."

Pete laughed. "Not sure we can find any women. But I am sure we'll find plenty of food and beer."

After months of training, Martin and the others stood tall, spines perfectly aligned beneath brawny shoulders and tucked chins, each man capable of one hundred push-ups and of marching for miles with a full pack. They could assemble a rifle in record time, knew the rudiments of Morse code and the theory behind more than twenty attack formations. Already close friends with Bill prior to enlisting, Martin now included Michel and Pete as friends he expected to depend on in battle.

Beyond the arch bearing Southampton's coat of arms, were cobbled streets along which medieval houses blended with newer buildings where shops and offices stood behind boldly painted doors. Soldiers from England, Australia, New Zealand, and India crowded the sidewalks, spilling out of the pubs they passed.

"God, it's great to be on land." Bill's grin stretched wide as he walked with a swagger. "Food first?"

"Suits me, as long as we can get a drink." Pete lifted an imaginary glass.

"I never thought getting off ship would feel so good. Did you see Spike?" Michel grimaced.

"Sick as a dog the whole way. Must've lost ten pounds," said Bill. "Thank God I sailed with my father every summer."

Martin nudged Bill. "Check that out."

Four heads turned to look across the street at a shop called Baltrey & Sons, where china and household items were displayed in one window and linens in the other. A woman had just left the store, and the men stared openmouthed, not only because she was beautiful but also because she was dressed in trousers, cinched jacket, and leather boots. Ignoring the looks she attracted, the woman mounted a motorcycle leaning against a lamppost, released its kickstand, revved the engine, and roared off.

Bill whistled under his breath. "Damn. Never seen anything like that."

"Well, gentlemen, no sense in gawking. She's not coming back," Michel said.

By late afternoon, they'd explored the main streets and visited several pubs, and as they returned to the ship, Bill and Pete sang "Keep the Home Fires Burning."

"Cigarettes, toffee, newspapers." The squawk of an old woman greeted them just outside the city gate. "Get 'em before you sail."

She wore a tweed jacket and a straw hat with a rose pinned on the front. Around her neck was a strap attached to a tray containing goods for sale, and beside her was a basket full of newspapers. Martin dug into his pocket for a few coins and took the newspaper she offered. Sale completed, the woman turned away, calling out to another group of soldiers. "Cigarettes, toffee, newspapers. Get 'em before you sail."

Just before nine p.m., the ship's engines came back to life, throbbing below deck like purring lions. In the officers' mess, Martin lingered over his newspaper, listening to glasses and plates vibrating in the galley next door. The headlines spoke of war:

BRITISH SUB SINKS GERMAN TRANSPORT. FRENCH CAPTURE TRENCHES AT SOUCHEZ. BRITISH ADVANCE AT GIVENCHY. TURKISH ATTACK AT GALLIPOLI. ZEPPELIN RAID ON LONDON.

He was used to the back-and-forth of battle reporting; one day the Allies made progress, the next day Germany or Austria held the upper hand. A single day meant nothing to overall progress; however, they all knew France and Britain were in trouble.

Still unable to sleep at two a.m., Martin found a quiet spot on deck and watched seagulls hover above the churning wake. Stars pricked the night sky, oblivious to the world's unfolding drama.

CHAPTER 4

June 1991

I left for France on the fourteenth of June, the day the space shuttle *Columbia* landed back on earth with three female astronauts on board—a positive omen for my trip, I thought. The flight was smooth, and after clearing customs and retrieving my bags, I drove northwest in a rented Renault from Charles de Gaulle Airport to Le Havre at the mouth of the Seine where my grandfather's ship had docked after crossing the channel. Honfleur followed Le Havre and then Hazebrouck, a stopover en route to his first trench deployment. From there, I drove farther north and stayed at a comfortable hotel in Ypres, a Belgian town that was the base for more than one epic battle during World War I.

After two days spent exploring Ypres and Passchendaele, places where unbelievable carnage took place, I drove to Bailleul, a town perched on a sweeping rise of land. By ten a.m., the heat had gathered, wispy clouds marking the horizon, crows squawking from a nearby tree. My trip to France was supposed to be a vacation, and six days of introspection amid the remnants of war had left me feeling morose, so I was taking a tour that morning with others for company.

The tourist office was in the central square. And that was where I saw him, the man with the straw fedora, a man I had first noticed on the ferry to Honfleur, when he'd taken a picture and then leaned against the railing as the boat gathered speed. I was almost positive the same man, minus the fedora, had also been in Hazebrouck, where I visited a replica of a casualty clearing station. A cold prickle crawled up my back.

I studied his appearance: middle-aged, belt underscoring a thickening chest, eyes concealed by sunglasses, biceps the size of my thighs. When he raised his head, I looked down at the tour brochure.

It can't be another coincidence. Or can it? Why would anyone be following me? I have nothing to hide and nothing of any real value. I shook my head to relegate the notion of being followed into the wild-imagination bucket where it belonged.

A petite woman holding a clipboard emerged from the tourist office.

"Good morning, ladies and gentlemen. I am Juliette Devere, your guide to historic Bailleul." She nodded at a few of us before continuing. "On our tour today, we will visit the Grand Place, the town hall, our famous belfry, and Maison de la Dentelle—the Lace House. Then we will travel a few kilometers to see our cemetery and memorial for the war. This is acceptable, yes?" Heads bobbed in agreement.

"*Alors*, I will begin. This area was originally settled in Roman times, however, Bailleul was officially designated a town in the twelfth century."

As Juliette spoke of the families who owned the land and the battles that occurred hundreds of years ago, I glanced again at the man wearing the fedora. He seemed to be listening attentively.

"During the Great War," Juliette continued, "more than ninety percent of Bailleul was destroyed, yet today we see it exactly as it was thanks to the determined efforts of our town leaders." Our guide beamed as though she had been personally responsible for this feat. "The belfry first, *mes amis*."

Juliette pointed across the cobblestone square lined with redbrick buildings toward the town hall, an imposing structure with a crenelated turret at one end and a belfry at the other. The French flag hung limply at the main entrance.

A woman with sensible shoes sauntered beside me. "Are you enjoying France?" she said in an English accent.

I turned my head and smiled. "Very much, although it's been less than a week."

"What brings you here? Most tourists never get to northern France, given the allure of Paris and the famous wine regions."

"I'm looking at World War One sites," I said, watching the man out of the corner of my eye. "My grandfather served in France, and I came to see where he had been."

"Sounds like me," she said, "but in my case, it's my father who served. I never knew him. He died in 1916, when I was two. My name's Pamela, by the way."

"Grace Hansen," I said. "From New York. Lovely to meet you, Pamela."

"New York is a wonderful city. My husband and I went there in 1985. But you don't sound like a New Yorker."

I laughed. "My English grandmother made sure of that. I had to pronounce my *r*'s and my *ing*'s. When I was young she would say, 'It's coffee, Grace, not *cawfee*.' Or dog, not *dawg*, or here, not *heah*. Drove me nuts. Even now she complains about the way Americans speak English."

Juliette called for our attention. "We are going to climb to the top. Many stairs, ladies and gentlemen, so if anyone feels unable to do the climb, please wait here. The rest may follow me."

She unlocked a wrought-iron gate and swung it aside so we could pass. Beyond the vestibule, stone steps led upward, winding around so many times I lost count. The walls and slit windows and the odor of damp cold conjured up a sense of long ago, and I imagined the clatter of soldiers' boots and the clang of swords as men fought their way up the tower. When we reached the top, I was out of breath.

"And here we are," said Juliette. "Let me explain a little. Belfries were built as watchtowers." She continued with a brief history lesson, then said, "If you look west, you see the spires of Hazebrouck, and looking north, you see Belgium. Ypres is just ten miles away, so you will understand why Bailleul was often threatened during the Great War."

While one of our group asked a question, I gazed at the land spreading in all directions, splotches of green in a multitude of shades mingling with pockets of trees and occasional bursts of reddish brown suggesting fields left fallow for the season. Roads meandered, each intersection marked by a cluster of houses surrounding a church steeple. A ridge embraced the southern horizon. Fedora Man stood a few feet away, seemingly absorbed in the same panorama.

A little later, as we walked to the lace museum, Pamela explained that her husband had passed away a year ago, and she had made a spur-of-the-moment decision to take a trip to the battlefields of World War I.

"Time to get on with life," she said. "I have my father's records, and I know he died near Ypres. My children think I'm slightly bonkers to have come on my own." She chuckled.

"No one understands why I'm here either, except my best friend, Joan. My ex-husband definitely thinks I'm crazy. Calls it a waste of money. Not that how I spend my money is any of his business. And my grandmother is annoyed with me."

"Was it her husband who served in the war?"

I nodded. "You might think she'd be pleased at my interest. But instead, she's concerned about herself. I suppose I shouldn't be surprised." I glanced at Pamela. "Sorry. You don't want to hear about my family problems."

"All families have problems," she said. "Human nature, I suppose."

"Perhaps we should talk about something else. Do you see that man over there with the straw fedora?" Pamela nodded. "Well, he keeps looking at me."

"That's not surprising. You're a good-looking woman."

I smiled to acknowledge her compliment. "I know this sounds crazy, but I think he might be following me. This is the third time I've seen him."

Pamela pursed her lips. "Surely not. Lots of men wear hats like that."

"I suppose they are rather common," I said. "Well, maybe you're right."

But I was almost certain she was wrong.

CHAPTER 5

June 1991

After Bailleul, I drove to Armentières, brooding about the man who might or might not be following me. He had left after the tour, making no attempt to speak to me, and I'd watched him amble down the hill until all I could see was the top of his hat. Had I let my imagination run wild? Grandmama would have said so; however, the notion of being followed refused to budge, and on my return trip to Ypres, I checked the rearview mirror so many times I was probably a danger to others on the road. When I arrived at Hotel Fleurie, I retreated to my room, hoping its restful green-and-white décor would soothe my worries.

Before going down to dinner, I called my sons. Michael's chirping voice and Paul's deepening grumble eased my growing apprehension. Stories about exams and end-of-school activities dominated, and I made only the occasional comment required of significant news. They failed to ask about my trip, and I chose to keep silent. Appalling wartime conditions were an unsuitable topic for boys of twelve and fifteen, although it occurred to me that Paul was only three years younger than many who had fought and died, some of whom were buried in well-tended cemeteries or commemorated in memorials dotting nearby hills and valleys.

After our conversation, I went down to the dining room, where fragrant smells of garlic and herbs and the unique ebb and flow of French greeted me.

"What do you desire tonight, madame?"

I glanced up to see Madame Thierry, the owner of Hotel Fleurie, in a blue dress and an apron the color of daffodils. She pushed a curl behind her ear and wiped her hands before pouring me a glass of wine.

"Sauté de veau chasseur, s'il vous plait, madame."

My command of French was limited, coming as it did from two years of high school classes, but I felt I should try. Who could resist the classic veal dish prepared with tomatoes and mushrooms and white wine? Madame Thierry disappeared, and I returned to my reflections.

Ypres had proven convenient for visiting several towns and villages mentioned in my grandfather's diaries. Each stop offered glimpses of French or Belgian tradition: churches with arched windows topped by tracery, houses whose intricately curved gables seemed straight out of fairy tales, remnants of medieval walls and turrets, and town squares hosting weekly markets full of colorful vegetables and oozing cheeses, freshly baked breads, and local specialties.

Wherever I stopped, I checked Martin's diaries. I thought of him as Martin now, not Grandpa, like a character in an unfolding story rather than a man I had known for more than thirty years. Having read the notebooks three times from beginning to end, I was familiar with the entries, yet I felt the need to honor his service at every opportunity. I now knew Jane was Martin's sister—a sibling whose existence had never been mentioned—and Alan Butler his captain for much of the war. The reason for including their letters in the tackle box remained a mystery.

A month after I announced my trip to France, Grandmama had produced a photo of Martin taken before he went overseas. The picture showed a man with wavy hair and a narrow frame, his face angular rather than handsome, as though waiting for him to grow into its contours. He had been twenty-one, far from the man he would become.

On the back, someone had written *Martin—May 1915—19th Battalion, 4th Brigade, 2nd Division.*

Le Havre, Honfleur, Ypres, Armentières, Bailleul, Abbeville, Hazebrouck, Eecke, Dranoutre, Vierstraat, Passchendaele, Cassel—all were mentioned in his diaries. Now that I had visited them and the unfolding countryside full of memorials and cemeteries marking the war's convoluted path, I felt closer to Martin. *So many places, so many young lives cut short.* This thought reverberated like an unending barrage.

Nothing I had seen so far provided even the smallest clue of how to solve the puzzle he had left me.

"Veal chasseur, madame." My host slid the plate in front of me, and I offered a vague smile. Perhaps sensing I was preoccupied, she didn't stop for conversation, and after savoring my first mouthful followed by another sip of wine, I returned to my thoughts.

A few days earlier, I had stood in a wide-open space just east of Eecke and, with Martin's diary in hand, had imagined a sea of white tents, men hurrying in various directions while others examined blisters, lathered whiskers, or wrote letters home slouched against their duffel bags. I conjured up men flinching at the first sounds of bombardment, fear registering in the twist of a gut or a tight swallow. Untested men, many with the fuzz of new beards and slim waists of recent boyhood.

Later, at the top of a hill near Vierstraat, I had spread a blanket beneath a chestnut tree overlooking a plain that in Martin's time was gouged with craters and strung with barbed wire, a plain full of misery and death, rattling with machine-gun fire and mortars, oozing smoke and blood and sweat. Now the view was peaceful: purple iris and red-tipped grasses swaying as fresh breezes chased away rain clouds. While orioles whistled and aspens shivered overhead, I reread an excerpt from Siegfried Sassoon's *Memoirs of an Infantry Officer* and felt anew the weary despair and grinding horror of war, imagining Martin rotating off the field for rest after losing men to one skirmish or another.

Listening to the haunting notes of the "Last Post" at the Menin Gate in Ypres, I wept for the thousands upon thousands of men whose names were etched there in stone. Walking through the museum at Passchendaele, full of pictures and memorabilia from 1917, I reeled at the utter devastation resulting from three months of battle where nothing except the skeletons of a few scorched trees remained. An entire town obliterated. On the path to and from the museum, name after name of those who had made the ultimate sacrifice echoed through loudspeakers with ghostly eeriness.

Who did Martin write his diaries for?

When I first read them, this question did not occur to me, but now I asked it repeatedly, wondering whether he wrote to document the weeks or console himself. Perhaps he needed a relief valve for all the pain and frustration. I could only speculate.

"You not hungry *ce soir*, madame?" said Madame Thierry as she cleared the table.

More than half the dish remained, mushrooms and sauce now congealed on the plate.

"I'm just a little tired. Perhaps I need something sweet?"

My host beamed, showing a ragged line of teeth, and bustled off, hips moving back and forth like round panniers. Unlike previous nights, the hotel's restaurant was almost full, a local crowd based on the familiar way they spoke to Madame. Chatter mingled with bursts of laughter.

Returning with a tray full of desserts, she described each selection as though they were beloved children: an éclair filled with custard cream, a tart with wine-poached pears and Armagnac glaze, gateau St. Honoré ringed with *choux* pastry and spun sugar, mille-feuille offering multiple layers of flaky pastry and custard topped with chocolate swirls.

"*Tous magnifique, madame,*" my host said with another glimpse of teeth. "I may also offer cheese." Her lips formed a slight pout.

"The tart looks delicious," I said.

Madame Thierry smiled and slid a generous slice onto a glass plate. "*Du café, madame?*" After I nodded, she bustled off once again.

I took a bite of dessert and closed my eyes as the silky taste of rich custard and soft pear slid down my throat. *If I stay in France too long, I'll regain all the weight I've lost.*

My dessert half-eaten, I extracted two more of Grandmama's photos from my bag. She had explained that although Martin had been born in Toronto, after the war they chose to settle in New York because it offered better job opportunities. And it had. Grandmama wore designer clothing and exquisite pieces of jewelry. They vacationed in all the right spots, bought expensive cars and an exclusive apartment. Growing up, I never lacked for anything.

In the first photo, my grandparents stood close together next to a rose garden and a wooden bridge that crossed a sunken pond. Grandpa's arm was around Grandmama's waist. My grandfather was in uniform, and Grandmama looked beautiful—hair curling against her shoulders, a calf-length skirt that buttoned down the front and a tailored blouse both emphasizing her slender waist. Though her face was turned toward Grandpa, her dazzling smile was clearly visible.

I'd seen the second photo before: it was a wedding picture taken of my grandparents on the steps in front of the Church of the Holy Cross, Grandmama's childhood church. A young couple who had been so deeply in love they had waited two years to be together.

MARTIN'S DIARY

June 19, 1915

Channel crossing was very smooth. Didn't think I got much sleep, but when I woke, we were in Le Havre. Ships everywhere—I counted more than twenty-five troopships from different parts of the world and at least six hospital ships. Watched a group of wounded men limp onto one of them. Assuming troopships carry roughly 1,000 men, 25,000 soldiers in port. I expect we're in for something major. Took a while to disembark. Marched to the base depot about four miles away. Children followed us for a while asking for coins. Some lighthearted grumbling from my men about their packs. They weigh at least sixty pounds—greatcoat, heavy underwear, extra shirt, several pairs of socks, handkerchiefs, mess tin, shaving gear, towels, housewife, sleeping cap, woolen scarf and gloves, plus reserve rations consisting of hardtack, bully beef, and various packs of powdered stuff. And, of course, bayonet, entrenching tool, and bullet pouches.

CHAPTER 6

August 1915

Led by guides from another battalion, Martin and his platoon were marching to Eecke for an overnight stop. Soon Hazebrouck was behind them, cobbled streets replaced by dirt roads connecting villages consisting of no more than a few houses—La Creule, La Brearde, Le Peuplier, Caestre. Windmills and sleepy cows marked their route, and the noise of more than four thousand marching men brought children and women out to wave as they passed by. In a wide-open field outside Eecke, he saw row upon row of canvas tents, gray and sagging from more than a year of use. In a bellowing voice, Martin's sergeant called out tent assignments.

"Don't get too comfortable, boys," Nully said. "Ten miles tomorrow. Reveille at five thirty."

Nully had been with Martin since training camp. A boisterous man when off duty, when on duty Sergeant William Nullford was deadly serious, growling at the enlisted men, insisting on discipline and close attention to orders. Now, just as Nully finished speaking, a roaring boom erupted. Martin steadied his face. Fear flickered in the eyes of his men, in the sudden jerk of a head, in the fumbling of fingers unpacking for the night, in taut lips and drawn brows. Shelling was occurring at the front, and each man knew they would soon be in the thick of it.

"I'll have everything shipshape in less than an hour, Lieutenant."

"Thank you, Nully. Butler wants me at the officers' mess. I'm sure I won't be long."

On the way to the mess, Martin collected his friends. Having Bill, Pete, and Michel in the same battalion was proving to be a blessing, a relief valve when Martin's frustrations mounted and a steadying influence when reality swarmed his imagination.

"We're heading ten miles closer to those shells," said Pete as they walked past a long row of tents, explosions echoing in the distance. Although he had an enormous appetite, Pete was skinny, and they'd begun to call him Knobby because his elbows and knees showed no discernible flesh.

Bill tugged on one side of his mustache, its hue a cross between ginger and copper. "Well, Knobby, this is what we came for."

A week later, Martin sat at a rough table recording recent events in his notebook. He and his friends were billeted just outside Dranoutre with an old woman whose low-roofed cottage looked more suitable for animals than humans. They slept on pallets filled with straw, but at least their bedding was dry and without fleas. His men were housed nearby in a converted factory that smelled of tallow and leather, a building with few windows and two stoves, one at either end, to provide slim bits of warmth against cool September nights.

Each morning, Martin heard the shuffle of Madame's sabots on the wood floor as she readied the fire to boil milk and coffee for breakfast and to heat a bowl of water so they could shave by candlelight before leaving for duty. She smiled a gap-toothed grin when they stumbled out of bed and motioned for them to wash outside before eating. Martin thought she resembled one of the witches in his childhood book of fairy tales, but she looked after them with tender care.

At six thirty, he led his platoon to a field full of mock trenches for training, and by midafternoon met Bill and Pete near the firing range. Within minutes, Michel and Captain Butler, their commanding officer, joined them. They planned to walk four miles to get into position, then wait until dark to approach the trenches.

Martin was beginning to like Butler. At first, the man had seemed overbearing, strutting like an angry bear whenever he appeared in front of the troops, his voice booming orders, his steely gaze missing nothing. But when Martin had been unable to sleep while crossing the Atlantic, he had often found his captain pacing the decks, and the two had fallen into long conversations exploring military life and the necessities of command.

"I sent your sergeants on ahead," Butler said, tossing his cigarette to the ground, where it hissed in a pool of water. "They'll take a first look at things."

Martin glanced at Bill, who shrugged. Butler clearly felt no further explanation necessary, and he turned and began walking briskly northeast. Although frequently brusque and impatient, Butler treated them well, acting tough but fair, apportioning tasks so that each of his lieutenants had an equal share of drudgery and challenge. After seven months, Martin trusted him and fell into line behind his captain.

The sky was a late-summer blue, cloudless and without haze. Overhead, a British airplane thrummed, scouting the lines from south to north. Three puffs of white burst in its wake like a painter adding a few clouds to an idyllic scene.

"Except for the shelling, this doesn't look the least bit like a country at war," Michel said.

"Wait till we get over the next rise," Butler said.

The group fell silent. Their captain was unusually curt, and Martin wondered whether he too was nervous. They passed a dilapidated hut, its thatched roof full of holes, then crossed a stile into a harvested field thick with mud. Geese flew overhead, their honking almost obliterated by menacing rumbles of artillery and staccato bursts of machine-gun fire.

Butler motioned them to halt. "Just about there," he said. He undid his flask and took a drink of water. "Keep low," he added, crouching.

Beyond the next rise, the war burst into view, a zigzagging patchwork of Allied trenches facing German lines. The scene looked nothing like Martin had imagined. Instead of deep, carefully constructed trenches designed to protect their men, uneven ditches were connected together in haphazard fashion, with mounds of earth and sandbags marking the lip of every section, and soldiers standing guard at uneven intervals. A sudden breeze carried the smell of mud, sewage, rotting flesh, gunfire, and death.

As far as he could see, the land had been blown to bits, leaving nothing but brown and gray and black, devoid of vegetation except a pocket of shattered tree trunks to the far right. Great rolls of barbed wire and deep craters partially filled with water defined the space between the lines. No-man's-land.

A dog barked. Shots rang out.

Nearby—and well behind the lines—was a stone hut with ammunition crates stacked against one wall. On the ground just a few feet away, a single boot lay encased in mud, the tongue flipped forward as though some soldier intended to return for it.

Holy Christ, Martin thought.

"Listen up," Butler said. "Second Division is taking over from the First, who've been in place for months. They're decimated and exhausted. Our line extends north and south from here, and we'll have responsibility for roughly a mile of it. British units are holding the line north of us." He gestured to a line of trenches marked at one end by a concrete bunker and a point at the other end where Canadian and German troops were so close it seemed their barbed-wire entanglements intersected. "Second Bavarian Corps opposes us. They're tough and vigilant. On our left is Third Brigade, and on our right a cavalry brigade. No use for horses in this shit, so Alderson turned them into an infantry unit."

A burst of gunfire erupted followed by innocent-looking drifts of smoke. *Tomorrow that will be us under fire,* Martin thought.

"Lines have moved back and forth since December with no significant change," Butler continued. "Germans have that ridge southeast of us. The high point gives them an advantage. The Brits are launching a new offensive at the end of the month. We'll be lending a hand. Until then, our objective is to hold the line."

"What do the Brits need us to do, Captain?" Pete asked, looking more fervent than Martin expected.

"Mainly create a diversion. We won't know details until a few days in advance, and even then, things can change up to the last minute."

Their escort showed up at eight p.m., four of the filthiest men Martin had ever seen, and they wasted no time setting off toward the line, following a deeply rutted path through a stand of trees before emerging onto a track behind the trenches. As they passed the remains of a small house, he saw bright bursts of flame shooting high, arcing across no-man's-land.

"Get down!" shouted the lead guide as he threw himself to the ground. Martin dove into a deep ditch just in time to hear a bullet zing overhead and thwack against the mud. His blood raced. His mouth ran dry. *Fuck, they're trying to kill us.*

A few minutes passed before the lead guide beckoned them forward, moving on the double across a field, rifle slung in the ready position. More bullets whizzed by, crossing where they had been moments before, and Martin cringed as a horse screamed followed by the sounds of a wagon overturning. The group continued single file along a ragged path. No one spoke until they stopped in front of muddy stairs, crudely reinforced with wood, heading down into one of the trenches.

"Devlin, you're here. This communication trench leads to B trench." Butler motioned to the steps. "Corporal Sundin will take you down."

Martin nodded.

"Best draw your pistol, sir," the corporal said in a low voice as they descended the stairs.

After twisting and turning for what seemed like an age, Martin and the corporal arrived at a wider section of the trench where ragged sandbags lined the top. Here and there, sections of the dirt wall had crumbled while other sections had been scooped out, forming small pits where soldiers sat or slept. Down the middle were duckboards, so covered in mud as to be barely distinguishable from the earth below. Martin shivered as a rat scurried over his boot.

MARTIN'S DIARY

October 10, 1915

Our diversionary action involved smoke sacks thrown over the parapet at four-yard intervals well before dawn followed by heavy bombardment. Enemy seemed confused, shooting wildly and shouting. Overall, we gained little ground at great expense. But I'm glad to have the first rotation behind me. Nully's Boer War experience is useful. He's very resourceful. Most of the men coped well. A ration of rum helps. McBride was killed and Milford wounded. Both excellent men.

December 29, 1915

All leave canceled. We now have eighteen days in the line followed by six days in the rear. The stress is taking its toll in carelessness. Lost Burton in a trench raid yesterday. I sent Gordon out to bring him back, but there was too much sniping, and he returned empty-handed. I hate the thought of Burton's body slowly rotting in the mud. What will I tell his parents? These are my men—mine to protect, mine to lead. They're also mine to bury. Life back home seems so remote, as though I were a child then and now I've grown up.

March 1, 1916

Holding the line again under continuous enemy shelling and excessive rain. Have to make constant adjustments, so my time is spent roaming up and down our little section looking for weak areas. Artillery runs nightly bombardments to hamper enemy repairs. Steel helmets are being issued to all ranks. Haven't changed my clothes for six days. Received a package from Jane containing socks, chocolate, razor blades, and cigarettes. She says Mother and Father are very worried.

CHAPTER 7

March 1916

Martin was in the cellar of a house partially destroyed by shelling that was serving as brigade headquarters, a distinct improvement over the dungeon they had occupied in December. Smelling of dried bat droppings and ancient slime, the air in that deep, dark space had created a feeling of doom, as though echoes of torture had only recently faded. He shivered, not from the cold, but from the memory.

Bill, Pete, and Michel sat with Butler at a makeshift table while Martin and the captain's adjutant leaned against the wall. Slickers hung from hooks next to the entrance, dripping dregs of sleet onto a packed mud floor.

"We're gearing up for a major offensive," said Captain Butler. "There's an enemy salient near St. Eloi." Butler stabbed at the map. "We're part of the force ordered to eliminate it."

"What are those, sir?" Michel pointed to several numbered circles on the map.

"Craters."

Pete scratched the rash at the base of his throat. "Who occupies them?"

"That's the problem," said Butler. "We thought we occupied four and five and could attack craters two and three from those positions. Turns out the Germans still hold them. Our battalions couldn't tell one crater from another. Fucking mess. We go in tomorrow night to relieve the Sixth."

Captain Butler spent the next two hours explaining the operation and answering questions. Trench reinforcements would be the first objective, their brigade augmented for this task by two thousand reserve troops. A series of bombardments and infantry attacks would follow with the aim of securing four of the largest craters.

"Fucking mess is right," Martin said to Bill as they returned to their dugouts, slogging through the mud, the wind whipping rain against their cheeks. He wiped his eyes and squinted. "I can barely see."

"The situation sure doesn't look promising," Bill said.

"If the Sixth lost almost fifty percent, you can imagine what we're in for."

On March 29, Butler ordered Martin's and Bill's platoons out of the line, saying they were so fatigued they would do more harm than good if they remained, and after twelve hours' sleep in huts that were little more than lean-tos, they were in the officers' mess. Bill stood close to the stove, hands wrapped around a mug of hot tea, while Martin sat on a wooden box changing his socks. Fresh socks and underwear were difficult to get, worse for regular ranks than officers, but nonetheless he could hardly remember when he last had a fresh pair. He stripped off the old socks and held them up for inspection. Nothing but a mass of holes and filth.

"Did you see what happened to Michel?" Martin asked Bill.

"No. All I saw were stretcher-bearers taking him to the clearing station. He was covered with mud but too far away for me to check on him. One of his men said they took a hit while securing positions along the crater lip."

"Bloody fucking Hun," Martin said.

Bill slurped a mouthful of tea. "Butler will find out if Michel's okay. Hopefully, it'll be something minor and he'll be back soon."

"Hopefully, I can't imagine our battalion without him," Martin said. "I know it's ridiculous to think that none of us will be hurt in this hellhole, but I suppose I've been thinking just that. You and Pete better not go anywhere." He pulled on a sock and wiggled his toes, now encased in thick brown wool. "Received these from Mother last month. I only have one pair left. Where's Van Leuven?"

"He's still out there."

"I lost Jimmy and Snowy this time. Both went down in the same scramble up the far side of the crater. Nully and I dug them out, but we couldn't get any medics in time to save them. Snowy knew I was with him at the end." Martin shook his head.

"We don't seem to be making any progress, do we, Dev?"

"Nope. Captain said aerial photos show all craters are still in German hands. He's infuriated that communications didn't get through in time."

The door opened, admitting damp, frigid air along with two senior officers. Martin and Bill stood and saluted.

"As you were, men. Are you just in?"

"Came in yesterday, sir."

"What was it like out there?"

"Bloody awful, sir," said Martin. "The enemy didn't want to give any ground. Artillery tried to work them over, but I don't think they had the right coordinates. The Boche took their unhappiness out on our front line, and we had a hard go of it."

"Interesting, Lieutenant . . ." The man paused, waiting for Martin to supply his name.

"Devlin, sir."

"Interesting, Devlin. We heard it was a successful attack."

Martin knew from Bill's frown that he should mind his tongue, but Michel, Snowy, and Jimmy deserved something other than silence.

"No, sir," Martin said. "Not at all successful, not so far as the infantry is concerned. We lost a lot of men because our artillery misjudged the distance. Can't imagine what idiot coined the phrase *friendly* fire."

"Well . . ." The lieutenant colonel cleared his throat. "Well, enjoy your tea."

The door opened again, and a chaplain entered, the only evidence of his role a stiff white collar. With a brief nod to the gathered group, he headed for the stove to hold chapped hands above its blazing warmth.

Bill waited until the officers retreated to the far corner. "Awful cheeky, weren't you? You're lucky he didn't dress you down for that."

"It needed to be said. Bloody staff officers think their maps are correct and then order the artillery to bombard the wrong locations. Just because they draw a new trench line on a map doesn't mean we control it." His whisper scraped like rough sandpaper, and the chaplain turned to stare.

Martin shoved his boots on and sat down once again to tie laces now stiff with mud. Heavy bombardment began again.

"Let's hope Pete's not in the midst of that."

CHAPTER 8

June 1991

As soon as the Renault crossed the railway tracks in the village of Gosnay and rounded the bend, thick walls standing over six feet high appeared, marking the hotel's western boundary. To the north, a stand of poplars lined the ridge behind the property; across the road, a windmill spun like an aging ballerina, and bulrushes mingled with purple flowers along the road's edge. Grandmama would have called it bucolic.

Just past a sign announcing Chateau Noyelle in gold letters, I turned left and stopped the car, enchanted by the graceful building and surrounding gardens lush with color and texture. Ceramic planters containing boxwood clipped to resemble enormous birds flanked the front entrance, where an open door offered a glimpse of white-tiled floors and a vase full of gladioli on a pedestal table. A young man dressed in black pants and a crisp white shirt emerged from the hotel to take my bags.

After settling in, I left my room with *The Shell Seekers* tucked under one arm. Dinner was more than three hours away, and a good book would allow me to escape from Martin's world and the man with the straw fedora.

Stopping in the bar to order an espresso, I admired the plush chairs and sofas organized for intimate conversations and several large windows embraced by silk overlooking the gardens. Next to a tall curio cabinet, a display of sepia photos caught my eye, and I peered at one, a shot of the building before it had become a hotel, taken at the front of the chateau. Two women held umbrellas edged in lace and wore long skirts and blouses with wide sleeves and tight cuffs. *Nothing sexy about those outfits,* I thought. Beside them, a young boy held a hoop in his hand. A straw hat—the kind Grandmama called a boater—lay on the ground nearby. Below the picture, a silver plaque announced *Chateau Noyelle, 1879.*

Below that photo was a framed certificate bearing the American coat of arms. Curious, I bent my head to read the inscription: *The President of the United States has directed me to express to Andre Justin-Gabriel Constant the gratitude and appreciation of the American people for gallant service in assisting the escape of Allied soldiers from the enemy.* Underneath was the signature of Dwight Eisenhower as *General of the Army.* How extraordinary. My imagination went to work: spies lurking in the corridors, an underground passage through the woods, secret doors behind . . .

"Your *café,* madame."

Smiling at the young bartender whose intense brown eyes reminded me of Michael's, I took the small cup and saucer he offered and inhaled the fragrant aroma. I was having a love affair with espresso. Its deep, rich, complicated taste and thick, smooth feel inside my mouth were like no other coffee I'd ever had. The experience made me feel adventurous and sophisticated, a woman of exotic tastes.

On the patio, lounge chairs arranged beneath striped umbrellas invited guests to linger. White pots marked each corner, some full of lavender, others with a mix of colors and trailing vines. At one end, a stone bench was home to a collection of blue watering cans.

"I wish my garden looked like this," I said, settling into one of the chairs.

I spoke out loud and quickly checked to see whether anyone was listening, wondering about a crazy American talking to herself. Traveling alone, I'd grown accustomed to my own thoughts for company and was amused when I voiced one out loud. I even talked to Martin from time to time, as if he might hear me from beyond the grave.

I opened the book and turned to page one.

The sound of coughing woke me, and for a moment I kept my eyes closed, hoping to recapture the languid feel of a dream slipping away like early-morning mist. After another spell of coughing, I lifted my head.

"I am sorry if I have disturbed you." The accent was a confusing mixture of British and French.

I smiled briefly at a dark-haired man stretched out on a nearby chair wearing wrinkled linen pants, then straightened my blouse and resumed reading, stealing another glance at my neighbor. The man made no further attempt at conversation but sat calmly without a book or newspaper, from time to time tapping his fingers and frowning. I must have dozed again because when I next looked to my left, he was gone.

Before going down for dinner, I called Grandmama. Although I had promised to talk to her once a week, I hoped she might be out because it was early afternoon in New York. But after three rings, Philomena answered and said Grandmama would be delighted to speak with me.

Philomena had worked for my grandparents as long as I could remember. A kindly, spirited woman with skin the color of creamy coffee, she declared often, and with a vigorous nod of her entire body, that her great-great-grandfather had been a plantation owner in South Carolina who became a senator at a time when slave rebellions, like the one led by Nat Turner, endangered many lives. Without Philomena's care, the early months of living with my grandparents would have been unbearable.

The conversation with Grandmama began well. I described the landscape, small villages, and war memorials and tried to amuse her with a few anecdotes about the people I'd met. In turn, she asked questions about the hotels and restaurants I had enjoyed and my impressions of France.

"Where are you now?" she said.

After mentioning Chateau Noyelle's elegant style and grand exterior, I asked my grandmother what she'd been doing.

"I went to a gallery opening down in the East Village. I cannot imagine why anyone would want to have a gallery in that beastly part of the city, but Sally Rockford said many new artists are exhibiting there because prices in Soho are too high. Dreadfully crowded, and they were playing some awful noise that young people these days call music. I couldn't hear a thing."

"Were the paintings interesting?"

"Hmm. One or two were quite distinctive. In a modern Japanese style, I would say. But nothing I wished to purchase." Grandmama prattled on. She stayed abreast of politics and gallery happenings and missed being part of the crowd surrounding the latest artists and designers.

"Ben Portelli came to see me yesterday," she said.

"That's nice." I made a mental note to send Uncle Ben a postcard with my thanks. "How is Uncle Ben?"

"Don't you think it's well past time to stop calling him Uncle? He's not related to you."

"I know, but he's been in my life since I was little. What did you two talk about?"

"Just the usual gossip. He keeps me in touch with the art world."

With a thick chest, bushy hair, and a tattoo on his right forearm, Uncle Ben had initially seemed scary to a five-year-old. But when he had gotten down on his hands and knees and let me climb aboard for a ride around the living room, I had squealed with laughter. He had been Uncle Ben ever since. As a junior and senior in high school, I'd often sought his opinion, and it was he who advised me to attend business school, telling me I should find my own passion rather than adopt my grandfather's.

Over the last twenty years, Ben had established a reputation as an authority on nineteenth-century European artists. He bought for himself and on behalf of wealthy collectors whose names he never revealed. His was a word-of-mouth business. In the past, Grandpa had often complained when he went to one of Uncle Ben's events—"shindigs," he called them—but he always came back with stories.

"Ben said he had lunch with you before you went away. Did you ask him to check up on me? You know I am perfectly able to look after myself. And Philomena is here if I need anything."

I imagined Grandmama straightening her back as she spoke, wrinkles cutting across her brow like furrows in a dry field. "We did have lunch, and I know how capable you are, Grandmama. I really should go now. It's time for dinner."

No point in mentioning the conversation with Ben about Grandmama's increasing frailty. He'd told me not to worry, that he would call in to see her from time to time like he always did.

"When will you return?"

"I've only been gone six days."

"A week, counting the day you left."

"Yes, you're right, a week." An edge crept into my voice. "I have no intention of being rushed. The boys are fine with Jim."

"Humph." I knew that sound, a snort that implied both dissatisfaction and disagreement, used frequently when I was an unruly teenager. "Your mother isn't well," she continued.

"Really?" *Two can play this game, Grandmama.* "Did you speak with Dr. Hildman?" I made my voice brisk.

"No. The nurse called."

"Well, speak to the doctor. He'll know if there's anything serious to worry about."

"You know I don't like talking with doctors."

"I'll call you next week. You can tell me what the doctor said. Bye, Grandmama." I hung up the phone and muttered out loud, "Why is she always so difficult?"

After my father's death in an airplane crash, grief had overwhelmed my mother. Despite the emotional ups and downs that ensued, she had looked after me, so when my grandparents took me away, I'd been bewildered. Though my clothes and toys had moved with me, nothing else had. Not the yellow sunflower pillow from the sofa where I lay while my mother read bedtime stories, nor the Winnie-the-Pooh cup I used for juice even though I was old enough for a glass. Not the wiggly bathroom stool that made me tall enough to turn on the tap and brush my teeth, nor the red lacquer jewelry box where I spent hours modeling necklaces and earrings to draw a smile or occasional laugh from my mother. When asked for these treasures, Grandmama would sniff and say, "We left those for Mummy" or "Mummy needs that," and for a while I had believed her, assuming that one day my mother and I would be reunited.

Days had become months. On one occasion, my mother spent two weeks living with us at my grandparents' apartment, a time of sharp conversations, hysterics from my mother, and slammed doors. One day, Grandmama took me out for ice cream. When we returned, my mother was gone.

Months became years. I went to school, made friends, attended birthday parties, received new clothes, learned to ride a bicycle, and spent hours with my grandfather at his art gallery. By the time I was ten, my earlier life was a hazy memory. Although Grandmama rarely mentioned my parents, Grandpa shared stories of happier times, and when I was ten, he revealed the truth about my mother's fragile state caused by my father's death and the subsequent depression that had overwhelmed their daughter, the alcohol abuse, and the places she went for treatment. Despite my grandparents' support, she never again lived independently. When she was diagnosed with Alzheimer's at age sixty-three, I moved her to a secure facility called the Willows. Though I visited almost every week, she no longer knew who I was.

Every second weekend until I was fourteen, my father's parents looked after me, and from them I heard many stories about my father, David Pickford, and a few about my mother, Lily. Those visits stopped after my paternal grandfather had a stroke. I often wondered how different my life might have been if my father had lived, and equally often I wondered whether losing a parent to grief was worse than losing one to death.

Grandmama and I had a difficult relationship, filled with arguments and criticism. She was anything but warm, never like the grandmothers my friends described, the kind who baked cookies and knitted sweaters and offered unquestioned affection. One day when I was about twelve, Grandmama found me standing in front of a mirror comparing myself to a picture of my father.

"Do I look like him?" I had asked.

"You have his coloring. And his chin. The chin of a stubborn man, if you ask me. You've inherited that too. You would be prettier if you looked more like your mother."

I could always rely on my grandmother's honesty.

CHAPTER 9

June 1991

Le Sommelier, the restaurant next door to the hotel, offered a tranquil refuge from thoughts of my mother's wasted life and Grandmama's demanding personality. Lace curtains billowed in warm summer air; sconces provided diffused lighting. Along one wall, copper pots hung from a horizontal rack, and throughout the restaurant, paintings of circus clowns added a touch of whimsy. I sat at a long banquette anchoring several tables for two and ordered a glass of white Burgundy. The French custom of drinking wine with almost every meal suited me perfectly.

That evening I wore a black skirt and sleeveless pink top that crisscrossed in front to show a hint of cleavage. According to my ex, I never wore sexy clothes, so on Joan's advice, I'd purchased a few items for the trip to prove him wrong. The current fashion of fluorescent colors and tight leggings or cargo pants was definitely not my style, but my legs were slender enough for the short skirts displayed in the latest style magazines—and the black skirt was definitely short. Usually I brought a book or a crossword or one of Martin's diaries for dinner companionship, but tonight I had none of these crutches with me; instead, I perused the menu, then watched the other diners.

An intense conversation between a man and woman across the room made me think of Rossini's, a Maplewood restaurant that used to be a favorite. An Italian place with delicious food, Rossini's had been ruined for me when Jim used one of our Friday night dinners there to ask for a divorce. A cowardly approach that still made me livid.

When the waiter returned for my order, the man from the patio was being seated at the next table.

"Bonsoir," he said.

"Bonsoir, monsieur." My earrings swayed back and forth as I turned to acknowledge him.

Close up, I now saw his features more clearly: gray eyes flecked with bits of green, a dark shadow on his face suggesting he might shave more than once a day, and strong, square fingers. *Not handsome exactly, but rugged and definitely appealing,* I thought.

Aware of the man next to me, I sipped my wine, savoring its crisp flavor, and forced myself to concentrate on other diners and the rhythmic motion of waiters approaching and leaving tables like actors entering and exiting a stage. A family with teenage daughters sat nearby, the girls feigning boredom, mother and father carrying on as though nothing was out of the ordinary.

At the far end of the room, a priest sat with a middle-aged man and woman. He seemed to be encouraging conversation with frequent nods, occasional comments, and a commanding tilt of his head, and I wondered whether he was related to the couple or whether they were parishioners in need of care.

After the waiter delivered my appetizer of smoked trout with crème fraiche, I picked up my fork.

"Who are you watching?"

"Pardon?" I turned to look at the dark-haired man.

"Which people interest you?" he said.

I inclined my head toward the teenage girls. "Those two girls look like they're being difficult. And the priest, I can't figure out whether the man and woman are his relatives or his parishioners. What do you think?"

"Teenagers are selfish beasts. Indeed, there are four or five years when they are intolerable. My mother assures me I behaved that way. Do you have children?"

His observation was so unexpected I laughed. "Two boys. One is twelve, the other's fifteen. Selfish beasts is exactly what my friend Joan calls them, and she has two of similar ages." I paused to savor another bite of trout. "And you?"

"Me?"

"Do you have children?"

"No. No children." His voice was curiously flat.

I chose a different topic. "What's your theory about the priest?"

"Hmm, the priest. No doubt marriage counseling. We French think delicious food and wine will solve every problem. During appetizers, he will remind them of their vows; over dinner and an excellent bottle of Bordeaux, he will talk about family responsibility and their many years together. Then he will leave before dessert so they can complete dinner *tout seuls*. Alone." He snapped his fingers. "Voilà."

I laughed again. "You must be a storyteller."

"Nothing so creative. My name is Pierre Auffret. I'm a museum curator." He held out his hand.

Auffret. There's something familiar about that name, I thought. *Have I seen it somewhere before?*

"Grace Hansen." I shook his hand, not with a firm grip, as I would have done in business, but a brief, light touch. My cheeks grew warm. Blushing is my curse, occurring whenever I feel awkward.

"Grace is a lovely name. The same in French as English. So, Grace, why are you visiting this part of France?"

I liked the sound of my name in French, the *a* less sharp, the *c* drawn out softly. When I was younger, I hated my name. Too old-fashioned for my teenage years, caught in that time of acute angst when

I felt anything but graceful. Grandpa always said it suited me perfectly, and Grandmama said she only hoped I would improve with age. More recently, divorce had obliterated any sense of grace accumulated in adulthood, although grief and anger had now eased.

Without mentioning divorce or the puzzle Grandpa had left me, I related the story of the diaries and my decision to retrace Martin's steps.

"My grandfather also fought in World War One. He never spoke about it, and I was too young to ask him." Pierre motioned to the chair opposite me. "May I?"

"Please," I said.

After he settled himself and we both took a sip of wine, I asked Pierre to explain his job.

"It's a bit of a story." He arched his brows, seeking permission to continue, and I offered an encouraging look. "I used to work in Paris for an international bank. It seemed a sound place to begin a career. My father had a few connections, and I did well."

Pierre explained that after a number of years, he wanted to leave banking and find an environment beyond numbers and finance; a world with more soul, he called it. After a long search, he found a job in Amiens working at the museum there.

"I love this work, bringing beauty, history, and creativity to the public. There's an estate collection in Arras I wish to examine. It's reputed to have several treasures. I will decide which ones to purchase and have a *petite vacances* at the same time."

"My grandfather would have enjoyed your story. He owned an art gallery in New York and shared your love of creativity. He taught me about beautiful things."

The waiter had adjusted his timing, and our main courses arrived together: sole Normande sprinkled with parsley and thin slices of truffle for me, duck breast with raspberry sauce for Pierre. Both looked like works of art.

As we ate, conversation flowed, one topic cascading into another.

"Where will you explore next?" Pierre asked after draining his coffee.

"Tomorrow I'm going to Thiepval and Courcelette."

"Thiepval was part of the battles near the Somme. Very bloody battles."

My shoulders sagged. "I know. So many tragic deaths." I tilted my head toward the waiter standing next to the bar yawning. "Time to go, I think."

He nodded. "We seem to be the last ones here."

The gravel walkway crunched beneath our feet as Pierre and I crossed the short distance from the restaurant to the hotel. Thinking of the pleasant dinner and conversation, I remained quiet as we walked along. I felt his presence beside me, calm and assured, quietly humming a tune I did not recognize.

"Sleep well, Grace Hansen," he said as we parted.

MARTIN'S DIARY

June 6, 1916

Hill 60, severe German attack. Eight killed, twenty-two wounded in our battalion. Four from my platoon gone. The men try to be stoic, but I see the way they look at each other, wondering who will be next, as though they're in line for the guillotine and the executioner draws names from a hat. I think some of them fear going on more than death. Throwing more and more men across no-man's-land will never win this war. Pete and I debate tactics endlessly, and he agrees. The men who put us in these places should be made to go over the top with us; then they might make different decisions.

July 30, 1916

Conducted a daylight raid yesterday to secure evidence of mine shafts and gas cylinders. Killed our share of Germans, but I've been here so long I don't think about those I kill anymore. Used to agonize over every one of them. Lenny and Simpson wounded but safe. Had time to write letters home today. I'm running out of ways to keep them positive.

August 13, 1916

General officer briefing on the Somme. As far as I can tell, it's going to be worse than Ypres. Pete and I are trying to figure out the big picture. Turned camp over to the 10th Infantry Brigade. Long columns of men coming in while we made our way out of the line. They stared at us, and we stared back.

August 16, 1916

Intense bombardment yesterday. Apparently, we were putting on a show for the king. I wonder how many died just so he could see some live action? Whoever made that decision is a fucking idiot.

CHAPTER 10

August 1916

From the train station at Doullens, they marched quickly to reach billets before sunset, the whump of boots and attendant cloud of dust marking their passage. Unlike low-lying Flanders, the land was different here, with hills surrounding valleys carved by tributaries flowing into the Somme, the earth loose and pebbled rather than red with clay.

As they approached Toutencourt, Martin saw the town's church spire framed by dense forest to the south. They passed an ivy-covered chapel guarding a cemetery and thatch-roofed houses flanking the road; a canvas-topped motor truck was parked near a group of old men making barrels. The street climbed toward the church, a rise insufficient to slow the men's pace.

"Where are we going, Lieutenant?"

"Far side of town."

Martin preferred not to make idle conversation while en route. Although he didn't discourage his men from talking, he felt he should set an example. While marching, he imagined angry conversations with senior officers about the futility of their efforts, accusing them of carelessness and stupidity, then suggesting strategies for better results. More recently, his thoughts dwelt on the increasing certainty that he and his friends would die.

Artillery rumbled in the distance, although not loud enough to interrupt his attempts to recall the map showing trench lines in the area. Germany had pushed west, creating a significant bulge near Albert that threatened supply lines originating from Amiens. Their objective was to flatten this bulge, and Butler assured them each company, battalion, and brigade had a role to play. For the next week, preparatory tasks would strengthen trench positions and the fitness of every man. He tried not to think of the coming casualties.

After making camp, Butler called his lieutenants together. Martin leaned against a fence made of flat stones loosely cemented together, watching Simon Duncan, the lieutenant who had replaced Michel Diotte, tear petals off a clutch of white daisies. They now knew that Michel's left leg had been amputated and he had been sent home to Canada. Simon was nothing like Michel, and Martin spoke to him only when necessary.

"We're taking over from First Brigade," said Butler. "Launch date is September fifteenth. Our goal is to advance the entire front with particular focus on the salient. We have the portion between Martinpuich and Courcelette, about half a mile. We're to take the enemy second line trenches and the Sugar Factory, where beets used to be processed into sugar. It's now a German stronghold, so we're expecting it to be defended with determination.

"Our initial task is digging attack trenches. Others will be digging new communication trenches and reinforcing existing lines. We'll be closest to the enemy and likely under fire. Attack trenches will ensure we can reach the German front line in less than three minutes. When action begins, you and your men will go over in waves from the attack trenches, one man per five yards. Four platoons wide."

"Who will go first, Captain?" Pete asked.

"You sound like you're spoiling for a fight, Pete," Martin said.

"Bloody right, I am."

"We're all spoiling for a fight," Butler said. "As to who goes first, no word yet. With at least a week to go, many things can change. Artillery will be deploying a creeping barrage, and for the first time we'll have tanks going alongside our advance. Haig wants them tested during the assault. Expectations are optimistic, but the tanks are to serve only as tactical accessories designed to take out machine-gun posts and strongpoints. General Byng has made it clear we are not to depend on them; responsibility for achieving objectives still rests with the infantry."

"So if they can help us, fine, but if not, we proceed as usual?"

"That's right, Devlin. During the first wave, you and your platoons are to use the barrage and cross no-man's-land before the enemy emerges from cover. The Sugar Factory is the second objective, and there we'll have tank support. After we secure it, other battalions will proceed to Courcelette. I'll have an update in a day or two."

Pete thought the whole affair far too ambitious and said so after Butler dismissed them. "Haig is throwing everything he can at the Boche, looking for one last chance to prove his strategies are sound. After what happened in July, his neck is on the line, but that means our troops might be sacrificed for the sake of his pride."

"Bloody idiots," Martin said. "Maybe those tanks will provide some protection. Did you see them rolling in yesterday? Can't believe how huge and noisy they are."

"I don't care how big they are," Bill said. "You won't catch me volunteering to sit inside one of them. Way too claustrophobic." He pretended to shiver. "Makes me think of sausage meat being stuffed into its casing."

❧

A week later, bombardment began in the shadowy murk of early morning. As they waited for the signal to advance, the air over Martin's head filled with the booming, sighing, whining, and screaming of thousands of shells raking enemy lines. The ground trembled.

All he could see were sheets of flame and belching smoke, and for a time fear took over, fear for himself, his friends, and his men. Who could possibly design warfare with such viciousness? What leaders could imagine officers capable of carrying on when faced with month after month of stupendous brutality? A shell burst nearby. Clumps of dirt and shrapnel and God knows what fell to the earth. A man screamed. Martin shuddered and closed his eyes.

When they heard the signal to advance, Martin and his men clambered out of their attack trenches and lurched forward, screened by a moving curtain of fire and shrapnel. A light breeze blew dust and debris toward enemy lines. With sweat trickling down his back, Martin maintained a steady pace, advancing step by step, rifle at the ready, Nully on his right. He surveyed the scene—the ground before him little more than a mass of shell holes and dead bodies revealed in the breaking light of dawn. There was no time to consider those whose lives had ended; no time to imagine them joking before battle or preparing their weapons, taking a last look at photos of loved ones, or making the sign of the cross. He checked his watch. Timing was everything. By six thirty a.m., they were on their bellies within a few feet of a German forward trench.

"No opposition yet," he yelled at Nully to be heard above the noise.

"Maybe the barrage got them all," Nully shouted.

"Well, we're sure as hell not taking any chances. Give the signal to fire at will."

Martin fired steadily as he covered the remaining distance and slithered into the trench. Dead Germans lay everywhere and in every circumstance, those who had been sleeping or eating next to those who had fallen, rifle in hand. Some piled in heaps as though tossed from a great height. Some missing limbs or gutted by the force of an exploding shell. Some looked like they might wake at any moment. In one dugout, a dog's body lay on a man's chest as though comforting his dying master.

Many sections of the trench had been blasted away, requiring Martin to step over or around heaps of debris as he made his way along, prodding the occasional body with his boot or the tip of his bayonet in case one of the soldiers remained alive. Rifles, grenades, shovels, and lengths of corrugated metal lay about the trench, and he watched one of his men take the bayonet off a German rifle and stuff it into his pack.

"We're done here, Nully. Mopping-up parties will deal with anyone who's hiding down those shafts. Find out where Pete and Bill are so we can proceed to the Sugar Factory. I'll figure out who we've lost."

Roughly five hundred yards separated the trench they had taken and the Sugar Factory, but the terrain was full of craters and deep with mud. On the horizon, Martin saw a few rooftops of Courcelette, the division's next objective. Other than scarred tree trunks, only a few German bunkers marked the land.

"Christ," he shouted at a brief rendezvous with Bill, Pete, and Simon, "I don't like the look of that open territory. If the barrage hasn't taken out those bunkers, we could be in trouble."

"That's what the tanks are for," Pete said. "We're making progress."

"How many casualties?" Bill asked.

"I've lost four or five," Pete said. "If I thought prayer would help us, I'd be on my knees right now."

"What do you think the Germans will do next, Knobby?" Bill said.

"Retaliate. That's what I'd do. Throw everything they've got at us." He smiled a thin-lipped smile. "Maybe I should pray after all."

After Bill, Pete, and Simon returned to their platoons, Martin checked his map. "Have a look, Nully. We're here." He stabbed at a position marked with an *X*. "We keep south of this road until we reach the Sugar Factory. Pete and Simon are north of the road on our left, and Bill is on our right flank. Sixth Brigade will converge from the far left."

Nully nodded. "Got it."

"Tanks will provide some protection, but keep your eye on them. If they falter, we proceed without them."

Clanking and grinding, four behemoths lumbered forward, and Martin directed his men behind one armed with four machine guns and two six-pounders. Inexplicably, the tank's name was Crème de Menthe. Butler told them the Sugar Factory, along with Sugar Trench and Candy Trench, formed an interconnected series of dugouts and machine-gun posts that would be fiercely defended by the German Forty-Fifth Reserve Division. As they moved into position, the barrage began again.

Battle continued until just before midnight, when the Nineteenth Battalion was instructed to withdraw to brigade headquarters. After securing food and water for his men, Martin went looking for Pete and Bill.

"Did you see those tanks in action?" Pete said. "Like a dragon spouting fire in all directions."

"Yeah. And when the Boche saw them, they put their hands in the air. Surrendered just like that." Bill shook his head as though he still could not believe what he'd seen. "We need more of those beasts."

"Killed me some Germans today," Pete added. "A lot of Germans. Used my bayonet frequently, and I can't say I felt any remorse."

"Neither did I," Martin said. "Neither did I."

Ten days later, they arrived at the Brickfields, a billeting area on the outskirts of Albert where a former brick factory sat on an inhospitable area of chalky ground. On September 26, they moved to Tara Valley, then to Sausage Valley on September 27, and finally to Gun Pit Trench that evening.

"We've been assigned to Sixth Brigade for the duration of battle. Our orders are to push forward from Gun Pit Road and establish a new line well in front of the trenches you can see on the map here and here," said Butler. "Expect to encounter hostile parties in hidden strong points as you advance."

"Sounds grim," Martin said to Pete after the briefing was done. "Butler looks like hell."

"Worse than usual, I'd say. I wonder what he knows that we don't." Pete tossed a half-smoked cigarette onto the ground. "This next bit won't be easy. But we've survived worse."

By noon the following day, the battalion had completed a new continuous frontline trench and established observation posts and telephone communication with headquarters. That night, Fourth Brigade took over from the Sixth amid severe German shelling. Martin did not expect to sleep.

⌢⌣

"What do you mean he's gone?" he said to Bill the next morning.

"Gone. Dead. Killed by a bloody, fucking German howitzer. According to his sergeant, they took a direct hit in one section of their trench. Killed four others as well."

"No. No. No." Martin's voice echoed inside his head like a booming drum. His vision blurred as he began to shake. "Not Pete. It can't have been Pete. There must be a mistake."

Bill hung his head, shoulders slumped as if carrying an awful weight. "That's what I said. I wanted to pound something to smithereens when I heard. Left my platoon and went searching for Samuels. I knew Pete's sergeant would have the facts. It's true, Dev. He's really gone."

"But we were together just a few hours ago."

"I know." Bill gripped Martin's arm. "I know it's terrible. But it's true."

"Where is he? Let me go. I have to see for myself."

Bill tightened his hold on Martin. "You can't. You don't . . . Fuck, I'll give it to you straight. There's nothing left to see."

Martin's eyes went blank. Every part of his body sagged. He shook his arm free and rushed over to the side of the road and vomited.

CHAPTER 11

June 1991

I slipped out of bed the following morning with a smile on my face. A man had actually paid attention to me, and a French man at that. The angst of divorce—an amputation of sorts, not of flesh but of spirit—eased a fraction, and after a quick breakfast, I gathered my maps and notes for the day and placed Martin's diaries in my purse.

Beyond the hotel's front entrance, finches swooped from bush to bush while across the road a cluster of speckled brown cows grazed, lifting their heads from time to time as if watching those coming and going from Chateau Noyelle. A yellow van announced the arrival of the mail. The postman grunted as he lifted an overflowing bin from the back, straining buttons suggesting a figure that had once been trimmer.

After opening the car door, I placed a backpack, an umbrella, and a basket containing lunch on the passenger seat, then slid into the driver's spot. Two Porsches, one red and the other white, were parked next to my little Renault. While clearing the car of accumulated papers and refolding my maps for the day's journey, a man, a woman, and two teenage boys emerged from the hotel. They spoke rapidly in a language sounding nothing like French, then, with a son and parent in each car, roared off.

Imagine having enough money for two Porsches, I thought, pulling the seat belt across my lap. *Damn. I forgot my camera.* I went back to my room, and when I returned, Pierre was leaning against the Renault.

"Thiepval and Courcelette today?" he asked. I nodded. "Beautiful day for a drive." I nodded again, wondering why he was lingering. "May I come along?"

I hesitated. Dinner conversation had been easy, likely made even easier with the addition of wine; spending the whole day with a stranger could be a disaster.

"Perhaps I can find something about my grandfather as well," Pierre said. "And translate if you need help."

Refusal seemed churlish. "Having company would be lovely. Do you think you can take us to Toutencourt?" I asked. "Martin was billeted there for a few days."

"Bien sûr, madame." Pierre studied the map, a dense jumble of roads marked in red, yellow, and white, the colors differentiating highways from lesser roads and village routes. "Why do you call him Martin?"

One hand on the gearshift ready to back out of the parking area, I debated how to answer. "Because he doesn't sound like my grandfather in his diaries. He sounds like somebody else. Someone who's . . ."

Pierre waited a moment for me to complete the thought. "Who's what?" he asked.

"I don't know. I'm trying to figure that out."

As we neared Toutencourt, a church spire beckoned, its squat, unadorned shape suggesting lives ruled by the seasons with little time to create beauty for its own sake. Pierre directed me onto a paved road, and I was grateful to leave the dusty lane behind, a road so narrow I could have reached out the window to touch the wispy tops of wild grass and bushes sporting vivid yellow flowers. The Renault cornered easily, and within minutes we parked in front of the town's bakery.

"They say the windows here never stopped vibrating during the war," Pierre said as we left the car.

"Imagine living so close to it all. Every day I would wonder if it would be my last. When my grandfather wrote about going to Paris on leave, he said the best thing was the absence of noise." I paused and then chuckled.

"Something funny?"

"Not really. Well, yes, I suppose it's funny." Looking away from Pierre, I fixed my eyes on a group of young boys examining a broken bicycle. "His very next diary entry said that the best thing was being with a woman."

"Really? I wonder what he was referring to."

When I glanced up, Pierre's eyes were sparkling, and I felt a blush spreading across my neck and face.

"You're teasing me," I said, embarrassed to have mentioned something so suggestive to a man I had just met.

"I am."

Grandmama's voice bounced inside my head. Something about the art of conversation requiring deftness, imagination, and aplomb. I changed the topic. "Not surprisingly, war stories are usually about soldiers, not ordinary citizens. When I researched, I found several memoirs written by men who served. They helped me understand what Martin faced. I also found a small book by Edith Wharton called *Fighting France*, but she wrote from the perspective of a journalist, not an ordinary citizen. Still, it was very informative, and somehow she was able to get quite close to the front lines."

"I wonder how she secured permission for that. Was she not a famous American writer?" I nodded. Pierre pointed to a street on our left. "Let's walk toward the church. We'll have a view from there."

As we passed the town hall—a two-story structure flying the flag of Picardy with its red lions and gold fleurs-de-lis—a man in a rumpled suit emerged from the doorway clutching a stack of papers to his chest;

a little farther away, two women left a small store, one pushing a baby carriage, the other laden with shopping bags. Otherwise, the street was quiet.

Rue de l'Église was not steep, but the incline was steady. Halfway to the top, a bell began to chime, sounding the hour with somber clangs.

"Eleven o'clock," Pierre said.

"Seems quite a sleepy place. We've hardly seen anyone." I stopped just beyond the church and looked around. "Where would you billet more than a thousand men?"

"In the fields, I imagine. Maybe over there." He pointed away from the dense woods framing the town toward a gentle roll of green where roads spread like the spokes of a wheel to create oddly shaped fields. In the near distance, a small cemetery plot with simple white markers looked sadly unkempt. "Officers might have slept in local houses or barns. The village is too small to accommodate everyone else."

Although Pierre spoke with an accent, his English was impeccable, though he occasionally included oddly formal phrases, as if from another era. "I haven't asked where you studied English."

"London," he said. "My father sent me there for a few years. English is the language of business, he always said."

By the set of his mouth, I wondered if he resented his father's view. "Does that make you unhappy?"

"In a way. France used to dominate European thinking. We've lost our influence to your country. And previously to the British." He picked up a flat stone and threw it well beyond a fence on the far side of the road. "My father allowed the pursuit of success to dominate his life."

"And you?"

"There's more to life than money. But that's a topic to discuss over a glass of wine."

Pierre's smile did not light up his eyes the way it had last night, so I took his hint and pointed to a design painted on the peak of a house. "Look at that," I said.

"That is a *rose des vents*," he said, "a compass rose. I wonder why it's here. You usually find them on ships. I'll read you the sign." Pierre stood in front of a bronze plaque. "This building was once a café where soldiers gathered during the Great War to play cards." He turned to me with a grin. "This is what the sign says, but they probably did more than play cards."

I laughed. "You're being so helpful. I'm glad you came along."

Pierre made an elaborate bow, pretending to sweep off his hat as he dipped his head, and I laughed again and took pictures of the café and its compass rose, the church, and the countryside. We strolled farther, nearing the edge of town where the road curved and the land flattened.

"Maybe they camped here," I said, imagining a scene bustling with soldiers, tents laid out in regular rows, supplies rolling in on horse-drawn wagons, thin ribbons of smoke curling upward from the remnants of early-morning fires. Perhaps a football game under way on the flat ground across the stream and men writing letters home while leaning against their gear.

"Did your grandfather write about Toutencourt?"

"Only that they camped here on their way to the Somme. He writes at random intervals. For a while, he'll write every day, and then there will be a gap. Sometimes just a few words. Sometimes facts. Other times, he records impressions and thoughts."

"Must have been difficult to write in the trenches."

I nodded. "The other day, I was wondering who he wrote for and why. Do you think keeping a diary could have helped him cope?"

"I can imagine doing that."

"Me too."

When we returned to the Renault, Pierre suggested we visit a museum at Peronne before going to Courcelette and Thiepval. "It's dedicated to *la Grande Guerre*, and I've heard it has excellent exhibits to explain the war experience. We can have lunch afterward, if you wish."

Peronne was a larger town, its streets and squares decked with hanging baskets full of petunias and cascading ivy. Housed in a medieval chateau, the museum's collection was laid out sparingly for maximum impact. On the floor, surrounded by wooden frames, were full uniforms and kits for French, British, Canadian, and German soldiers. Similar frames housed rifles, ammunition clips, light trench mortars, medical instruments, ambulance supplies, and signaling equipment. In the next room, a display of camouflage techniques showed a hollowed-out tree trunk used as an observation post along with a range of ingenious materials used to disguise artillery and command posts. Along the walls were posters exhorting civilians to donate to the cause or help in some other fashion.

"What does this say, Pierre?" I pointed to a sign that seemed to be telling French citizens what to do during an air raid.

"Turn out all lights. Stay away from windows. If possible, retreat to the basement. To avoid being hurt by breaking glass, open the windows, but only if you have shutters."

"Well, that's quite clear, isn't it?" I said.

He chuckled. "We French love little rules and regulations."

Pierre and I followed two men, one walking with a cane, the other holding his companion's arm as they climbed a short flight of stairs. The men stopped in front of a wooden leg displayed on a shelf next to a pair of wire-rimmed glasses. When the older man tapped his left leg with his cane, I heard a hollow *thunk, thunk* and looked at Pierre. He drew his lips together and nodded.

Near the exit were two rough tables full of debris and a sign explaining that every item had been found in the trenches and battlefields of the Somme. Water bottles, helmets, boots, bully tins, pickaxes, knives, shovels, petrol cans, breastplates, barbed wire—all rusted and dirty.

I sucked in my breath. "My God. Seeing this makes it so real."

"It has almost as much impact as all the earlier exhibits combined," Pierre replied.

We said nothing more, merely stared at the remnants of war. These tangible items encapsulated all I had read and allowed me to imagine Martin's experiences in a visceral way. A lost helmet became a dead soldier lying in the mud gasping for breath; a pickax suggested a sapper tunneling deep beneath German lines; a bully tin made me think of meals where the food contained bits of mud and smelled of petrol; a tangled piece of barbed wire made me feel the jagged tearing of leg or arm or face. I shuddered.

"Do you feel like lunch?" Pierre said after a lengthy silence.

"Not really. I have some food from the hotel in the car. We can share it later, if you like."

"Would you like me to drive?"

I shook my head. "Driving will keep my mind occupied."

"Courcelette next?"

"Courcelette."

Pierre guided us cross-country, avoiding heavily traveled roads. Dense bush sprouting clusters of orange berries or tall chestnut trees marked the intersections. Cemeteries dotted the landscape. Clouds gathered on the horizon like a thick ribbon of mourning.

Courcelette contained chipped brick homes and narrow streets, nothing to distinguish it from other villages we had seen that morning. Nothing to suggest it had been completely leveled during the battles for the Somme. Beyond the town, we found the turn for its memorial at a long row of trees on either side of a graveled entrance. I parked next to a camper van with its roof propped open and rock music blaring. A red peace sign had been painted on the driver's side.

"Hippies visiting a war memorial?" I said. "Seems odd."

"Perhaps they wanted somewhere to sleep undisturbed," Pierre said with a low laugh.

"Good to know you have a sense of humor."

Beyond the parking lot, a stone path led to a low, square memorial, one side inscribed with the words *WITH SACRIFICE AND*

DEVOTION beneath a wreath of maple leaves. On the other side, an inscription commemorated the Canadians for their part in breaking German lines. We examined all four sides of the monument.

"Would you like to hear some of what my grandfather wrote?"

"I would be honored," he said.

We had moved away from the memorial to gaze at what had once been a battlefield but was now farmland. A line of trees defined a distant boundary, beyond which were glimpses of rooftops against a band of white clouds.

I described the beginning of Martin's diary and how his early entries were optimistic, imagining danger in the context of adventure. As I flipped through the pages, I read brief snippets, at times lighthearted, at other times morose or critical. My voice wavered as I read passages describing his increasing sadness and frustration.

"It's as though he's trying to figure out the military strategy. For months, his brigade has been near Ypres, where they measured advances and losses in feet. After Ypres, he comes here to the Somme."

"The Somme was a terrible place to be. Every French child learns about it in school."

"Here's the first entry at Courcelette." I showed Pierre the page I'd marked before leaving that morning and began to read:

"September 16, 1916. Nerves tight as wire before we began, but the sweat trickling down my back soon disappeared. Barrage began at 3:00 a.m. on the fifteenth. We went over the top at 6:20 and took several German trenches very quickly and many prisoners. By 7:40, we had captured the Sugar Factory. My section came under frequent fire with six casualties. Twenty-First Battalion has severe losses, many of them officers I trained with. We're very short of officers now, and some of the new ones have little experience. Intense enemy shelling all night and counterattacks on the sixteenth. Relief brigades coming in tonight.

September 17, 1916. General assessment: attack successful in our sector due to intense preparation and element of surprise. Other brigades failed to *advance as far as planned. Tanks had mixed success. Casualties were laid out like a sea of broken men. We can't sustain this level of loss. The day is a blur of images, and now nothing stirs. Nine of fifty men gone. At dusk, I watched the sky turn pink, then purple, and finally darken to a moonless smudge and wondered what tomorrow will bring. We begin again in a few days."*

"Nine men gone," Pierre repeated when I closed the diary. "How could they face each day? And what would he have said to his remaining men? I wonder if my grandfather had the same sort of experience."

"There are many entries like that."

"Everything is so peaceful now. It is difficult to believe how many died to save this land."

As we stood overlooking the rolling countryside, I debated telling Pierre about Grandpa's puzzle. Spending the day in his company, I felt safe, able to dismiss thoughts of the man in a straw fedora. Instinct told me he would treat the puzzle seriously. *But how would that help? He'll be gone in a day or two, and so will you.* Instead, I returned to the topic at hand.

"I know," I said. "Around Ypres, there were so many cemeteries and memorials I lost count. Everything else looked quiet and calm, like it must have looked for centuries."

"Shall we go on to Thiepval?"

I remained still, my gaze fixed on some distant point. Finally, I nodded. "Will you drive?"

Thiepval Ridge appeared innocent, wrapped in white with breaking bits of blue. In the foreground, rectangular patches of gold mixed with green and the deep brown of freshly tilled fields. After the car turned a sharp right, the memorial was suddenly visible, its great brick arch and massive base an invincible gateway to victory.

"I feel like a tiny insect," I said as we approached the looming edifice on foot.

Pierre gestured at the memorial. "Your guidebook says it is one hundred and forty feet high and that the foundations are nineteen feet thick."

"Look at the names." I traced a finger along the letters of *H. L. BOLTON*, wondering who he was and the circumstances of his death.

"There are seventy-two thousand names of soldiers who died at the Somme and have no known grave," Pierre read from a sign posted near the memorial. "Seventy-two thousand. And those are just the soldiers of the British Empire."

We walked beneath the towering arch and emerged on the far side, where precise lines of simple white markers stood like stepping-stones for sacrificial souls.

"I imagine Martin thought the ridge almost impenetrable. Do you think they could see any landmarks other than rubble and tree stumps?" I said.

"Probably not. And they would have heard the constant sound of explosions. What did he write about Thiepval?"

"He said it was a costly exercise. And that without Bill, he would not have survived. Bill was his closest friend. At the beginning, Martin had three close friends. Michel was wounded near Ypres. Pete died here at Thiepval. Blown to bits. They were all in the same battalion."

We walked around the thick limestone columns, pausing in front of a raised section at the heart of the memorial inscribed with the words *THEIR NAME LIVETH FOR EVERMORE*. A collection of poppy wreaths leaned against the stone like freshly spilled blood.

Pierre stood beside me. "If I had been an officer, I would have had difficulty sending my men into battle each day," he said. "French troops even mutinied at one point."

"By this point, my grandfather was losing hope," I said, wiping away a tear. "Let me read you what he wrote."

I took a deep breath before beginning. *"September 26, 1916. Another day of bombardment. Many operational orders issued. We have to attack to take the ridge, but when we do, the men become sitting ducks for enemy fire and artillery. Machine guns and tanks assigned with us. Shells are cascading like fireworks in the distance tonight. We synchronized watches at 10:50. This waiting drives me crazy.*

September 27, 1916. Kept on the move for two days. Machine gunners and tanks kept us company. Tanks proved useless—kept getting stuck in the mud. Attacks went back and forth, fighting for every square foot, using grenades to clear the trenches. Pushed my men to the limit, and I'm proud of them. Worked under heavy shelling and sniping to consolidate positions. Exploding shells lift great scoops of dirt and fling them toward the sky. At one point, a shell burst within two yards of my position, and the force of the explosion knocked me out; Davidson pulled me to safety. Enemy flares made night work difficult, but our position has stabilized. Germans so deeply dug in that our division was unable to take Regina Trench. Hundreds of casualties. Desolation everywhere. We are weapons now, not men. Men decide whether or not to kill. Weapons merely kill."

"I can understand why he said that," Pierre said. "The war was so brutal. I wonder what kept them going?"

"I don't know, and Martin doesn't say. I read somewhere most men kept going for the sake of their friends. But the following day, Martin's friend Pete died."

After Thiepval, Pierre drove us to Arras. He seemed to sense I needed a change and showed me the ancient Abbey of St. Vaast and its adjoining museum full of medieval sculptures, faded tapestries, delicate porcelain, and paintings from the seventeenth century. Though I said little, I was grateful to immerse myself in beauty. When it became clear that the museum was about to close, he took me to a bar located just off the

Grand Place. The lighting was soft, and dark wood lined the lower half of each wall while thick beams held up the ceiling. A bell clanged whenever the door opened. Pierre ordered two glasses of beer.

"You must try the beer. It's dark but has lovely hints of chocolate and coffee. A local favorite."

After watching him take a gulp and swirl it in his mouth before swallowing, I sniffed the beer's smokiness and took a sip, the liquid bubbling softly on my tongue, its light bitterness tasting vaguely of chocolate, just as he promised.

"Are you a connoisseur?" I asked.

"In this part of France, we take our beer seriously." He raised his glass and winked, but his face soon grew somber. "I have not seen the British memorials before. Did you learn anything about your grandfather today?"

"I don't know. I think he feels responsible. How could he not? And I suppose he feels helpless."

"Imagine leading your men into action knowing some would die. I'm not sure I could do that."

My shoulders slumped, and I turned my glass around and around. "I can't get over how many men died." My voice trailed off, and we sipped our beers in silence.

"I have a restaurant in mind, if you're not too tired," he said a few minutes later.

I shifted on my chair, considering his suggestion. Today's sights brought Martin's dilemma into sharper focus, a focus that demanded further contemplation.

"Or I can take you back, if you prefer." Pierre's left foot bobbed up and down.

"Dinner would be lovely."

At the restaurant, an intimate space of flickering candlelight and spicy aromas, sparkling glassware, and murmured conversations, Pierre ordered for me, which felt old-fashioned but seemed to give him great enjoyment. Oysters Mornay, vichyssoise, and quail with grapes and tarragon. By the time the soup was served, we'd settled into a discussion of art and artists as Pierre talked of his work and I shared stories about my grandfather's gallery. When two espressos arrived at the end of the meal, a slim, balding man wearing chef's whites approached our table with a smile. He clapped his hand on Pierre's shoulder and spoke in rapid French. Pierre laughed.

"My cousin Gerard. He says you're beautiful."

Gerard took my hand, and for a moment I thought he might bend over to kiss it like a courtier from long ago. Instead, he held it between his hands, callused and nicked from cooking.

"If he doesn't treat you good, you come tell me, mademoiselle. You like your dinner?"

"Delicious, Gerard. Absolutely delicious."

Still holding my hand, Gerard spoke once again in rapid French. I had no idea what he said, but a hint of pink appeared on Pierre's cheeks, and a rueful look crossed his face.

"Please visit again, Grace," Gerard said, releasing my hand.

Pierre stood and put an arm around his cousin, then walked with him across the room to the kitchen door. They spoke for a few minutes before Pierre returned to the table.

"You didn't tell me you know the chef."

"He's one of my favorite cousins. Actually, he owns the restaurant. Has done for years. Usually, his wife is here, but her mother is in the hospital, so she's away for a few days. You would like her."

Following dinner, our drive back to the hotel was quiet, and when we parted at the bottom of the stairs, he touched my cheek. Nothing more, just a brief touch with one finger—disquieting in the most tantalizing way.

MARTIN'S DIARY

October 17, 1916

The last view of Thiepval as we marched away is imprinted on my brain. I'll never forget and never forgive those bastards who killed Pete. Not just the Germans, but the higher-ups who gave the orders. Senseless slaughter. Just Bill and me left. God knows how we'll carry on.

November 21, 1916

We're seasoned troops now. Drummond said so after Sunday parade. He also said we compare very well with the PPCLI, who are known for their successes. Who gives a damn? Pete, Woody, Sherman, MacLeod? They don't fucking care. They're dead. I watched Woody get blown up. One minute he was there, and the next minute he was scattered into pieces no one will ever find. Same as Pete. I wrote Michel about Pete. Not sure if he'll reply, but I knew he would want to know.

We've been in the Somme three months—have taken a few hundred yards and pushed back the German salient, but the cost has been terrible. Forty percent of our battalion gone. We can't win a war like this, advance a little here and there, take a ridge, then lose it again two months later. I tell my men it can't get any worse, but I know that's a lie. At night, some of them tell stories and write letters and try to sleep; others simply stare at nothing. Death is on its own clock; nothing to be done but wait for it.

CHAPTER 12

November 1916

"Dev. Wake up, Dev." Bill shook Martin's shoulder. "We're wanted at brigade HQ. By the look on the sergeant major's face, something significant is going on. He said to hurry."

Martin lay on a lumpy mattress in quarters little more than a large cave, stone walls wet and clammy, the floor nothing but packed earth smelling like rancid meat. But at least they were dry. He shared the space with Bill and Simon, who was proving capable but prissy. So far, no one had replaced Pete.

Martin rubbed his eyes. "Fuck. I only just fell asleep."

"Come on, Dev." Bill offered his hand to haul Martin up. "Too early for foul language."

Martin shoved on his boots and followed Bill through a warren of connecting tunnels until they reached a meeting room jammed with officers. Along the way, they passed handwritten signs: *This Way to Heaven*, *Fine Dining*, and *Hooley's Bar*. Signs labeled *Throne Room* led to brigade headquarters, where chairs were few and reserved for senior officers. Martin and Bill leaned against the back wall and waited.

Brigadier Fenton stood next to a large map where solid lines documented the network of tunnels built by the Engineer Corps, and dashed lines estimated the locations of enemy tunnels. At a nod from his adjutant, Fenton began.

"We're planning a little show in three nights' time, and you boys will be front and center."

Martin hated terms like *little show* because they diminished the enormity of what soldiers did and the consequences. *If we used real words like* bloodbath *and* killing raid, he thought, *perhaps we could find a way out of this mess faster.*

The brigadier outlined a plan to blow up one of their own mines, which would in turn destroy several German mines. The operation would take place at night using four thousand pounds of highly explosive ammonal set in three different charges under and between two craters. Garrisons at crater posts and in nearby dugouts would withdraw before action commenced to avoid unnecessary deaths. Consolidating parties would be ready to rush forward and collar the lip of the newly formed crater to hold it.

"I don't have to tell you there will be a good deal of artillery retaliation."

Strange what men will talk about before battle, Martin thought, listening to his men banter and curse while waiting in a tunnel for the signal to begin. For the most part, no one grumbled, and except for the occasional dark stare, he observed little fear. His men spoke of letters received or last night's generous rum ration or a broken bootlace. They told jokes and shared cigarettes and punched one another in the shoulder, not a hard punch, just the kind friends exchange as a token of camaraderie. His face softened as he listened and then hardened as he imagined who might soon be missing.

At two a.m., Martin's orders came through, and in the deep of night, he led his now-silent platoon, following a scout he could barely see. Each man carried twenty-four hours of rations, one hundred twenty rounds of ammunition, a pack, a blanket, a waterproof sheet, hip boots, mitts, and a water bottle. On their heads were four-pound steel helmets, much heavier than those issued previously. The pace was slow as the men felt for solid ground with every step, from time to time making way for pack mules. His platoon was separated from Bill's by one hundred yards to prevent enemy artillery from killing too many with a single well-directed shell.

By three a.m., they were settled at the edge of a crater called Big Slide, the Boche on the other side less than forty yards away. Though the men were muddy and freezing, Martin's orders were to stay quiet until action began, with a penalty of court-martial for lights or cigarettes. Once the mines exploded, Martin's men would rush forward with sandbags, knife rests, and iron plates to collar the lip of the newly formed crater so it could be held against retaliation. Their battalion was on a precarious course, betting that the Germans would not blow their own tunnels first. He and his men had hours to wait, and Martin knew some would be wondering whether this time their number was up.

To keep his mind occupied, he thought of the last letters he'd had from home. The one that had arrived a few days ago, his mother had written in late September, and in it she spoke of the jams she'd made and the fruits and vegetables she and Jane had canned to take them through the winter months. His father's latest letter spoke of repairs to the roof and a recent poker game with a group of men he'd played with for more than twenty years. Jane's letters usually made him laugh—her latest was no exception—and a smile appeared as he recalled what she'd written.

As the sun breached the horizon, birds began to twitter, and Martin envied their freedom to escape the misery below. Looking up, he watched gray wings flap, dip like a grace note, then lift toward the beckoning flame of day.

That night, at exactly nine fifty p.m., a monstrous boom sounded, shrieking and roaring like nothing Martin had ever experienced. Directly in front of the German lines, the earth rose like a massive mushroom, and the trench where he and his men waited shook as though an earthquake were tearing apart the land, sucking mud and debris from its path. Bursts of flames emerged from the explosion. Artillery opened fire.

In less than twenty minutes, flares called them to action. Martin and his men skirted the edge of the crater, stepping over debris and slogging through pools of water to reach the forward lip. He motioned them into a crouch. Moonlight exposed a yawning hole more than thirty feet deep, the sides draped in dead bodies, arms and limbs skewed in every direction like dolls tossed onto a garbage heap.

"We need to work quickly," Martin said, "but the sides are steep, and the earth will be loose. Jackson's platoon is on our left. We'll work together toward the middle. Be careful and methodical. I don't want to lose anyone in that pit. Any questions?"

Protected by snipers and Lewis guns against enemy retaliation, they worked hard, building two new posts before being relieved by another platoon.

"Has anyone seen Murphy or Fitz?" Martin said, crawling among his men when they were back in the trenches, asking the same question over and over. In the chaos of securing the crater, no one had seen either soldier disappear.

MARTIN'S DIARY

February 5, 1917

What is the purpose of endless action, retaliation, and further retaliation? Our front at the Somme moves in and out like a wheezing accordion whose tunes we blindly follow. We are cold, exhausted men who must beg for clean socks and the luxury of a bath every thirty days or more. Duty and sacrifice, freedom for our loved ones—but what about us? I look into eyes robbed of humanity and into other eyes glazed with fear. Will building another trench or another mile of tunnel stop this madness?

February 22, 1917

We have moved to billets at Neuville-Saint-Vaast, not far from Vimy Ridge. Based on all the men and materials being assembled and the miles of tunnel being built, something immense is under way. The higher-ups must be planning a third attempt to take the ridge, which looms in the distance like a specter of doom. Last night, Bill and I went to a concert and laughed over several sketches mocking senior officers and the bungling of Sam Hughes. Bill called it gallows humor. Sent my usual letters home today. Had two from Mother this week and one from Dad with a few stories that cheered me up.

CHAPTER 13

April 9, 1917

Martin and his men assembled in Zivy Cave, a vast space where brigade and battalion staff waited along with hundreds of soldiers. Equipped with electric lights, running water, tables, kitchens, and telephones, the cave had been a hub for the Nineteenth Battalion, its spokes connected with all other battalions through a maze of trenches and tunnels. With so much snow and rain, the roof dribbled in sections, coating the floor with gray slime. The air reeked of tobacco and sweat.

At four a.m., they moved into Zivy Tunnel, where they remained jammed shoulder to shoulder for the last ninety minutes before the attack. Martin watched Butler moving around the tunnel, checking the men, clasping a shoulder here and there, his voice jolly, as though the day's objectives were nothing unusual. His captain looked like he could sleep for a month.

"Remember, men," Butler said, eyes sweeping around the darkened space, "we've practiced each step. You all know your parts and how to step in for others. Remember, the artillery conquers, and it's our job to occupy. You'll do well. I know you will. I'm proud of you all."

Butler often said, "Artillery conquers, infantry occupies," as though imbuing their role with grand purpose. Once Martin and Pete had discussed the validity of that phrase, trying to decide whether it somehow demeaned the infantry, whether their captain would have preferred being in the artillery to leading foot soldiers like them. Pete had observed the contradiction between a culture slavishly adhering to command and the chaotic disorder of battle. *Pete would approve of today's orders,* Martin thought.

Waiting for battle to commence, he briefly stretched his back to ease the strain of standing so long and shook his head to clear his mind; sharp powers of concentration were essential for what was to come.

At exactly five thirty, as a colossal roar of artillery began, the Nineteenth Battalion rushed forward. Having practiced every stage and every move a hundred times, Martin's men executed the opening sequence with precision. Within three minutes, they gained their first target and by five fifty-one crossed the German front lines. Exhilarated, Martin and his men pressed forward in preparation for taking their next objective.

The artillery barrage paused to allow reserve units to move up, and for a few minutes he could hear himself think. So far, enemy retaliation had been weak, and Nully confirmed with a quick nod that their platoon was intact. Looking right to check that Bill remained on his flank, Martin caught a glimpse of his friend's hefty shoulders, but as he turned left to look for Simon, German machine-gun fire erupted, forcing Martin and his men to take cover. When the guns fell silent, Butler motioned them forward toward Furze Trench.

Across the muddy sky, signal flares marked Allied advances while green rockets indicated German panic. Crouching low, stretcher-bearers fanned out to search for casualties, and through the mist, Martin saw a small cluster of prisoners straggle past.

"Bavarians," Nully shouted, to be heard above the barrage.

Martin nodded but said nothing. He was worried that decreasing visibility from the rain and sleet would hamper their efforts. German barrages still concentrated on positions they'd left more than an hour ago, but it wouldn't be long before they adjusted their sights to put the Nineteenth in danger. Continued movement was critical.

"Not much opposition," Martin said to Nully.

"Can't last, sir. Have to get on with consolidating our position."

"Right."

Martin heard the rumble of tanks advancing on their left and checked his watch. Beyond the hulking machines, he could see the vague outline of soldiers from another brigade. These men would leap-frog the Nineteenth and continue the push forward, leaving German forces almost no time to exit their deep dugouts and defend against the infantry advance. Once again, the sky filled with howling madness.

"Dig in. Over here, dig in," Martin shouted to be heard. "Bernstein, get your machine gun working. Hurry. I need it now."

Less than ten feet away, Bernstein knelt on the ground and flipped open the front legs that steadied the gun. Kirby stretched beside him and readied a belt of ammunition. The rest of Martin's platoon fanned out along a low ledge of sandbags. Nully crouched nearby waiting for orders. A group of signalers began to dig a cable trench, two of them carrying a huge roll of wire. Shells burst to their left.

"How are we supposed to know whether it's clear up ahead?" Nully's mouth was only an inch from Martin's ear.

"I don't fucking know, Nully. You figure it out. Kendal!" Martin shouted for his signals corporal, and the man wiggled close. "Can you reach Butler?"

"No, sir. Our lines aren't working yet."

The scene looked anything but orderly as clumps of men, scattered over a wide swath, made their way up the ridge. Martin and Nully looked at one another. Martin nodded only once. They would proceed.

In a sudden spit of rifle fire, Kirby toppled over. Bernstein's gun fired in return, spraying shells in a narrow arc at the source of German attack. Another man took up Kirby's post while Martin motioned for three of his platoon to take out the enemy's position. He watched them crawl forward, and upon hearing their grenades explode followed by the sound of screaming, twisted his mouth into a grotesque smile.

By nightfall, he and his men were situated on the crest of Vimy Ridge, the land behind them torn to bits, the land beyond the ridge showing evidence of massive German retreat. From time to time, a shell dropped far away, spurting mud in all directions, but otherwise the scene was calm. Farther east, shells were exploding on roads leading north to German-held territory and the towns of Lens, Avion, and Mericourt.

"We've won the ridge, haven't we, Lieutenant?" Nully said.

"Yes. Well done, boys. I'm proud of every one of you. I'll go check with Butler to see what's next. Nully, you keep this motley crew in order."

"Aye, aye, sir," Nully said with a grin.

"Any casualties other than Kirby?"

Nully's grin disappeared. "At least four others. Probably more. I'll do roll call and let you know when you return."

Martin nodded and headed north to the brigade's command post, situated in one of the German trenches.

"Devlin reporting, sir," he said to Lieutenant Colonel Drummond. "Objectives achieved."

"Well done, Devlin. Have a tot of whiskey. I'm gathering reports from each company, and I'll soon have a more complete picture. Sorry about Butler," he added. "An excellent man."

Martin stepped back a few paces. "Butler, sir? He's gone?" The pit of Martin's stomach heaved as though something had exploded within him.

"No. Wounded. Serious, I'm told. I'll know more tomorrow morning."

"Any word on Bill Jackson, sir?"

"Foxley!" Drummond shouted to be heard over the noise, a combination of exploding shells and the shouts of men. "Bill Jackson. Where is he?"

Captain Foxley held a clipboard in one hand and a hunk of cheese in the other. "We just had word. Lieutenant Jackson was killed taking Thelus. A very admirable effort, according to his sergeant."

Martin staggered, attempting to maintain his balance. A rush of acid clogged his throat, forcing him to swallow, once, twice, three times before regaining control. His vision blurred. *Not Bill. Not Bill. Anyone but Bill. Anyone.*

"Thelus?" he said. Foxley nodded. "Where is he?" Foxley consulted his notes and looked at his commanding officer.

"Friend of yours, Devlin?" Drummond intervened.

Fighting nausea, Martin moved his head up and down. Both Drummond and Foxley looked enormous to him, as though someone had pumped them full of air. His grip on reality felt tenuous. "Since we were boys," he managed to say.

"Foxley, get the lieutenant another tot of whiskey." To Martin, his CO seemed to spit the words rather than speak them. "Losing friends is hell," Drummond continued, placing an arm on Martin's shoulder. "Sit here for a minute, Lieutenant. Take as long as you need to compose yourself."

A tear slid down Martin's cheek and hung for a moment at his chin before falling to the ground. *When will this stop?* he wondered. His head felt as though something had crawled inside it, poking every cavity, scraping the bones of his cheeks. He had nothing left to give, and he whirled deeper and deeper into a bottomless pit of despair.

Faceless men stared at him as he staggered back to his platoon, and he saw nothing except the shit and the filth and the soul-destroying pulse of war and everywhere the reek of corpses. *What have we wrought?* he thought. *Through what twisted path of logic can we have justified the consequences of men pitted against one another like animals fighting over the putrid remains of a dead carcass? We are weapons. We are cannonballs and bullets and bayonet thrusts and fuses. We are nothing. I am nothing.*

Clouds hurtled above the treetops in the dead of night, and he imagined eyes all around him. The eyes of German soldiers preparing for battle. The eyes of the enemy cowering and terrified. The eyes of men he had killed in battle. He knew he could kill each one of them again.

CHAPTER 14

June 1991

All along the winding road, the tall pillars of the Vimy Memorial were haunting in their majestic simplicity, marking the ridge as a monument to sacrifice, duty, and the fading glories of time. When at last I stood in front of the mourning female figure representing Canada's grief for its fallen soldiers, tears ran down my cheeks.

In fields west and south of the ridge, remnants of trenches, craters, and tunnels made Martin's experience clearer. Did he zigzag over this particular patch of ground? Did he lead his men beyond that crater? I would never know.

After looking at old photos and maps showing battle plans displayed at the tourist center, I followed a guide through one of the underground tunnels that had been preserved so visitors could appreciate the conditions below ground. Narrow passageways; rooms the size of prison cells where bunk beds allowed moments of sleep; stone walls thickened with lichens; a stifling, primordial odor of stale air and mouse droppings. According to the guide, some of the tunnels had stretched almost as far as Mont St. Eloi, three miles away.

I knew from Martin's diary that zero hour was five thirty a.m., and I imagined him leading his men up the slope of the ridge amid the deafening blasts of artillery, dodging and weaving, firing his rifle, urging everyone forward. Did they have time to think, or did they merely perform well-practiced parts?

As I walked along a path leading to one of four cemeteries, the distant fields and clear blue sky felt at odds with what had occurred seventy-four years earlier. Standing in front of a sign honoring those buried beneath each small cross, I sucked in my breath as I read that graves had been dug prior to battle. To know that some military officer would have estimated the death toll in advance made me almost physically sick. Would I have been able to dig graves for men still living, men with hopes for the future? Would I have been too numb and disillusioned to care?

Was Martin afraid? He rarely wrote about fear, so I had nothing specific to consider, but how could he not feel its flickering surge with all that he faced? Surely his breath would quicken and his skin prickle with doubt. Surely his hearing would sharpen and his muscles tense. Perhaps fear had given way to acceptance of his fate.

Martin lost the last of his best friends here. After reading and rereading the diaries, I felt I knew them: Bill, who had been such a steadying influence; Michel, with his sense of humor; Pete, who, along with Martin, collected bits of information with which to debate battle strategy. All young men on the cusp of life who fought for the freedom of future generations. Not one of them had created the circumstances leading to war, but they followed their leaders, obeyed each order, and kept alive a tiny flame of hope.

Or did they? As far as I could tell, Martin had run out of hope after the Battle of Vimy Ridge.

I opened Martin's diary and ran my finger along words he had written so long ago. The page describing Vimy Ridge had yellowed like every other page, but the last few words stood out, thick and emphatic, as though he had pressed the pen hard against the paper. *I will carry the burden of their deaths as long as I live.* After Vimy, he stopped writing for more than a month, and I assumed grief had overcome him, but I knew from later entries that he also felt pure, blinding outrage.

Summer sounds of flickering insects and chirping birds mingled with the scent of freshly mown hay from adjacent fields. Visitors came and went, soft chatter mixed with the scrunch of footsteps, sharp laughter at odds with my sense of sorrow, the weight like a heavy blanket, confining rather than comforting.

I was in no hurry to leave. Indeed, the idea of rushing off after such a moving experience seemed almost sacrilegious. *The thousands who fought deserve more,* I thought, *so much more. Why didn't Grandpa tell me?*

Since first reading his diaries, I had asked this question over and over, regret filling me with intense longing for his strong face and wise words, his wry humor and gentle scolding. I missed him even more now than when he died, sensing that our relationship would have deepened further with time. But would I have understood if he had described his experiences? Would I have been patient enough to respect his feelings?

The sun disappeared behind a cloud, and I shivered and reached into my bag for a light sweater. Distracted by my thoughts, I was pulling the sweater over my head when I heard the crunch of footsteps approaching.

"I need to talk to you."

I whirled around at the sound of a male voice. Fedora Man, without the fedora. I clutched my purse tightly, holding it against my chest as if it could protect me.

"Who are you? Why have you been following me?"

"Keep your voice down."

"Why? Why should I keep my voice down?" I raised my voice more and glanced around. While there was no one in the immediate vicinity, a family was nearing the parking area—father, mother, and two sons who looked a little younger than Paul and Michael.

He grabbed my elbow. "We'll just take a little walk so I can explain."

"I'm not going anywhere with you."

During college, I had taken a women's self-defense course with my roommate because there had been several threatening incidents on campus. *Aim for the eyes first and the groin second* was the only piece of advice I remembered. His eyes were protected by sunglasses. But my shoes had pointy toes and I kicked with as much force as I could.

"Fuck," he said, letting go of my arm and bending over in pain.

I wasted no time and ran toward the family. Fedora Man did not follow.

CHAPTER 15

June 1991

The whine of a vacuum cleaner pulled me from a fretful sleep, groggy and not in the least refreshed. My first thought—the same one that had preoccupied me since the incident—concerned the identity of my assailant and the reason he had accosted me. Nothing made sense. The family I'd approached yesterday spoke little English; however, I had been able to convey a desire to walk with them to the parking lot. Once in the Renault, I'd wasted no time returning to Chateau Noyelle and had paced my room until seven o'clock. During dinner, which had consisted of more wine than food, a dark feeling had settled over me, a feeling I couldn't shake. Pierre, the only person I could think to talk to, had not appeared.

Questions filled the spaces between bites of food and sips of wine. Would the man with the fedora appear again? Why would someone want to frighten me? Was I in danger? My thoughts turned to my children.

At breakfast, I ordered a double espresso, and the buzz of caffeine made me feel more human; however, the idea of any food beyond a single slice of baguette turned my stomach. For distraction, I watched a nearby couple, the man slumped in his seat reading the newspaper, lower lip protruding into a pout—a pout large enough to hang a mustard pot on, Grandmama would have said. The woman across from him ate forkful after forkful in a determined fashion, eyes flitting around the room. Neither spoke.

"You must be daydreaming."

My coffee cup rattled as I set it down. "You startled me."

Thick eyebrows raised, Pierre rested one hand on the table, close enough for me to catch a pleasing scent of soap and aftershave.

"What were you thinking about?"

"I'm watching that couple. They've been here for more than thirty minutes and haven't said a word to each other."

"Perhaps they're fighting?"

"He scowls a lot. They've probably been married too long; no spice left now that their children are gone."

"That's imaginative." He sat down beside me. "What did you see yesterday?"

"Vimy Ridge. It was very moving." Tears pricked my eyes, and I blinked several times to keep them from falling. "But . . ."

"But what?"

"Oh, nothing." If I told him about Fedora Man, he'd probably think I was crazy. And besides, what did I really know about Pierre?

He frowned and waited a few moments before speaking again. "Where are you going today?"

"I haven't decided."

"Then you're coming with me. You've seen too many cemeteries and monuments. I have a meeting in Lille that won't take long. Afterward, I can show you the city."

I hesitated. He seemed so sure of himself, so certain I would go along with his plans, and a small part of me wanted to say no. Jim had also been sure of himself, an attitude I found attractive when we met, but Jim's self-assurance became dominance, and I had no desire for that kind of relationship again.

Don't be ridiculous. This isn't a relationship. Relax and enjoy his company. Much better than worrying why someone has been following me. Yesterday's encounter removed any doubt I had about *whether* someone was following me. The question now was why. And would he try again?

"That would be lovely."

Pierre's smile made him look boyish. "*Très bien.* Will you meet me outside in twenty minutes?"

We went in his car, a low-slung silver Peugeot that cornered easily and accelerated briskly whenever he passed another vehicle. En route, Pierre spoke little, and I followed his lead, enjoying the scenery and the comfort of having someone else worry about directions.

"We'll take more interesting roads on the way back," he said as we sped along the highway.

Pierre dropped me at the tourist center in Lille, where I picked up a pamphlet and map. While he went to his meeting, I walked through the ancient town, stopping first in front of a massive sculpture honoring soldiers and civilians who had endured two wars. The pamphlet described the German occupation of Lille in World War I as a time of heroism and suffering, the city having surrendered after three days of bloody resistance and widespread destruction. All around were buildings of brick and stone, their facades decorated with cupids, cornucopias, garlands, and lions, and I pictured them as they would have been then, ruined by heavy bombardment.

Following the arrows on the map took me through the Grand Place, dominated by an ornate clock tower, then past the opera house, where a group of backpackers congregated by a circular fountain, and the old stock exchange, each building grander than its predecessor.

The route turned left down a narrow street, then along a wide pedestrian boulevard, past windows hung with white duvets airing in the summer sun and around corners where café tables invited leisurely morning coffee and groups of men played chess. When I saw a shop full of chocolates piled into pyramids, I went inside and, smiling at the intense aroma, bought ten individual pieces of differing shapes and colors from a woman whose round middle and full bosom suggested a passion for her wares.

Outside the chocolate shop, I checked my watch and hurried back to the tourist office, where Pierre was leaning against the wall by the entrance, hands tucked into the front pockets of his pants.

"What a charming city," I said as we strolled along Rue de la Monnaie and negotiated our way past a woman securing her bicycle to a lamppost.

"It used to be Flemish. Louis the Fourteenth laid siege to the city sometime in the seventeenth century. He built the citadel. Later, the Austrians tried to take it but failed. It was occupied during the First World War." He shrugged. "The Lillois are a strong people."

"Where are we going?"

"I have an idea for lunch." He gestured at a narrow path on our right, which we followed until it opened into an oddly shaped plaza. "This is Place aux Oignons. The restaurant is just over there."

Pierre led me through a door decorated with etched glass into a tiny restaurant called Au Vieux de la Vieille. A bar dominated one end of the restaurant while wooden shelves filled with white-and-blue crockery dominated the other. Smells of ripe cheese and spicy sausage stirred my hunger. Crowded tables filled the room, and I could barely hear the clock chime over the buzz of conversation.

"Why is this called Onion Place?" I asked once we were seated.

"A long time ago, it was called Place Donjon. *Donjon* means 'castle keep,' but the name became distorted over time. *Oignons, donjon.* They sound alike, do they not?"

"How do you know these things?"

Pierre sipped his beer before replying. "I guess I am a student of trivia." He drew the corners of his mouth down. "Historical trivia."

"Why the frown?"

"My father didn't approve of my fascination for history. He still doesn't."

"At least you have a father. Mine died when I was five."

"Oh. I'm sorry," he said. "What happened to him?"

"It was a plane crash. A small plane. I never really had a mother either. She fell apart after Daddy died, and now she has Alzheimer's. My grandparents raised me. I suppose you would call it an unusual upbringing. Grandmama was strict and disapproving. Grandpa was the one who offered affection and reassurance and taught me so much. He used to say things like, 'Truth shall be your shield' and 'Make sure you live without regrets.' One of my favorites is 'Ideals are like stars; if you follow them, you will reach your destiny.'" I laughed and, encouraged by Pierre's smile, continued. "I used to wonder about my destiny, and now I wonder why I didn't ask him more about his own life." I stopped. Why was I telling Pierre so much about my past? "You don't want to hear any more of this," I said, forcing a wide smile to my lips.

"On the contrary, your grandfather sounds like a wonderful man."

"You'll have to tell me more about your father and why you scowl whenever you mention him."

Pierre drained his beer. "Perhaps I will another time."

When we left the restaurant, he said he had a destination in mind, and a little while later, we stood in front of several connected buildings blending different architectural styles. "This is the Hospice Comtesse. The original hospital was built in the thirteenth century by the Countess of Flanders inside the walls of her palace. She hoped God would notice her charity and return her husband, who was a prisoner of the king of France. Now it's a history museum."

"And did he?" I asked.

"Did he what?"

"Did her husband return?"

"He did, but not for twelve years. She ruled in his place."

"Can we go inside?"

Pierre grinned. "I was hoping you would ask."

The interior was larger than I'd expected, full of tapestries and paintings, antique furniture, and musical instruments, some from the fourteenth century, others from the sixteenth and seventeenth centuries. In what was once a hospital ward, we stood beneath a vaulted ceiling of paneled timber while he explained that each square of the ceiling represented heraldic arms of the hospital's benefactors. I watched Pierre's animated face as he talked about these treasures.

"The craftsmanship is exquisite."

"True," he said. "Unfortunately, most craftsmen were terribly poor."

I nodded. "Would you want to live in that world?"

Pierre leaned over to examine a case displaying ancient coins and jeweled plates and cups. "I don't think so. Far too likely I would be someone's servant, desperate to earn enough to feed my family."

I wanted to ask about his family, but something in his voice suggested the time still wasn't right. "What's in the next room?"

By the time we left the hospice, heavy clouds had dimmed the city's charm, and Pierre set a brisk pace, taking shortcuts through narrow alleys and interior courtyards, dodging traffic en route to his car. Just as we reached the parking lot, it began to rain, small drops turning within seconds into fat splotches.

"Quickly," he said, grabbing my hand and sprinting toward the Peugeot.

The car cocooned us from the elements, rain pounding the exterior like drummers beating a war dance, spiraling toward the edge of control. Through fogging windows, I watched lightning flash followed by a split of thunder.

"Does it always storm so suddenly?" I asked.

Still feeling the warm clasp of Pierre's hand, I kept my voice cool and hoped he would assume my blushing cheeks were the result of running. I was acutely aware of his hand resting on his thigh and his eyes watching me.

"Sometimes. We'll have to wait until it eases." He reached in front of me to open the glove box and extracted a small cloth to wipe the fog from the front window. "I promised to take you on the back roads. There is a place I want to show you."

"Where's that?"

"It is a surprise."

"You seem to like surprises."

"You are correct. I do."

Gradually, the drumroll softened to a pitter-patter. "I think we should go before it's too late," he announced.

Too late for what? I wondered but did not ask.

Pierre drove with concentration. Tires swooshed through puddles that had gathered in asphalt depressions along the road's edge. Drivers honked as cars inched forward and jockeyed for position.

We were in the countryside when the rain stopped and dark clouds lifted as if their time on stage were over. Cows sheltered beneath trees as birds dipped and dove for their supper. The land glistened and mist lingered, hinting of mystery and magic.

"You were upset this morning," Pierre said, glancing at me as he negotiated a tight curve.

"I was," I said, wondering how much to tell him. "Partly it's all the memorials and cemeteries I've seen. They're overwhelming. So many lives destroyed. And such horrible conditions." I shivered. "I don't know how Martin did it."

"Did what exactly?"

"Endured. Killed people. Watched his friends die. Saw unspeakable things." I shook my head and reached in my handbag for a tissue.

"Most of them never spoke about it," Pierre said. "My grandfather rarely said anything, though I wish he had."

"My grandfather spoke through his diaries. Maybe that's why he gave them to me. And . . ." I turned away and stared out the window.

"And what?"

"After Vimy, he's so angry. His best friend was killed there. And his captain was horribly injured. All his close friends were gone. He loses hope. Ultimately, something terrible happens, I'm sure of it. He left me with a mystery to solve, and each place I visit, I hope there might be a clue of some sort. Probably a ridiculous idea. I thought I might find something at Vimy. But I'm beginning to think I'll never solve it."

Pierre shifted gears. "What is the mystery?"

I hesitated. Something about Pierre invited disclosure, but Grandpa's puzzle was private, like a precious trust received from beyond the grave. The quest to solve it brought him back to me. Every day, I felt like I was talking to him, his reassuring presence walking right next to me. Would disclosure interfere with that feeling?

"He left me a box of mementos. I found them while clearing out the attic in my house. The diaries were in there along with an odd collection of items."

"An odd collection of items." Pierre echoed my words. "What sort of items?"

"Oh, you don't want to know about all that."

"I do. I'm interested in things about you."

I hesitated. He smiled as if to encourage me. *What harm could it do to tell him,* I thought.

"Letters from his sister—a woman I never knew existed. A letter from Captain Butler, who went to England to recover after Vimy. A soldier's belt and two brass buttons. A hand-drawn map. And . . ."

"And?" he said.

"When I opened the diaries, I found a small slip of paper my grandfather addressed to me with the words 'Read carefully, I never should have taken them.'"

Pierre gripped the wheel as he maneuvered the car around a tight corner, his face unreadable. "How unusual. What does he mean by 'taken them'?"

"I have no idea. That's the puzzle. I thought I might find some clues by coming to France."

"You said you were close to your grandfather. What about your grandmother?"

I tilted my head side to side before responding. "Grandmama is . . . difficult. I suppose that's the right word. She means well, but she always criticizes and rarely showed affection when I was young. And she discouraged my father's parents from taking much of a role in my upbringing. They're dead now too. Grandpa made room for me in his life. He was really the only parent I had."

"You still miss him."

"I do. I miss him a lot. Now that Jim is . . . Well, I won't bore you with all that."

"You're not boring me. Perhaps I can help with your mystery, but for now I think you need a distraction. I will tell you of my surprise. We are going to see the chateau that once belonged to my grandparents. During the First World War, it was occupied by German soldiers who destroyed many valuable family possessions. During the Second World War, our family experienced more loss, and eventually my grandfather had to sell the chateau and live in a house in the village. I don't think he was ever happy again. My father moved to Paris and married well. He has been quite successful in business. I think I inherited my grandfather's love of art, certainly not my father's love of business."

"And your mother?"

"She is a typical Parisian. I love her, of course, but her world and the things she values are so different from mine. She was not pleased with me when I divorced. We are on much better terms now, but I don't see her often."

"What about brothers or sisters?"

"I have two sisters. We talk regularly. I am closest to my younger sister."

Pierre pulled into a parking area in front of a graceful sandstone building. On the ground floor, mullioned windows created a look of stately elegance, each curtained in delicate lace. Smaller second-story windows had arched tops enhanced by wreaths of sculpted stone. Carefully pruned trees housed in marble planters were spread evenly along the walkway leading to the front door.

"It's magnificent, Pierre." I dropped my voice to a whisper. "Who owns it now?"

"It is a Relais and Châteaux hotel." He must have noticed my puzzled look, for he went on to explain. "A luxury hotel that meets a certain standard of excellence. My grandparents would be pleased to know it's well looked after. For a while, it was used as a retreat for people with addictions and looked very shabby. Shall we go inside?"

In the lobby and salon, a mix of antique and modern furnishings created a feeling of fashionable comfort. Gilded mirrors and soothing paintings, crystal wall sconces, and silk curtains drawn back with sashes gave the impression of a time when cares were few and every whim indulged.

"I like to imagine them sitting here with a fire crackling on a cool autumn night. Perhaps sipping Calvados or a glass of red wine," Pierre said as we stood in the salon next to a fireplace with an ornate marble surround.

"Such a big house for two people."

"When my father was little, the house was full. Papa had five siblings, and with a cook, a few housemaids, a governess, a gardener, and a man who tended the horses, the place bustled. My great-grandfather owned many acres of land and had a tenant farmer who looked after the dairy cows and a few crops."

"Excuse me, sir. Can I help you?" A thin man with wispy hair stood by the door.

"Bonjour, monsieur."

Pierre spoke in French, gesticulating with his hands, lifting his shoulders and raising his eyebrows to emphasize various points. I was intrigued. When he spoke English, he was restrained. But when he spoke French, his movements were animated, as though putting his whole body into the message. The thin man listened and began to nod, then broke into a smile. He replied in rapid French and nodded in my direction.

"Bien sûr, monsieur. Enchanté, madame."

"He is content for us to look around. Not the second floor, but here and in the gardens. I explained about my grandfather, and he knew the story."

Close to the house, the gardens were immaculately tailored; size, shape, and color laid out with precision around a patio full of white umbrellas and chairs grouped for conversation. Spreading oaks at the back of the property framed the garden's tranquil beauty.

"I don't remember how the garden looked many years ago," Pierre said. "I was quite small when Grand-père sold the house."

As we passed through the reception area once more on the way back to the car, he explained that the Germans stripped out much of the furniture during the war and lined most of the rooms with mattresses.

"You must be pleased that it looks so charming now."

"I am." Pierre took a deep breath and let it out in one long sigh. "But I wish it had remained in the family."

Leaving the chateau, we meandered along back roads, from time to time stopping to gaze across fields and valleys or admire an ancient farmhouse. While we waited by an abandoned church for another heavy storm to pass, I pulled out the package of chocolates.

"Which one would you like?" I said.

Pierre selected one with a dollop of red on top and told me about the candy bowl his grandfather kept in the living room. "We were only allowed to choose one each time we visited. I took so long to choose my sisters always complained." Pierre laughed and took another chocolate.

"Pierre?"

"Mm-hmm," he said, mouth full of chocolate.

"Can I tell you something else?"

"Of course."

"I think someone is following me."

"What? Following you? Are you certain?" I nodded slowly. "Well, you must explain it."

I told him about the occasions I had seen Fedora Man and his encounter with me at the Vimy Memorial. "I kicked him in the . . . I kicked him and was able to get away."

"Mon Dieu," he said. "It could be serious. Why do you think he's following you?"

"I have no idea."

"You should not go out alone."

"But how is that possible? I'm here on vacation by myself."

"Let me think," he said. "But for now it is getting late and we should return to Chateau Noyelle."

Pierre insisted on escorting me to my room.

"Lock the door," he said. "Will you be down for dinner?" I nodded. He touched my cheek. "May I kiss you?" I nodded again.

His kiss was gentle at first and then more insistent as he moved closer and put a hand behind my neck. My mouth curved easily against his, and I was certain he could hear the thumping of my heart. Heat spread through my body.

Pierre let his hand trail down my back. "I will see you in the restaurant."

He kissed me again after dinner, a long slow kiss that made me long for more. Afterward, I held two fingers against my mouth and gazed into his eyes.

"I think . . ."

"I do not think we should do that again. Not unless you wish to invite me in."

"I . . . I don't know."

He touched my cheek. "Sweet dreams, Grace. And lock your door."

As Pierre walked along the corridor toward the red-carpeted stairs, I pulled the key out of my purse. It required a bit of wiggling before I heard the click and tumble of the lock. Still in a daze from the warmth of Pierre's kiss, I opened the door and walked into my room.

"Holy shit," I said, unable to form a coherent thought.

Someone had been in my room. The bedsheets were in disarray, drawers hung open, shirts and underwear on the floor. In the bathroom, I could see toiletries scattered across the vanity.

This can't be happening, I thought, stepping farther inside. The wardrobe had also been ransacked, dresses and skirts in a heap on the floor, hangers and shoes tossed aside, my shawl balled up in the corner. A sound came from the corridor, and I whirled around. No one there. Heart thumping, sweat pooling, with a hand on my mouth, I ran out to the hallway.

"Pierre, can you hear me?" I shouted.

Nothing.

"Pierre!"

Rapid footsteps descended the stairs. I heard him call my name, and in less than a minute he arrived, took one look at me, and held me close. "What happened?"

"My room . . ." I pulled away and grabbed his hand. "Someone has been in my room."

"Merde," he said forcefully. "Who would do such a thing?"

"The window's open." I pointed across the room. In my initial confusion, I had failed to notice the window ajar and my pearls on the blue velvet chair nearby.

Pierre picked up the phone. "I'm calling the front desk."

I blinked several times, swaying slightly from light-headedness, and reached for the desk chair to steady myself. I breathed in and exhaled slowly.

The manager arrived, followed fifteen minutes later by two police officers, bulky men with almost identical mustaches, which on any other occasion would have made me smile. I answered questions; Pierre translated as required. The officers took notes, poked around, checked for fingerprints, spent a long time looking out the window—the presumed method of entry and exit—asked more questions, and examined my passport.

"Grace, you should tell them about the man who has been following you," Pierre said. I did as he suggested and the two officers took more notes.

"C'est tout?"

"Oui," I said. "That's all."

One of the officers said they would make inquiries and return the following day.

When the manager offered to move me to a different room, I quickly agreed, and he disappeared, promising to bring another key in a few minutes.

"I will stay with you, if you would like," Pierre said. "Nothing romantic. I just want to make sure you are safe."

"Yes, please." My voice was timid. Not at all like my usual assured self.

"You are shivering." The warmth of his arms released some of the tension from my body.

"I am. It's not every day I experience such excitement."

"You should not joke about it, Grace."

"You're right."

"Perhaps you should go to another hotel, not merely another room," he said.

"I'll consider that in the morning. Right now I feel too unsettled to make any decisions."

"All right. But promise me you will think about it in the morning."

"I promise."

MARTIN'S DIARY

April 14, 1917

Vimy was successful, if you can call the bloodbath we experienced successful. But Bill is gone. Killed taking Thelus. I can hardly believe it and still expect to see him every time I turn a corner. He has been part of my life for so long. We grew up together, shared our hopes and dreams, boosted one another up. We even prayed together not long after Pete died. No friends left here except Nully. It feels as though my family has died. Butler is badly wounded and is on his way to England for treatment. Twelve of my men killed. Twelve! I will carry the burden of their deaths as long as I live.

CHAPTER 16

June 1917

Martin slumped beside the river, his back propped against a boulder. Though shelling spit and grumbled a few miles away, here the birds chirped happily and bulrushes swayed in the breeze. Nature did not stop for grief, nor notice the passing of friends. Its rhythms continued, turning winter into spring and spring into summer. The sun blazed with warmth, and he'd rolled up his sleeves and opened his collar to feel the heat on his skin. He thought of taking off his shirt, but Captain Lindsay had already made known his feelings about appropriate dress, especially for lieutenants, who should be role models.

Lindsay was a hefty man with a thick brown mustache and a nose that must have been broken at one time because it had a sharp bump on the bridge and was a little off center. When he smiled—a rare occurrence—his mouth disappeared into a thin line. Martin felt Lindsay was barely half the soldier Butler had been and disliked him from the very beginning. He knew his dislike stemmed from the deaths of Bill and Pete and Butler's severe wounds and Michel's lost leg, but he had yet to forgive Lindsay for replacing one of his friends.

Still a little drunk from last night's encounter with a bottle of brandy stolen from the colonel's quarters, Martin tossed a stone into the river. He tried to bring Michel's face to mind, but it was elusive now that more than a year had passed. They had exchanged a few letters, but Michel's were often morose and Martin had little cheer to offer. Pete's and Bill's faces were sharper, although he wondered how long it would be before they too faded from memory. He smacked a fist against his forehead. If he couldn't remember them, who else would? And what was the fucking point of their deaths if no one, not even their closest friend, could remember them? He was the only one left. He had to remember.

He could still hear Pete's laugh, though. A boisterous sound that had cheered them all even as they prepared for battle. Martin tried to recall the last time he had heard someone laugh. Maniacal laughter did not count.

The men he met now—new recruits, hastily trained lieutenants, captains whose reason for promotion was death, not merit—would never be friends because he would never allow himself to care for anyone again. He had made a pact to honor his friends, and now all that was left was emptiness. He was a vessel of sorrow. A man who sent soldiers out to die.

To keep sane, he indulged in small acts of insolence and insubordination. Failure to address Lindsay properly was one of his favorites, an act that made the man grit his teeth in exasperation. Being late for meetings was another. Occasionally, he indulged in behavior that put his life at risk.

At the sound of a twig snapping, Martin glanced over his shoulder.

"Sir, Captain Lindsay says you're needed to review new operational orders," said one of his fresh recruits.

Tom Smith still saluted when addressing his lieutenant. He was loose limbed and rocked from left to right as he walked. Martin found him slow to understand tasks. Nully said he would improve with time, but Martin doubted the man would survive that long.

"Relax, Smith. Wanna smoke?"

"No, thank you, sir."

"Your mother's not here to scold you, Smithy." Martin's laugh scraped the air as he thrust a cigarette in the young soldier's face. "You'll be smoking soon. They all do. Calms the nerves. Just like the booze."

Ignoring Smithy's discomfort, Martin unrolled his sleeves and took another long drag of his cigarette, exhaling slowly before tossing it in the river, where it spun round and round before lodging against a clutch of branches. Finally, he rose to his feet and followed the young soldier along the path toward camp. Artillery screamed in the distance. Smithy's shoulders twitched. Neither man spoke.

When Martin entered the dugout housing the battalion's officers, Lindsay lifted his head.

"Good of you to come, Devlin," he said.

Simon Duncan was there, as well as Morgan Bennett and Frank Jervis, the men who had replaced Bill and Pete. The day Bennett and Jervis arrived, Martin got so drunk he could hardly stand. Fortunately, Nully kept him away from Lindsay; otherwise Martin might have been demoted.

Lindsay motioned them to gather around a map spread out on a case of ammunition. "We're conducting an attack in three days' time," he began. "The objective is to seize a small bluff less than five hundred yards from our front lines, then clear and occupy it in preparation for a larger action. HQ feels the timing is excellent because three enemy observation balloons have been destroyed, and we've silenced a significant number of enemy batteries in the last few days."

Martin had an imaginary conversation with Bill and Pete about the logic of connecting downed balloons and silenced batteries to a mission's success. Bill would have said that the intelligence folks were nuts, as usual, and Pete would have dismissed it as a lame exercise in boosting confidence.

"You have forty-eight hours to prepare your men. Go in with minimal gear so you can move quickly and get it done. That's all." He waved them off but said, "Devlin, I need you to stay."

Slouching against a wooden beam, Martin waited for his captain to speak. Lindsay sorted some papers, stacking them into three piles, then made a note on a piece of paper and attached his signature. When he turned to face Martin, he was scowling.

"I've spoken to the CO. After this action, you're going to England to rest." He held up his hand as Martin opened his mouth. "Drummond and Fenton say you're a man with leadership potential. Can't say I agree with them, but it's their decision. I know about your friends and about Butler. We've all had losses to deal with, but failing in your role as lieutenant and being an insubordinate ass doesn't bring them back." Disgust clouded Lindsay's face. "When you return, I'll expect a new attitude and your respect. I may not be Butler, but I'm a bloody good officer."

Lindsay stared at him as if looking for some spark in the depths of Martin's eyes.

"Are we clear?"

Martin nodded once. "Yes, sir."

One week later, after a successful push against the Germans, Martin left camp. He rode in an ambulance to Hazebrouck and from there caught a train to Boulogne that shuffled along the tracks, stopping so often to make way for incoming trains he missed the boat across the channel.

After a night in a hotel that looked and smelled like it hadn't been cleaned in over a decade, Martin's eyes were gritty when he awoke. In the bar, where both food and drink were served, his stomach rebelled at the greasy pool of sausage and stewed tomatoes thumped in front of him by a red-lipped barmaid whose breath made him cringe. After one bite, he pushed the plate away and swilled a mouthful of coffee to clear the taste.

Goddamned fucking war.

He was still smarting from Lindsay's criticisms. When Martin had complained to Drummond, the battalion's commander had said, "You could be a fine officer, Devlin, but you seem to have lost your way. I'm worried about you." In a patronizing manner, the man had gone on to say that rest and reflection would do him a world of good. Martin imagined that *reflection* was a euphemism for *getting his act together*.

"Probably good for you to get away for a bit, sir," Nully had offered when told about the leave.

Martin's sergeant had covered for him on numerous occasions, and he was grateful. Nully had become a friend, not merely his sergeant but he couldn't yet confide in Nully the way he could with Pete, Bill, and Michel.

"There's nothing wrong with me," Martin had replied.

"I'm sure that's the case. Still, it's good to get away."

His leave consisted of two weeks at Chumley Park, a place for officers with psychological problems, and one week in London. When he read the orders, the full weight of Bill's and Pete's deaths and the absence of Michel and Butler descended once again, a weight he had pushed aside by being nasty and defiant, as if pretending to be someone else could smother his grief.

Leaning against the railing, Martin watched the water churn behind the steamer, reflecting thick gray clouds that spread across the horizon. He flicked a cigarette over the rail. Seagulls cawed, and the ship's motor clanked and sputtered, making him think he would be lucky to reach England at all.

"Not that I care," he muttered, his words blown away on a gust of wind.

At the dock in Hastings, a boxy vehicle was waiting for him, *Chumley Park* written in white letters on both sides for all to see. Martin slung his duffel bag over his shoulder and crossed the street.

"Lieutenant Devlin?"

Martin nodded.

"Waiting for one other bloke," the driver said, poking his head out the window.

Preferring fresh air to idle chatter with a man who looked old enough to be his grandfather, Martin remained on the street until a colonel whose left leg did not bend approached the car. Remembering what Lindsay and Drummond had said, he saluted.

Chumley Park, a rambling two-story building that might once have been a school, or perhaps a hospital, stood at the end of a very long driveway bordered by a stone fence on one side and a line of poplars on the other. Martin's room was clean and simple, containing a single bed, a child-sized chest, and a wooden chair that wobbled and squeaked. "Not much bigger than a prison cell," he muttered, dumping his duffel bag in one corner. Through the narrow window, he saw a paddock where three horses grazed, a pond spotted with water lilies, and a patch of forest beyond. He opened the window, letting in a light breeze and the scent of early summer. The contrast to where he had been could not have been greater.

At the sound of a discreet cough, Martin turned.

"Hello, Lieutenant Devlin. I'm Sister Yolande. I've come by to make sure you are settling in and to tell you that tea will be served at six. You might call it supper, but we call it tea. Do you have any questions?"

Martin shook his head.

"Excellent. You're free to explore in the interim. Dr. Berger will see you at ten tomorrow." She smiled and left with a swish of her long gray habit and boots tapping on the wooden floor.

CHAPTER 17

July 1991

When I awoke after a restless night, Pierre was sleeping on a chair by the window, his feet propped on the padded bench at the foot of the bed, a blanket draped over his body. For an instant, I wondered why he was there, and then I remembered, last night's events rushing through my mind like a giant wave raking the shore, tossing shells and debris this way and that.

It was inconceivable that someone had deliberately set out to follow me, let alone ransack my room. It was a small group of people who knew I was in France: family, work colleagues, close friends, Uncle Ben, and my neighbor, who had agreed to take in my mail and give it to Jim once a week. And Jim, of course. None of this would be happening if Jim hadn't asked for a divorce.

I couldn't imagine any of them wanting to harm me or having me followed. Jim might no longer want to live with me, but he would never harm me.

I picked up my watch from the bedside table. Quarter after seven. The police said they would return in the morning but had given no indication of time. I knew I should get up and shower, but the thought of doing so with Pierre in the room was disturbing—pleasantly so, but disturbing nonetheless.

"Are you awake?" Pierre said a few minutes later.

"Mm-hmm." I propped myself up on one elbow. "Thank you for being here last night. Did you get any sleep?"

"*Un peu.* A chair is not exactly the most comfortable way to sleep."

"I'm sorry."

"No, no. I am not complaining. Just making a little joke. What we call *une petite blague.*" He threw off the blanket and stood up, stretching both arms above his head. "I should return to my room. Will you be down for breakfast?"

I nodded. "After I shower and get dressed. The police said they would be back this morning. Do you remember if they mentioned a time?"

"Nine, I think, but knowing our local police forces, it will more likely be closer to ten." He came over to my side of the bed and dropped a kiss on my forehead. "I will see you in thirty minutes or so."

"Pierre, there's no need for this matter to intrude on your day. I'm sure you have better things to do than wait around for the police."

He smiled. "We can discuss that over coffee."

Walking along the corridor toward the stairs to the lobby, I passed room 209, the only evidence of last night's episode a door tag saying *Ne pas déranger.* Do not disturb. No outward sign that anything had happened. With a sense of unease, I quickened my pace, escaping down the stairs to reach the breakfast room slightly out of breath.

"Here you are," Pierre said, setting aside his newspaper.

While we ate, he steered the conversation away from yesterday's events, making no mention of our time together or the break-in. Instead, we spoke about French nuclear tests occurring in the South Pacific and international reaction.

I drank the rest of my espresso and set the cup down. "What else was in this morning's papers?"

"An article about the ending of apartheid in South Africa. Some are predicting that Nelson Mandela and the ANC will form the next government. I've heard it's a beautiful country."

"Would you go there?"

"Possibly. But"—he thrust out his chin in a manner I was beginning to recognize as typically Gallic—"it will have to become safer than it is today. And now we must discuss other things. Have you thought about changing hotels?"

"I would prefer to stay here. My family has my itinerary, including the phone numbers for each hotel. Making a change would require that I let them know, and that would only generate a lot of questions."

"I see," he said. "To be safe, I think you should consult with the police when they come this morning."

"I can do that. Pierre, about the police. I'm sure you have plans for today, and I don't want to interfere. I'll be fine on my own."

"Are you certain? I can rearrange a few meetings."

"No, you should go. Do what you planned. Perhaps I will see you tonight."

With a brief lift of his shoulders, Pierre said, "*D'accord*. As you wish." I couldn't tell if he was pleased to be free of obligation or annoyed that I insisted he attend to his own affairs. When we parted, all he said was, "Perhaps tonight, then."

By noon, the police officers had also departed, their questions mainly a repeat of last night's, although they did ask me to check my belongings for stolen items. When I did so and assured them that nothing had been taken, they seemed somewhat deflated by the news. They said an investigation would be conducted; however, I doubted they would find anything.

A staff member helped shift the rest of my belongings to room 224, and the manager sent a bottle of Burgundy with a note of apology for what he called "the incident." Once again, I unpacked my belongings, my hands jittery as I placed clothes in the dresser and hung others in the closet. Seeing familiar items gave me comfort, but I remained uneasy, returning time and again to the questions of who had been in my room and whether Fedora Man was in any way involved.

Sitting at the desk, I made a list of everything that had happened since finding the items in my grandfather's tackle box. Two theories emerged. Either someone wanted to harm me, or someone wanted an object I had in my possession. Neither theory offered any consolation.

Why is someone following me? I wondered. *What are they looking for? And why here in France?* Were these incidents in some way connected to Martin and the note he left for me? Was it the same person or two different people? The implications of that thought made my hands shake.

MARTIN'S DIARY

June 15, 1917

Chumley Park

CHAPTER 18

June 1917

Martin counted thirteen closed doors until he found the one marked *Dr. Gerald Berger* at the end of a plain green corridor. Before knocking, he paused to look out the window, where a badminton net and a croquet course anchored opposite ends of the lawn. A man sat on the patio reading a newspaper while two others played badminton, rallying back and forth until one leapt into the air and smashed the birdie toward a far corner. Sighing, Martin turned away and rapped on the door.

"Come in. Come in."

Wearing a white lab coat over a brown suit, Dr. Berger leaned across his desk to greet Martin with a firm handshake. "Lieutenant Devlin?"

"Yes, sir."

"Sit down. Yes, please sit down. Perhaps that chair, it's not so rickety. I've asked for new chairs, but with this bloody war on, there's no money for things like that. Should probably just bring one in from home. Are you comfortable? Would you like a cup of tea?"

Martin shook his head.

"Well, now. I'm glad to see you have no physical problems. Some of the chaps who come here are in such a dreadful state I don't know where to begin. Bodies are delicate constructions, and mind-body interactions are unpredictable. Definitely unpredictable. Don't you agree? Now tell me, why are you here?"

Caught off guard, Martin said nothing. Why he had been sent to Chumley Park was Berger's problem to solve. He did not plan to make the man's job any easier.

Dr. Berger rustled a stack of papers, attempting to pull them into a neat pile. Sniffing, he rubbed his nose and picked up a book covered in red leather, then swiveled his chair, stood up, and took a few steps toward a set of bookshelves spanning one wall. He slid the book into position among a collection of other red leather books, each labeled by year, the last labeled *1916*. The doctor remained silent, and Martin wondered if this approach was some kind of game for which he had yet to learn the rules. Berger returned to his chair, took another sip of tea, and stared at Martin, his eyebrows raised a fraction beyond their resting position.

"I have no idea," Martin said.

"Come now, man. Of course you do. They wouldn't have sent you here unless you were causing a problem and they're worried about your mental state." He flipped open a manila folder and placed a finger on a piece of paper marked with an official-looking seal. "L26, it says. War stress." Berger gazed at Martin with unexpectedly steely eyes.

"Hmmph. We're all under stress. They don't need to give it a bloody code," Martin said.

Berger scribbled something in his notebook and looked up again.

"You try living in the conditions we have for almost two years. You'd be under stress too."

Berger made another note and underlined a few words twice. "Let's go back to the beginning. When did you enlist?"

For the next hour, Martin recounted his time in the army, from basic training to France and the front line. At some points he faltered, and at other points he spoke with ease. Once, he laughed while relaying a story about Michel, who had turned upside down with his pants around his ankles while sitting on a tree branch. The doctor filled more than two pages with notes.

At a knock on the door, Berger put down his pen. "That's all we have time for today. I'll see you tomorrow. Ten o'clock."

On the third day, Martin finally opened up. As usual, he had arrived a few minutes before ten and glanced out the window. Low-lying mist shrouded the ground, reminding him of a morning when fog delayed an attack in the Somme and forced his platoon to wait, his men growing more and more anxious as the minutes ticked by. The day Diggy and Thompson died.

"Where were we?" Berger began flipping through his notes. "Ah. Yes. You just arrived at the Somme. Messy business, the Somme. I've had quite a few from there." The doctor sounded like he was referring to a collection of stamps.

"Much more than messy. I would use the word *slaughter* myself," Martin said, articulating each word with sharp clarity.

"You sound angry."

"You'd be angry too if you lost one of your best friends there."

"Who was that?"

"Pete Van Leuven."

The doctor propped his chin on his hands and leaned forward. Staring at Berger's long fingers, the nails cut blunt, dark hairs sprouting between each joint, Martin debated waiting him out: a test of wills he knew he was strong enough to win, but what was the point? He allowed himself to consider sharing his burden. He looked away, seeing Pete's weary face that day, as they tossed jaunty words of encouragement back and forth. "First one back gets the best mattress" were his last words to Pete.

"We trained together," Martin said, "and swore to protect each other."

"I see." Berger did not press. He let the silence gather, and for the first time since Vimy Ridge, Martin felt a shred of comfort.

"Pete and I debated tactics. That's how we got through each day. At first, we knew so little our opinions were laughable, but over time we understood more. He was amazing at ferreting out information. When we weren't in the trenches, we'd draw diagrams to consider the bigger picture. Lieutenants aren't told much more than what affects their few hundred yards of the front. Pete and I . . ."

How long had it been since he had spoken Pete's name without hesitation? After Thiepval, in the unspoken way of men, Martin and Bill had agreed not to mention him. Neither could acknowledge that their friend had been blown to pieces, the image far too awful to contemplate. Then after Bill died and Butler was shipped to England, no one but Nully understood the intensity of their friendship, the bond of four young men shipped out together, determined to be strong and fearless.

"I . . . I would have taken a bullet for him."

Berger set down his pen. "And your friend Bill?"

Martin's eyes blurred. "Bill too. He was killed at Vimy. I didn't know until the end of the day. I couldn't even comfort him as he died. I had my own men to lead. To protect however I could. Twelve of my men died that day. Twelve of them."

Martin slumped in his chair and stared into the distance, sorrow thrashing his soul, throat aching with unshed tears. Footsteps echoed in the corridor and then grew fainter as the clock on the doctor's desk ticked the seconds away. Berger picked up his pen, removing and replacing its cap again and again.

"War's a terrible thing," said Berger, his voice soft and low. "And this war is more dreadful than most. I know I'm not supposed to say so, but it is. In some ways, surviving is harder than dying. Leading is more difficult than following. You're a leader and a survivor, Martin."

"There are days when I wish otherwise."

"I can imagine. Lieutenant Colonel Drummond writes very favorably about your skills. But you're the only one who can decide whether you want to survive. I'd like to talk about that some more tomorrow, if you're willing."

Martin did not reply.

After leaving Berger's office, he swam lengths in the pool. His objective was one length for every one of his soldiers who had died, but after seventy-three, his arms felt like lead weights, and his breath came in such shallow bursts he began to choke. Later, he found a punching bag and danced around, jabbing right and left. He missed lunch and in the afternoon borrowed a book from the library to avoid the clamoring in his head. That night, he dreamt of his friends setting up camp like they did outside Le Havre—Michel playing his mouth organ while Martin chopped wood in time to the music, and Bill and Pete laughed.

"We were going to talk about survival," Dr. Berger said. He paused as if waiting for permission, and Martin's head wobbled, neither a nod nor a shake. "I imagine you wonder why you've survived while your friends have not." Berger sipped his tea and leaned back, the chair squeaking in protest. "As I said yesterday, surviving is harder than dying. Many of your men will feel the same. They'll want to give up because their reservoir of courage is empty. And what's your job? You have to help them find new courage, and to do so, you have to be strong.

"Remember, Devlin, you can't get through it alone, and the sooner you understand this, the sooner you'll find others who can help you like Pete and Bill did. This kind of support isn't weakness, it's strength, the kind of strength that will ultimately cause our enemy to lose their will to fight. You need to rediscover your strength.

"Believe me, I've treated enough officers to understand your pain. Losing your men is like losing a child. Losing your friends is like losing your family. But what the army needs from you is initiative and decisiveness, and you've lost those qualities. As a result, you put your men at risk. Not just yourself." Berger tipped forward. "Do you care about your men?"

Martin nodded. "I suppose so."

"I've counseled others just like you. Caring for your men will ease your grief. Help them take pride in their unit, train them well, keep them physically strong, fight for them to get the necessary rest. Whenever you can, give them information rather than keeping them in the dark. These are the tasks of a leader. If you lead well, you'll regain your sense of purpose and will to survive."

Martin picked at a callus on his palm until he loosened a piece of skin and pulled it off. "Even if what you say is possible, it won't work for me. I've lost their respect. Lindsay called me an insubordinate ass, and he's right."

"Well, Lieutenant, you have to stop feeling sorry for yourself and get on with the job you were trained for." As Martin began to protest, Berger thumped his hand on the table so hard his teacup rattled. "Damn it, man. Don't you see? Young soldiers need their lieutenants. My son is out there somewhere, and I know he's scared. Christ, he's only nineteen. He needs someone like you to get him through it. We've all got to get through it, and the only thing I can do for him is help men like you get back to the front. You've got what it takes if you'll only let yourself care again.

"If I could go myself, I'd take my son's place in an instant, but I can't. So you, Lieutenant Devlin, you with your brains and your quick wit and your ability to lead—at least that's what your profile says— you have to help us win this bloody war." Nostrils flaring, the doctor thumped the table again.

By the time Berger had finished, Martin's eyes were wide. "Yes, sir," was all he could think to say.

Berger wiped spittle from the corners of his mouth and mopped his forehead. "I'm sorry, Devlin. I shouldn't lose my temper. My wife has always scolded me for doing so. She says it's my least attractive trait." He cleared his throat. "Let's forget that last bit and return to what I said earlier. If you lead well, you'll regain your sense of purpose, and ultimately, your friends' deaths will have some meaning. A man could be proud of that."

Martin felt he had to say something. "Powerful thoughts, Dr. Berger."

"I want you to stay the full two weeks. Rest and relax. If you need to talk with me again, let Sister Yolande know. Otherwise, I'm going to pronounce you fit for duty. You've suffered acute stress, but I don't judge it debilitating." Berger scribbled something in his notebook and snapped it closed. "I understand you're to have a week in London, which I hope will help. I keep promising my wife we'll take a little trip there soon, but the cases here keep mounting up."

"That's war, sir."

Both men stood, and Martin offered his hand. "Thank you, Dr. Berger."

"Good luck, son."

On the train rolling through the countryside from Chumley Park to London, Martin noted the calm of land unscarred by battle and bombardment. Although he knew soldiers would be training in nearby camps, and pilots preparing for raids across the channel, what he saw were fields dotted with crops, grazing animals, and trees and bushes in full leaf. After so many months of mud-soaked terrain among the ruins of buildings and the skeletons of trees, he felt a faint stirring of normalcy and the possibility of a future. If only he could summon the desire to hold on.

Closer to London, buildings surrounded by rubble pitched him into despondency once again. Walking from the train station, he passed flag-draped statues and sandbags piled high to protect underground entrances. With pedestrians wearing black armbands and black bunting draping so many windows, the city felt like a morgue. He bought a newspaper from a red-cheeked boy calling out the latest tragedies:

AMMUNITION FACTORY EXPLODES. RUS-
SIAN FLEET MUTINIES. ENEMY TAKES
MOUNT ORTIGARA. TWENTY THOUSAND
ITALIAN SOLDIERS LOST.

Newspaper and duffel bag in hand, he continued toward his hotel. Everywhere he looked, women were dressed in the uniforms of tram conductors, nurses, traffic police, and factory workers. They moved not with slow, swishing steps or plodding fatigue but with long, confident strides, as though released from lives of boredom and drudgery. They made him think of Jane. His sister had always rebelled against the confines of society's expectations, and if she lived in London, he was certain she would have a job.

Martin had dinner at a pub called the Sheep's Horn before finding his way to the bar at the Mercury Hotel, where Bill and Pete had gone after Courcelette. They'd told him it was a place to forget the war in the company of lively young women. A visit to the Mercury would be his silent eulogy to their bravery and friendship.

With uniformed men from various countries standing two or three deep at the bar, he nudged his way in, careful to avoid any movement that could be taken as aggressive. Soldiers on leave, fresh from months of trench warfare and with instincts sharpened by brutal combat, were quick to respond with their fists. He'd reacted that way himself from time to time, but tonight he planned to honor his friends in peace and quiet.

Next to a rack of beer pulls, a group of men clustered around a woman wearing a red dress. Martin noticed a hint of cleavage that deepened when she leaned forward as a British soldier lit her cigarette, and he admired the way she tossed her head back and laughed. Another time, he would have found an opportunity to persuade her onto the dance floor. Tonight he merely nodded to acknowledge her beauty and carried his whiskey to a corner. While he was nursing his third drink, she appeared at his elbow.

"Bad night?" She stood with a hand on her hip, slim legs inviting.

"You might say that."

"Do you need someone to lend an ear?"

Martin liked the lilt in her voice, soft and melodic. Excluding a nursing sister and the slovenly barmaid in Boulogne, he hadn't heard a woman speak for months. "Now why would you want to listen to a soldier talk about his little corner of hell? Don't you hear enough of that?"

"Not really. Most of the men only want to laugh or talk about their wives. They don't come to the Mercury to be serious."

"I see."

"I could tell you were different as soon as you walked in."

Martin cocked his head but said nothing.

"It's your eyes," she continued. "They're so very sad."

Bill would have said, "What are you waiting for?" But Martin held back. He wanted to reminisce, not indulge in mindless flirtation. "If you're here tomorrow, I might be in a better mood," he said, swirling what little was left of his whiskey.

"Suit yourself."

The woman in red lifted one shoulder in a brief shrug and walked away, the rustle of her dress like feathers brushing silk.

CHAPTER 19

June 1917

Martin bent low to see his face in the mirror. Normally, his appearance was of little consequence as long as his pistol was at hand and his helmet on, but for the first time in two years, he actually cared. *God, I look awful.* Sagging cheeks and sallow skin gave the impression of sickness.

He dabbed a little Harrison's on his fingers and smoothed his hair, then straightened the knot of his tie. Peering at his forehead, he wondered if his hairline had receded. *Doesn't matter, she won't be there anyway.*

Though it was eight o'clock, light still lingered at the edges of rooftops as Martin walked to the Underground. Few people were on the streets, and the fading smells of cabbage and onions and the sound of mewling infants suggested that Londoners had finished their tea. He imagined women gathered in sitting rooms, tethered by aprons and knitting needles, young boys playing with metal soldiers, and old men grumbling. He would give anything to see his mother's smile and his sister's bobbing curls and his father puffing on a pipe while reading the evening paper. They sent letters, of course, with cheery bits of news and exhortations to be careful and come home safe, his father's more stoic than his mother's, and Jane's more humorous than serious, an effort Martin appreciated. But words on a page did not comfort like a warm embrace, a linked arm, or a soft touch on his cheek.

A man huddled on the steps to the Bakerloo line, coat draped over his shoulders like a ragged cape, one foot encased in an army boot with no laces, the other in a dirty plaid slipper.

"Are you all right?" Martin said.

The man looked up, confused eyes clearing for a moment. "Yes, sir," he said, straightening his shoulders and squaring his jaw. He lifted his hand to form a salute, then dropped it again. "Enemy sniping, sir. Stay down." The man ducked his head and whimpered like a frightened child.

Martin dug in his pocket and crouched down. "Here's a few shillings, soldier. Why don't you get a hot cup of tea? Can I help you find a place?"

The man bit one of the shillings, then shoved the rest in his pocket and scuttled away.

"Hey! Hey!" Martin shouted. "Don't run off. Let me help."

The soldier stopped, his face barely visible in the gloom. He tipped his head left, then right, and let out a wild cackle before disappearing down a narrow alley, the slap and thud of slipper and boot fading with each step.

The man made him think of the bleak, weary men at Chumley Park and Dr. Berger's quiet face and probing questions. Martin had avoided conversation while he was there. He had no desire to become entangled with those broken by war whose spirits might never heal and, equally, no desire to place battle strategy beneath a microscope, debating what could or should have occurred while cursing those in command. He had more than enough of those conversations inside his head already.

A yapping dog interrupted his thoughts, and he turned back toward the stairs to the Tube station where accumulated heat and the noxious smell of burnt brake dust assaulted the senses. As the Underground juddered and screeched from station to station, he tried not to think of anything except the potential pleasure of seeing the woman in red. Few were on the train, and those who were paid no attention to the neatly dressed soldier whose doleful eyes and muscular physique indicated more than a few months of battle experience.

At the Mercury, the dance floor was packed, music spilling onto the street. Martin stood at the doorway watching a jumble of colors and uniforms whirl past amid laughter and sweat and swirling skirts. *Clearly,* he thought, *Friday is more popular than Thursday.* Weaving his way through dancing bodies, he reached the bar and, while waiting for a beer, scanned the crowd. Though he expected the woman to wear a different dress, each time he caught a flash of red, his hopes rose, only to fall a moment later when the face turned. Beer in hand, he circled the room like an outsider looking in.

When he had almost completed one rotation, he felt a tap on his shoulder.

"Are you looking for me?"

She was dressed in soft yellow, which was less provocative than red but more alluring. "I am." There was no point in pretending.

"Do you dance?"

Martin put his beer down. "I'm out of practice," he said.

"No matter. I can lead if you like." She lifted her arms as though they had danced together many times, and he held her, not close, but close enough to smell her perfume and feel her hair brushing his cheek. Her nearness softened the hard line of his mouth and loosened his shoulders. He thought of Bill and Pete and hoped they had found similar comfort.

"What's your name?" he asked as the last note of a clarinet faded away.

"Cynthia." She paused a moment, a flash of indecision crossing her face. "Gibson."

"Cynthia. That suits you. I'm Martin Devlin." Realizing he was still holding her although the band had yet to begin a new song, he released her and stepped back a few inches.

"Why would you think it suits me? You know nothing about me." Her tone was light and a little mocking. "It could be the name of my widowed aunt who tyrannizes the family because she happens to be wealthy. Or the name of my father's younger sister who died before she was twenty. Or the name of a famous British suffragette." She arched her eyebrows and folded her arms.

Martin laughed. "Are you trying to scare me off?"

"No, but all of those things are true, and sometimes I hate my name. I should have been a Juliette or Genevieve or even a Catherine. Much more sophisticated."

Before he could respond, the band started up and he stepped toward her. She slid into his arms, and this time he pulled her closer. For more than two hours he held her, through slow dances and fast, ignoring others attempting to cut in, rarely speaking except for brief phrases murmured mouth to ear. His body hummed with longing.

The air-raid siren began at eleven twenty-two p.m., its sound at first indistinct above the noise of the band. But when the music stopped, the surging wail broke through.

"We shall have to go," she said.

"Where?" Tension returned to Martin's face and shoulders.

"There's a shelter a short distance from here. I know the way."

Cynthia took his hand, and they moved with the crowd surging toward the door like a wave through a narrow crevice. Afraid to lose her, he held tight. Out on the street, the siren was louder and more insistent, its crescendos more frequent. People hurried in all directions, purpose evident in long strides and somber faces. No one shouted or panicked, even though they knew the zeppelins could be deadly.

"Here we are. Down these steps. Hurry. We need to hurry," she said.

Searchlights fanned the sky and antiaircraft guns fired as Martin and Cynthia disappeared beneath the ground into a pit of darkness. Inching past women and children huddled against the wall, he led the way, feeling more comfortable now that they were off the streets. The cellar was much wider than the tunnels at Vimy, and his eyes soon grew accustomed to the gloom. From his left, he heard giggling.

Martin gripped Cynthia's hand tighter and was reassured by her answering squeeze. Eventually, they found a corner beyond the crowd, and he draped his jacket around her shoulders and sat beside her on the stone floor.

"What is this place?"

"An air-raid shelter. A friend told me it's actually a tunnel connecting two hotels that used to be owned by the same man. Staff could go back and forth, and somewhere there's an old wine cellar."

"Doesn't seem to be used anymore."

"No. The owner died. His son sold the hotels to two different buyers."

"Have you been down here before?"

"Just once. With my girlfriend Lucy."

"Were you afraid?"

Cynthia nodded, and he put his arm around her.

He was puzzled at his feelings of possessiveness and pleased that her slender frame fit so well against his side. "Will your parents be worried about you?"

"Mm-hmm."

"Will we hear the all clear?" He felt her nod against his shoulder.

With Cynthia's warmth pressed against him, he inhaled her scent, one that was both floral and spicy at the same time, and pulled her closer. She was soft and tender, and younger than he'd originally thought. As he held her on the dance floor, long-buried emotions had stirred. Maybe, just maybe, life could be worth living.

"May I kiss you?"

She nodded again.

CHAPTER 20

June 1991

Drenched in sunshine, the patio felt like the perfect oasis, and for a while I did nothing but listen to the cooing of a dove and the occasional chirp of crickets. A light wind stirred the treetops, and a calico cat daintily crossed the flagstones before settling in the shade of a wide stone bench. After a while I picked up my book and allowed the story to calm my nerves.

When I returned to my room, the message light was flashing. The woman at the front desk said Monsieur Auffret had left a message and would like to meet me at eight for dinner. Pierre had been gone for three days, and I was oddly annoyed that he had not disclosed his plans or left me a note.

Entering the restaurant, I saw him perusing the menu at a table overlooking the garden. He looked different: less relaxed, his clothes crisper, and his curly hair less floppy. Having tried on almost every combination in my limited wardrobe, I had settled on a light blue dress with thin straps and a scooped neckline, and a simple strand of pearls that were a graduation present from my grandparents. Joan called my clothing style traditional, and although I had checked the fashion magazines for ideas before coming to France, I was not the least bit interested in wearing leggings or tight leather pants with wide belts or short, form-hugging dresses. If that made me traditional, so be it.

I caught Pierre's eye and resisted the urge to smile, fingering the pearls as I crossed the room, aware of the spicy scent of L'Air du Temps clinging to my neck and wrists.

He held the chair as I sat down. "Are you all right?"

"I am."

"I had to go to Paris for a few days. I am sorry I did not tell you."

"Is everything all right?"

"Yes. Just a little family matter. Now tell me what has happened with the police."

"The police came and repeated the same questions from the night of the break-in. They said they will investigate further, but I don't expect much. It's likely a mystery that will never be solved."

"Perhaps a small-time thief looking for money or jewelry."

"You're probably right. My pearls were on the chair. Whoever was there must have dropped them before going out the window."

Pierre rested his chin on one hand. "Can you think of any other reason someone would go through your things?"

"That's what the police kept asking. I don't think so. It's bizarre, really. Why don't we talk about something else?"

Pierre tilted his head and tapped one finger against his lips. "All right. Where did you go today?"

"Nowhere. I stayed in the hotel and gave myself a break from war memorials. Spent a very pleasant afternoon reading on the patio."

He smiled. "Would you like some wine? It's a Chablis I enjoy." I nodded, and Pierre poured a generous amount into my glass.

I took a moment to straighten my cutlery, aligning knife and fork handles so their bottom edges were even. "I keep thinking about the diaries. The one from June 15, 1917, is the most puzzling. A whole page and the only words he wrote are 'Chumley Park.' I've spent hours trying to find a reference to Chumley Park. I keep thinking there's something threatening about the deliberateness of that entry."

"Do you think it was a place he wanted to remember or forget?"

"Good question. My grandmother appears not long after that, and I know they corresponded regularly until his demobilization. As far as I can tell, Chumley Park has nothing to do with Grandmama. She might know what and where it is, though."

"Did you ask her?"

"No. My grandmother has always been rather uncommunicative on the subject of the war and his service. Who knows why? Although she did give me a few photos and a couple of my grandfather's letters from the war."

The arrival of our appetizers provided a diversion, each meticulously arranged on the plate like works of art. I slid a piece of scallop into my mouth, savoring the contrast between crisp exterior and soft interior with a drizzle of delectable white wine sauce. "What did you do today?" I asked.

Pierre described a visit to Arras to review an estate collection, telling me about a few of the unique pieces he found there, including a seventeenth-century clock made by Thuret, clockmaker to Louis XIV. To his surprise, three other curators were also reviewing the estate, which made him more cautious about expressing interest to the agents hovering in the background.

"I prefer to avoid bidding wars," he said.

I nodded. "Did you buy the clock?" His experiences were intriguing, such a different world from mine.

"I did." He grinned. "Also a sketch done by Adélaïde Labille-Guiard in preparation for one of her more famous paintings."

"A female painter?"

"Eighteenth century. She was quite successful and even had her own academy. And she lobbied on behalf of women painters."

"I would never have imagined eighteenth-century France to be so . . ."

"So liberal?" he said. "We have a small collection of female artists in the museum. I will have to show them to you."

While our waiter served dinner, I considered the promise that statement implied and how conversation with Pierre differed from that of my ex-husband. Jim would have talked about baseball or a fancy sports car he had seen or complained about someone at work. I would have talked about the boys or jobs we needed to do around the house. It was as though we made statements rather than conversation and operated on different planes.

"You have that puzzled look on your face."

I laughed. "You know my looks already?"

He reached for my hand. "Come with me to Amiens tomorrow. You can see the old town, and I will show you my museum."

"I would love to." I left my hand in his.

Dusk had given way to dark, the flickering candle making our corner feel more secluded as the restaurant shifted from the hustle and clatter of peak serving time to a quieter mood. Our conversation flitted from topic to topic like a hummingbird unwilling to linger in any one spot, and a certain tension grew as the table was cleared and only a few sips of wine remained.

As we walked to my room, I knew he would kiss me again. And then what? At the door, he tilted my chin and looked into my eyes.

"Would you like to come in?" I said.

Once inside the room, Pierre enfolded me in his arms and kissed me. Uncertainty dropped away. He traced a line from cheek to neck, then slipped off one shoulder strap and bent to kiss the curving slope. I thought of nothing except the stirring sensation of his lips.

He gazed into my eyes and kissed me again, his tongue tasting of wine and spice and something uniquely him. His arm tightened on my waist, and for the first time, I touched his hair, winding my fingers in its springy softness. I pressed closer, feeling his body and its urgency against me. When he drew back, I took his hand and led him to the bed.

His hands were gentle, releasing my clothing as if slowly unwrapping a gift, stopping to draw my nipples into his mouth, then lingering with lips and soft breath here and there. When he asked to explore further, I moaned in agreement and he stripped off his clothes in order to lie against me. I stroked his back and shoulders, his buttocks, and the soft skin at the top of his thigh. When neither of us could wait any longer, he pulled me on top of him.

Later, as his fingers traced a pattern across my body, he murmured French phrases I wished I could understand.

I must have fallen asleep, and when I stirred, Pierre was on his side, one arm draping my body, the other tucked beneath his cheek. As soon as I moved, he woke.

"Don't leave," he said.

"Hard for me to leave; it's my room."

"Oh, I forgot."

"What else did you forget?"

"Not one thing." Pierre's silence made me wonder whether he had fallen asleep again. Finally, he said, "Do you want me to leave?"

"No."

"Good."

MARTIN'S DIARY

July 4, 1917

Met a woman named Cynthia at the Mercury Bar. She's young and pretty and loves to dance. Probably nothing serious, but I'm enjoying her company. We seem to be able to talk about anything—even the war. First US troops arrived in France at the end of June. Apparently, the US army has plans to recruit one million men. Many think this will be the beginning of the end. I hope so, but I'm not optimistic.

CHAPTER 21

July 1917

During the remainder of his leave, Martin spent as many hours as possible with Cynthia. Though her time was restricted by work and her parents' rules about what was seemly for a young woman, they managed to see one another every day, and he soon discovered she was the eldest of five children, her father was a painter, and her parents had married for love.

"My mother was a real beauty who had many suitors," Cynthia said as they walked along Threadneedle Street, stopping from time to time to examine shop windows. "Mama told stories about them. One was the son of a wealthy industrialist—I think his name was Robin Dunbar—and there was William Wainwright, who had already made a fortune at the age of thirty-five. And a man called Jeremy Sheridan, who ultimately inherited acres and acres of farmland. But once she met my father, she refused to consider anyone else."

"Was that a problem?"

"Well, he was an artist with no standing in society, and my grandparents looked down on artists. I suppose you would call them snobs. Papa paints beautifully, but he has no business sense. And once they had spent Mama's dowry, we lived from painting to painting. We still do." Cynthia sighed. "She could have had a wealthy life."

"Did you have a happy childhood?"

"For the most part. But there's never been money to spare for the right clothing or outings or any extras. Now that I work, I have a little of my own."

"What about your grandparents? Do they help?"

"No. My grandfather informed Mama she would have her dowry and nothing else. Perhaps she expected he would change his mind, but he never did. My mother's sister, Aunt Anne, helps. She sends clothes my cousins have outgrown and books and toys. I think she also gives Mama a little money from time to time." Cynthia frowned. "I should not be telling you all this. My parents would be mortified. What about your family?"

"No artists in my family. My father's a bank manager. He's done well. Better than his father. When I was in school, he always said if I worked hard enough, I could be a banker like him." Martin pursed his lips. "I'm not sure it's the life for me. I have a younger sister, Jane. You would like her. She's high-spirited and smart and a great storyteller. My mother . . ." Martin's voice trailed off.

"What about your mother?"

"I was just remembering her last letter. She wrote that my uncle George had died of pneumonia. He was her favorite brother. I won't ever see him again."

Cynthia squeezed his arm, and they walked on in silence, past a woman selling fruit and vegetables toward the corner where the Royal Exchange stood opposite a branch of the Bank of England. They waited while a double-decker bus bearing an ad for Tatcho rumbled by, then hurried across the road in front of a wagon drawn by a plodding gray horse.

"Do you have any other siblings?" Cynthia asked when they reached the far side of the road.

"No. We had a baby brother, Geoffrey, but he died of scarlet fever when he was eighteen months old."

"That's dreadfully sad. Mummy miscarried when I was ten and I still remember how much she cried."

Heading toward them was a boy pushing a three-wheeled cart containing a metal dispenser and a sign for Cowley's Dairy. The boy whistled a brisk high-low sound, and a dog appeared, his tongue hanging out, one ear pointing up, the other flopping over.

"What do you think he's doing?" Martin asked.

"Selling milk. Many of the dairies sell door to door. Used to be the men who pushed those carts, but they're all away now." After waving the boy over, Cynthia asked for a half-cup measure, then offered it to Martin. Drawing two small coins from her handbag, she gave them to the boy, who flashed a wide grin.

Martin took a drink and grimaced. "That's strong. Are you sure it's milk?"

"Straight from the cow." Cynthia handed the measuring cup back to the boy and linked her arm once more with Martin. "Do you remember your little brother?"

"Not really. Just an image of the three of us playing on the beach. I think he was a happy little fellow. Jane and I were left on our own after he died. My mother was in tears for months, but we were too young to understand."

Strolling along the busy street, Martin took pleasure in the sounds of the city and the rush of traffic. "Tell me about your job. I know Jane wants to find one, but my parents don't approve."

"Neither did mine," Cynthia replied. "It caused quite a kerfuffle when I told them. Papa said it was his responsibility to look after me, and Mama said it would ruin my chances for a decent marriage. I think that's rather hypocritical of her, don't you? At any rate, many of my friends have jobs, so I asked around and found an opening at

Woolwich Arsenal. It's a munitions factory in southeast London. I'm in the typing pool."

"How do you like it?"

"The work is fine and the other girls are quite jolly, but Miss Stanhope is terribly strict. She's my supervisor. Some days she walks about the room with a long ruler and raps on the desk of anyone who makes a mistake. The first time it happened to me, I nearly fell off my chair. I'm hoping a job on the factory floor opens up. The pay is much better."

"The factory floor? I don't like the thought of you working with the ammunition itself." He gripped her arm a little tighter.

Cynthia's face turned serious. "I doubt it would matter. If we were to have a serious accident, we would all be in danger. I try not to think about it."

"Promise me you'll be careful."

"I shall."

A milky moon shimmered across the water as Martin returned to France. Elbows resting on the ship's railing, he wondered at the wisdom of becoming entangled with a woman. He knew men with wives and sweethearts who lived for letters that never came or brought news of fading love. Some of his men gave him their just-in-case letters for safekeeping, letters he had sent on numerous occasions despite knowing the terrible sorrow they would cause.

Martin fingered the handkerchief and brooch Cynthia had given him as keepsakes from the last night they spent together. Since coming to France, he had thought about his previous girlfriend from time to time, initially with regret and ultimately thankful she had not agreed to wait for him. But he felt differently about Cynthia. He wanted her in his life. She had promised to write, and he was already anticipating her first letter.

As the boat drew closer to the coast, his thoughts turned to war. Lindsay would expect him to behave. Drummond would not tolerate another lapse without stripping him of his rank. Berger's words and the anguish he expressed when speaking of his son returned to him: young soldiers need their lieutenants. Perhaps he could hang on to that, not merely for his own sake, but for that of Michel and Pete and Bill.

CHAPTER 22

June 1991

We had forgotten to close the curtains, and sun glinted through a tall tree next to the window, casting dancing patterns of light across the bed. Pierre had turned in the night so his back faced mine, brushing my skin whenever he shifted, and I lay still, preferring not to disturb him. Thoughts burst and scattered like a kaleidoscope. Sleepy warmth prompted images of tangled limbs, taut nipples, and the pulsing throb of orgasm. Pierre's lovemaking had been at times gentle and at times demanding. I had responded without hesitation.

"Are you awake?" he whispered.

I turned over and nestled against him. "Yes."

He reached for my hand and tugged my arm tightly around him as if claiming possession. "I want to make love to you again."

It was later than expected when we left the hotel, and Pierre drove quickly along the main roads to Amiens, occasionally resting his hand on my thigh. I wondered what he was thinking, his face tightening from time to time followed by a smile or brows drawn sharply together. My own thoughts jumped from recalled moments of passion to sudden worries about impulsiveness and whether I would end up getting hurt.

Rebound. That's what this is. I'm on the rebound from a failed marriage, pleased that any man at all is paying attention to me.

He's not any man, the other half of my brain said. *He's interesting and kind and attractive.* The skeptical half replied, *But being on the rebound never works out, and besides, it's too soon to take anyone seriously. And he lives in France. Just think of it as a fling. That's what he's probably thinking. Some loose woman from the States.*

Pierre's voice pulled me out of my reverie.

"Pardon?"

He touched my fingers. "You were lost somewhere. What were you thinking about?" He did not wait for my reply. "I just said we will not be much longer."

I smiled and nodded. Having Pierre direct my day suited me perfectly, to say nothing of being able to talk to him and touch him, making the previous night real. In my current dreamy mood, I was likely to get lost.

"How are you feeling about what you have seen?" he asked, turning off the main highway and following the exit ramp to a roundabout.

"I never expected to feel so connected to my grandfather. Being here has allowed me to appreciate the enormity of what he endured. Brings the reality close, I suppose. So much closer than reading a history book. Even though it all looks so peaceful now, when I look at particular places and then read his diaries at the same time, I can imagine what he did and how it affected him."

"Does that make you sad?"

"How can anyone visit these places without feeling sad? A whole generation wiped out. And for what? We did it all over again twenty years later."

"I know, and France was destroyed again."

We were silent for a while, the Peugeot speeding past lush green land that had once been part of that destruction.

"What happens after Vimy?" Pierre said after a while.

"He becomes depressed and insubordinate. Perhaps more than insubordinate."

"What does his diary say?"

"When he came back from three weeks in England, he was in a better mood. That's because he'd met Cynthia, my grandmother. But it doesn't last very long. He writes things about how many methods we create to kill people and that they are all just pawns in the game."

"The game?"

"I think he means the way generals and politicians conduct war."

Pierre nodded.

As we spoke, the Gothic spires marking Amiens grew more and more visible, and soon we exited the highway. In the city proper, flat-fronted buildings three or four stories high lined the streets. Calm canals, framed by weeping willows and dotted with kayaks, and cafés spilling onto sidewalks instilled a sense of romance amid the bustle of pedestrians and midday traffic.

"And after today, where else are you planning to explore?"

"I have a few more places to see, and then I'm going to Cologne, where he served with the Army of Occupation."

He pulled a face. "Do you have to go that far?"

I flashed him a smile. "I'll return if you want me to." Bold and impulsive were not my normal style, but the words had appeared almost of their own accord. And why not? I was on vacation, on my own, and Pierre made me feel good. Very good.

He pulled my hand to his lips and kissed it. "That would be wonderful. I live here in Amiens, you know. Gosnay has been a little holiday for me too."

"I'm sure I could enjoy a few days in Amiens," I said.

"It is a lovely town. You will see."

Pierre drove along a wide boulevard filled mainly with office buildings, but as he turned onto a smaller street, I saw an imposing structure surrounded by wrought-iron gates, the façade adorned with sculptures and a mansard roof framing a central dome. A cluster of French flags flanked the main entrance.

"What's that building?"

"That is the museum." I saw pride in his face and something else, an intensity that comes with purpose.

While we walked from the parking lot to the rear entrance, he told me that the building had been constructed as a museum during the reign of Napoleon III and is a well-known example of Second Empire architecture.

"You could spend hours here, but today I will show you just a few of my favorite galleries."

Though the entrance was modest, it opened into a grand hallway where doors were labeled with the names of various departments: archaeology, antiquities, fine arts, membership, finance. Pierre gestured at closed double doors with a plaque to one side bearing his name. "That is my office."

Stepping out of our way as we passed, a woman greeted him. *"Bonjour, monsieur. Avez-vous retourné?"*

"Pas encore, Marie, mais bientôt."

We turned down another corridor, past a central lobby where a group of tourists were waiting for their guide to purchase tickets. Pierre continued into a high-ceilinged room.

"This is our sculpture room," he said, sweeping his arm to one side like an actor poised to take a bow.

White marble sculptures set on raised platforms were arranged along both sides of the room. Marble columns stretching from floor to ceiling and one deep red wall created a sense of drama.

"What a wonderful display," I said.

"*Merci.* We have sculptures from as early as the twelfth century. Sometimes I come here at night when it's quiet and imagine them talking to one another. Look at this one."

He led me to the figure of a naked woman sitting on a tree stump, one knee on the ground, a hand resting on the other. Her wistful face was turned a little to the side, and she was reaching for a tiny bird. The artist had created an impression of haunting innocence.

"She's beautiful."

He leaned close. "Almost as beautiful as you."

The intimate tone of his voice made my insides shiver. How long had it been since a man called me beautiful? And how sad that I could not remember. I caught his eyes in mine and hoped they conveyed a bit of what I felt.

As he described another sculpture, this one a black marble warrior, sword and shield held high, a rotund man in uniform approached.

"*Excusez-moi, monsieur.*"

After a voluble exchange during which Pierre's face went from calm to puzzled to annoyed, Pierre sighed and explained that he was needed but would return in a few minutes.

"Why don't you continue to explore? Beyond this room is our display of religious artifacts and paintings. I will come find you as soon as I am done."

I wandered from sculpture to sculpture, appreciating their exquisite detail and varied subjects. Some pieces encased in glass frames were antiquities, but most were from the eighteenth or nineteenth century. In the next room, I picked up a brochure to look for a diagram of the museum's layout and on the second page found Pierre's picture alongside a word of welcome to visitors. *Good grief, he's in charge of the whole place.*

While examining a series of carved religious figures, each one gilded and about half life-sized, I heard brisk footsteps approaching.

"I'm sorry I had to leave. There has been an unexpected resignation. I think it will be fine. They know I am on holiday."

"There's no need to apologize. I've had a wonderful time exploring. What a magnificent collection, Pierre. Are you sure everything's all right?" He nodded but still looked distracted. "If you're needed, I can amuse myself. You don't need to look after me." I waved the brochure at him and raised my eyebrows. "And you failed to mention that you're the man in charge."

Pierre shrugged, as though being the head of a major museum were nothing. "I don't like to boast."

Beyond the next doorway, we entered a room covered in red wallpaper sprinkled with fleurs-de-lis. "This is our grand salon," he said.

The room itself was a work of art, the walls topped by a two-foot cornice carved and painted with heraldry and floral motifs, the ceilings arcing high to allow ribbons of light from a domed skylight, doorways enhanced with sculpted stone. Paintings encased in elaborate gold frames hung at wide intervals. Though I had been around works of art all my life, I could not think how to describe the room's emotional impact. I could only turn and look and turn again.

"Do you like it?"

My head bobbed like a loose-necked puppet.

"We feature many artists here, with a bias to those from our region. It is a huge collection, less than twenty percent on display at any one time. Let me show you some favorites."

Captivated, I allowed him to pull me through an archway into another equally striking room, where he pointed at a small group of pictures.

"My grandparents used to have four of these," Pierre said. We stood only inches from the canvases. "Look at the detail. Can you feel them draw you in?"

I moved close, absorbing texture and color, the vivid reds and rich browns of one contrasting with the creams and yellows of another. Though each painting was different, there were similarities in setting and composition: the slow curve of a river, a farmhouse nestled against a stand of trees, a church spire and rolling hills in the distance.

"Exquisite," I said. "Simple yet compelling."

"They are. Luras did many portraits, but he is most famous for his landscapes."

"My grandfather loved landscapes. He had many in his gallery and several in his personal collection. Where did Luras do these paintings?"

"Northern France, for the most part. I think that's why my grandfather liked them. He had other works, but nothing as valuable. It saddened him a great deal to lose them, and he spent a lot of money trying to locate them after the war. Money he should have saved for living." A shadow briefly passed over his face, but then he brightened. "Let me show you some other artists."

After lunch, we toured a few highlights of Amiens, then strolled alongside the canal, where colorful houses with steeply sloped roofs mingled with cafés canopied under canvas. By six o'clock, I was exhausted.

"I don't think I can absorb any more history."

"I know what you need."

Without disclosing our destination, Pierre linked his arm with mine and turned away from the canal, passing through a walled courtyard where a fountain trickled into a shell-shaped bowl and thick moss grew in cracks between the cobbles. Beyond the courtyard was a rectangular bit of grass surrounded by oak trees and a bench shaded by a trellis of white flowers. A few minutes later, we approached a three-story brick house with a bold blue door.

"This is my house," Pierre said.

"Your house?"

I was surprised. I had imagined an apartment with crisp, masculine lines, not a cheerful-looking place with flower boxes and a stone cat on the front porch. Inside, the house revealed Pierre's enjoyment of simple pleasures as well as fine art and ancient artifacts. In his sitting room, I saw family pictures and comfortable cushions, a newspaper folded to an unfinished crossword, a pile of books next to one of two comfortable armchairs, a pair of glasses on the coffee table. The kitchen also looked lived in, not sleek or modern, but pleasing, with a wide window overlooking the back garden.

"Do you like to cook?"

"Mm-hmm. Great therapy after a day in the office." He held my shoulders and kissed me lightly. "What you need is a soak in the bath." When I began to protest, Pierre held up his hand. "No arguments. I will get a few groceries and make us something to eat. You will find everything you need upstairs."

When I returned to the kitchen, Pierre was chopping onions and had various ingredients set out on the counter: chicken pieces, apples, lemon, butter, celery, a bottle of some sort of liquor, and a small bag that might have contained flour.

"What are we having?" I said.

"*Poulet Vallée d'Auge.*"

I laughed. "Well, I'm a lot wiser now. And what is that, monsieur?"

"A classic chicken dish from Normandy. With Calvados." He held up the liquor bottle. "I will use chicken stock in the sauce, but some use apple cider and call the dish *poulet au cidre.*"

"What can I do to help?"

"You can pour us a glass of wine. I have a Sancerre being chilled." He waved his knife in the direction of the fridge and pointed me at a drawer for the corkscrew.

The dish was delicious, the sauce a silky blend of savory and sweet. Afterward we sat outside as light faded from the sky and I could sense Pierre's relaxation, as if, having invited me into his personal space, he could dispense with caution and be himself. While we talked of nothing in particular, I heard neighborhood sounds: a door shutting, a dog barking, music drifting from a nearby window, a greenfinch calling her mate. When the air cooled, I shivered, and he reached for my hand.

"Time for bed," he said.

CHAPTER 23

July 1991

Lying in bed the following morning wearing one of Pierre's T-shirts, I asked about his plans for the day.

"I have another collection to see this afternoon, but we do not have to rush." Leaning on one elbow, he trailed his fingers through my hair. "What about you?"

"I have a few more places I want to visit—the ones I had originally planned for yesterday."

"They will make you sad again."

"Probably. But I feel that's the least I can do in his memory."

"Why don't you read something else from Martin's diary? His experiences make me think of my grandfather."

"I could read you the ones from Passchedaele, although Martin's mood is pretty grim."

"I can imagine," he said, propping his pillow against the headboard and settling back to listen.

"*October 24, 1917. We are back near Ypres fighting over the same god-damned land as before. If the newspapers reported the truth, if they wrote about the mud and filth and the body parts littering the ground and how young men look old before their time, would we still be here? The ground is a morass of water and shell holes that will drown you if you aren't careful. Our artillery is about to make it worse by shelling the hell out of it again. We move up to the line tomorrow for an assault. Thank God for Cynthia's letters. She has written almost every day, and I write to her. When I close my eyes, I imagine us together.*

November 1, 1917. Worst fighting yet. The first day, we were seriously bombed but suffered few casualties. Then it went from bad to worse. Sloan, Nelson, Harris, Paton, Birdy, Darcy, and Usher are gone. Fleming is missing. Lindsay says our battalion strength is less than half what it was before. CO is satisfied because we took our objectives. We go back of the line tomorrow. This isn't war, it's slaughter.

November 15, 1917. The only positive news is that the Americans are beginning to have an effect. But even that news is dimmed because Russia has been lost, and Germany can now bring its full strength against our western front. We are holding the line rather than attacking, so casualties are fewer. The rain is endless and driving me mad.

November 30, 1917. There's nothing left of Passchendaele. Absolutely nothing. A whole town gone. I'm to see the CO tomorrow. I suspect it's my promotion. Too many men had to die for me to be promoted. If I could refuse, I would, but what's the point?"

Several moments passed before Pierre spoke. "What a terrible experience. It is impossible to imagine what they endured. Your grandfather sounds depressed."

"He does. Very depressed. Cynthia kept him going, I think."

"What's she like?"

"Formidable. Sharp-tongued. Quick to find fault. Hard to love." I made a face.

"What did he see in her?"

"She was gorgeous. And probably different then. She was only eighteen when they met."

"How old were you when you met your husband?"

"Ex-husband."

He stroked my arm, eyes half closed. "Ex-husband."

"I was twenty. Twenty-three when we married. Why do you ask?"

"I am curious."

"What about your marriage?"

"Her name is Vivienne. We divorced six years ago. She was my father's choice, not mine, but it took me a long time to understand that. We got along but had no passion. I left the bank right when we separated. My father still doesn't understand."

"And you said no children?"

He nodded. "Vivienne had two miscarriages." A wistful look appeared. "But you have two boys."

"Paul and Michael. Paul's fifteen. Michael is twelve. Jim's looking after them while I'm away, but normally they live with me."

"You must miss them."

"I do. But I'm enjoying being on my own."

"Oh. Have I intruded?"

"Not at all." I leaned close enough to kiss his cheek.

"And what about your grandfather's puzzle? Have you solved it?"

I made a face. "No progress. Nothing at all in terms of clues. I suppose it was silly of me to think being here would provide answers. Grandpa wouldn't have expected me to travel to France, so he must have assumed I could solve it at home."

"But you came to France anyway."

"I did." I wanted to say that if I hadn't come to France, I would never have met him, but it seemed too soon to say something like that.

Pierre looked like he was assessing something. "If he wanted you to know, why did he make it so difficult?"

"I don't know. I've never asked myself that question. He often set puzzles for me when I was younger, so it didn't seem odd to me."

"Perhaps he wanted the puzzle to be too difficult for anyone else to solve."

"Too difficult for anyone else. That's an interesting thought."

"Perhaps it involves a lot of money or something terrible he did during the war."

"Maybe you're right. Whatever it was, I'm beginning to think Grandmama must have known about it. But I can't imagine him doing something terrible. He was such a successful man with a wonderful reputation."

"Success can lead to greed or entitlement."

"Grandpa wasn't like that, Pierre. If anyone was, it would have been my grandmother. Maybe she wanted to keep the secret and Grandpa didn't." My thoughts filled with the image of the man with the fedora. "Do you think the man wearing the fedora also broke into my hotel room?"

Pierre nodded slowly. "Yes, I have that suspicion. Can you think of any reason someone would do that?" he said in a somber tone, a deep frown appearing between his eyebrows.

"No. No reason at all."

"Promise me you'll be very careful and you'll let me know if you see that man again."

Promise me. Pierre's protective stance offered comfort and something more. Something I wasn't ready to think about.

"Now, we really should get out of bed," he said, though his hand on my thigh said otherwise.

On the return trip to Gosnay, Pierre talked animatedly about plans to enhance the museum's collection and reach new audiences. Having never thought of a museum in business terms, I found his perspective fascinating.

"In the spring, there will be a major exchange of treasures with a museum in Chicago. We want to take French culture to different parts of the world, so we are also in talks with museums in Dublin and Hong Kong." As he spoke, his face filled with anticipation.

"I wish I were as excited about my job," I said as we passed through a small town.

"What's wrong with your job?"

I paused for a moment. What exactly was wrong with my job? My boss gave me lots of scope. I had been promoted on several occasions. The company was in the midst of a major merger.

"I suppose I've been there too long. I'm at that point where every project feels like something I've done before. In the beginning, it was challenging and I kept getting more responsibility. I work in marketing . . . actually, I'm the marketing director." Having discovered the nature of Pierre's role, I saw no need to hide my own success, and I said these last few words with a hint of pride. "I guess I've realized that insurance is a staid business that attracts relatively boring people."

"Perhaps you need a change?"

I snorted. "Don't you think I've had enough change? Divorced a husband. Looking after two boys on my own. Taking leave to come here. Some people think I'm crazy." My face softened. "Not Paul, though. He understands."

"He's your eldest?"

"Yes, and more like me than Michael is." I clasped my hands together. "I'm ashamed that I've hardly thought about them lately. And Grandmama will be furious I haven't called."

"Sounds like a reason not to call."

I laughed at his logic. "I should call the boys, though."

"Would I like them?" He sounded hesitant and a bit sad.

"I think you would."

From my hotel window, I watched Pierre drive off. Yesterday's heat had turned oppressive, early sunshine giving way to a shroud of thick gray clouds, suggesting a storm would soon erupt. On my list of places to visit were Cambrai, Valenciennes, Mons, and Canal du Nord, each included in Martin's diary, some with more significance than others. Would one of these towns provide insights into the fury gathering in his thoughts and emotions? Not likely, but at least seeing them would allow me to pay tribute to the sacrifices he made.

Martin's words now spoke to me more than ever. What I had taken for criticism was bitterness, what I had taken for cynicism was shock at the ineptitude of leaders. And his disillusion was really the deep, deep despair of a man without hope.

Only Cynthia gave him hope. I shuddered, imagining what Martin might have done without her. *Perhaps he would have flung himself into battle wishing for death, trading bravery for recklessness and caution for carelessness.* I put a hand to my mouth. *Maybe he had, but death had laughed at him and tossed him back to the living.*

A crack of thunder made me jump. I loved watching storms unfurl: the drama of darkening sky and eerie yellow light, the pungent smell of rain about to fall, the quickening wind tossing twigs and discarded scraps. At a lakefront cottage one summer, Grandpa had driven the motorboat to shelter in an abandoned boathouse as lightning split the sky followed by booming bursts of thunder. Now, as this storm broke with sudden fury, I recalled his tight lips and worried frown in the boathouse, and understood why he had flinched.

I had come to France with two missions: to understand my grandfather's war experience and to solve the puzzle he left for me. Exploring the countryside, visiting memorials and cemeteries and museums had helped with the first objective, but not the second. *I never should have taken them.* Everywhere I went, Martin's words lingered just below the surface. Never could I have imagined words like *deceit* or *theft* associated with Grandpa. Never.

Would Grandmama know? This was a question I pondered time and again and the main reason I was avoiding the telephone. Intuition told me she would have the answers, but since I hadn't mentioned the diaries before coming to France, I didn't want to disclose Grandpa's puzzling note now. Once back in New York, I planned to confront my grandmother, but for now I continued to hope for a clue to unlock the puzzle.

One outcome of my time in France had not been in my plans: self-discovery. Unfamiliar surroundings prompted examination of the path I had been on—education, marriage, children, and career—a logical progression unfolding just like so many other conventional lives. Grandmama had insisted on a business degree, and I had acquiesced, imagining such skills would prove valuable in the short and longer term. When Pierre had spoken of finding a job he loved, something had stirred inside me. Something I needed to examine.

As a college student, I hadn't questioned my grandmother's advice nor imagined she might have harbored regrets. As a newlywed, I never imagined being more successful than my husband.

And now I understood. I understood that Jim was not strong enough to cope with my success, and that Grandmama wanted to be more than the wife of an art gallery owner. I understood that their daughter's failed life and the loss of their son when he was two years old were heavy burdens for my grandparents, burdens that caused Grandmama to be demanding and resentful, and my grandfather to surround himself with young artists. Understanding them helped me understand myself.

Rain tumbled in blinding sheets. *I'll go out tomorrow,* I thought, and collected my maps and Martin's diaries and my half-read copy of *The Shell Seekers*. Before going down to the salon to curl into one end of a comfortable sofa, I changed into jeans and brushed my hair, remembering Pierre's house and how he'd looked at me in the midst of making love.

The sharp double ring of the telephone interrupted my thoughts. I put down the brush and moved briskly to the bedside table.

"Hello?"

"Well, finally my granddaughter answers. Where have you been? I called twice yesterday, and you weren't there either time."

"Hello, Grandmama. How are you?"

My grandmother snorted. "You don't need to hear about all my aches and pains. Where were you last night? The second time I called would have been well after ten in France."

"I was out for dinner." Technically, that was the truth.

"You must have had a very late dinner."

"Is everything all right, Grandmama?"

"Yes. But you promised to call. Tell me where you've been."

"So many places." I recounted the last few days, mentioning various villages and towns I had visited. I described a few of the memorials and cemeteries and the museum at Peronne. "Have you been to any of these places?"

"No. What have you found?"

"What have I found? Did you think I was looking for something?"

"Don't be silly. That was merely an idle question. Have you met anyone?"

Mentioning Pierre would only lead to questions I didn't wish to answer. "Not really. Just shopkeepers and waiters and a few other tourists. What have you been doing, Grandmama?"

I did not mention the man who might or might not be following me, or my ransacked room. I needed to gain some distance before revealing what had occurred—merely thinking about them made me jittery, causing me to look over my shoulder, and I worried that fear would curtail my travels.

While Grandmama talked about seeing her friend Sally Rockford, I debated whether to ask about Grandpa's war experience. A misstep could easily arouse her suspicions. Grandmama had a sixth sense when it came to fibs or even the briefest hesitation when I attempted to dissemble.

"What are you keeping from me, Grace Louise?" she would say when I was young. "You have that fibbing look, and you know I will not abide any lies." I never really learned the calm, clear-eyed gaze required to tell a lie or avoid the truth until I was an adult.

"What did Grandpa tell you about the war?" I asked with as much nonchalance as I could muster after Grandmama finished her story.

"Most men never spoke of the war. It was such a dreadful time. Your grandfather was in the infantry. He became a captain before it was all over."

"I know the story of how you met, but when did you see him again?"

"Not for many months," she said. "The fighting was fierce in 1917, and his leaves were often canceled. I wrote to him three or four times a week, but I didn't see him again until the following March. By the end of the war, he was a different man."

"Different?" I echoed. "Different how?"

"When he returned to England, he was desperately depressed. He had so many deaths to cope with." Grandmama's voice grew distant, as though she were talking to herself. "Everyone he cared for was gone. I tried to help, but nothing seemed to work. At one point, he even said he no longer wanted to get married."

"But you did get married."

"Yes, we did."

"And what happened after you married?"

"We sailed for Canada almost immediately and eventually moved to New York City."

"What else happened?"

"Why do you think there should be something else?" Her tone sharpened.

"No reason, Grandmama. Just a question."

I was accustomed to her testiness, but I heard tension in her voice now, perhaps even fear, which was at odds with her usual imperious attitude.

"Tell me again why you're in France," she demanded.

"Grandmama, you know the answer to that question."

"Well, tell me again."

"I'm here to see where Grandpa was during the war. Don't you remember? I wrote away for his war records, so I know the towns where he served. And I needed a holiday."

"Have you found anything interesting?"

"Everything's interesting. But I'm not looking for anything in particular. I'm just enjoying myself."

"I wish you'd come home."

"I will. In a few weeks' time."

Each time I replayed the conversation, I had the same feeling. Something in her questions sounded strange. *Don't be ridiculous,* I thought. *She's just getting old.*

MARTIN'S DIARY

December 4, 1917

Games day. Now that I'm a captain, I don't participate, just hand out prizes and encourage the men. Church parade on Sunday. Cynthia tells me she no longer goes to the Mercury with Lucy because it makes her feel lonely, and she misses me too much. Have to confess that this makes me happy. I wish we'd had more time together—then I would have even more to hang on to.

December 15, 1917

Jane has written with news that by January or February, she'll be nursing with the Red Cross in Belgium or France! Had a letter from Mother as well saying they had tried to forbid her to go. Mother should have known such an approach would only make Jane more determined. Unthinkable that my lovely sister will be amidst this horror. I am going to request leave to visit her and try to convince her to go home or at least do her nursing in England.

We are training for new assault formations that will give more authority down the line so we can attack and counterattack rapidly. Keep the Boche off balance, according to Drummond. Another Christmas in this godforsaken place. With my new rank, I know a bit more of future plans and general strategy. A few days from now, we will be back in the line for one more rotation, then we return to the Vimy area. I'm not looking forward to that.

CHAPTER 24

March 1918

After two and a half years, a man should be used to this, Martin thought as he ordered two platoons to deepen a line of trenches so they could move about more safely in daytime. The Germans dug in opposite them were a considerable distance away but close enough for sniping, and he had already lost two men to their bullets, picked off just before dawn.

"They should have known better," he muttered, "always the worst time for sniping."

Over hill and valley, across rivers and canals, skirting towns and villages, they occupied a zone of deadly stealth. Day after day, week after week, they lived in a place where men seldom spoke above a whisper, where coughing brought enemy fire, where unexpected movement might prompt the end of an existence so horrible they hardly spoke of it. The cracking, popping, sizzling, clanging, thundering sounds of artillery and snipers and machine guns came and went, disturbing the furtive silence at times for mere moments, at other times for hours. Harsh warrior cries and the moaning of those beyond help defined their days and nights.

Martin and his men were dug in just west of a town their artillery was gradually blowing to bits. He had orders to constantly harass the enemy and keep them guessing as to when and where the next attack would come. In retaliation, German shelling increased, and Lindsay sent word that a shell had exploded in one of their gun emplacements, killing four and wounding seven highly trained gunners. According to Lindsay, replacement gunners were proving too green to be useful. "Fucking useless" had been his exact words.

These days, Martin thought often of Dr. Berger. Though he resented Lindsay, Fenton, and Drummond for sending him to Chumley Park, Berger's fervent plea on behalf of his own son had pierced the armor of despair following Bill's death, opening a sliver of compassion for his men. They needed him. For the most part, Martin did not care whether he lived or died, yet from time to time, he heeded the unspoken plea in a soldier's eyes and offered words to bolster courage or soothe the doubts that filled each day.

Since his promotion to captain, he and Lindsay were on better terms. Both commanded four platoons, each platoon roughly fifty men, and they often collaborated on attacks. Sometimes they held the line while at other times they went on the offensive. But these were only skirmishes and rarely made material difference. In three years, their lines had moved only a little here and there, nothing that would break the stalemate along the western front. Yet every day brought casualties, and occasionally a day recorded casualties in the hundreds if not thousands. Martin had written so many condolence letters he had lost count, a circumstance unimaginable at the beginning. No doubt, he would soon be sending more.

When Martin and his men were out of the line again, their brigade commander assembled all officers for a briefing. Fenton was austere and rarely betrayed emotion, but his eyes missed nothing. According to Fenton, the strategy would be to reduce the proportion of frontline troops and pull reserves and supply dumps back beyond artillery range.

"The forward zone will be held by snipers, patrols, and machine-gun posts. Our battle zone will be those units just out of range. They will be responsible for resisting the enemy. Farther back, we'll have a rear zone with reserves ready to counterattack or seal off German penetrations."

"What do you think?" Lindsay asked Martin as they walked back to camp.

"Makes sense. More flexibility with the potential for less carnage. But why has it taken them so long to change the way we operate?" Martin said.

"Because pompous generals and useless staff officers have been running things."

Lindsay's criticism surprised Martin. "I'm beginning to like you, Lindsay."

That night, he and Lindsay debated what the generals would do next amid swirling rumors that Germany was planning a major spring offensive to break through Allied lines.

"Are they strong enough to break us?" he asked, deferring to Lindsay's experience, although, in truth, Martin had become the better tactician.

"Depends where they hit. If they head northwest, they could push through and take Dunkirk and Calais, maybe even Boulogne. But if Ludendorff gets greedy and attacks on a wider front, they could fail."

"If he attacks on a wider front, we'll be in the thick of it again."

Pulling out a silver cigarette case that had once deflected a bullet, Lindsay grunted. "If they attack where the British and French armies meet, we're vulnerable. Let's hope the Americans get more men on the ground soon. Where's your sister?"

"Longuenesse. Just west of Hazebrouck. Far too close for my comfort. I wish I could send her home."

"Will Drummond give you leave to see her?"

"He says he will, but . . ."

"But every time you see him, he has another excuse. I know the drill. Promise whatever will soothe. Never deliver."

"I'm worried about her. She's with a casualty clearing station, not at the front but close enough. Who knows what they have her doing. She could be out with the ambulances for all I know. Christ, I wish she hadn't come."

"Sounds gutsy."

"She's got guts, all right. It's her common sense I'm worried about. You'd like her."

"Maybe I'll come with you." Lindsay laughed and nudged Martin. "Don't worry. Drummond would never let both of us go at the same time. I'll speak to him on your behalf. It won't hurt to add my support."

MARTIN'S DIARY

April 10, 1918

Lindsay is dead now too. He was assigned to the forward zone and taken out in the first wave of attacks. His sergeant said he went down fighting, which I know he would have preferred. He always talked about snipers being nasty cowards, not real fighting men, and hated the thought of being caught by something random. There's no point in friendship in this mess. You make friends and they die. It's that simple. God knows why I'm still alive. At times I even think of throwing myself in front of a bullet, then I remember what Berger said about my men needing me.

We held them off at Arras, but today Drummond said the British Fifth Army is in trouble. Rumors are 20,000 dead on the first day of battle. Total numbers will never be known. Inconceivable. Some generals should be shot. Does anyone remember what we're fighting for?

April 15, 1918

Finally received permission to visit Jane. Three days leave beginning tomorrow.

CHAPTER 25

April 1918

Martin took a supply truck to Hazebrouck and from there found transport on a farmer's wagon, sitting on the wooden seat beside a gray-haired man who spoke no English and whose French was incomprehensible. After following three ammunition trucks over what was left of the cobblestone streets of St. Omer, the farmer left him at an intersection, and he walked the last mile to the casualty clearing station in Longuenesse where Jane was stationed. A cool mist accompanied him along with the intermittent crump of shelling.

The German offensive that had begun in March had faltered; otherwise his battalion commander would never have given Martin permission to leave. However, Drummond had only granted him three days, and only because he had denied all Martin's requests for leave since January.

He walked along a dirt road traversing fields still thick with winter mud, passing a farmhouse of brick-and-stone construction and a barn reeking of manure. Now that the mist had cleared, Chateau Sainte-Croix was visible atop a gentle rise surrounded by trees. Jane had written about the chateau, currently used as a casualty clearing station, and he could see its ornate roofline and charming turret as he drew closer.

He cocked his ear, appreciating the chirping of birds and the peacefulness of land undamaged by war. The midday sun warmed the earth, and while unwrapping his scarf, he caught the glint of low-flying airplanes heading in his direction. Martin shaded his eyes as, one by one, they landed on a wide strip of tarmac, bouncing and swerving until coming to rest.

Nearing the chateau, he saw nurses, white headscarves flapping as they hurried toward one of the nearby huts, and a group of uniformed men standing on the steps leading to the front door. Three ambulances were parked beside a picket fence, and wounded soldiers lay on stretchers placed in rows on the ground.

"Martin!" A gray-clad nurse with a navy cape ran toward him.

He swept his sister into his arms and hugged her tight. "You're safe."

"Of course I am. We're all safe here in Longuenesse."

For the next hour, Jane showed him around the clearing station, explaining each area's role in treating the wounded: the resuscitation ward, the X-ray hut, the surgeries, the nurses' quarters, and the officers' mess.

"We triage each case, sending those with more serious wounds by train to transport ships headed for England. Last month, we conducted more than six hundred operations, but that number is low. It's usually much higher. Once, we dealt with more than three thousand patients in a twenty-four-hour period."

"That's unbelievable," Martin said. "What are your duties?"

"I'm usually in the resuscitation ward. It's very difficult work, Martin. To see men dying in such numbers is ghastly. Their conditions are appalling. Sometimes those who are conscious smile grimly at me, and I know they are glad to be wounded and finished with war. Yesterday a man pleaded with me to remove his boots, which he said had not been off his feet for over a week. I suppose you can imagine the smell when I took them off."

Martin nodded.

"Sometimes the soldiers who aren't as badly wounded help by holding the torches so we can work at night. Many times I've been on duty more than twenty-four hours at a stretch until Matron forcibly sends me off to bed."

"Why don't you go home? Or at least go to England. Mother and Dad are so worried about you."

"I can't, Martin. You know I can't. They need me here. I'm well trained. Just yesterday Colonel Francis said I was doing splendid work, and I've made such an important contribution since I arrived. You only have to be here during a major battle to know how much people like me are needed."

"So I can't persuade you."

"No, you can't. Now tell me what you've been doing. I can see in your face the stress you've been under."

While having tea in one of the chateau's sitting rooms, Martin told her everything, each disclosure easing the weight of his burdens. He described the conditions they lived with, the men under his command, the nerve-racking wait prior to battle, and the condolence letters he wrote afterward. He spoke about Michel and Pete and Bill and Butler, and described his time at Chumley Park and conversations with Dr. Berger. A brief smile lit his face when he mentioned Cynthia.

"She writes to me several times a week," he said.

Jane laid her hand on his. "She sounds lovely. Perhaps I'll meet her when this is over. Major General Burstall was here last week," she said. "Our CO invited as many of us as could be spared to hear him speak, and since I wasn't on duty, I went along. Burstall had encouraging news about the spring offensive and even hinted it might all end soon."

"Well, I think we have many months left. Germany is still fighting hard. But the Americans are finally making a difference."

"Promise me you won't do anything foolish, Martin. I want us both to go home in one piece."

That evening they walked into St. Omer to attend a concert given by one of the army's traveling comedy teams—an evening full of skits and songs and card tricks and even a bit of dancing. Martin smiled as Jane swirled around a patch of open floor with one soldier after another, tawny curls swinging back and forth, her eyes bright with laughter.

While Jane was on duty the following day, he wrote to Cynthia and his parents, describing the casualty clearing station and avoiding the grimmer aspects of the work she did, and that evening he and Jane talked until well after midnight. With rain so fierce he could see little beyond fifty feet, Martin was fortunate to discover a senior officer returning to Hazebrouck the next morning who offered to give him a ride. Jane followed him down the front steps and hugged him tightly.

"Make sure you come home, Martin Devlin," she said. "I don't know what I would do without you."

CHAPTER 26

July 1991

Power outages caused by the storm meant Le Sommelier served only a limited selection of food that evening, and I chose a seafood platter nestled on crisp greens and a glass of Chablis to remind me of the previous night. Candles flickered on every flat surface, casting quivering shadows in keeping with my mood. As the dining room emptied, there was still no sign of Pierre, and I retreated to my room, disappointed not to have seen him and worried whether something had happened.

He was there when I came down for breakfast. "I'm sorry about last night," he said after kissing me on the cheek. "The storm was so nasty it was unsafe to drive. Where are we going today?"

"We?"

"I want to spend another day with you. Is this a crime in America?"

I laughed. "Cambrai, Valenciennes, Mons, and Canal du Nord are all on my agenda. I was planning to see them yesterday, but the storm got in the way."

From my research, I knew that four of the last major actions fought by the Canadian army occurred in these locations, a hundred days of

further bloodshed and massive losses on both sides resulting in significant German retreat and a demoralized German army.

"Excellent. I will drive, and you can enjoy the scenery. I suggest we
go to Cambrai first. I know a café where we can stop for an espresso."

Having concluded I would not find clues to Martin's puzzle by
visiting the sites where he had served, I relaxed, appreciating Cambrai's
main square and clock tower and its massive gate—the remnants of a
wall that had once surrounded the city—for their beauty and history.
After walking around, Pierre and I sat outside enjoying espressos along
with the warmth of the sun, linking hands from time to time for the
simple pleasure of touching one another.

Valenciennes had a different feel to it, busier and more modern,
which Pierre explained was due to an almost complete reconstruction
after World War II. We did not linger, and after a brief look at a memorial for Canal du Nord, we proceeded on to Mons in Belgium, where we
lunched beneath a yellow umbrella at a restaurant on the Grand Place.
And that was where I saw him again—the man with the straw fedora.

"What is wrong?" Pierre said when I gripped his hand.

"Don't look around or make a sudden move," I replied. "I've just
seen the man who was following me. He's leaning against the entrance
to the pharmacy on your left."

"Are you sure?" Pierre kept his eyes on me.

"Perfectly sure. I had a very close look when he confronted me at
Vimy. And he's wearing the same hat."

"I see. Do you think if I shifted my chair a little, I could take a look
without attracting his attention?"

I shook my head. "Perhaps it would be better if you went to the bar
and ordered another beer. More natural that way." I gripped his hand
again. "Don't let him know you're watching."

"He looks rather harmless," Pierre said upon his return, the waiter
following with a glass of beer balanced on a circular tray.

"What should we do?"

"Well, maybe you should leave. Then if he follows you, I can follow him."

"What if we lose each other?"

"We shall rendezvous back here. But I do not plan to let you out of my sight."

Pierre's concern reassured me. "All right. You should probably drink some of that beer first."

After Pierre paid the bill, I kissed him on both cheeks in the French way and left our table, passing a series of boutique shops and cheerful restaurants spilling onto the sidewalk beneath brightly colored awnings as I made my way toward the town hall. I slowed my pace, stopping to look into windows that caught my eye and snapping a few pictures as any tourist would. Taking pictures allowed me to observe the man with the fedora, who followed at a reasonable distance. While taking a picture of the town hall, I noticed Pierre staying well behind as promised.

Crossing the square, I proceeded beneath a Gothic arch marking the entrance to a narrow street where trailing vines and second-story balconies blocked the sun. About fifty yards away, the alley opened onto another plaza, and I stopped to look at the map, twisting it around more than once as if checking where I was going before taking the first left. With as much confidence as I could muster, I continued walking. My plan—naïve and possibly dangerous—was to walk a little farther, then turn around to confront the man, demanding to know his name and why he was following me. Hopefully, Pierre would be right behind him.

Grateful for flat-soled shoes, I walked along the cobbles past grimy street-level windows and metal doors secured with bulky padlocks. At what looked like the back end of a restaurant were several garbage cans and a cat licking remnants from a plastic container. I heard footsteps behind me but forced myself to continue on. Water dribbled from a spout emerging from the narrow space between two buildings; graffiti marked a blue door that sported several buzzers and no names. As the sidewalk narrowed I realized I'd taken a dead-end street.

I hesitated. If Pierre was not behind me, I was in more danger than I'd bargained for. More footsteps. I walked farther. At the end of the street a car was parked against the wall. I took another few steps and stopped, pretending to look at my map once more.

Do it now, I thought, and whirled around, startling the man with the suddenness of my movement.

"Who are you?" I shouted, fear galvanizing into anger. "And why are you following me?"

Pierre was nowhere in sight.

"Well, Grace," he said, drawing out my name into two syllables, "that's none of your business. You got away from me before, but not this time. Now hand them over to me."

The accent was odd, American with a slight European twist, and hearing my name spoken aloud by this man was more than disconcerting; it was frightening. "Hand what over to you?"

"You know what I'm after." He took a step closer, and despite the dim light, I could see that his eyes were the strangest color of gray, a gray as pale as fog.

Stall, Grace, stall. Pierre will be here soon. "Are you the one who broke into my hotel room?"

"Maybe." The twitch of a smile appeared.

"You're not very good at what you do," I said. "I've seen you three times before, but if you hadn't worn that hat, I might not have noticed you today. Stupid thing to do, if you're trying to be invisible. Did someone tell you to follow me?"

In the distance, Pierre rounded the corner. I forced myself not to shift my gaze. The man was facing me, and I wanted to keep it that way. I took a step forward, which seemed to surprise him. And another. Pierre inched closer.

"Now why would I tell you that?" He reached out one hand. "Give me your purse, Grace."

"There's not much money in it."

"I want the diaries. Give me the purse, or I'll take it from you."

"The diaries? Why would you want the diaries?"

Without making a sound, Pierre stepped closer.

"Wouldn't you like to know?"

Think, Grace, think. I had to do something to keep him from hearing Pierre. I gathered saliva in my mouth and spit, landing a thick gob just beneath the man's right eye.

"Shit," he said. "You bitch." The man wiped his cheek, and as he backed away, Pierre grabbed his arms tightly.

"Why are you following her?" he said, anger flaring across his face as he shook the man hard.

The man struggled, breaking one arm free. Using all his weight, Pierre pinned him against the wall, and I heard the smack of flesh against stone.

"Fuck! Let go of me," the man said.

Pierre uttered a stream of French words and smacked the man against the wall a second time. "Who sent you? Tell us who!"

"You think I'll tell you who sent me? No way. No bloody way."

The man went still for a moment, then shoved one foot against the wall, knocking Pierre off balance. He wrenched free and scrambled to get away, feet slipping on the cobbles. Pierre regained his footing and lunged just as the man thrust his body sideways and knocked me to the ground. Pain shot through my knee and wrist.

Pierre hesitated. The man turned and began to run while I remained on the ground holding my knee, blood dripping down my leg.

"Are you all right?" Pierre said.

"I think so."

Pierre helped me to my feet as the man, shoes slapping hard against the cobbles, put more and more distance between us. I watched him turn the corner. Tires squealed. A loud shout followed, then a sickening thud and the crunch of metal slamming against stone.

CHAPTER 27

July 1991

"What the hell was that?" I said.

"You stay here. I will find out." Pierre hurried off.

By the time I limped to the corner, a small crowd had gathered around the man, who lay in a heap on the street, one arm flung wide, face covered in blood, and legs pinned beneath a dark green Citroën. The straw fedora had rolled away and now leaned against a battered garbage can. An older man in a dark gray suit stood next to the car looking bewildered. People chattered loudly, gesturing at one another. As a police officer pushed his way through, the crowd grew silent.

Sirens wailed. More police arrived, followed by an ambulance that barely stopped before the doors burst open and two paramedics rushed out. One of them checked for a pulse and shook his head. He covered the man's face with a blanket.

What had I done? Was I responsible in some way for this man's death?

For the next few minutes, Pierre spoke to one of the police officers, a man with thick hair and a hooked nose who scribbled in a pocket-sized notebook as he asked questions. I understood nothing of what was said, although the tone was serious and occasionally the officer gestured at me with a tilt of his head.

"Ask him to check for ID so we know the man's name."

Pierre relayed the question, and the police officer checked each pocket in the man's clothing.

"No identification. You no speak French, madame?" he said to me.

"No, monsieur," I replied. "I'm sorry. What will you do next?"

"I am Inspector Casale. Monsieur Auffret very helping." He continued on in French and then paused for Pierre to translate.

"They are taking the body to the morgue. I said the man was following you and your room was ransacked, and I explained that we had confronted him just a few minutes before the accident. Inspector Casale has our names and the hotel telephone number and expects to contact us again."

I nodded and attempted to smile at the officer. *"Merci, monsieur."*

"De rien, madame." Inspector Casale put his notebook away and shook our hands.

We stood on the sidewalk watching the police officers gather up their belongings. Somewhere a clock began to chime.

"Four o'clock," Pierre said. "I think you need a cognac. You are as white as a ghost."

❦

"Do you think it could be my grandmother?" I said to Pierre on the drive back to Chateau Noyelle. "Who else would want the diaries or even know I had them?"

"I thought your grandfather did not want your grandmother to know about them."

"That was my assumption. Why else did he leave them in a tackle box at my house? But maybe she already knew of their existence. Maybe she found them a long time ago and never told Martin. Or . . ."

"Or what?"

"Nothing. I'm sure it's a crazy thought."

"Why not tell me anyway."

"Well, the night my grandfather left the tackle box, Jim was the one who put it in the attic. Suppose he looked inside and saw the diaries. And maybe the note from my grandfather as well."

"What if he did?"

"He might have confronted my grandfather to find out what the note meant."

"Then why would he wait so long to do anything about it?"

"I don't know. I said it was a crazy thought."

"We should leave the matter to the police," Pierre said as we drove into the hotel parking area. "They will investigate. Now stay there. I will come around to help you out."

I was glad to have Pierre's help as I hobbled through the front door and along to my room.

"I'm going to take a nap," I said.

"Bolt the door after I leave," Pierre said. "Will you be down for dinner?"

"I will." I managed to smile at him.

That evening we sat by a window looking out on the garden, crimson streaks filling the horizon as the sun continued its journey west. I felt wobbly but was determined not to spoil what would probably be our last night together.

"It's so beautiful outside," I said.

Pierre nodded. "What are you doing tomorrow?"

"My plan is to drive to Cologne and visit a few German towns where Martin was with the Army of Occupation."

"I do not think that will be possible. The police expect to speak to us again. You should come to Amiens instead. You can stay with me."

"I can't stay at your house."

"Why not?"

I looked down at my plate and slowly cut a piece of sea bass. "You hardly know me."

"Maybe I want to solve *that* puzzle." His mouth twitched, not a smile exactly, but a hint of amusement, and I wondered which puzzle Pierre was referring to. "Tell me what you expect to find in Germany," he continued. "You haven't found anything in France, and that's where Martin fought. Remind me what his note said."

If Pierre knew me better, he would have realized that a certain narrowing of my eyes signified stubbornness. "'Read carefully. I never should have taken them.' He's referring to reading the diaries." I kept my voice even.

"How will cemeteries and memorials and places in Germany lead to clues?"

"I don't know."

"Maybe this is a puzzle you won't be able to solve. Have you thought of that?"

A splash of annoyance crossed my face. "Yes, I've thought of that. But for now I'm not admitting defeat. My grandfather loved giving me puzzles when I was little. He wouldn't have set one that was impossible for me to solve. Not if . . ."

"Not if what?"

"Not if he really wanted me to solve it."

"I have an idea." He swirled his wineglass. "Stay with me for a few days. That will give the inspector time to contact us again. If you still think you should visit Germany, go after that."

The time I had spent at Pierre's home had put me at ease. And he was a different person there, more relaxed, willing to sit in warm silence. Lying in bed that night at his house with Pierre sleeping next to me, I had listened to the pitter-patter of rain and thought of how tumultuous my life had become, so much more complicated than a few weeks earlier. An inner voice told me to be impulsive.

"All right," I said. "I'll come to Amiens for a few days. And thank you, Pierre. You're being very kind to me."

A cluster of birds streamed overhead, stretching into a V formation, wings flapping furiously as they headed west before banking south. High gray clouds shaped and reshaped, revealing occasional glimpses of blue. A tractor rumbled, tilling the fields across from the hotel, and cicadas hummed in the early-morning heat.

Pierre hoisted my bag into the trunk.

"We should go. I have a meeting at ten. I will drive slowly so you can follow me."

I waited while he settled into his Peugeot, a map lying on the passenger seat beside me in case we became separated. I noted his license plate number and started the car. Pierre pulled ahead and signaled with his hand that he was off.

Once we settled onto the highway, I let my mind wander. The shock of yesterday's encounter and ensuing accident had eased; however, my nerves still jangled, my thoughts refusing to settle on any one thing. Who was that man? Who had sent him to follow me? Why did he want Martin's diaries? The idea that either Grandmama or Jim could be involved seemed preposterous.

I was no closer to knowing why I was being followed, and one person who might have been able to tell me was dead.

Shoving that thought aside, my mind turned to Pierre. Why had I allowed him to convince me to come to Amiens? Intellectually, I knew it was too soon to feel anything other than friendship for him. Lust perhaps, but certainly not love, and as far as I could tell, he had given no indication that our arrangement was anything more than a casual affair. I tried not to think of how happy he made me feel.

Traffic was light and the road damp from overnight rain. Pierre's Peugeot shifted left to pass a lumbering truck preparing to turn onto a dirt road between two fields of corn. I eased the Renault behind his car and followed him back into the right lane. We resumed our modest pace, and I allowed my wandering thoughts to take over again.

I never should have taken them. What had Martin taken? And why? In some curious way, I knew that my future was bound up in the answer to this puzzle.

Perhaps it has nothing to do with the war, the diaries merely a convenient spot to hide a note. But then why would he use the diaries? Why not leave me a letter? I tightened my lips and frowned. Grandpa always said to examine the clues, even the little ones. So what are the clues? One is the note. Another is the diaries. And then there are the items in the tackle box. Round and round I went. Nothing made sense at all.

MARTIN'S DIARY

April 30, 1918

The enemy has stopped their advance and must be regrouping. In order to hold them off, we abandoned the area around Ypres that claimed so many men last fall. To die for victory can be considered noble; to die over territory that is then abandoned is a shameful tragedy. Bloody senior officers never acknowledge responsibility. I'd like to see one of them out on the line. Wouldn't last more than a minute.

May 11, 1918

From the bits of information flying around, it looks like the Germans might soon give up on this offensive. They've gained territory but at enormous cost in manpower and supplies, and now they have to defend several exposed salients and a longer front line. While we also lost thousands, our manpower is now reinforced by the Americans.

I've put in for leave. If I don't see Cynthia soon, I will go mad.

CHAPTER 28

May 1918

In London, the threat of rain thickened the air, and the streets smelled of soot and sweat and unwashed clothing. Martin stepped around a steaming mound of horse manure as he made his way toward Piccadilly Circus, where Cynthia would meet him at six o'clock. He had promised to take her out to dinner, and tomorrow, if all went well, he would meet her family.

Rain did not bother Martin. Nothing could bother him as long as he was away from France and the bloodiness of war. Everyday noises surrounded him—the jangle of bells and squeak of trams, the shouts of a newspaper boy, the whoosh of passing traffic. Women were every-where—young and old, tall, thin, short, and plump—and groups of children dashed about as though they had no cares. One step removed from war, the city offered life and laughter and a normalcy he had forgotten.

Will I ever return to a life like this? he wondered.

After stopping to ask for directions, he walked north along Haymarket Street, where horse-drawn vehicles and automobiles jock-eyed for space and late-day shoppers hurried home, skirts showing more than six inches of leg above neatly tied shoes. Two blocks farther and he caught a glimpse of Eros, the winged statue at the center of Piccadilly. He quickened his pace. When he saw Cynthia, wearing the same red dress she wore the first time he saw her, he ran the last few feet and kissed her despite the disapproving glance of an elderly woman.

Cynthia's lips were soft and willing. With his arms around her, he deepened the kiss, and she responded without hesitation, leaning against his chest, one hand clasping his arm. Martin felt like a man suddenly released from quicksand.

All through dinner, he wanted to kiss her again but instead held her hand across the table, squeezing every few minutes. Though he had promised himself not to talk about France, he couldn't avoid the place he lived and breathed with such ferocious intensity. Cynthia listened to every word, emotions flying across her face as he spoke of daily horrors and fears, of disgust and sorrow. When he talked of his men, those who died and those who survived, tears ran down her cheeks.

"Tell me about your sister," she said. "You wrote little about your visit with her. I cannot imagine her bravery."

"Idealism is more like it. They're so short of nurses; the hours she works are punishing. The clearing station is about twenty-five miles southeast of Calais and thirty-five miles west of Ypres."

"Is she in danger?"

Martin paused before answering. Nowhere in the vicinity of Ypres was truly safe, but the Germans had never been close to Longuenesse. "I suppose she's safer than me."

"Perhaps I shall meet her someday."

"You would like her. She's funny and kind. When we were young, my mother called her a tomboy because she was always getting into scrapes with me."

"I find it hard to believe your parents let her come."

Martin snorted. "Based on the letters I've received, they're horrified and very worried. But you don't know my sister. She's even more stubborn than you."

"Now you're being unkind." Cynthia tapped his knuckles with her spoon. "I'm glad you tell me these things. You wrote that Lindsay was killed. Was he the captain who sent you to England?"

"Yes." Martin's face sagged even more. He stirred his tea around and around.

"Without him, you would never have come to the Mercury that night."

"I used to hate him because he took over from Butler. But we'd become friends. Now I don't have any friends left except Nully."

"Who is Nully?"

"He's my sergeant. We've been together since the beginning. Nully and I seem immune to enemy fire, as though our bodies instinctively know how and when to twist and duck and hide. I used to wish a bullet would find me so it would stop. The war, I mean. Stop for me at least. Before you and I met, that's what I planned to do. Put an end to the voices inside my head."

His voice had grown fainter, each word labored. While speaking, he had looked away because he could not bear to see Cynthia's thoughts reflected in her face. Would she think him a coward? Would she reject him?

Cynthia held his hand. "Are the voices gone?"

He turned back to look at her. "Some of the time."

༄

Martin stepped off the tram next to the Cock and Crown as a man wearing a bowler hat opened the tavern door, spilling conversation and smells of tobacco onto the street. A bustling crowd signaled late afternoon as women bearing baskets and shopping bags hurried home, and men dressed in suits or the rough clothes of laborers entered their favorite pubs. In contrast to London proper, Hackney felt more like a small town, a place where one would greet friends at local shops and stop for a chat, a place where people walked wherever they needed to go and where families had lived for generations.

To Martin's left, faded awnings were fully extended to provide a canopy of shade. He turned right, following Cynthia's directions to number sixteen Northwold Road.

On Northwold, narrow doors topped by arched windows marked identical family homes. Martin passed a limping man wheeling a wagon full of discarded metal and a young woman bending over a baby carriage. On the far side of the street, lime trees sprinkled shade on a scruffy bit of park, and in the distance, he caught sight of Cynthia waving.

Cynthia led Martin into the sitting room at the front of the house and introduced him to her parents. Despite her age and number of children, Lydia Gibson looked more like Cynthia's sister than her mother, even though fine wrinkles marked the corners of her eyes. Compared to his willowy wife, Thomas Gibson was tall and thick. Long fingers covered with daubs of paint caught Martin's attention as the two men shook hands.

"I'm very pleased to meet you," Martin said in a voice loud enough to be heard over shouts coming from the second floor.

"Our daughter has spoken about you so often we feel we know you already." Lydia Gibson's smile was warm. "I'm sorry about the noise. Charles and Timothy are practicing for the school play." She turned to Cynthia. "Please run upstairs, dear, and tell them it's time to stop."

Though the exterior was drab and nondescript, the interior of Cynthia's home was full of color. No matter where he turned, Martin saw unframed canvases, some stacked three or four deep leaning against the fireplace and beneath both windows.

"Father's gallery," Cynthia said as they moved into the dining room.

Martin was surprised at the Gibsons' courtesy and the wide-ranging conversation that took place during his visit. He was surprised too that Cynthia's father insisted on taking him for a walk after supper, the two men smoking cigarettes as they ambled along the pathways of nearby London Fields. Thomas Gibson was sizing him up.

"You live in Canada?"

"Yes, sir. My family has been there for several generations. Originally from Manchester. My father is a bank manager."

"And you? Your trade?"

"Early days, sir. I worked at the bank before the war. But it doesn't really appeal to me. I hope to try something else when this"—Martin waved his arm as if the right word would materialize out of thin air—"this business is over."

"Hmm. Lydia and I married for love, not wealth. I expect my daughter has already mentioned that." He chuckled and threw his cigarette butt to the ground. "We're happy despite our circumstances. But I know my Cynthia; she will not be content unless she has more." He stopped and held Martin's arm for a moment. "I would not normally be so blunt, but I've seen the way she looks at you and the way she lights up whenever your letters arrive. Can you give her what she needs?"

"I don't know, sir. It's all too . . ." Martin wanted to say that it was too soon to know what he would do after the war. If he survived. "Too unpredictable."

Thomas Gibson grunted. "Well, you've heard my opinion. You seem like a good sort. Shall we make our way back?"

On Sunday, Martin's fourth day of leave, Cynthia met him at Regent's Park in the early afternoon. She brought a wicker basket containing a picnic lunch, and Martin carried a thick wool blanket over his shoulder. He planned to find a secluded place.

Beyond numerous gardens and a pond offering rowboats for rent, the park was home to a zoo and an American Red Cross hospital, where nurses pushed wounded soldiers in wheelchairs along curving pathways. Wanting nothing to remind him of war, Martin steered Cynthia in the opposite direction, and eventually they found a sheltered area next to a low stone bridge over Regent's Canal.

"I have to go soon," Cynthia said much later.

They were lying on the blanket, Martin's arm cradling her head, the length of their bodies touching. Each kiss had eased Martin farther away from war, releasing his tensions and reminding him of what it felt like to be alive. He traced a circle at the base of her neck, and when she shivered, he pulled her closer.

"Do you have to? I wish we could stay here forever."

"Forever?" She slipped her fingers into his. "But I have work tomorrow."

"Damn, tomorrow's my last day. Will I see you after work? We could dance at the Mercury."

At six the following night, Martin waited by the bar. Each time the door opened, he looked up, expecting Cynthia, and when she had not appeared by six fifteen, he went outside and prowled up and down until finally, at six thirty, she stepped out of a taxi.

"Where have you been?"

"Mother is having one of her bad days, and I had to help Daddy with supper. Don't be angry with me. I've just spent money I cannot afford on a taxi so you didn't have to wait any longer." She flicked her eyelashes and held his hand. "Buy me a drink, soldier?"

Martin chuckled. "You know exactly how to make me laugh, don't you? Do you want a drink?"

"Not really. I'd prefer to dance." She held out her hand.

Oblivious to anything except the music and the woman in his arms, Martin felt the heat between them grow from song to song.

"Will you come to my hotel?" he whispered into her ear.

Cynthia drew away and looked at him. "But I . . ."

He put a finger on her lips. "Trust me," he said.

Their lovemaking was all he had imagined and more. Afterward, they lay together, limbs tangled, skin caressing skin. A feeling of great gentleness overwhelmed him. A feeling of completeness, of coming home.

"You have given me one of the greatest gifts I've ever received," he said as Cynthia buttoned her dress and made to leave.

"Come back to me, Martin Devlin. Just make sure you come back to me."

In the days and weeks that followed, that memory kept him going. Her nakedness on the narrow bed, her hair spilling across the pillow, the small gasp when he penetrated her, the feel of her soft breasts and her nipples taut with desire. He polished each detail into bright images to remind him of what the future might hold.

CHAPTER 29

August 1918

The sun rose, a red orb hovering behind German lines. Even at dawn, the heat promised grueling sweat. Oblivious to human tragedy, birds chirped a lazy melody. Not a breath of wind stirred the air.

Preferring to sleep near his men rather than back of the line, Martin had endured a restless night in a hole not much bigger than a trash can, close enough to offer encouragement, a nod of approval, or a hand on someone's shoulder. Just the other day, he'd told Nully that the new soldiers needed a steady hand from time to time. He shook himself awake and unraveled stiff limbs, stretching one leg at a time. As he hunched into a sitting position, his back felt sore and creaky.

"Any orders, Sergeant?" he said, words garbled by a groaning yawn.

"Bringing it to you now, sir."

His eyes filmy with fatigue, Martin blinked slowly. He yawned again. "Just read it to me."

"Company B will clear German positions in zone 3.C.1 tomorrow. All useful material to be secured. Prisoners to be handed over to guard details upon completion."

"What do you think, Nully? Are they really retreating?"

"Gotta say, sir, that it seems so. Christ, it's bloody well time. Sorry, sir."

"No apologies, Nully. We've been friends far too long for that." Martin bent backward to get the kinks out of his body. "Gather the officers and NCOs, will you? I'll take a piss in the meantime."

Yesterday they'd cleared German bunkers but found little of note, just pieces of damaged artillery and a few scared soldiers, cheeks still flushed with youth. As the Germans moved back to more secure lines, they destroyed everything that might possibly be useful: barrels, beds, stoves, shelves, telephone equipment, crude chairs, and tables.

The face of Corporal Vincent now appeared, a wire from his headphones stretching back around the corner to where it connected to the company's Fullerphone.

"What's up, Jimbo?" Martin used the corporal's nickname.

"Odd message came through just now, sir. It says you're to report to Drummond without delay."

"Shit. I wish they'd make up their minds. First I'm ordered to clear German positions, then it's go see Drummond. Nully, you get things started. I shouldn't be long."

Martin made an attempt to straighten his clothes and grabbed his service revolver and gas mask before heading along a zigzagged path, shoulders hunched to keep below the parapet. Though he heard sporadic artillery, none of it was close, and as he loped along, he passed small groups of men preparing for the day by rolling up their blankets or shaving or eating a meal. After a short while, he turned and followed a communication trench heading west toward battalion headquarters. This trench was deeper, so Martin walked almost upright. Drummond's location was two miles back at battalion headquarters in the small town of Fontaine, far enough to avoid German artillery range. He hurried; he did not want to leave his men for long.

Martin found Drummond in a church cellar sitting on a bale of hay.

"You needed to see me, sir?" He attempted to keep the annoyance from his voice.

"Sorry for the unusual summons." Drummond pointed to a second bale of hay. "Sit down. Would you like some tea?"

Tea? Why is Drummond going on about tea? Martin thought. *He knows we're preparing for action.* "I shouldn't stay long, sir. We have orders to clear German positions starting at dawn tomorrow."

"Hmm. Yes, I know. Sent those earlier, then this came in." He held out a folded piece of paper. "You better read it."

Martin reached out. The paper was wrinkled, as though someone had crushed it at some point. Though his mouth was steady, Drummond's eyes seemed unfocused, and a muscle twitched in one cheek. The slip of paper slid into Martin's hand. He knew the news would be bad.

Jane Devlin killed 7-29-18 during enemy bombing raid. Telegram sent to next of kin. Ensure Captain Martin Devlin is informed with condolences. His sister was a great asset to our troops.

The paper fluttered to the ground as Martin slumped forward and covered his face. He tried to breathe but could not seem to gather any air into his lungs. Shaking his head, he looked up at Drummond.

"Goddamn. Goddamn. God-fucking-damn. This fucking war." His voice grew louder and louder. His eyes burned with fury.

"I'm sorry, Devlin. I can't begin to imagine how you must feel. Let me get you a drink."

Drummond pulled on one earlobe as he moved toward a small chest where a bottle and two glasses were waiting. He poured a double measure for Martin and a smaller one for himself. Martin's hand shook as he gripped the glass and took a large swallow of whiskey, some of which dribbled down his chin and onto his jacket.

"Everyone's gone now. Everyone but me and Nully." He tossed the rest of the whiskey down and threw the glass against a wooden beam so hard it shattered into pieces. Martin sat for a moment, staring at nothing.

"Devlin, you need to—"

"Will that be all, sir?"

Drummond tried again. "Martin, I'm sorry . . ."

Martin climbed the stone stairs leading out of the cellar without looking back. He had little recollection of where he went before returning to his men. Little recollection at all. But when he did stagger in, Nully took him by the arm and muscled him into a dugout where officers slept or conferred over tactics.

"What the hell happened? You've been gone for hours."

Martin said nothing.

"You look like shit. And you've been drinking. What on earth did Drummond say?" Martin still said nothing. Nully grabbed his lapels and shook him. Martin's head bobbled back and forth.

"I'm going to throw up." He pushed Nully away and fell to his knees, retching onto a pile of damp bedding. When he was done, he sat back on his heels and wiped his mouth. "My sister's dead."

Nully kept the men away until late afternoon. Martin had no idea what his sergeant said, but when his lieutenants did appear, they were quieter than usual, and Nully did most of the talking, explaining each platoon's responsibilities while Martin had only to grunt or nod. Before dismissing his officers, Martin gathered himself together enough to tell them to proceed with caution.

"Intelligence reports suggest the enemy is long gone, but they've been wrong before. I want one day without casualties. Just one fucking day. Do you all hear me?" Five heads nodded.

They departed early the following morning, Nully with Genton's platoon on the far left and Martin with Morelli on the right. His other lieutenants, Connelly and Snider, were in the middle. The men fanned out, leaving gaps between each platoon, and began to advance. Taking proper safeguards, they would need more than an hour to reach their target.

Cynthia's latest letter was in Martin's left pocket, the piece of paper bearing news of Jane's death in his right. He loved them both, and now one was gone, and he felt like someone had kicked every inch of his body. *How many more can I lose?* Cynthia had promised to wait for him, and for a moment he pictured her naked on his bed and failed to notice a cluster of birds rising from the scrub no more than two hundred yards ahead. By the time Snider shouted, it was too late.

The explosion burst in front of Connelly's platoon, spraying chunks of mud and smoke in a high, wide arc. Every member of B Company ducked, waiting for the next shell to fall. Martin whispered instructions for Morelli to send two men to check for casualties while others fanned out along abandoned German trenches and readied their weapons.

"What the fuck's wrong with our intelligence? They should've known Fritz's artillery was still here."

Jimbo was attempting to reach Connelly. "Nothing yet, sir."

"Morelli. Get your men in position. We're going to get those bastards." He crouched next to Jimbo. "Send Nully a message. Flanking left and right, center holds."

Nully had been with him from the beginning, and like a quarterback and receiver, they knew each other's plays. Nully, with Genton's platoon, would come at the German position from the left while Martin and Morelli would tackle from the right with the intent of surrounding the enemy or forcing them backward.

Through his periscope, Martin saw a haze of smoke drifting across the land. As another shell whistled its unknown trajectory, rifles flashed about three hundred yards away. Morelli nodded at Martin's raised eyebrows. Their target was clear. The shell exploded well behind them.

"Let's hope it's an isolated group," Martin said to no one in particular.

"Two dead," Jimbo reported. "One wounded. Connelly's okay."

Martin gave the signal to advance.

Intent on their target, he paid little attention to remnants of enemy occupation: gray uniforms, black knee-high boots, trench signs marked in German, unfamiliar packs and equipment. He crawled over dead soldiers with no thought to their humanity. After he had covered roughly half the distance, Genton's machine guns opened fire, drawing German attention away from Martin's platoon, and he began to imagine revenge.

With no regard for his own safety, he fired at enemy soldiers attempting to retreat and closed in on the German trench just as another rattling burst of fire erupted. He paused an instant to watch bullets tear into a group nearing the shelter of a wooded area. Only a few feet away now, Martin lobbed a grenade into the trench and smiled—a demonic smile—when he heard men scream.

He was thirsty, but there was no stopping for water. His eyes narrowed, nothing but a desire for annihilation occupying his thoughts. Each step, each shot bore that purpose.

A shell whizzed by. He heard it thud into the mud behind him without exploding. Shouts came from his left, but he kept moving toward the next German trench. He fired again. A soldier flung his arms out and pitched forward. Martin fired at the man once more to be sure.

He shifted left to avoid a shell hole where a German lay moaning, one leg bent like a broken doll. He fired again, taking satisfaction from the way the man's body jerked before slumping into stillness. Crouching low, he stopped to reload and shifted onto his belly, feeling the wet seep through his clothes and gagging at the smell of rotting flesh as he wriggled forward to the edge of the trench. Martin checked the scene below before slithering down the side.

Behind a barrel, two soldiers huddled over a wireless machine while a third stuffed papers into a rucksack. Though two were armed, neither had his rifle at the ready, and he briefly wondered why they had remained behind.

"Stop," he shouted.

The signalmen paid no attention, and Martin fired twice, watching them slump and fall. Another grim smile split his face. He stepped beyond their bodies and shoved the third man to the ground, holding his rifle against the soldier's chest. Ignoring the man's pleading eyes, Martin lifted his foot and kicked. The German curled onto his side. Another kick followed by a moan. Another kick. Another. The young soldier tried desperately to roll away.

This one's for Bill, Martin thought as his boot connected with the man's belly. *And this one's for Pete.* Martin aimed at the groin. *Here's one for my sister.* He swung his rifle at the soldier's head and nodded at the satisfying thunk of metal on flesh. The man's mouth twisted with pain as he tried to move away. Martin kicked him again and again and again. Finally, he aimed his rifle.

"That's enough, sir. Captain! That's enough," Nully shouted.

With Morelli looking on, Nully pulled Martin away. "Get a medic, if you can, Lieutenant," Nully said.

The German moaned. His face was a mess: one eye swollen shut, blood leaking from his mouth, purple bruises already forming, and his nose cocked at an odd angle. He tried to move his left leg and moaned again.

Martin could hardly think, pulsing adrenaline making him both jumpy and nauseous. Nully's lips moved, but the words echoed in his ears as though the two men stood at opposite ends of a tunnel. His sergeant forced him to sit on a wooden crate, then knelt beside the battered German. Threads of awareness crept into Martin's consciousness.

"I would have killed him if you hadn't stopped me. He wasn't even armed."

For a long moment, Nully said nothing. "Happened to me when I fought against the Boers. A blinding rage took hold one day. Couldn't control myself. Must have offed at least seven of them. I never told anybody. There's a demon in war, Martin, and sometimes it takes over. You'll have to live with what you've done. That's punishment enough."

In three years, Nully had never used his Christian name, always *sir* or *Lieutenant* or no name at all. Martin lifted his head and looked into his sergeant's eyes. Eyes that were normally sharp and fierce now exuded compassion. Finally, he nodded.

Nully remained at his side until stretcher-bearers came to apply rudimentary first aid before carrying the soldier off to join the ranks of German prisoners.

"We have a job to do, sir. Better get at it." Nully's voice broke the silence.

For the next four hours, they cleared a long stretch of trenches, finding boxes of ammunition, stick bombs, binoculars, entrenching tools, a ceremonial sword, and several German helmets. In one dugout, they found a Victrola sitting on top of a chest alongside tins of ham and an empty bottle of wine. Gradually, Martin assumed a more normal demeanor, although the men kept their distance, and his lieutenants spoke to him only when necessary.

With one small section still to clear, they bedded down for the night. German trenches were larger, with more alcoves for sleeping, but the smells of so many men lying in the damp and dirt were the same. And the sounds were soon familiar, the snuffles and snores and occasional muttered groans, the shifting of men from side to side, and the clank of metal. Martin had his own corner but did not sleep. Instead, he relived the last two days beginning with Drummond's news.

He imagined Jane bloodied and broken, her eyes lifeless, her skin clammy. The idea of her no longer alive, no longer smiling, made him choke. He imagined his mother's grief and his father offering comfort all the while frozen by his own unspeakable sadness. How would they bear the loss knowing that their son could also disappear at any moment? Their only remaining child.

What was the point of living? Could he endure year after year of memories that would never fade? Memories that could strike at any moment, returning him to this hell on earth. *Worse than hell,* he thought. Could he ever stifle his thoughts or calm his fury? He wondered if Cynthia could save him or if she would turn away from what he had become.

Martin relived his morning rampage, the recklessness with which he'd proceeded to shoot his way from place to place. At the time, some portion of his mind knew he should have stopped, and yet he had decided to continue killing whoever got in the way. Never had he felt such uncontrollable fury.

A fine drizzle and dull booming marked the following morning.

"Sounds like artillery," Morelli said.

"Pretty far away, I think. Better find out, though," Martin said.

Thirty minutes passed before Morelli returned with a message confirming their orders to continue clearing the area. After Morelli left, Nully came by.

"Just checking on ammunition."

"Cut the crap, Nully. I'm fine," he said. "We both know what I did, but there's no need to hover over me." Martin cinched his belt tighter. "I won't lose control again. Show me where we are and where we're supposed to go."

Along with Genton and Morelli, he huddled over a tattered map as Nully pointed to a section of German reserve trenches. Martin studied the contours, noting a creek to their left and low-lying hills stretching south.

"That's an ideal spot for snipers to hide," he said.

"Agreed, sir. Shall we stay clear?"

"Yes. Plenty for us to do beyond the creek. We can work together or split up."

"Together is safer, sir," Morelli said.

"Right, then. Everyone ready in thirty minutes."

In the last trench they cleared, Martin found a stack of journals, each entry dated and handwritten, and a long, tubular map case. Knowing staff officers might glean some intelligence from such documents, he slung the map case over his shoulder and tossed the journals into a box for a young private to carry. He would hand the maps over to Drummond, but not until he had a chance to look at them first.

CHAPTER 30

July 1991

With the Renault parked in the lane behind Pierre's house, I opened the trunk and reached for my suitcase.

"Let me do that. You are still limping." Pierre took my bag and led the way through a wooden gate into his small garden.

"I keep an extra key in case I am locked out," he said, lifting a clay flowerpot situated near the back door. "You can use it while you're here."

He took my bag straight upstairs and plopped it on his bed. "Why don't you hang your things in the spare room? There is also a chest of drawers you can use."

"All right," I said, oddly aware of the intimacy implied by unpacking my clothes in this man's home.

He tipped my chin up and kissed me. "I would prefer to stay with you, but I have to work." We went down the stairs and into the kitchen. "There's not too much food in the house. A bit left over from the dinner we had."

He seemed awkward, and I wondered whether coming to Amiens had been a mistake. "I'll go shopping. Don't worry about me."

Pierre pulled me into his arms. "I want you to feel at home. Explore whatever you would like. There's a cat called Frou who likes to sit on my window ledge. She is always looking for a bit of milk. If you do go out, you will find some nice shops near St. Jerome's. You can see it from the street. I should be home around seven." He kissed me again. "I will call Inspector Casale to let him know where we are. Will you be all right?"

"Of course. I'm fine. Really, Pierre. Don't worry."

He straightened his tie, then opened the door and disappeared down the steps. A few moments later, his car roared off.

How strange to be in Pierre's home on my own. Unsettling, in fact. I turned around and then back again, uncertain what to do, yet certain I would inevitably disturb the equilibrium he had created. Was that what he wanted—someone to disturb his equilibrium? Should I settle in as he'd suggested, hang up my clothes and make myself a coffee?

Through the front window, I noticed a few men and women dressed for work walking along the sidewalk. I made a slow tour around Pierre's living room, bending close to look at pictures of family and friends, running a finger along a wooden statue of an old man with a cane, examining books in both French and English and a bowl with an inscribed silver medallion on the front. *Well, Grace Hansen, you have at least eight hours, so you might as well be productive.*

I looked up from the kitchen table strewn with maps and Martin's diaries to watch Frou Frou lick one paw. The cat had arrived soon after Pierre left and had already devoured the milk I set out on a small saucer, front paws tucked close to her body as though ready to leap, a small dab of pink on an otherwise black nose. Now Frou Frou's white-tipped tail swished back and forth.

Earlier, in the midst of hanging my blue dress in the closet, I'd returned to the thought that Martin's secret must be in the diaries themselves, not the places where he fought and trained or went on leave. Since his note said "read carefully," that was what I would do. And ever since, I had been rereading Martin's diaries, searching for clues in repeated words and unusual phrases, trying different combinations, jotting notes on lined paper to see if I could find a key to unlock his message—all to no avail. Nothing, absolutely nothing. Now it was one o'clock, and my brain felt like mush.

"Time for lunch," I said out loud.

Except for the occasional car driving past, Pierre's house was quiet. I rummaged in the fridge, finding a few vegetables and some leftover chicken, which I placed on a plate alongside a slice of bread. I was intrigued to see two sets of china when I opened the cupboards, a traditional set in deep blue with white accents and another set in cream and gold that seemed too fussy for his taste. This thought amused me. What did I really know about Pierre's tastes after such a short time?

I shook my head. *Concentrate, Grace.* I poured a glass of water and picked up the first diary again, Martin's words and script so familiar I could almost recite the entries by heart. "Begin at the beginning," Grandpa had always said.

February 5, 1915

Enlisted today. A whole mess of forms to fill out. Looks like I'm signing my life away. Guess I shouldn't joke about that. Went down with Bill Jackson, who's been chomping at the bit to get in the fight. Last September, everyone thought the war would be over in a few short months. Reality is somewhat different. Mother won't be happy to hear the news, but I feel duty bound. If we don't stop the Hun, who will?

He did sign his life away, I thought. Grandpa's life had been changed forever by what he experienced. I read the rest of the entry, and suddenly there it was, something I'd never noticed before: a small dot beneath the letter *d* of the word *duty*. I held the diary closer, trying to determine if the dot was significant, then read further, more slowly than before, searching each word for another dot, finding nothing until March 1, 1915, under the letter *e* in the word *we're*. Several more dots and corresponding letters followed.

"DERTITTHA," I said. "That makes no sense at all."

Perhaps the marks meant nothing. After all, the diaries were seventy-five years old. Paper and ink might deteriorate after such a long time. Maybe frustration was clouding my judgment; Grandmama always did accuse me of having an overactive imagination. But instinct prevailed. Page by page, I searched for tiny dots, making a note of each letter and corresponding diary date on my notepad. By three o'clock, I had thirty-six letters and no idea at all what they meant.

Pushing back from the table, I rubbed my eyes and stretched. Now what? Why did he mark these random letters? *I could spend all day and still not know what Martin wants to tell me.* I paced the kitchen. There was only one person who might know the answer: Grandmama.

My eyes stung. My head ached. I needed a breath of fresh air. Taking the spare key and a cloth bag from a hook in the pantry, I went out to shop for dinner.

The street perpendicular to Pierre's featured two-story houses with shutters in various shades of blue, green, and terra-cotta red, antique streetlamps posted by every fifth or sixth house. Farther on, the streets widened, populated with four-story buildings, a pleasing mix of residential and retail. I passed a well-dressed woman and her minuscule dog and wondered how she could possibly traverse such rough cobblestones wearing four-inch heels.

Around the corner from St. Jerome's Church, I found a grocer and butcher and purchased several items, including plump chicken breasts and mushrooms smelling of damp earth, a gnarly piece of ginger, some onions, and four apricots. A few shops past the butcher's, I discovered a bakery whose shelves were rather depleted, but nonetheless I bought croissants for breakfast and a round, crusty loaf. The woman behind the counter waddled back and forth, wrapping the bread in paper before taking my money and returning with a small handful of change.

"Au revoir, madame," she called out as I left the shop, a jingling bell announcing my departure.

"Au revoir."

Across the street, a flower shop caught my eye with buckets of cheerful colors arranged like an arresting landscape. On impulse, I bought a large bouquet and, shopping bag in one hand, flowers in the other, retraced my steps to Pierre's house.

This everyday outing gave me a different appreciation of Amiens. As a place to live, its modest scale and artful blend of new and old, its canals and cobblestones, made the city seem charming. Pierre's neighborhood invited friendly conversations and leisurely browsing. *No wonder he lives here,* I thought.

❧

A few minutes after seven, I heard Pierre's car, and a moment later the back door opened.

"You look tense," I said after kissing him.

"I am. You might think my staff would allow their problems to wait another day. But instead they trooped in one after the other, presenting me with issues." He loosened his tie. "Something smells delicious."

"I've made dinner. We can sit in the garden while you unwind. I chilled a bottle of white wine. Do you mind?"

"Of course not. You open it while I change."

Though I had cautioned myself it was premature to tell Pierre of my discovery, after less than twenty minutes, I was blurting out the story of the tiny dots and the time I had spent trying to decode them. He didn't interrupt or make me feel the least bit foolish, and when I finished, I leaned back and took a sip of wine.

"Sounds crazy, doesn't it?"

"Not from what you have told me about Martin. May I see the diaries?"

I went into the house and returned with the first diary and my page of notes. "See, here's the first dot. I think he put it on the first page so I would notice it. But I was too busy reading the words to look for anything else."

Pierre examined that page and the second one I showed him. "They are quite faint. Easy to miss. If you like, I can take this to the museum and ask my archivist to determine whether the ink on the dots is different from that of the diary entries."

My eyes widened. "You can do that?" He nodded. "If I knew the ink was different, I would know for sure Martin wanted to tell me something important and wouldn't care how long it takes to figure it out."

"Tomorrow, then. I will take just the first notebook. You can work on the others." He grinned. "You are becoming obsessed."

"I'm sorry. We should talk about something else."

"Shall we have dinner?"

Warm aromas filled the kitchen, not the classic smells of Italian or French cooking, but something sweet and more exotic. Pierre took an appreciative sniff.

"Is that ginger?"

"Yes. And cinnamon and cumin and coriander. I've made us a Moroccan dish."

Afterward, as streaks of color faded from the sky, we walked his neighborhood, a mix of narrow streets and broader boulevards. Night sounds settled around us, the clink of glasses and bits of laughter, the thud of shutters and rustle of curtains, the rush of footsteps and cries of children put to bed. Jasmine mingled with the smell of the land releasing the day's heat.

Pierre held my hand and later wrapped his arm around my waist. When we returned to the house, he led me upstairs and took off my clothes, piece by piece, kissing each newly revealed bit of skin. My wrist, the nape of my neck, the small of my back, behind my knee. I shivered, not with cold, but because his breath was warm and my body full of desire.

"Lentement," he said in response to my swift intake of breath and unspoken demands.

As I lay on my stomach, he massaged my shoulders, legs, and feet. When he rolled me gently onto my back, he touched my nipples and traced a line down my body until he found my moist center. I closed my eyes and felt the pressure gradually build into an intensity I could not resist.

CHAPTER 31

July 1991

Pierre kissed the top of my head. "I'm sorry I have to leave so early. I have a full day of meetings ahead, and someone distracted me last night."

He looked handsome in a dark blue suit, French cuffs showing just a quarter of an inch below the jacket sleeve. His tie was the only flamboyant item, red with small blue turtles, which from a distance looked like swirls.

"Will you be all right?" he asked.

"I'll be fine. Head down looking for tiny dots. My eyes will be bloodshot by the time you return. I'll get some more groceries."

"We could do that when I get home. Or go out for dinner. Oh," he said, "I forgot to mention Inspector Casale. He plans to visit either tomorrow or the next day."

"Will he and I be able to talk without you here to translate?"

"He said something about a colleague from Paris who speaks English."

"I see." I smiled to show Pierre that the thought of further conversations with the police did not disturb me. A lie, of course. "I hope you have a good day."

I wondered at our easy domesticity. That morning I'd prepared fruit and a piece of toast for his breakfast, enjoying the look of surprise when he found them waiting on the kitchen table along with hot espresso. I sat across from him with my own coffee, enjoying its bracing flavor and pungent aroma. I'd passed him the paper, as though this were our regular practice, and watched him scan the front page.

"There's a headline about Russia and the United States negotiating nuclear weapons reduction. Can you tell me what the article says?" I asked.

Pierre read a little further before responding. "Gorbachev and Bush will meet at the end of July to ratify a treaty that has been under development since 1982. The treaty they are now expected to sign preserves nuclear parity." He read a bit more. "They have also agreed on limits for fighter aircraft, tanks, artillery pieces, and attack helicopters."

"After years of cold war, it sounds like a step in the right direction."

"Only if the Russians keep their word."

I continued nibbling on a piece of toast after Pierre left. Then, once the kitchen was tidy, I took Martin's second diary and continued searching for dots, noting each letter and diary date as before. By late morning, I had two more columns of letters, the process made quicker by a magnifying glass Pierre provided. I examined my notes, parsing letters into words, trying various substitutions. Each time I thought I had the right decoding method, it turned out to be a dead end. I could find words, but not sentences, and no consistent pattern.

By midafternoon, I needed a break and again went out to shop for dinner, my travels taking me farther afield as I explored Amiens using the map Pierre left for me. I found a fish store and an outdoor market selling cheeses and vegetables and a wide selection of fruit, and I felt relieved to be in the bustle of a city, away from reminders of war.

"How was your day?" Pierre asked, arriving just after six. "Productive?"

"So-so. I found many more dots in the other diaries, but no key to decipher them. A bit frustrating. But I had another lovely walk to the shops. And you?" As I spoke, Pierre flipped quickly through a pile of mail.

"It was a long day. Remember those museums I mentioned? The ones we are arranging exchanges with? The director and his chief curator from Hong Kong came for a visit. Difficult to spend an entire day listening to English spoken by someone whose mother tongue is Cantonese." He chuckled. "I remember someone telling me that today's language of business is broken English."

"Does that bother you?"

"A bit, I suppose. But if I could not speak English, how would I have found you?"

His words suggested that finding me was of significance. He hadn't spoken that way before, and warmth spread through my body. I stepped closer and undid his tie, then took hold of both ends and pulled his face close.

"I'm glad you found me," I said, my lips brushing his.

As we sat down to dinner, Pierre placed Martin's first diary on the table. "I forgot to give this back to you. The dots were definitely written with different ink. My lab technician says they are more recent, though he cannot give an accurate date. He checked more than one, so you are not imagining them. Sounds very devious, your grandfather."

"I can't figure him out. He seems to be three different men: the young idealist going off to war; the angry, desolate man when it ended; and the grandfather I knew. My grandfather didn't seem the least jaded or morose or angry."

"What did his note say again?"

I repeated Grandpa's words to him. "I've read it so often I've memorized it." My lower lip quivered, and I knew I was on the verge of tears.

"Never should have taken them. And that is all?"

"Only the date. April 3, 1972."

"'Read carefully.' That sounds like he is trying to tell you to concentrate on the diaries." He squeezed my hand. "I am sure you are on the right track."

"Enough of my grandfather and his diaries. Tell me something about your family or your father, if that topic isn't too sensitive. You make a face every time you talk about him."

"My father. Hmm. He is a workaholic. Obsessed with status. Dogmatic. Opinionated. We get along best when I stay away. I am his only son, so I think he expected me to follow his path, and when I was younger, I went along with his ideas. I even married Vivienne because of him; however, after ten years of marriage and banking, I wanted something else."

"You said to me once, 'There's more to life than money.' What have you found working at the museum?"

"Purpose and a meaningful role. The museum is so much more than one individual. It has permanence and beauty and will endure as a place to celebrate culture and history long after I am gone. I hope that doesn't sound pompous. I really enjoy what I do."

"You're not the slightest bit pompous. I'm jealous."

Two days later, engrossed in my dot-finding mission, I was startled when Inspector Casale knocked on the door just before ten. Standing next to the inspector was a man with thin lips and shaggy hair who introduced himself as Detective Boudin of the French National Police. After a few awkward pleasantries, I invited them into Pierre's living room, where they settled into chairs flanking the sofa.

"Madame Hansen?" Boudin spoke my name as though it were a question.

"Yes."

"We are still verifying his identity, but can you tell us what you know about the man you say was following you?" Boudin's English was heavily accented but nonetheless clear.

"I can't tell you very much. Not really. The first time I saw him was on a ferry traveling to Honfleur." I proceeded to mention the second and third time I had seen the man, his distinctive straw fedora, the encounter at Vimy Ridge, and the occasion when my hotel room at Chateau Noyelle had been disturbed. "I don't know who broke into my room, although the local police did check for fingerprints. I heard nothing else about the matter and did not see the man again until that day in Mons when he . . ."

"When he was killed," the detective said.

I nodded.

"And why do you think he was following you?"

I pictured the scene in the dead-end alley. "He said he wanted my purse. I told him there wasn't much money in it, and he said something like, 'I'm not after your money. I want the diaries.' And that's when Pierre arrived. Monsieur Auffret."

"What else was in your purse?"

I smiled, a brief lifting of my lips to acknowledge the proverbial male question. "Just the usual things a woman keeps in her purse. Wallet, lipstick, brush, a few papers, my passport. And my grandfather's diaries."

Detective Boudin turned and spoke to Inspector Casale for a few moments in French. "What kind of diaries?"

"They were written during the war. World War One."

Another burst of French ensued.

"Will you be staying in Amiens very long?"

"Only a few days," I said, although in reality I had no idea how long I would stay. So much depended on Pierre. "I have to return to New York, where I live."

"Please write down your address and telephone number for us. We may need to contact you again."

"Do you know anything about this man? Does he have a name?"

"We are conducting preliminary inquiries, madame. Confidential, of course."

"I want to know if you find something. Anything at all."

"We will do what we can, madame."

Detective Boudin closed his notebook. He was clearly the more senior officer, and Inspector Casale deferred to him in a manner that had nothing to do with his own limited English. I thanked both men for coming and escorted them to the door.

During the rest of the day, I was distracted and made little progress; however, I hid my disappointment from Pierre, who took me for a stroll along the canals before dinner. Long punts uniformly painted blue trolled the narrow waterways where weeping willows bent low as if taking a sip. Grassy banks and bobbing flowers edged the canals, and every now and then, a small house with a red-tiled roof marked a turning spot.

As we walked, Pierre explained that Amiens had been a Roman town, located where the Somme intersected the Selle and Avre Rivers, and because of its marshy surroundings, many canals were built to drain the land and serve as a mode of transportation.

"When the railway connected us to Boulogne-sur-Mer, the city expanded beyond the river into the hills. But these canals remained, and now they are a tourist attraction."

I observed the pleasure in his eyes and expressive gestures as he described the history of Amiens, the kings who fought to rule its rich land, the nobles who built the churches and grand chateaus and who dominated the city's ancient textile industry.

"You love history, don't you?"

"I do. You should stop me before I get too boring."

For a moment, we watched a mother duck herd her little brood into the water accompanied by stuttering cheeps and a few loud quacks. Once in formation, the ducklings paddled obediently behind her, keeping close to the banks, occasionally disappearing from view beneath overhanging grasses.

"I used to look like that with Paul and Michael and one or two of their friends straggling along behind me."

"Perhaps I should call you Ducky," he said with a grin.

"Don't you dare."

"Better than *Canard*." Pierre laughed at his own joke and tucked my arm through his. "We should go now or we'll miss our dinner reservation. It's a popular restaurant."

"Does another cousin own it?"

"No. I have told Gerard he should buy it, but he says his hands are full right now, which is true. He barely has time for his wife and two children as it is."

"I wasn't serious, you know. Would he really consider buying it?"

"We have talked about doing it as a joint investment. Don't you think owning a restaurant would be a romantic thing to do?"

"Hard work, long hours, difficult to make a profit. It doesn't sound romantic to me."

"Well, the French look on it differently. I think I need to help you develop a French soul. You Americans are far too practical."

We continued our light banter over dinner but fell silent on the walk home. A comfortable silence that made me acutely aware of how entangled I had become.

MARTIN'S DIARY

November 11, 1918

The war is over. Words I have longed to write. Over at last. Nothing can bring my friends or Jane back, but at least no one else needs to die. When we heard the news, the roar up and down the line was so fierce, so jubilant, I wanted to weep. My men rose from deep, wet holes and built fires to warm their emaciated bodies. Singing broke out, at first ragged and then stronger as platoon after platoon added their voices to the swell. A sound I will never forget. That and the hopeful faces around me imagining a future they had assumed would never occur.

My own future feels heavy with uncertainty. After so much loss, what will I do? Can I live with what I've done? I long to set down my burdens and calm my rage. I long for Cynthia but wonder if her love can survive the great void of my existence.

April 4, 1919

After three months of duties with the Army of Occupation and two months in Belgium, I have orders to return to England and await transport home. Nully left last week—the only friend still alive. I wouldn't have made it without him. How will I go on? What is the point of living after everything I've done?

CHAPTER 32

April 1919

The skies were crystal clear and as blue as the iris in his mother's garden when Martin disembarked at Southampton. Not even a wisp of cloud obscured the ship as it steamed into port, turning like a graceful but aging ballerina, flags flapping cheerful colors in the wind. Martin's cheeks were hollow, his shoulders slumped as he descended the ship's wide, bare plank among a jostle of soldiers whose eyes sought the embrace of a familiar smile or an encouraging wave. Leaving the war behind was proving difficult for him.

Expecting no one to greet him—he had told Cynthia expressly not to come—Martin looked straight ahead. Inner wounds had settled deep, a gaping fissure tearing him apart. He was not worthy of her. Not worthy of love. Pain had rooted so deeply in him that without the routine of soldiering, he knew he would fail at life. He was nothing. A carcass of bone and skin and muscle and blood, nothing else.

She should know my feelings from my letters, he thought.

For months now, the words he wrote had lacked tenderness. He no longer spoke of love or their future together and instead wrote as if to his mother, avoiding intimate topics, remarking on the weather or the stew he had for dinner or a tasty glass of wine. He mentioned inconsequential details, like how many hours he slept and whether he won or lost at cards. Days went by, sometimes weeks, before he responded to her.

And yet there she was, standing on the dock amid the crowd, wearing a purple hat with a feather at the front. Martin looked away. He could not bear to see her smile, her face full of expectation. She would fling her arms around him, and that would remind him of making love, of watching the surprise on her face and the intense shudder when she climaxed. He could not think of that. No, not that.

A seagull landed on the railing and opened its beak, twisting its head back and forth, eyes black and beady. Cynthia waved. Martin took another step down the plank. And another.

"I told you not to come," he said, brusque and distant. Duffel bag in one hand, map case in the other.

Cynthia's astonished tears softened some of Martin's rigid composure, enough that he dropped his bag and put one arm around her shoulders. "Shhh, don't cry."

"But how could you think I would not come? I love you. I have waited for your return all these months." She clung to him, speaking through heaving sobs and pent-up emotion. "All I want is for you to love me. We can sort out everything else if we love each other."

Martin shouldered his duffel bag once again. "I can make no promises."

After Southampton and the inept bureaucracy of demobilization, he stayed in London, not because Cynthia pleaded with him, but because he couldn't face going home to his mother and father, to a home without Jane.

Instead of his soldier's garb, he adopted a new uniform: white shirt, striped tie, gray flannel trousers, and a navy-blue sweater with two missing buttons purchased at a rummage sale. When Cynthia offered to buy him a new sweater, he refused. He wouldn't let her visit the room where he stayed, a run-down place with a sagging mattress and a single chair, the fabric faded and worn, a hole in one armrest where tufts of stuffing poked out. He bought cans of beans and ate them cold, he downed pints of beer at the local pub, and he refused Cynthia's invitations to the Gibson family home.

Every weekday afternoon, he boarded a bus and traveled to Hyde Park Place to visit the Daughters of the Empire hospital. Captain Butler had been treated there, and Martin had sent him many letters in the months after Vimy Ridge. Most of those letters had remained unanswered, and it was only in late April when Martin had spoken to Matron Crockett, a thin woman with chapped hands and a brisk manner, that he had learned the truth. Butler had committed suicide not long after being released from the hospital.

"We did our best for him, Captain Devlin, but our best was not enough," the matron said.

Martin cocked his head, waiting for her to disclose more information—a technique he had learned from Dr. Berger at Chumley Park and had successfully deployed on many occasions since.

"His wounds were severe," she continued. "One arm and one leg lost as a result. Plus damage to his face. I wrote to his family, asking that someone come to England to be with him, but they had no funds to do so. Family and friends can make all the difference, you know." Although she spoke briskly, her face looked ragged and worn and older than Martin judged her to be.

Hearing of Butler's fate, he wanted to escape. The sooner he found a pub, the better; however, good manners and respect for his former captain had prevailed.

"How many officers are still here?" he asked.

"We have eleven now, mostly Canadian, but two are from Australia and one from New Zealand. Captain Creighton says the hospital will close in September, and hopefully everyone will be fit to travel home by then. If you have a little time, perhaps you would like to visit the wards?"

"I only came to see Captain Butler," Martin said.

"Well, Captain Devlin, your visit came too late for him, but I'm sure a man like you could cheer a few others." Matron Crockett's gaze was unrelenting.

"I don't have a lot of cheer to offer, but I suppose I could say hello to one or two," he said.

Hands clasped firmly behind his back, he followed Matron along the corridor to the front entrance, where a grand piano sat in the far corner and wide curving stairs led to the second floor. Hyde Park, bursting with new growth and flowering bushes, was visible from four arched windows facing the street.

"We have one large ward and four smaller ones," she said as they mounted the stairs. "Colonel Gooderham and his wife purchased the house in late 1915. I arrived soon after, and we received our first patients in February 1916. Ever since, we've been dedicated to treating wounded officers. Here we are."

Sunlight streamed through the windows of the room, each wall painted lavender-gray with panels outlined in white. Bed screens framed in white separated white beds and tables from one another, and beside each bed was a gray mat patterned with pink roses. Martin wondered who had chosen such feminine décor for a room full of military officers.

"Hello, Captain Williams," Matron said to a man in a wheelchair facing the window. "I've brought Captain Devlin with me to see our little operation. He's just been demobbed and was looking for a friend who used to be here."

When Williams swung around to face them, Martin saw the man's pajama pant rolled up to reveal a stump bound in white gauze. He quickly lifted his gaze to the captain's face.

"And where were you, Devlin?" said Williams after shaking hands.

"Ypres, the Somme, Vimy Ridge, and others, of course. I was also in Cologne with the Army of Occupation and then Belgium waiting to be released. And you?"

"Similar. Got this blighter at Cambrai. But at least I'm alive. Matron says I'm to be fitted for a fake leg any day now."

"In two days' time, I believe, Captain Williams." Matron smoothed the front of her skirt. "Gentlemen, I'm late for afternoon rounds. Captain Devlin, it's been a pleasure speaking with you. Make sure you say hello to some of the other chaps while you're here."

Though he remained in the ward until late afternoon, Martin had had no intention of returning to the hospital. And yet he had. Something about Williams's determination and the hopeful way he'd asked Martin to come back to see his new leg had broken through Martin's deliberate solitude. From time to time, other officers joined their conversations, and when David Williams took his first unaided steps, Martin and the entire ward cheered.

The question of what to do with Cynthia remained. When they were together, he was remote and unbending, harsh and irritable, refusing the kindnesses she offered. He told her repeatedly that his plans for the future were indefinite, that he was not the man for her, and still she persisted, traveling from Hackney every Saturday afternoon to meet at the local pub and cajole him into a walk in the park, a cup of tea, or a trip to the museum, which was free to former soldiers.

On one of those Saturdays, gloomy clouds had given way to a fine drizzle as Martin and Cynthia walked along, and soon a more serious storm erupted with gusts of wind that blew Cynthia's umbrella inside out.

"Take me back to your bedsit," Cynthia said. "This rain is ruining my shoes."

"No," Martin said. "It's not a seemly place for you to be. Your parents would be horrified."

"I don't care. I came all this way to spend the afternoon with you. Besides, they will never know. Please, Martin. We haven't been alone together since you arrived. I want—"

"Not everything is about what you want."

"Martin Devlin! What a beastly thing to say. I've been patient with you, kind, considerate. I've tried everything I can think of to erase the gloom from your face. Why can't you do something for me? You visit those men at the hospital. You're kind to them. Why can't you be kind to me? Where did the man I fell in love with go? You keep pushing me away, but I know you need me. You do, Martin. You need someone. I love you. I still love you. I think I will always love you." Her face reddened as tears formed and rolled down her cheeks.

Martin softened enough to put one arm around her as he considered Cynthia's words. Visiting the hospital required little emotional investment while allowing him to be with men who had shared the experience of war, officers like him who had sent others to their deaths. They demanded nothing from him except a little conversation and a knowing shrug when the talk became difficult. They knew his pain. They all did. No one judged him, and for the hours he was there, his numbness eased.

What he wanted most was for the pain to go away. Every day, he woke to the same dull throbbing ache. The same lethargy overtaking his body such that he had no desire to even get out of bed. No desires at all. An empty, hopeless life stretched in front of him. Cynthia deserved better.

"All right," he said. "You can come to the bedsit with me."

CHAPTER 33

July 1991

With all four diaries thoroughly examined and eleven pages of individual letters noted, I once again shook my head at Grandpa's puzzle. I knew I should return to New York in a day or two. I had been gone almost four weeks, the length of time Jim and I had agreed on.

Instead, I had lied to my ex-husband, making up a story about getting sick and needing a bit more time to complete my plans. He had been solicitous and assured me that a few more days would be fine; he and the boys were getting along fabulously. That was the very word he used: *fabulously*. I reminded myself that I had to let the boys go in order to hold on to them, a notion picked up from a parenting book our family physician recommended as Paul had entered his teenage years. I'd also called my grandmother, bracing for another tirade, and was relieved when Philomena informed me Grandmama was out for lunch. "Tell her I'll be home soon," I said.

Leaving Pierre would be difficult. After only a few weeks, I felt he understood me better than anyone except my grandfather. Not only did he understand me, but our time together flowed so easily, quiet mixed with laughter and conversation both deep and light. And he knew my body better than anyone. Jim had never explored it with such care and caresses or discovered so many ways to give me pleasure. In return, I too sought ways to bring a knowing smile to his face and prolong the intensity.

But he lives in France. I wrote these words on my notepad followed by three exclamation marks, then crumpled the paper and threw it in the wastebasket. *Why did I ever come here? If I had stayed in New York, I wouldn't be in this mess. But then, I would never have met him.*

Despite my uncertainty, I felt more alive since being with Pierre than I had in years. I savored the feeling, recalling last night's lovemaking and the quiet pleasure of sleepy conversation afterward. Pierre did not mention love, and neither did I. Instead, I tried to tell him how I felt in other ways, gently rubbing his nighttime beard with my fingers, curling my body around his, touching his toes with mine.

I sighed and idly picked up my grandfather's note—4/3/72. I leaned closer to the note. "What if that's a one, not a seven?" I muttered, picking up the magnifying glass. *Oh my God, maybe that's it—4/3/12. Grandpa made it look like a date, but it isn't. Maybe he's telling me how to decode the letters.* I sat up straight and set to work, Pierre momentarily forgotten.

I found the first dotted letter from diary four—*m*—then the first one from diary three—*y*—and the first from diary one—*d*. Working frantically, flipping back and forth from my notes to Martin's diaries, a message began taking shape. *My dearest Grace.*

Words tumbled out, sentences gradually formed. Occasionally, I made a mistake and had to find the sequence again. Choose a letter from diary four, then three, then one, then two. I did this over and over as the minutes passed, turning into hours. Finally, Martin's puzzle lay before me, and I sat back, shocked at the story, my grandfather's dilemma laid bare, my own just beginning.

My dearest Grace,

This is a story that has haunted my life.

Once the horror of war became apparent, my friends kept me going. Then I lost them all to the war.

I kept thinking, why not me? Take me next. I could not bear the burden of killing more, of watching more death. I became depressed, even suicidal. I showed no kindness to my men.

The final straw was Jane's death in a bombing raid. Possessed by rage, I killed as many Germans as I could. And I beat one so savagely he almost died. I kept remnants of that episode in a tackle box so I would never forget.

Next day, I found a map case in a German bunker. Inside were four stolen paintings. At first, I planned to return them. But I never gave them back. Your grandmother knew they were valuable. We agreed to use them as collateral for the gallery. Over time, I realized I kept them as compensation for what I had endured and to make something of my life on behalf of those who died. A terrible lapse of morality.

Your grandmother gave me hope. She was beautiful. Kind, funny, beguiling. I loved her then and love her now. But life changed her. She never got over the loss of our first child, and when your mother fell apart, another piece of your grandmother crumbled. She was afraid to love you like she loved them.

When the gallery became successful, I wanted to return the paintings. I had discovered they belonged to a French family called Auffret. But your grandmother refused to let them go, so I hid them.

With this one exception, I believe I am a man of integrity, but I live with regret. You have made me proud, Grace. You have been so special to me. Do one last thing for me. Return the paintings to their owners.

I will always be your loving Grandpa.

I gasped out loud when the name Auffret appeared and covered my mouth in horror, remembering how much money Pierre's grandfather had spent trying to find those paintings. The coincidence of meeting the grandson of the man who owned the paintings my grandfather had taken was unbelievable. Had fate intervened? Grandmama would scoff at that notion. Pierre would never forgive me.

For the next two hours, I agonized over what to do, finally concluding I would tell Pierre nothing about the letter. Instead, I would fly home immediately to confront my grandmother and get the paintings back to him.

"Let me understand. There's an urgent family situation you cannot tell me about and you have to return to New York." Pierre's voice was clipped, his accent heavier than normal, nostrils flared.

"I will tell you. I promise. But I have to do something first."

"I see." His eyes narrowed.

"Pierre, please don't be angry. In all this time, you've never been angry with me. I'm so sorry. You need to trust me."

"I need to trust you. Is trust not a two-way street?"

"I'll tell you as soon as I can."

"And you have to leave tomorrow. Just like that, with no warning. You have been enjoying my hospitality and"—he snapped his fingers—"just like that, you disappear. A little fling with a charming Frenchman. You did find me charming, did you not?"

"I find you more than charming. You know that. I'm not the kind of woman who sleeps around."

Pierre tossed his napkin on the table. "And I'm not the kind of man who invites just any woman to his home. I wanted us . . ."

"What, Pierre? What did you want us to do?"

"Never mind. It does not matter anymore. I am going out. Do not bother to wait up." He picked up his keys and wallet and walked out the door, slamming it behind him.

But I can't tell him, not until I speak to Grandmama. Not until I can return the paintings to him. If he would only be patient. But why would he? He has no history with me. A debate raged inside my head. Part of me wanted to run after him. The other part worried that if he knew the truth, he would be even angrier.

Feeling numb, I cleared the table, storing leftover food in Pierre's fridge, corking the wine bottle, wiping away crumbs, the excitement of solving Grandpa's puzzle obliterated by Pierre's reaction. Footsteps on the sidewalk brought me to the window, but the man passing by was a stranger. Nonetheless, I stood there waiting as night mist gathered, at first mere threads of moisture, then ultimately thick and impenetrable. When all I could see was a vague glow surrounding the streetlight, I climbed the stairs.

I woke suddenly and for a moment could not remember where I was. Footsteps crossing the living room floor were followed by the sound of water splashing in the sink and then a glass set down hard on the granite counter. Pierre had returned. The stairs creaked. The bathroom light clicked on.

"Pierre?"

"Go back to sleep," he said, leaning against the doorjamb.

"Please, Pierre. Can't we talk?"

"There is nothing more to say, and I have had too much to drink. I will sleep in the guest room."

"Don't do that." I slipped out of bed and held his face in my hands, attempting to get him to look at me. "I don't want to go home, but I have to. I would much prefer to stay with you. I promise you'll understand. I promise."

"You already said that." He was glassy-eyed, his speech a little slurred, but he didn't draw away. "Leave me be, Grace. If I am going to function at all tomorrow, I need to sleep."

"Won't you at least kiss me?"

"I don't think so."

In the morning, he took clothes from the closet and disappeared without a word to shower and shave. He was in the kitchen drinking espresso when I came down.

"Here's my phone number and address in New York." I placed a piece of paper on the counter.

"I have to go," Pierre said. "Put the key under the flowerpot when you leave."

Afraid I would burst into tears, I nodded, and he left without another word. From the window, I watched as he got into the Peugeot, backed down the drive, put the car in first gear, and roared off.

CHAPTER 34

July 1991

New York was a steam bath. Tempers flared, from the attendant at the baggage carousel to the taxi dispatcher. On the highway, a stalled car in the center lane caused traffic to jam, and people honked and shouted their impatience. *Ah, New Yorkers, I've missed you.*

In Maplewood, glistening patches of tar and a ghostly absence of shoppers and neighbors greeted me. With straggling petunias hanging limply in the flower boxes and bits of paper dotting the front yard and driveway, the house on Brookfield Lane looked as forlorn as a grieving widow. The door was dusty and the curtains neither fully closed nor open, as if no one cared enough to acknowledge the passing of day and night.

Since the boys were on a fishing trip with Jim's father, I would have the house to myself for three days, and for that, I was grateful. Being alone would allow time to deal with my grandmother and my feelings for Pierre. Neither would be easy.

A wall of hot, stale air greeted me, and I moved swiftly to the family room to turn on the air conditioner. After twisting the dial to *COOL*, I absorbed the feeling of home, the place where I had lived more than fifteen years, shaping a space for my family. Except now my family was missing a limb. For a moment, the pain of divorce felt sharp and oddly fresh.

"Keep busy," I muttered, hauling two suitcases up the stairs. After dealing with my clothes, I went through the house opening curtains, plumping pillows, tidying magazines and other items left in disarray. While I worked, my mind probed troubling topics and soothed them into manageable choices so I could see them not as churning seas but as small streams to cross.

Jim and I might no longer be a couple, but as parents we could work together. Grandmama was disappointed with some of life's twists and turns. With continued patience, perhaps I could ease her mind despite the confrontation I was expecting over Grandpa's request. As for my job, it had taught me many skills while providing security when my children were young. I knew with unexpected certainty it was time to apply those skills elsewhere.

Pierre was a different matter. One for which I had no simple resolution. Every time I read my grandfather's letter, my stomach churned.

Return the paintings—my grandfather's last words to me. But why hadn't he disclosed where to find them? I shook my head. The only person who could possibly know was Grandmama.

"Hello, Grandmama. How are you?" I said, twisting the telephone cord around one finger.

"Are you back?"

"Yes. Last night." I twisted the cord again.

"Well, good. I was telling Sally Rockford yesterday I had no idea when you would return. She was surprised, of course. And asked me if there was something wrong with you."

I ignored her implied criticism. "I'd like to see you." By now the cord was wrapped around my wrist. "This afternoon."

"This afternoon? I don't know if—"

"This afternoon. It's important. I'll be there at two o'clock." My voice remained flat and clipped, and I heard the sound of Grandmama's cane tapping the floor.

"Two o'clock, then, if you insist, but this is Philomena's day off."

"Then I'll make the tea. Bye, Grandmama." I unwound the cord and hung up the phone.

Since waking at five, I had been busy with laundry and cleaning, attempting to keep my mind clear of emotions, but as I climbed the stairs to the second floor, a memory of the first night at Pierre's came to mind, his hand resting on my waist and his gentle but insistent pull toward the bedroom. I closed my eyes and paused on the landing, waiting for the sadness to subside. I had already shed many tears. My grandmother would notice puffy, red-rimmed eyes and ask far too many questions, and I needed to be unemotional for the conversation that would take place. Not only did I plan to discuss Grandpa's letter, but I also planned to confront her about having me followed. I felt certain it had to be her, but I could not fathom the warped thinking that would have caused her to do so. And what would she think now that Fedora Man was dead?

By eleven o'clock, I had finished my chores, showered, and changed, choosing white pants and high-heeled sandals and a fitted red top before adding a chunky gold necklace and dark red lipstick. Grandmama would consider the combination far too bold. In my teenage years, she would have called such a look trashy. At noon, I grabbed my purse and left the house.

CHAPTER 35

June 1919

Martin read the letter again, the slanted script as familiar to him as his own. Earlier letters had been more solicitous, as if his father understood Martin's need for solitude upon leaving the army. This time, his father was more direct. *You must come home, son. Your mother needs you. Only you can ease her grief. I will cable travel funds as soon as you advise me of bank details.*

Would they ever forgive him for being the one to survive? He should have protected Jane, convinced her to return to Canada instead of nursing on the front lines or to deploy her talents in England rather than France. If he had, his parents would not be suffering such anguish. Martin crumpled the letter in his fist.

Earlier that morning he had opened the map case and placed the four paintings on the bed. On the bottom right corner of each canvas was a signature. Luras. Was the painter famous? Whom did the paintings belong to? Not to the German officers who had them in their bunker, and certainly not to him. Did that make him a thief? *No, not a thief,* he thought. *I'm just looking after the paintings until the rightful owner can be found.*

Martin stared out the window. Although early summer was evident in blue-washed skies and in the floral prints and pastel shades that women were wearing, he remained locked in gloom, existing only in shades of gray, living each day still encased in the cold, rotting shelters of trench and tunnel, pelted by rain and hail and sleet, where mists unrolled to deliver terror and the unasked question, "Will I see the dawn?" Etched in his mind were a thousand eyes: lifeless, hungry, thirsty, fearful—always fearful. The eyes of men fearful of death and fearful of life, living—if one could call it that—amid the hiss and thwack of bullets and the ominous roar of exploding bombs. Only those who were there understood.

Steps on the stairwell. A knock on the door. He did not move.

A second, more persistent series of knocks. "Martin? It's me."

Damn.

"Martin. Please open the door. I know you're in there. I saw you by the window."

He moved to the door and cracked it open. "Why are you here?"

"It's a lovely day. Come out with me."

"Shouldn't you be at work?"

"That's the wonderful thing. The factory is closed for a week of refitting. No need for ammunition any more. According to Mr. Everett, we will soon be making engines. The kind they use for motorbikes and small boats. So I can spend the whole week with you." While speaking, Cynthia's smile had gone from wide to tepid. "You look strange," she said. "Are you feeling ill?"

"No."

"What's wrong, then?"

"You wouldn't understand." Martin had yet to invite Cynthia in, but now he stepped aside. He knew how persistent she could be.

"I know the war was awful," she said, pulling at each white-gloved finger one by one before removing her gloves entirely. "And you don't like to talk about it. I know being a civilian again is a difficult adjustment for you, but together we'll get through it. Have you heard from your mother and father?"

Martin nodded.

"Are they pressing you to return to Canada?"

He nodded again.

Cynthia moved beyond the doorway. "I'll come with you. As your wife. Lucy and her Frank arranged a license in five days. We could be married by the end of next week." She turned to him with soft, pleading eyes. "You used to want to marry me. You remember that, don't you?"

"But things have changed. I've changed. I don't . . ."

"You don't love me anymore." She looked straight at him.

"That's not . . . I don't . . . Do you really want to have this conversation?"

Cynthia nodded. "We must. We cannot continue like this. I cannot go on watching you destroy yourself."

Martin lifted his arms, then let them flop. "I don't know how I feel about us. Most days, I feel nothing except dull, empty pain. But I am certain of one thing. I won't be able to make you happy."

"Why can't I be the judge of that?"

"Because you'll make the wrong decision."

Cynthia touched his cheek. "When we met, your eyes were haunted, just as they are now. I had spoken to enough soldiers at the Mercury to know you were suffering, but you let me in. And we were happy. Don't you remember? You said I gave you hope. Let me in again, Martin. Let me at least try to help."

She stood so close he could see a tiny vein pulsing at the base of her neck. No more than a few inches separated their lips. *It would be so easy,* he thought, allowing himself to remember the time a few weeks earlier when she had insisted on coming to his room. He hadn't been able to resist her then, had crushed her to him, drowning in the taste and feel of her and the fervent coupling that left them bruised and panting. Afterward, he had cursed himself for losing control.

Today he stepped away.

Cynthia's gaze did not falter. "Well, the least you can do is come walking with me. But you'll need to dress properly. Not in that dreadful sweater with the missing buttons." She turned. "Why are there paintings on the bed?" she said, crossing the room. "My goodness, they're stunning, Martin." She bent to look closer. "What wonderful technique and color. Where did you find them?"

He knew she was putting on a show for him, pretending that everything was all right between them. "They're nothing to do with you."

"You should show them to my father," she continued, as though he had not spoken. "They might be valuable."

Martin took the canvases from the bed and rolled them together, securing the bundle with a shoelace tied around each end. He slid the paintings into the map case and snapped on the lid.

"I'll get my jacket," he said.

With his father's funds deposited in the bank, Martin knew he had to book passage home. Having remained so long in England, he had forfeited the right to travel on one of the many troopships sailing out of Southampton and now had to find a commercial ocean liner instead. Despite his resistance, Cynthia was still talking of coming with him. He tried to imagine married life with a house and children and a steady job. The thought filled him with panic.

The previous day he discovered the RMS *Adriatic* leaving Southampton for New York and the *Aquitania*, a Cunard liner, offering discounted rates for the same journey. Tomorrow he planned to book a ticket without telling Cynthia. Today he would end their relationship.

"But you can't leave me," she said as they sat on a park bench beneath a chestnut tree heavy with fruit.

He had spoken as gently as possible, reiterating previous conversations about his unsuitability and how the war had affected him. "My future is so uncertain," he said now. "Far too uncertain for me to jeopardize yours as well."

"Well, you already have," she said. "I'm going to have your child, so my future will be even worse if you fail to marry me."

Martin covered his face with both hands. "Christ almighty. That can't possibly be."

She lifted her chin, hands balled into tight fists. "Well, it is. I've known since last Monday and was waiting for the right time to tell you. I even thought it might help you look to the future. I so want to make you happy, Martin. The baby and I will give you a fresh start."

"Can't you see that I'm not right for you? I've tried to tell you in so many ways." Martin closed his eyes and shook his head. A baby was the worst possible situation. He could barely get through the day, let alone be responsible for a wife and child. Today's conversation was supposed to end their relationship, not add further complexity to it. "I'll give you the paintings. You said they're probably valuable. You can sell them and go away for a while, then give the baby up for adoption. My cousin did that, and later she married a fine man, and now they have four children. No one was supposed to know about the adoption, but Mother told me when I was dating a girl before the war. I think it was her way of warning me to be careful."

"You should have listened to your mother's advice." Cynthia pulled a handkerchief from her handbag and wiped away the tear trickling down her right cheek.

"Is it mine?"

The slap on his cheek resounded like distant rifle fire and hurt more than he imagined a woman of Cynthia's size capable of. Her eyes glittered with anger.

"You are being an ass. A bloody ass, and I will not deign to answer that question. Do you think I want to be pregnant? Did you imagine I planned this to trap you into marriage? The last few months have only served to show me what a mistake it was to fall in love with you. But I'm not going to give this baby up, and I'm not going to be an unwed mother. You, Martin Devlin, are going to be an honorable man."

The next day, he booked two second-class tickets home and cabled his parents to expect them in early August.

Eleven days before the *Aquitania* sailed for New York, Martin married Cynthia in a ceremony attended by her immediate family, her friends Lucy and Frank, and Cynthia's two aunts. His own parents sent a poignant telegram and arranged for a wedding cake to be delivered to the Gibson home. In the days leading up to the wedding, he experienced brief moments of optimism followed by the crushing certainty that failure and heartache lay ahead.

"You still have the paintings," Cynthia said as Martin placed their suitcases on racks at the foot of each narrow bed. Their cabin had little else to offer except a small sink and mirror, several hooks for hanging their clothes, and a three-drawer chest. Two portholes let in a little light, and above each bed was a reading lamp anchored to the wall.

Before leaving, Martin had debated what to do with the paintings. He knew the right thing was to turn them over to the military, but he imagined they would then sit for years in a dusty storage facility waiting for someone to decide how to repatriate them. Worse was the thought that they might be destroyed or end up in the private home of an undeserving general who had remained behind the lines throughout the war, making the kind of incompetent decisions that had resulted in the deaths of his friends and so many others.

"I'll tell you about them sometime, but not now," Martin said. A horn sounded, followed by the ringing of bells. "Let's go on deck as the ship pulls away."

As they stood at the railing with a crowd of other passengers, Cynthia linked her arm with his. Martin was beginning to accept what had happened. Here they were, bound for New York, to be followed by a train to Toronto. In less than six months, he would be a father.

Cynthia still looked as slim as she had at the Mercury bar, although he thought he detected a little fullness to her breasts and just the smallest amount of thickening at her waist. The first time they slept together after the wedding, he had awakened wondering where he was, but now having her lying next to him, her body brushing his whenever she turned, felt almost natural. Martin watched as the *Aquitania* pulled away from England's shore and hoped he would never return.

∽

"You seem to be improving," Cynthia said a few days later as they walked the promenade deck, shielded from buffeting winds by a wall of windows enclosing the starboard side.

"How so?"

"You're less grumpy. Do you realize you actually smiled when I teased you about your sweater this morning?"

"I did?"

Cynthia became serious. "Will we be all right together, Martin?"

"I'm sure I can find a job."

"That's not what I mean. Will we be all right as husband and wife? I don't want you to resent me or wake up one morning and wish you'd never met me."

She was seeking reassurance, and Martin wondered how much he could offer. "Why don't you ask that question again a few months from now? I want to be able to say yes, and it's still too soon."

"In a few months, then," she said, withdrawing her arm from his.

Martin sought a topic to please his new wife. "Would you like to know about the paintings?"

"I suppose so."

"I found them in a captured German trench not long after Jane was killed." Martin relayed the story. "When I looked inside the map case and discovered what was there, I kept them. I still don't know why. I suppose I've done something illegal, or at least the army would consider it conduct unbecoming an officer. Whenever I look at them, I wonder who they belong to. It's clear the Germans stole them, but there are no markings to indicate ownership. I imagine they were hanging on the walls of one of the many French or Belgian homes they requisitioned."

"So the paintings are not yours."

Martin shook his head.

"What are you planning to do with them?"

"I don't know."

"They might be worth a lot of money."

"Yes, but I can't sell them. That would be . . ." Martin debated what word to use: *wrong, illegal, irresponsible, reprehensible.* All of those words combined, he supposed. "That wouldn't be right," he said finally, imagining at some future date searching for their rightful owners.

CHAPTER 36

July 1991

"Hello, Grandmama," I called out after letting myself in.

I listened for her voice but heard nothing. My high heels clicked along the front hall, and my keys jangled as I dropped them onto a lotus leaf–shaped brass tray that sat on the console table. I glanced into the living room and proceeded to the kitchen.

"Here you are." I bent over to kiss my grandmother's cheek. "I had such an interesting time. You didn't tell me France is so enticing."

Grandmama harrumphed. "Well, you were in the countryside. Paris is much more enticing," she said. "My, my. That's a flashy combination you're wearing."

I ignored her comment and described my visit to Lille while getting the kettle and tea organized. After the water boiled, I carried the cups, saucers, teapot, and lemon on a silver tray into the living room, and we settled into our accustomed places. I chewed my lower lip, then cleared my throat.

"How are the boys?" Grandmama asked before I could begin. "No doubt they're pleased to have you back."

"I . . . I haven't seen them yet. Jim's father took them fishing. But they sounded fine on the phone. Jim did too. He said they had a lot of fun together."

"I'm sure he spoiled them terribly. Where were you this past week?"

"So many places." I wasn't going to mention my time with Pierre. She would be scandalized. "I'll tell you another time."

"Did you meet some interesting people?"

"I did, and I spoke a bit of French."

"What was your favorite place?"

I was about to say Amiens but stopped. Any reply would only prompt more questions, and I was beginning to think Grandmama was using this tactic to avoid the questions I might ask of her. Since my cup was empty, I poured more tea and lifted the pot toward my grandmother. She shook her head.

Once more, I cleared my throat. "Grandpa left me his diaries. I took them to France with me and traced his route."

"His diaries?"

"Yes. His war diaries."

"I see. Did you find them interesting?"

Nothing in Grandmama's demeanor indicated surprise, and I experienced a flash of anger that she had never mentioned them. I had certainly asked enough questions about Grandpa and the war before traveling to France. If she had known about them, she should have told me. If she had not, then she was lying to me now. And then, of course, there was the question of the man who had followed me. I decided to assume she had known about them all along.

"Very. I'm sure you've read them and know how at first he's young and enthusiastic, but gradually he becomes angry and depressed. He mentions you, of course, as you no doubt know. I visited memorials and cemeteries overlooking the battlefields and all sorts of little villages and towns where he stayed. Being there was very moving, Grandmama. The whole experience made me sad. I wish he had talked about it."

"Most men refused to speak about it. It was too horrible."

"Grandpa also left me a letter."

"A letter?" Her eyes narrowed, and she looked nervous, although I might have imagined that. "May I see it?"

"I didn't bring it with me. Actually, his letter was disguised as a puzzle."

"A puzzle."

I nodded slowly. "Remember when we did puzzles together on Sunday nights? Grandpa loved to make them for me and give me little clues whenever I got stuck. Remember, Grandmama?"

She tilted her head but said nothing.

"I had to work hard to solve this puzzle. Very hard. I'm sure you know what it's about."

"I doubt it." Grandmama looked down, carefully folding the pleats of her skirt. "He certainly said nothing about a puzzle before he died." Her tone was imperious, her English accent more pronounced than usual. "Your grandfather could be peculiar, you know."

"Well, he was certainly clear in his letter. He said he had taken some paintings at the end of the war that didn't belong to him. And that you knew all about them. He said they'd always haunted him, and he wanted to make amends. He asked me to find a way to return them to their owners." I kept my face neutral. "Is that why you had me followed, Grandmama?"

"Followed? In France? Don't be preposterous. Why would I have you followed? You're my granddaughter. You've always had the wildest imagination." Again, she sounded nervous.

"Don't try to bluff your way out of it. It couldn't possibly be anyone other than you. He even ransacked my room one night."

"Ransacked your room? I have no idea what you're talking about. Was anything taken?" I shook my head. "Perhaps this divorce has affected you more than you know." She took a slow sip of tea and set her cup down. "And as for paintings your grandfather took, he never mentioned any paintings." Grandmama's cheeks were almost as red as the poppies I had seen leaning against the Thiepval Memorial.

"He was very specific. He even knew the name of the family they belong to."

"He did, did he? Let me see that letter."

"I left it at home. And now you need to tell me the truth, Grandmama."

She frowned and shifted in her chair. "My back hurts. Fetch me that blue pillow." When I complied, she put the pillow behind her back. "There." She shifted once more. "Let me tell you about your grandfather. He was always weaker than me. I'm the one who convinced him to keep them. And where would we be without those paintings as the starting point? No bank would have given us a loan without collateral. Where would you be? This well-brought-up life you've had. Have you thought of that?"

"So you did know about the paintings. Why did you just lie to me?" I crossed my arms and stared at her. "You made him live with deceit his whole life. Didn't you know what that cost him?"

"He never minded the social standing we had."

"Grandpa never cared about social standing. You did. You're the one who wanted that life."

"He liked what money could buy."

"He bought those things for you. Because he loved you. He said so. He said you gave him hope."

Grandmama's face softened for an instant before she straightened her back and set her mouth.

"The paintings must remain a secret. Do you hear me? If you say anything, I shall . . . I shall sell them. There have been plenty of people prepared to buy them in the past."

"Sell them? You would really do that?" I opened my eyes very wide and slowly shook my head. "So that's why you had me followed. You didn't want me to find out about the paintings."

"What rot. I told you, I did not have you followed. You were probably imagining things. As for the paintings, would you risk your grandfather's reputation by returning them to someone you don't even know? And risk the gallery? It still brings in a tidy sum every month. Most of it will be yours when I die."

"I don't care about the money. I care about Grandpa. He asked me to do this for him."

"You're weak." She almost spit the words at me. "Just like your grandfather. And just like your mother."

My hands shook. I opened my mouth, then clamped it shut again. "We'll see about that," I said, glaring at my grandmother before I stood up, turned on my heel, and left the room.

"Grace, come back. You can't walk away from me."

I kept going. A moment later, I slammed the door behind me.

Though I had remained calm for most of the conversation, by the time I reached the parking garage, I was shaking, adrenaline pumping through my body like a blaze of fire. I fumbled with my keys before managing to unlock the car and, once inside, leaned my head against the steering wheel and squeezed my eyes shut. Grandmama was infuriating.

She's a witch, I thought. *Not just a stubborn old woman, but also a nasty one.* Having me followed. What kind of grandmother would do that? And threatening to sell the paintings, that was the worst possible outcome—an outcome I had not anticipated. I had imagined a difficult discussion, but not one that left me feeling trapped in a dead end.

Is this what you expected, Grandpa?

I raised my head. Maybe he expected me to explore the diaries after Grandmama died? In that case, I would have the freedom to do what I thought was right. He could never have anticipated my meeting Pierre. *What do you want me to do, Grandpa?* I had no one to turn to. Pierre was the only person I could imagine asking for advice, and he was furious with me.

Like an automaton, I put the key in the ignition and started the car.

CHAPTER 37

July 1991

The next morning, the heat was unrelenting, the city's smog looming in the distance. Dressed in faded shorts and a Yankees baseball cap, I was on my knees in the garden, pulling weeds and turning the soil. Gardening had always been my time to think.

Yesterday's meeting with Grandmama still made my blood boil. But I was also puzzled. Twice, she denied having me followed. Either she was lying or she was telling the truth. While it was unfathomable to me that she would take steps to have me followed, if she had, what was her motive? If she hadn't, then who else could have sent someone after me? I didn't know which scenario was worse. It had to be someone who wanted the diaries, although I could not imagine anyone else solving the puzzle, and, having read them several times, I knew there was nothing incriminating in the text of the diaries.

What possible motive would Grandmama have for hiring someone to follow me, particularly since she clearly knew about the paintings?

Grandmama can't win this battle. Grandpa expected me to convince her to go along with his plan. But why didn't he give them back himself?

Was it love that stayed his hand or misguided loyalty? Or cowardice? No, he was never a coward.

Now more than ever I understood his bravery. So was it love or loyalty? Or both? His letter said my grandmother had suffered disappointments and insisted on keeping the paintings, and if Grandmama had given him the strength to go on, maybe he felt he could not turn his back on her. I returned to my earlier question: Why would she have me followed? If she already had the paintings, there was no need to hire someone to take the diaries.

Maybe she doesn't have them.

This thought made me sit back on my heels. But if Grandmama did not have the paintings, why would she threaten to sell them? Did Grandpa hide the paintings from my grandmother? If so, she might not know where they were. And if that was the case, how would I ever be able to return them to Pierre?

I thought about all this while snipping dead roses, tossing withered brown petals into a basket, working my way along the rose bed. Pierre was never far from my thoughts. I had his phone number, but it was too soon to call. And I had nothing tangible to remember him with except the pamphlet from the museum with his picture on the inside cover. Why was I so enamored with someone I had known such a short time?

I brushed a tear from my face with the back of my hand and bent to sniff a newly opened blossom, remembering the cemetery near Thiepval where roses marked the end of each line of crosses, as though the beauty of nested pink blooms could somehow take the sting out of death.

As I put the gardening tools away, I made my decision. I had to confront Grandmama again. She was the only person who could help.

Three hours later, I was heading into New York, the traffic so slow it was almost noon when I finally arrived. Philomena looked puzzled when she opened the door.

"Is Miz Devlin expecting you?" she said.

"No."

"Well, I'm glad you're here. She sure is poorly this morning. Hasn't even got out of bed. I tell you, I don't like the way she looks." Philomena bobbed her head up and down to emphasize the point. "You go on down to see her. I'm making tea and toast. She won't have anything else."

When I peeked into the bedroom, Grandmama's eyes were closed, a slow-moving piano piece drifting from the radio on her bedside table, drawn curtains preventing the sun from lessening the gloom. Hints of lily of the valley reminded me of watching her put on one of the many fancy gowns that used to fill her closet. On those occasions, if I had behaved, I was permitted to brush her hair or fasten a favorite necklace.

"What are *you* doing here?" Grandmama said.

Her voice scratched like rough sandpaper, and I wondered if I detected a hint of anxiety, or perhaps it was fear. "You're still in bed. Didn't you always say morning is the best time of the day?"

Grandmama's eyes flicked open then shut again. "I didn't expect to see you. Have you come to badger me?"

"We shouldn't be at odds. Grandpa would be sad to see us like this."

"How do you know? Maybe that's exactly what he planned. Driving a wedge between us."

While Philomena plumped the pillows and settled a tray in front of my grandmother, I opened the curtains, ignoring her protest that the light was too strong. Pulling a chair next to the bed, I sat down and waited. Grandmama stirred her tea.

"I've learned a lot about Grandpa and the war. And the friends he lost. And his sister, Jane. Why did he never talk about her?" I paused for a moment, but Grandmama didn't respond. "Did he tell you they sent him for psychiatric care? Or that he was planning to step in front of a bullet?" Again, I waited for the words to penetrate her stubborn attitude and experienced a brief feeling of satisfaction when her face lost what little color it had. "Meeting you was the only reason he carried on."

My grandmother remained silent. Frustrated, I stood up and looked out the window. How could I get through to her? I paced, stopping in front of the dresser to touch a silver-handled brush and its matching comb. I picked up a tube of lipstick and daubed a splotch of ruby color on my wrist, then wiped it off with a tissue. I arranged six pill bottles in a straight line. All the while, neither of us spoke.

Finally, I took a deep breath and puffed out my cheeks as I exhaled. "Grandpa wanted to make amends. You have to see that. I'll read you what he wrote." I pulled the letter out of my bag and unfolded its pages.

"*When the gallery became successful, I wanted to return the paintings. I had discovered they belonged to a French family called Auffret. But your grandmother refused to let them go, so I hid them.*

With this one exception, I believe I am a man of integrity, but I live with regret. You have made me proud, Grace. You have been so special to me. Do one last thing for me. Return the paintings to their owners."

"As I said yesterday, if you insist on this course, I shall sell the paintings." Grandmama spoke with her usual directness, but something was missing. Conviction? Certainty? Or perhaps something else. She seemed agitated, on edge. I ignored the underlying emotions and kept pressing my case.

"That doesn't make sense. Grandpa's letter says he hid them away. So unless you found them, you're lying to me. And now you have to help me find them. If you refuse, I will tell the story publicly, and your reputation will be damaged too."

As I spoke, my grandmother's face tightened. She clutched the blanket, alternately grasping and letting it go.

"You will not do this. Not to me. Who would you be without me? A girl with one parent dead and the other helpless." Grandmama wagged her finger. "I took you in. I raised you. You owe a duty to me."

"I'm grateful for what you did. The home you provided. But Grandpa was the one who taught me love and gave me confidence. He was the one who brought laughter into my life. He said . . ."

"What? What did he say? You two always had secrets you wouldn't share. Tell me." She was almost shouting, her mouth twisted and her chin thrust forward. She seemed on the verge of bursting, her breath coming in short, shallow gasps.

"Grandmama! Calm down. You can't catch your breath unless you calm down."

I hurried to the doorway and called for Philomena, then returned to the bedside and took my grandmother's hand. As soon as Philomena entered the room, she grabbed a bottle off the dresser, twisted it open, and slid a small yellow pill beneath her employer's tongue.

"Her heart medicine," Philomena said. "Dr. Williams showed me what to do. Now, Miz Devlin, everything will be fine soon. What were you thinking, getting yourself so riled up?"

My grandmother lay like a rag doll, eyes glassy, silver hair damp with sweat. Philomena wiped her brow with a cool cloth while muttering brief, soothing phrases in a singsongy voice, like a mother comforting a distressed child. Gradually, Grandmama's breathing slowed, and her body relaxed into sleep.

"Grace, you need to take care with your grandmother. She's not strong anymore. Doesn't have much fight left in her."

"You're right, Philomena. I should have realized how fragile she is. But you know what Grandmama's like. So stubborn and domineering. I wanted her to do something important, and she refused. It was like the fights we used to have."

"Oh, I remember them all right. Hollering and banging and sulking till one of you gave in. You were a real pair." Philomena's broad smile flashed for a moment, and then her face turned serious again. "She's lonely, honey. Ninety-two's not an easy age, and she misses your grandpa. Talks about him every day. Just little stories. Sometimes I think she forgets I'm here."

The idea of my grandmother telling stories to Philomena because she had no one else to talk to overwhelmed me with sadness.

"I've been so tied up worrying about myself that I've neglected her."

"Now don't you go feeling guilty. She's a difficult woman. Always has been. But she loves you. It may not always seem so, but I know she does."

I nodded and blew my nose. "Thank you, Philomena. And thank you for looking after her. I think I'll wait in the library until she wakes up."

After tiptoeing down the hall, I entered the library, taking comfort in its dark, glossy furniture and my grandfather's familiar things. I pulled on the drawstrings to open two sets of heavy silk drapes and fastened their tiebacks so they hung in elegant swoops, the way my grandmother preferred.

Beyond the confines of the apartment, everyday life continued. A taxi drove slowly past the building, then quickly performed a U-turn and parked next to a fire hydrant while two middle-aged women laden with shopping bags clambered in. On the corner, a group of teenagers lingered, jostling one another as they waited to cross the street, the boys dressed in cargo pants and the girls in short skirts and fluorescent tops, undeclared uniforms of the young. High in the sky, a kite fluttered, its long tail pulling against the wind, and I watched it dive and soar in random patterns.

I wondered what to do. Only Grandmama could help me find the paintings. I could not push her any farther without risking a heart attack or worse, and since I did not know where they were stored, I could not take matters into my own hands. Stalemate.

CHAPTER 38

July 1991

When Paul and Michael returned on Sunday, I hugged them close.

"Stop, Mom. You're embarrassing me," Paul said, drawing away, although Michael continued to hug my waist as they waved good-bye to Jim and we proceeded into the house. In a little more than four weeks, Paul had grown, and both looked tanned and healthy. For the next hour, I listened to stories about living with their father, the summer baseball league they had joined, an enormous bass Michael had snagged fishing with his grandfather, new skateboards purchased with money earned clearing out their grandparents' basement, and outings with a woman called Miranda.

Though I assumed Miranda must be Jim's girlfriend, I chose not to ask about her. A twinge of regret pinched my heart, but who was I to pass judgment, having been attracted to Pierre since the moment we met. Time would reveal if this woman was someone special.

Almost immediately, the house resumed its clutter of skateboards and basketballs, thumping music and boisterous chatter. Nothing could have pleased me more. Nothing except having Pierre with me as well.

Before going to bed that night, I wrote him a letter, tearing up many sheets before being satisfied with the result. In it I explained that Grandpa's puzzle involved a terrible secret, which I felt bound to deal with immediately. I apologized for leaving so abruptly and told him I thought about him constantly and hoped to see him again as soon as possible. And I signed it *Love, Grace.*

I returned to work on Monday and immersed myself in merger activities at Colonial Insurance. When I left after five p.m. to rush into the city and visit my grandmother, Pierre's words followed me: a world with more soul. Was that what I wanted? Joan Patterson, the friend who had consoled and counseled me during the divorce process, called that evening to hear about my travels. When we got around to the topic of work, she said I deserved to do whatever was right for me.

"But that's the problem," I replied. "I don't know what's right for me. All my certainties have become unhinged. Maybe it's a delayed reaction to divorce. I really don't know. France has made me see things differently. I can't explain why."

"You'll sort it out, Gracie. You're a smart woman. Give yourself time."

Nights were lonely. I sat outside, pretending to read, or went for long, solitary walks thinking of Pierre, imagining his comings and goings and recalling the intimate details of how he lived. I wondered if he had found my earrings, slender gold hoops I normally reserved for evening wear. Only a few days earlier, I realized they were missing and remembered placing them on his bedside table the night before I solved Grandpa's puzzle.

"He probably threw them out," I muttered, ducking beneath a drooping willow overhanging the sidewalk.

I wondered if Pierre missed our conversations, the easy ebb and flow mingled with gentle teasing and intimate glances. On several occasions, I picked up the telephone, then replaced the receiver without pushing one button. He would soon have my letter; I would call after that.

Uncle Ben and I had dinner about ten days after Grandmama's heart incident. We met at his favorite restaurant on Mulberry Street, the kind of place you might choose to bypass because of its drab exterior unless you knew that the food was authentic and so delicious I always wished I could lick my plate.

"How's my best girl?" Ben said after I sat down. "Are you beginning to get over the divorce?"

I smiled. "Much better than I was the last time we got together."

"I said France would be good for you, didn't I? You're a charming woman. Trust me, you'll find someone else."

"That's a laugh. When you live in a little place like Maplewood and have worked at the same company for over fifteen years, finding someone is hard. You know, Ben, there's not one single man at Colonial who interests me. Married or otherwise."

"Give it time, sweetheart." He patted my hand and poured me a glass of wine. "What would you like? Luigi is bringing some calamari to get us started, and I'm having the scaloppine. The best in New York City." He paused for a minute while I scanned the menu and gave my order to the waiter hovering nearby. "Now tell me about your trip," he said. "Your grandmother had her shorts in a knot the whole time you were away."

I laughed. Ben loved old slang phrases. He said things like "Don't take any wooden nickels" or "She's the cat's meow" or "Don't cast a kitten," adding them to conversation more frequently after having a few drinks.

"You remember I told you about Grandpa's diaries?" Ben nodded. "Well, I went to many of the places Grandpa mentioned. It's so sad seeing the memorials and cemeteries in France and Belgium."

"I've been to some of them. Very sobering. And in World War Two, we did it all over again."

"Where did you serve?"

"Italy mainly. But we're not here to rehash my war experience. Did you ever tell your grandmother about the diaries?"

I didn't answer because our calamari arrived, steaming hot and smelling of garlic and spices. "Eat while it's hot," Ben said, and the next few minutes were occupied with chewing tender morsels of calamari cooked with finely chopped tomatoes, onion, and fennel and sprinkled with parsley, basil, and Parmesan cheese.

"Delicious." I set my fork down. "I'd better stop or I won't have room for the next course."

Ben chuckled. "I love this place. Luigi and I have history together. But back to my question about Cynthia. Did you tell her?"

"I did. She pretended to know all about them, so why would Grandpa have given them to me hidden in an old tackle box? It doesn't make sense."

"Maybe she's being cagey with you?"

"Could be. Grandpa wrote about the terrible things that happened. I'll have to show them to you. At the beginning, he was optimistic about what they could accomplish. By the end, he sounded like the war had destroyed him. I find it difficult to compare that man to the one I knew. Did he ever tell you anything about his experiences?"

Ben wiped his mouth and shifted his chair so he could cross his legs. He was sixty-nine, his hair almost white, his nose splayed with a spiderweb of veins that Grandmama often said was the result of too much drinking. Over the years, the thickness of his upper chest had settled into his belly, but he remained an attractive man, one who had never married but always had a woman in his life.

"Not really," Ben said. "It was 1946 when we met and he was in his early fifties. I was looking for a job. You know the story. I answered an ad in the newspaper for someone to learn how to keep the books at an art gallery. I was good at sums and needed a start. Planned to save some money and go back to school, but the art world got into my blood.

Your grandfather was what my mother called a real gem. My father was long gone, and Martin treated me almost like a son. When we parted company, he was disappointed, but I wanted to go out on my own. I suppose I was prepared to take more risks than he was." His mouth curled in a lopsided smile.

"And did you? Take risks, I mean."

Another lopsided smile. "I did. Moreover, we remained friends. I count your grandmother a friend too. Strange that he didn't want her to know he had given you the diaries."

"Did he have any secrets that you know of?"

Before Ben could reply, Luigi arrived with our main courses, and once more we settled into the business of eating. When he was growing up, Ben's family had very little money, and his mother worked two jobs to make ends meet. Ben was one of six children and food was a serious matter in the Portelli household, every morsel chewed with deliberation until nothing was left. Sometimes they went hungry. According to Grandpa, Ben's upbringing made him who he was.

Without any preamble, Ben resumed where we left off. "I don't know of any secrets your grandfather had. Working together all those years, we were pretty close."

"He was very fond of you," I said, and Ben smiled. "Can I tell you something?"

"Of course."

"While I was in France, someone was following me."

"Good God. What . . . why . . . why on earth would someone follow you?"

"I don't know. Well, I guess I do know. He wanted Grandpa's diaries. And that's just so strange to me, Ben. I can't imagine why someone would want them. I thought it must be Grandmama, although even that seems bizarre. But she denied having anything to do with it."

"Did you contact the police?"

"I did."

While we lingered over coffee, I told Ben all about the man with the straw fedora, including his demand for the diaries and the car accident.

"Christ, that's an incredible story. I'm so glad you're all right. Sounds like a very nasty character. And Cynthia denies having anything to do with it?"

"Vehemently. In fact, the second time I accused her was when she ended up having a heart episode."

"But who else could it be?"

"That's the sixty-four-thousand-dollar question."

CHAPTER 39

August 1991

Between five and six most days, I visited my grandmother. At first, she was too weak to talk, and I read snippets from the newspaper or one of the many magazines that arrived with her mail. As time wore on and I had apologized more than once for agitating her, I broached the subject of Grandpa's desire to return the paintings and read the entire letter aloud to her. She remained so still, her eyes shut and mouth slack, I thought she must have fallen asleep, but she winced when I read the part about their son's death and daughter's instability, and her fear of loving me.

Without warning, Grandmama started to speak. "He was right. I was harsh with you and demanding. And when I saw how you adored him, I was jealous. For a while, you caused a rift between us. I could see it developing, but I'm a stubborn woman, and I let that rift widen. I wasn't always that way, but time has a way of changing you.

"I grew up poor. Never destitute, although my parents had very little and nothing to spare for extras. But I knew about art. That's one thing Papa taught me. He let me watch him paint, if I was quiet and stayed very still—as still as a church mouse, he used to say. While he worked, he talked about subject matter and technique and colors. Oh, Grace, the colors." She widened her eyes as if seeing them once more. "And the way he put them on canvas, sometimes a stroke so fine the brush barely touched the surface. And then he would hurl himself at the picture and daub furiously, as though his body were possessed. It was dazzling to watch.

"Once, he painted me. I pretended to be a statue, hardly daring to breathe until my legs turned numb. I wonder where that painting is?" My grandmother's eyes opened wide again, as if expecting me to know the answer. Then she closed them and resumed talking. "On summer Sundays, we took his paints to the park, and Mother would watch him work while I looked after my brothers and sisters. She always loved him. Before I married your grandfather, she said I would be fortunate if I loved him as much as she loved my father. And I did then."

Philomena's head peeked around the doorway, and I waved her away.

"What about the war, Grandmama?" I kept my voice low, almost a whisper.

"The war. The war almost destroyed Martin. When we were together the second time, I thought he could hang on. The Germans were starting to fail, and people said only a few months to go. Then Jane was killed. Her death was the worst blow. He thought it should have been him. 'How could my sister die, but not me?' he said over and over. I remember . . ." A frown crossed her face, and she closed her eyes once more. "I'm tired, Grace."

"That's all right. We can talk more tomorrow." I smoothed the covers and stooped to kiss her cheek before leaving the room.

The following day was much the same. Grandmama talked and I listened, wishing I had a tape recorder to capture the stories word for word. With a hint of pink in her cheeks, she lay on the sofa, propped against two pillows, looking like a china doll. She wore a long, blue dressing gown, and her eyes were bright.

"You were talking about Jane's death and Grandpa's visit to see you. Didn't Jane die after Grandpa's visit?"

My grandmother looked confused. "Jane. Jane. Jane," she said. "Yes, you're right. She died after his visit. Maybe August. I think it was August."

I nodded encouragement.

"I never met her. Martin said you looked like her, but he wouldn't have any pictures of her in the house. He told me he couldn't stand the guilt of being the one who lived. After Jane died, he wrote to me, and I knew he was in a dreadful state. And then for a while, his letters stopped. I thought he was dead or wounded, and since no one knew that I was his sweetheart, I'd never know what happened. I didn't know what else to do, so I kept on writing, and I heard from him again in October. I remember as though it was yesterday. My mother brought the letter to me, and she was smiling, such a brilliant smile. And there was his handwriting. Black ink on a blue envelope."

"What did he say?"

"He said it was a bad patch. And he was sorry to have worried me. But he also said I would be better off without him. How could he have said that? I refused to believe him and kept writing to him as before. When he finally returned to England, he was in a dreadful state."

"The last diary entry is April 4, 1919, so he must have landed in England in early April. Is that right, Grandmama?"

Clutching a fold in her dressing gown, her blue veins pulsing like a burrowing animal, my grandmother ignored my question. "He wrote that I should not come to the dock, but Lucy said I should surprise him. When he walked down the ramp, he didn't see me at first, but I could see him, with his thin cheeks and slumped shoulders, wearing a uniform that was far too big. He didn't wave or smile. When I rushed over, all he said was, 'I told you not to come.'"

I took her hand, feeling the cool loose skin, and touched each gnarled finger, along with the sapphire-and-diamond ring next to my grandmother's simple wedding band. "I'm sure he didn't mean that."

"He did. I know he did. He stayed in London, not because I pleaded with him, but because he couldn't face his family. Not with Jane gone. I assured him his parents loved him and always would. I didn't know what to do. I knew he should return to his family, but I couldn't let him go. Not like that.

"I thought once he was out of uniform he would start to put the war behind him. Instead, he wore a different uniform: white shirt, gray trousers, and a tattered sweater with two missing buttons. When I offered to fix the buttons, he glared at me and shook his head.

"Occasionally he wrote to William Nullford. Martin said the man had been his sergeant. And he wrote to Michel Diotte, one of the other lieutenants in his original battalion. I think he wanted to be in touch with others who had survived, but he never told me much about them. We visited Michel in Toronto after your grandfather and I married, and I think seeing him helped. But for the most part, when he was in London after the war, all Martin did was smoke and stare and pick at his fingernails, and every afternoon he disappeared for hours."

"Where did he go?"

"He was incensed when I asked and wouldn't tell me, so one day I followed him." A bewildered look crossed her face. "He went to a veterans' hospital where a man called Butler used to be."

"Captain Butler?"

"Yes." She cocked her head. "Martin's diaries must disclose a lot."

"They do. Would you like me to read them to you?"

"No. I don't think so. I don't think I could bear it."

"What did he tell you about Captain Butler?"

"Nothing at first. Eventually, after he showed me the paintings, he disclosed Alan Butler's suicide."

I held a hand to my mouth. "Oh no. That wasn't in his diaries. Grandpa must have been devastated."

"He was. But he kept on going to that hospital. He said the officers there understood him and the pain of survival." She closed her eyes.

While I waited for my grandmother to continue, I watched a billowing cloud form and re-form. Grandmama had agreed to have the curtains open that day, a change I thought hinted at improvement. She had even allowed me to rub cream on her hands and arms, a task Philomena normally performed. Traffic stopped and stuttered on the streets below, and an ambulance wailed in the distance.

"You look tired, Grandmama. I'll come back tomorrow, and we can talk about the paintings."

"Stay. Just sit with me a little longer. I'm going to die soon. Then you can do whatever you want with them."

"Don't say that. Besides, you're the only one who can tell me where they are. What happened, Grandmama? I need to know."

"You don't *need* to know. You *want* to know."

I smiled. I had missed that haughty, scoffing tone. Perhaps Grandmama was getting better. "You're right. I want to know. Please."

"Will you be staying for dinner, Miss Grace?" Philomena came into the living room with a glass of water and three pills in her left hand. "Time for your pills, Miz Cynthia."

"I have already had my pills, and they're so large I can hardly swallow them."

"That was yesterday, Miz Cynthia. Be good, or the doctor will be upset with you."

"Fiddle-faddle. I can do whatever I want."

"Leave them with me, Philomena. I'll give them to Grandmama. But I can't stay too much longer. I promised to take the boys shopping for clothes."

Philomena left the room like a stately battleship, accompanied by the rustle of stockings and thump of thick-soled shoes. I set the glass of water and pills down on the coffee table and waited, hands folded in my lap.

"Oh, all right. You'll just pester me until I tell the story, won't you?"

"Mm-hmm."

"This is all so long ago. Hardly relevant now." Grandmama leaned back against the chair and closed her eyes. "I suppose he would want me to tell you." Phlegm rattled in her throat as she sighed. "For weeks after he came back, I didn't know how to get through to him. I tried everything and finally I convinced him to make love to me. I thought being intimate would help somehow. Instead, I became pregnant. Your grandfather was furious. He said I had tricked him, but nothing could have been farther from the truth. I was frantic. Not even twenty-one and pregnant by a man who acted in no way like the one I had fallen in love with. What would you have done?" She opened her eyes for a moment to glare at me, as if I were in some way responsible. "I said he had to marry me, and that's when he showed me the paintings. He said I could have them, that they must be worth something and would see me through the pregnancy. I asked him, what then? And he said I could give the baby away and start fresh. Our baby, he wanted to give our baby away.

"I knew the paintings were excellent. They were French landscapes full of color and motion. One showed a windmill on a hill, another had a young couple gazing at the sea. Beautiful compositions. When your grandfather was out one day, I took them to a friend of Papa's, who said they were by an artist named Luras and worth a lot of money. So I made a plan. I pleaded with Martin to marry me. After the wedding, we left England and visited his parents. I thought we would settle there, but Toronto had too many painful memories for your grandfather, so we came to New York. He used to say a person could reinvent himself in New York. And we did, I suppose. I left behind my upbringing, and he left behind the war. But we needed money to get started, and although his family was comfortable, they didn't have the kind of money to help us out. So I convinced Martin to use the paintings as collateral for a loan. Day after day, I badgered him until he agreed. Mother would have called it a bargain with the devil if she had known the truth.

"For a while, I was the strong one. I kept us going that first year or so. And then, after your uncle Lucas died, he kept me going."

"Oh, Grandmama. What a sad story. He loved you. I know he did."

She nodded. "And I loved him. But we had a lot of sadness. Life was not easy." She wiped a tear from her cheek. "Enough of that. Now you know the story."

"But what about the paintings? Where are they, Grandmama?"

"It's complicated, and you've tired me out. I'll finish the story tomorrow. I need to rest now. Give me my pills, will you, dear? Philomena will be upset if I don't take them."

There was no point in pressing her. My grandmother was too stubborn. I would just have to wait another day. After getting her pills, I kissed her brow, and she squeezed my hand.

Driving home, I tried to imagine a young Cynthia, pregnant and in love, desperate to salvage her relationship. For a woman who was normally brusque and domineering, her candor had been surprising. I wondered whether the paintings had been worth the cost.

The following morning, heat shimmered on city streets and hovered over the Hudson River, where seagulls rested on worn pilings and motorboats trailed white froth in their wakes. Although many bikers were out, it was too early for sailboats or kayakers, and the river looked peaceful, almost sleepy. I knew Grandmama would still be eating breakfast, but I was anxious to hear about the paintings, and afterward I could decide what to do about Pierre.

Philomena was dressed in yellow with lipstick in a shade I can only describe as purple. Slices of orange and kiwi were arranged on a plate, and the toaster popped a moment after I entered. Ever since Grandmama's heart had acted up, Philomena had moved into the spare room so she could be on hand at night; just a temporary precaution, the doctor said, overriding my grandmother's protestations.

"What are you doing here so early? I've barely had time for juice, and you know I like to eat breakfast in peace."

I had invented a story for this very question. "I know, Grandmama, but I promised to take the boys to a baseball game, and I have to be back by noon, so it seemed sensible to come now. I'll just have a cup of coffee while you eat."

She gave me a withering look, turning her lips into a wrinkled prune in the process.

"All right, but don't pester me until I finish eating."

I tried to look innocent as I took a mug from the rack beside the sink and helped myself to Philomena's coffee—a rich brew with a hint of vanilla—while listening to the rhythmic scrape of knife on toast. Grandmama took small bites and chewed each one as though she had all the time in the world. I remember her telling me once that chewing thoroughly and drinking lots of water were the best things anyone could do for their nutrition. I poured a small amount of cream into my coffee and wondered if my patience would hold.

My grandmother lingered over her breakfast for at least forty minutes, and before setting out for groceries, Philomena poured each of us another cup of coffee. Since this was my third cup, I was beginning to feel edgy.

"You were going to tell me where the paintings are, Grandmama."

"Well, the truth is, I don't know."

I set my mug down with a clatter. "What do you mean, you don't know?"

"I told you yesterday that it was complicated." She wore a look of anxious uncertainty.

I took a deep breath to contain myself. "I'm sorry, Grandmama. I'll try not to interrupt again. Please just tell me what you know."

Grandmama stared off into the distance. "At one point, the paintings hung in our living room on Second Avenue. But your grandfather insisted on moving them before a journalist came to the apartment to interview him. He was supposed to be some sort of expert on European landscapes, and Martin feared he might recognize the artist, so we hung them in our bedroom instead. I loved looking at them and insisted they be somewhere I could see them. One evening, I came home late from the opera . . . no, I think it was the symphony. Yes, the symphony. At any rate, it doesn't really matter where I was. When I went into the bedroom to change, the paintings were gone.

"I was furious with Martin. How could he take them away without telling me? They were our good-luck charms. But no matter how much I pestered him, he would not tell me where he put them."

"But you must have some inkling where they are, Grandmama. You must."

Grandmama was tapping her fingers on the table, and I stared at her, attempting to determine whether she was telling the truth.

"No, I don't have any idea. It's the one secret he took to his grave."

I shook my head. Unbelievable. After so many weeks trying to solve the puzzle and another long wait to hear my grandmother's story, I still didn't know where the paintings were.

CHAPTER 40

August 1991

On Sunday, I took Michael and his friend Timmy to the local fair. Though rain threatened all afternoon, the boys were oblivious, caught in the thrall of rides that flipped them upside down, rolled them sideways, and made them shout with delight. When it was almost six and they had each earned a prize at the shooting gallery, I convinced them to leave by promising pizza for dinner. Turning down our street, I caught a glimpse of Paul pacing the driveway.

"You need to go to the hospital right away," he said. "Nana had a heart attack. Philomena is with her. I called Dad. I was going to take the train into New York, but he said to wait here for you."

I clutched a hand to my mouth. "Oh no. When did it happen?"

"Early afternoon. You go to the hospital. Michael and I will be fine by ourselves."

"Thanks, sweetie, but I might have to stay all night. Give me a moment to think." As I rushed into the house, I called over my shoulder. "You two walk Timmy home. I'll phone your father."

Rain broke as I emerged from the Holland Tunnel, thick drops that drummed hard against the roof and obscured the view ahead such that motorists slowed to a crawl. Puddles spread as water gathered too quickly for the city's drains. New York streets were always congested, but with pedestrians running for shelter and taxis double-parked to let passengers in and out, they became a nightmare. I watched the traffic light turn red once again and calculated it would be another ten minutes before crossing the intersection. The hospital was still many blocks away.

I turned on the radio, punching the preprogrammed buttons, rejecting rock and roll, talk stations, and show tunes until I found one playing jazz. My left leg jostled in time to the music as I inched the car forward. "I could've walked faster than this," I muttered.

Room 504 was on the west side of the hospital, past the nursing station and opposite a door marked *Showers for Patients Only*. Philomena was waiting in the corridor, and I stepped into her arms for a brief, fierce hug. Inside the room, two nurses and a young-looking doctor surrounded my grandmother's bed. An instrument panel showed three lines—one red, one green, one blue—recording the rhythms of Grandmama's heart. Her eyes were closed. She wore an oxygen mask and looked tiny and fragile and very pale.

"How is she?" I asked after introducing myself.

"Stable," said the doctor, a sturdy woman with curly hair. She turned to look at me. "We've just had a little scare. But she's rallied." The doctor issued a few instructions to the nurses and gestured for me to follow her into the hall.

"Her housekeeper was very smart. She called an ambulance straightaway, gave Mrs. Devlin nitroglycerin, and brought all her medications along, which made our job easier. I've spoken with Dr. Williams, so we're aware of her condition. Given her age, I'm not optimistic, but I've seen others recover from this sort of attack."

"You mean she might not make it."

The doctor nodded. "I'm sorry to be so blunt. I'll be back in an hour to check again."

I opened the door, then shut it behind me, taking care to make as little noise as possible. Drawing a chair close to the bed, I sank into it. Philomena stood beside me and squeezed my shoulder.

"She's been asking for you."

"I took Michael to the fair. If I'd known, I would have been here sooner." I held my grandmother's hand. "Thank you for being here with her. She would have hated being alone."

"The attack came on suddenly. One minute, she was telling me what she wanted for dinner, and the next minute . . ." Philomena made a vague gesture and reached for her handkerchief.

Grandmama did not move. As time passed, we listened to the hiss of oxygen and the slow click-click of the heart monitor. Occasionally, a nurse came in to check the instruments, noting a few numbers on the chart that dangled at the foot of the bed. At nine, I convinced Philomena to go home and left my grandmother briefly to get a sandwich and call the boys. Jim answered the phone and assured me that he would stay all night if necessary.

"Is Cynthia all right?" he said.

"Hooked up to various machines. She seems to be sleeping. Do you think that's a good sign?" I didn't wait for Jim's response. "She hasn't said a word."

When I returned, nothing had changed, and in between bites of sandwich, I carried on a one-way dialogue with Grandmama, occasionally patting her hand or smoothing her brow.

With no recollection of falling asleep, I was startled when a bell began to ring, its insistent chime bringing first one nurse, then another, and then the doctor to the room. I stood aside as they gathered around the bed, feeling helpless and fearful among the instruments and acronyms and sharp medical language. One of the nurses administered a needle into Grandmama's arm while the doctor listened with a stethoscope. The second hand of a wall-mounted clock measured time as if the world were spinning in slow motion. When the doctor turned away from the bed and put the stethoscope back into her pocket, I knew my grandmother was gone.

CHAPTER 41

August 1991

The funeral was a solemn occasion attended by many in the art community and the handful of Grandmama's close friends who were still
alive, as well as a few of mine. My mother was also there, a befuddled
presence who remained glamorous, and Jim attended as well. I was
surprised at how pleased I felt to have him sit in the front pew with our
two sons, my mother, and me. I knew his presence would have pleased
Grandpa, though Grandmama would have said something less than
kind. Dressed in suits and ties, Paul and Michael suddenly looked older,
and I found myself imagining a time when they would be all grown up
and I would be alone.

Before the service began, people had congregated in the foyer, and
every time the door opened, I looked up, hoping against all reason to
see Pierre. Not only was there less than an infinitesimal chance he would
have seen the notice of her death, but also we had not spoken since I
left Amiens almost six weeks ago. I had called once and left a message
saying I hoped to hear from him. And I called to let him know about
my grandmother, but he wasn't there that time either. I knew my hope
was futile, but hope I did.

Philomena joined us in the front pew. I told her she was family and Grandmama would want her with us, and she hugged me hard before sitting down.

"I miss her so much, Grace. What am I going to do with my days now that she's gone?"

"Maybe it's time to retire. Have you thought of that?"

"I surely can't retire yet. I'm only seventy-two."

"Let's talk about it later. The minister is about to begin."

"That's a fine idea. And I have something to talk to you about as well."

I had steeled myself for the funeral and the reception that would follow, determined to remain composed, just as my grandmother had at Grandpa's funeral. It was only three days since she died, and during that time I had alternated between efficiency and tears, the tears arriving at totally unexpected moments. *She's gone,* I told myself over and over. *Never coming back.* Whenever that thought occurred to me, fresh tears erupted. Despite her brusque ways and criticisms, I loved my grandmother. Now there was no one to anchor me to my childhood, no one who loved me as unconditionally as she and Grandpa had.

The reception was held in the church hall, a spacious room next to the nave that allowed easy mingling, where the church ladies served tea and tiny sandwiches along with an assortment of desserts. Sally Rockford cornered me early on, and I was grateful for the way she made me laugh with stories of my grandmother's more outrageous antics. Although Sally's glass looked like water, I knew it was straight vodka. Still, she was only a little tipsy, the ice rattling as she waved her hand back and forth with yet another tale. Ben Portelli was a reassuring presence, acting almost like a host as he helped greet the guests so I could make the rounds, listening to anecdotes and thanking people for their kindnesses.

Almost everyone had left, and I was talking with Ben when Philomena approached.

"A fine funeral, Grace. Your grandmother would have been pleased."

"Thank you, Philomena."

"You know, I've been thinking about what my mother said after her father's funeral."

"What was that?"

"She said death is like reading a long book, and suddenly it's over, and the friends you made while reading are gone."

"I never thought of it that way. I'm so glad you were her friend."

Philomena laid her hand on my arm. "Before I go, I have something important to tell you."

"I'll leave you two to chat," Ben said, stepping away to speak with Jim, who was waiting patiently to drive us home.

"Your grandfather left me something to give you after your grandmother's death."

"He did?" Could this be a final clue to the paintings' whereabouts? "What is it?"

"I don't know. He left it in a sealed envelope. But I can bring it over to the apartment the next time you're in the city."

"I'm coming by this Saturday and Sunday, if that's convenient. But I could drop in at your apartment instead to save you the trouble."

"There's no need for that. Besides, I want to see the apartment one more time and return my key. Now make sure you get some rest. You're looking too pale for my liking."

Settling my grandmother's estate would require endless meetings and mounds of paperwork over the months ahead, and I wondered whether my boss would allow further flexibility. Like a transplanted flower, the merger was beginning to blossom on its own, my role in it almost complete. In a few months, I could step aside, and in the meantime, I could consider my options. My time in France and now Grandmama's death made me see life differently.

Money was no longer a reason to work. Grandmama's will made it clear that the entire estate would come to me, aside from an annuity my grandfather set up twenty years ago to look after my mother, along with a generous bequest for Philomena. My share of the gallery was estimated in excess of five hundred thousand, and the apartment would sell for well over a million. Though significant, these amounts paled in comparison to my grandparents' personal art collection. The painting that hung above the living room mantel alone was valued at two hundred fifty thousand dollars.

"You're a very wealthy woman," John Thurman, my grandmother's lawyer, said as he and I accompanied an art appraiser through the apartment and John recorded each estimate in his leather notebook. After the living and dining rooms, the tally was over two million.

I had rarely considered my grandparents' wealth. During childhood, the topic of money was discouraged—there are some things you just don't talk about, Grandpa would say. To fit in at college, I bought inexpensive clothing and secondhand items, much to my grandmother's annoyance. Once Jim and I married, we adopted the cheap and cheerful lifestyle of other young couples and declined offers of assistance from my grandfather. We wanted to make it on our own.

And now I never needed to worry about money again. But the question of my future remained.

Before Grandmama passed away, my thoughts had turned to the gallery. When Grandpa retired, he sold sixty percent of the business, and I'd already made a discreet inquiry through a third party to see if the majority shareholders might consider selling. I kept this possibility to myself and was still waiting for an answer.

One person I could talk to about the gallery was Ben; he knew so much about that world and my grandparents' past. We met at the Bull & Bear, another of his favorite restaurants. As I passed through the sumptuous lobby of the Waldorf Astoria, I wondered how many deals had been made over lunch or dinner at this particular restaurant, a meeting place for businessmen since the early thirties. Polished wood paneling and shiny brass fittings along with discreet tables covered in navy linens reassured patrons of their importance. The Bull & Bear was a man's choice.

"There you are." Ben rose to greet me as I approached his corner table. "Julian will get you a drink. What would you like?"

Julian held the chair, sliding it forward as I sat down. I turned to him and smiled. "I'll have the same as Mr. Portelli."

"Certainly, madame." Julian nodded and slipped away.

"Since when do you drink Campari?"

"I've never tried it, but maybe it's time for something different. I'm feeling adventurous these days."

"Must have been that trip to France. You haven't shared any of the details. Did you have fun?"

"I did," I said, allowing a small smile to touch the corners of my mouth. *Other than being followed and leaving Pierre furious with me,* I thought. "I'm so glad you had time to meet. I want your advice. I'm trying to decide what to do about the gallery, and that's not an easy decision. I keep asking myself what Grandpa would want."

"He always hoped you would take it over. After you went into the insurance business, he would mutter to me sometimes about wasting your talents. He thought you had such a good eye for art and could charm just about anyone." Ben held up his hand when I began to protest. "I know there were valid reasons. Didn't I encourage you? But now it's different."

My drink arrived, and Ben offered a toast. "To Cynthia," he said. "A feisty grande dame."

"To Cynthia," I echoed. "*Feisty* is a good word for her."

Ben smiled. "Yup. Bet your ass, she was. Now tell me about the gallery."

"I've been in touch with Ian Whittaker and Brian Smiley," I said, mentioning the majority owners.

"You have? That was quick work. Are you going to make them an offer?"

"I'm thinking about it. I'll need help to learn how to run it."

"Whittaker and Smiley might be prepared to stay on as advisers," Ben said. "They've run it well, and they'll want compensation for that. Let me ask around to see if I can find out approximately what the gallery's worth. You'll want a professional appraisal, of course, but it doesn't hurt to be prepared."

All through dinner, we talked about the business of running a gallery, and I was surprised at how knowledgeable Ben was about valuation, attracting top artists, securing international deals, and marketing. At one point, I started taking notes, and I'd filled four pages by the end of our conversation.

"This has been amazing," I said, lifting a cup of espresso to my lips. I took a sip. "Doesn't taste like the ones I had in France."

"Never been a fan," Ben said. "Too strong for me. Anyway, I'm glad I could help. Let me know how things proceed. You must be inundated with lawyers these days. Have you decided what to do with the apartment? It's probably worth a bundle." He rubbed his hands together.

"I hope you're right. I thought about keeping it, but with the boys still in school, it doesn't make sense, so I'm going to put it on the market. Lots to clear out before I do. That's what I'm planning to do this weekend."

A man with long sideburns—the kind that had gone out of style ages ago—stopped at our table to say hello to Ben. After introducing him as a fellow art lover, Ben excused himself for a brief conversation.

"And what are you planning for your grandparents' art collection?" he said when he returned. "I'm sure I could get you a ton of dough for some of them."

I laughed. "I'm sure you could. But I'm not ready to sell any of them. Not yet. And there are a few Grandpa had that I can't find." Though I hadn't disclosed the missing paintings to anyone except Grandmama, I thought Ben, given his long association with my grandfather, might know of them. I knew I could trust his discretion.

"Really? How do you know?"

"Grandpa left me . . . he left me a letter."

"Wow. That sounds mysterious."

"It does, doesn't it? You know a lot about landscapes. Do you remember Grandpa having any by an artist called Luras?"

"Luras? Hmm. French, I think. I've heard of him, but not in connection with your grandfather's collection. Are those the missing ones?"

"They are."

"I could make some inquiries."

"No need for that. I'm sure they'll turn up."

CHAPTER 42

August 1991

Convinced my grandfather wouldn't ask me to return the paintings without providing a clue to their whereabouts, I planned to use the weekend after the funeral to do a thorough search of the apartment. Philomena promised to drop by Saturday afternoon.

Around six on Friday, I left Paul and Michael at Jim's. With a slow-down in the tunnel, it was almost seven thirty by the time I arrived at the apartment. After disabling the security alarm and turning on a few lights, I carried a small suitcase to my old bedroom, footsteps echoing along the hallway. Without Grandmama and Philomena, the space felt deserted, its mood flat and lonely.

Returning to the front hall, I took a cooler of fresh food to the kitchen, placing several items in the fridge. Bread, tomatoes, and bananas I put on the counter along with a bottle of wine. Then, with a frozen pizza in the oven, I poured myself a glass of Merlot and walked into the living room. Two real estate agents were coming the following weekend to appraise the apartment, and I wanted to tone down the heavy, overdecorated look.

Art dominated the living room. Eighteenth-century oils mixed with twentieth-century watercolors and Oriental scrolls nearly five hundred years old; Russian, French, Chinese, Japanese, British, and American painters coexisted in careful arrangements designed to look random. Some referred to the Devlin personal collection as stunning; for me, each piece was like a longtime friend.

My favorite was a small Pahari depicting three women with slender waists and long hair dancing in the moonlight. When Grandpa had hung the picture, I had been mesmerized by the exotic women dressed in flowing garments and the jeweled elephant dancing nearby. Now, I stood in front of it for a long while, appreciating the delicate shapes, graceful movement, and dramatic colors. This one I would never sell.

Wineglass in hand, I turned once more to my task. Since the living room had far too much furniture and decorative accents, it was the obvious place to begin. In its current state, it looked as though Grandmama had decided to surround herself with every expensive piece of furniture she'd ever purchased. I wanted the room to feel spacious and quickly identified three chairs, a footstool covered in needlepoint, a lacquered chest, and two ornate tables as surplus and put red stickers on those items for easy identification. An antiques dealer promised to take the surplus furniture tomorrow, so I needed to work quickly.

"Less is more," I muttered as the kitchen timer announced that the pizza was done.

By the time I finished three slices and two glasses of wine, many items in the dining room and living room sported red stickers, and I was tired. My watch showed ten p.m., enough time to tackle the guest room before bed. I would clear my grandmother's bedroom and my own tomorrow morning. Grandpa's library would be last.

After a restless night, I got up at six and made a piece of toast and cup of tea and took them to what was once my bedroom, attempting to view it through the eyes of a potential buyer rather than those of the young woman who last occupied it. Two windows covered with paisley curtains looked down on an enclosed courtyard. The room looked tired and dated.

Munching toast, I stared at a row of books. The *Oxford English Dictionary*—according to Grandmama, the only proper dictionary—sat among a collection of coming-of-age novels, including *The Catcher in the Rye* and *Anne Frank: The Diary of a Young Girl*, works questioning society like *The Fountainhead* and *1984*, and several other novels, plus a selection by Agatha Christie chosen for sheer pleasure. I thought of the summer I had turned fifteen and read *Gone with the Wind* over an entire weekend, and *Valley of the Dolls*, my first book containing explicit sex, which I had kept hidden beneath a pile of shoeboxes for more than a year. At the far end of one shelf, *Curious George*, *Babar*, and *Winnie-the-Pooh* reminded me of bedtime stories. That my grandmother had been sentimental enough to keep these reminders of my childhood brought tears to my eyes.

I tagged the bookshelf and desk with red stickers and made a mental note to purchase a bedspread and curtains to freshen the room, then placed the storybooks and the dictionary in a box of mementos to take to Maplewood.

Grandmama's room was next. Although Philomena had removed my grandmother's clothing, her jewelry and other personal things remained. After pouring myself a second cup of tea, I took a deep breath and began.

Finding an array of small boxes lining the shelf in Grandmama's cupboard, I opened one and discovered a bundle of letters. The second, third, and fourth boxes also contained letters, each one seemingly in its original envelope. I put these aside to peruse at a later time.

Over the next few hours, I sifted through photo albums full of unfamiliar faces, receipts and bills with dates as long ago as 1928, a collection of city maps, medical insurance claims, books, costume jewelry, fans and hat pins and brooches, theater tickets, notepaper, warranties, and a box full of my mother's school papers. In the bedside table, I found Grandmama's appointment calendars from 1970 to 1991.

Twenty years of theater outings, luncheons, gallery showings, parties, doctor appointments, and other events that had filled her life. A set of small books spanning no more than eighteen inches when lined up one by one.

Flipping the pages of this year's calendar, I noticed one of the last entries was *SR at OB 1:00 p.m. SR* would be her longtime friend Sally Rockford, and *OB* likely referred to the Oyster Bar, a favorite restaurant because Sally loved their oversized martinis. *BP* also showed up several times, and I assumed the initials referred to Ben Portelli. Occasionally, she wrote a name or place in full. It saddened me to think of reducing someone's existence to a series of one- or two-hour outings.

After the antiques dealer had come and gone, removing all the red-sticker items, I rearranged what remained, creating spaces for individual pieces to gain prominence rather than being lost in the clutter. As I worked, I kept a tight rein on my emotions. When I caught myself daydreaming about childhood, a memory prompted by a gold-rimmed vase or a piece of china shaped like a lady's shoe or my grandfather's antique horse brasses, I shook my head and quickly wrapped the piece in paper. My grandparents were gone, their era dying with them. My mother was gone too, though her body still lived. I felt like an orphan.

I went for a brisk walk to get away from the feeling that Grandmama disapproved of what I was doing. My head clamored with imagined criticisms and my own silent replies, and I was weary of such thoughts. When I returned, I went to the library.

For years, Grandmama had refused all offers to help cull Grandpa's files, contained in a wooden credenza and two matching filing cabinets. Although the task felt daunting, I was buoyed at the prospect of discovering clues about the missing paintings. To begin, I opened each drawer in turn: tax forms, financial statements, bank statements, receipts, insurance information, invoices organized alphabetically, and an entire drawer devoted to the gallery. I found a file labeled *LILY* with report cards and swimming certificates, piano awards, school photos, and a few letters written in a childish scrawl. Such poignant reminders of my mother's frailty made me weep.

As I returned my mother's file, an idea took shape. *If Grandpa kept a file on my mother, he might have kept a file on the paintings.*

I opened the top drawer again, lifting each file folder one by one, working on the premise that my grandfather would have disguised the name of any such folder with clues intended only for me. Behind a folder labeled *ENGLAND*, I found one labeled *Nineteenth Battalion* and searched page by page, article by article, from front to back before concluding that it held no secrets.

I closed that drawer and opened the one below, the drawer full of gallery files with faded labels. For someone as organized as my grandfather, I was surprised that these files were in no particular order; files by artist mingled with files by painting, none of them alphabetical. I checked each one until my eyes felt dry and scratchy and then, hiding in the open, found a file labeled *CHUMLEY PARK*.

"Grandpa, why did you make it so difficult?"

I knew the answer: Grandpa wanted to keep the information from Grandmama. The more disorganized he left his files, the less likely she would be to conduct a thorough review. I took a deep breath. *Slow down, Grace. Slow down.*

Within the Chumley Park folder, Grandpa had enclosed each item in individual plastic sleeves. The item on top was a picture of four young men, on the back of which my grandfather had written *Bill Jackson, Pete Van Leuven, Michel Diotte, and Martin Devlin, May 1915*—the same picture as the one he'd left in the tackle box. Bill was short and stocky with dimples in each cheek, while Pete was the tallest with fair hair and an angular face. Michel was thin, his dark looks and even features making him the most handsome of the group. Two dead, one crippled for life, and one burdened forever by survival.

Behind the picture of these young men was one of a solid, utilitarian building sitting among wide, sweeping lawns. Grandpa had written *Chumley Park* on the back. Next, I found a postcard from a small hotel in London and a cocktail napkin stamped with the figure of Mercury surrounded by the words *MERCURY BAR* in swirling script; a touch of faded red that might have been lipstick marked one corner. Other sleeves contained train tickets and restaurant receipts, a photo of my grandmother taken in a park, a letter from someone called Anne Gibson, a faded copy of my grandparents' marriage certificate, and the birth record for my uncle, who had died when he was two. Finally, at the very back, I found an envelope. Written in block letters was the word *AUFFRET*. Nothing else, just *AUFFRET*.

Taking care to preserve the envelope, I opened it and extracted a few sheets of paper. One was an article about the Auffret family dated 1980, on the occasion of the death of Philippe Auffret. Another, dated October 1920, contained an appraisal of the four paintings. Clipped behind that was a copy of a bank loan also dated October 1920. And finally, a handwritten letter from my grandfather.

The telephone rang. I looked up. No one except Philomena, Jim, and the boys knew I was here. A second ring. *If it's important, they'll call back later,* I thought, and began to read.

> *My dear Grace,*
> *I know it will be you reading this letter, for your grand-*
> *mother would never have the patience to go through my*
> *files. A trait upon which I am depending. I assume too*
> *that you have solved the diary puzzle. If not, then you*
> *need to know I found the paintings referred to in this en-*
> *velope during the war and kept them rather than return-*
> *ing them to their rightful owners, the Auffret family. You*
> *might say that I stole them, an act which I have regretted*
> *for more than fifty years.*
> *You will find—*

I stopped and lifted my head. Someone was knocking on the door, and I thought I heard my name being called. A male voice. *Strange. Who on earth would come to Grandmama's apartment?* As I walked down the hall, the voice grew louder and more familiar. Frowning, I pushed a strand of hair behind one ear and peeked through the peephole. Eyes wide with astonishment, I keyed in the alarm code and opened the door.

Pierre stood there, slightly disheveled, as though he had just awakened from a nap, but otherwise exactly as I remembered, exactly as I recalled every night before going to sleep. I wanted to reach out my arms and feel the warmth of him.

"What . . . what are you doing here?" I said.

He stepped into the apartment and pulled me close. The familiarity of his embrace felt exquisite. Except for my sons, no one I cared about had held me since my grandmother's death, and I allowed myself to rest against him, absorb his strength, and think of nothing.

"*Mon Dieu,* I've missed you," he said.

"I can't believe you're here. In New York. But why are you here?"

"I had your message about your grandmother's death and knew how upset you would be. When I arrived, you were not at your home, so I persuaded your neighbor to tell me where to find you."

"You came all this way because of my grandmother?"

"No. Not really. That was merely the excuse. I came all this way because of you. But that doesn't mean I'm not upset with you for leaving."

"You have every right to be upset." His arms were still around me. "I behaved badly. I should have disclosed everything. I'm so sorry, Pierre. You have no idea how often I've regretted that. But . . . but I have something to show you. It's about the puzzle I was working on."

"Are you still obsessed with that puzzle? I have come all this way, and you want to talk about a puzzle." He sounded insulted.

I shook my head. I was done with secrets and the havoc they wreaked. This man was too important to me to keep secrets from him anymore. "It's about your grandfather's paintings. They're the reason I returned to New York."

"My grandfather's paintings?"

"Come with me." I pulled him by the hand. "First, you need to see the puzzle I solved at your house."

Once in the library, I gave him the letter I'd decoded and watched the growing look of confusion on his face as he read it. I knew exactly when he came across his family name because Pierre's eyes went back and forth and back again as he gripped the paper. His head lifted, his eyes demanding a response.

"I had no idea. You have to believe me, Pierre. Truly, I had no idea until I solved that puzzle."

With a curt nod, he returned to reading, then nodded again when he came to the end of Martin's letter.

"My grandfather's paintings," he said in a thin, confused voice. "I can't believe it."

"Here's another letter. I was beginning to read it when you knocked on the door." I stood beside him so we could both see Martin's writing. Pierre smelled of aftershave and another scent that reminded me of his home.

> . . . you will find the paintings in a special stor-
> age facility that is temperature and humidity controlled.
> Philomena has the key. And there's a tackle box stored in
> your attic with additional information. The Auffret fam-
> ily used to live in northern France near Lille, although I
> have no idea where to find the descendants.

"Locked away in a storage locker for . . ." Pierre looked at the date on the letter and shook his head, "for more than fifteen years. Unbelievable. Who is this person called Philomena?"

I touched his arm. "She's been our maid since I was a little girl. And she's promised to come over this afternoon with an envelope Grandpa left in her keeping. I hope it's the key to the storage locker." I checked my watch. "That's strange. She should have been here by now."

CHAPTER 43

August 1991

I called Philomena immediately, but her telephone just rang and rang. We waited an hour and called again. No answer. In between calls, I told Pierre everything I knew, including Grandmama's revelations and the hidden documents contained in my grandfather's files. Around seven o'clock, I suggested we make dinner.

"I'm sure there's a reason why she didn't come today. I'll call again after dinner, and if I still don't reach her, we can go to her apartment tomorrow. And then . . ."

"And then what?"

Pierre's gaze searched my face, and I looked away. "And then I can ask you to forgive me."

"I do forgive you. I came to New York because I finally admitted to myself that you must have had an important reason to leave without telling me why, and I needed to know what that was."

I took his hand, stroking each finger gently with my thumb, and he pulled me close, kissing me with such urgency I could barely think. When he raised his eyes to mine, I nodded and led him down the hall to my bedroom.

~⌒~

Philomena didn't answer the phone in the morning either, so I left a message on her answering machine, and we drove to Maplewood instead. We passed a leisurely afternoon as I showed Pierre the neighborhood, stopping for ice cream at Carmel's before buying steaks and corn for dinner. Being with him was just as comfortable as it had been in Amiens.

"Hi, Mom," Paul yelled as he came in the front door. "Dad said to tell you that he wants to take us to Philadelphia in two weeks. Is that—" Paul stopped talking as soon as he entered the kitchen, frowning when he spotted Pierre. Michael followed a few paces behind.

"I'm starving," Michael said. "What's for dinner?"

"Pierre, these are my sons, Paul and Michael," I said. "This is Pierre Auffret. We met in France."

"I'm glad to meet you," Pierre said as he shook hands with each of them, and I was grateful they had enough manners to greet him politely.

"Are you staying for dinner?" Michael asked.

"Yes, he's staying for dinner." I kept my voice light and even, as though inviting men for dinner were a routine occurrence. "We're having steak and corn on the cob."

"Oh, good," Michael said. "I'm going upstairs. Are you coming, Paul?"

"Nope. I'm going to stay with Mom," Paul said, directing another frown at me.

An awkward conversation ensued, Pierre or I asking questions, Paul providing one- or two-syllable answers. When I declared it was time to light the grill, Paul finally left us alone.

"Is he always so intense?" Pierre asked.

I laughed. "No, I think he's protecting his mother."

During dinner, Pierre captured Michael's interest with stories of World War II flying aces, but Paul remained wary, his eyes darting frequently to mine, as if checking to make sure I was all right. He had always been my sensitive child, attuned to the emotions of others, and I found his behavior touching and vaguely amusing; the son watching over his mother, who had been damaged by divorce. Paul had been the one who checked on my feelings every day after Jim left, the one who sat beside me on the couch while watching TV. He had even endured my hugs when I needed the reassurance that my little family still existed despite the gaping hole of Jim's absence.

Pierre insisted on clearing the kitchen after dinner while I helped the boys put away their belongings and sort through dirty clothes. With school beginning the following day, I agreed to a movie on TV and sat with my sons on either side of me while Pierre occupied the corner chair, tossing amused glances my way. When the subject of going to bed came up, Paul asked Pierre where he was staying.

"He's staying here," I said. "In the guest room."

Early Monday morning, Pierre found me in the dining room sorting Grandmama's letters into piles. Although I had contemplated creeping down the hallway to the guest room after the boys were asleep, some inner voice cautioned me to respect Paul's discomfort at having another man in the house. I hoped Pierre would understand.

"You're up early," I said.

"Mm-hmm. Jet lag."

Dressed in jeans and a rugby shirt, he looked tousled, dark whiskers shadowing his face. He leaned over and kissed the back of my neck.

"Did you sleep?" he said.

"More than I had expected." I turned around to kiss him properly.

"And what are all these things?"

"My grandmother's letters. I found them in her cupboard. At least ten boxes full of letters from as early as 1921. I never imagined her being so sentimental. She kept all sorts of papers too, and I want to see if there's anything important in them. Do you want coffee? It's not espresso."

"Yes, please."

When breakfast was over and the house quiet once more, Pierre and I sat at the kitchen table with second cups of coffee. The phone rang, and I swallowed a quick gulp before answering it.

"Hello?"

"Is this Grace Hansen?" The voice sounded curt and rather official.

"Yes."

"This is Officer Jensen of the NYPD Queens division. Do you know a person called Philomena Walters?"

"I do."

"Someone broke into her house and took something she says belongs to you."

"What?"

"Someone broke—"

"This is shocking. Is Philomena all right? Can I speak with her?"

Pierre had stopped reading the newspaper and was looking at me with concern.

"Yes, but we'd prefer to speak with you in person."

"In person?"

"Yes, Mrs. Hansen. Standard police procedure. Can you come to the precinct office?"

"Of course I can."

I grabbed a pen and wrote down the address, then listened to a few other instructions before the call ended.

"You won't believe what's happened."

"It must have been shocking," Pierre said. "Your face lost its color."

As I explained about Philomena, I raked my fingers through my hair. What was going on? As far as I knew, the only thing Philomena had that belonged to me was a key my grandfather gave her before he died—the key to a locker containing Pierre's paintings.

"I have to go right away," I said. "Will you . . ."

"Of course. But I thought you had to go to work."

"Philomena is more important than work."

On my way to the precinct building in Queens, more than one driver honked at me, and one even gave me the finger when I cut in front of him with little space to spare. I was silent for most of the drive, my thoughts a scrambled mess. The waiting room at the precinct—one of those utilitarian rooms bereft of personality and painted a pale shade of green—housed an assortment of people looking either confused or belligerent. Officer Jensen did not appear for fifteen minutes, by which time I was as anxious as a woman going into labor.

Jensen asked Pierre to remain behind and led me through the bull-pen to a corridor marked by closed doors. He opened the door to room 21, where Philomena sat beside her sister in a cramped space no more than ten by ten, with a long table, six chairs, and a sofa that had seen better days. A bandage covered most of her forehead. I hugged her tight.

"I'm so glad you're here, honey. I was worried sick that man might have gone to your house too. Do you remember my sister, Charmaine?"

"Yes, I do. But are you all right? What did he do to you?"

"Well, mainly he frightened me. I was in the kitchen and heard a knock on the door."

"Told you never to open your door," Charmaine muttered. "Told you a thousand times."

"The chain was on," Philomena said with a pointed look in Charmaine's direction, "but as soon as I cracked the door open, the way I do when I'm not expecting someone, he pushed his way in. Broke the chain too."

"I told you that chain was too flimsy," Charmaine interjected once again.

"Did you recognize him?" I asked.

Philomena shook her head, a slow, deliberate movement. "He wore one of them ski masks. All I could see was brown eyes. Mean brown eyes."

"We've asked Mrs. Walters all those questions," said Officer Jensen. "The intruder put tape across her mouth and tied her wrists behind her back. He had a pistol and forced her to give him the envelope your grandfather left in her care. Apparently that's the only item he took. Then he knocked her out with the butt of his pistol before leaving." Jensen flipped through a few pages of a tattered notebook before closing it. "The question I have, Mrs. Hansen, is what is the significance of the key?"

For a moment, I debated whether to deny knowledge of the key. The paintings were a matter for Pierre and me to resolve. Police involvement would only add delay and complication. But Philomena had been hurt guarding my grandfather's secret. She deserved not only my loyalty, but also my honesty.

"The key opens a storage locker containing four valuable paintings." I hesitated.

"Go on, Mrs. Hansen."

"My grandfather had these paintings in his possession since the end of World War One." I spent the next five minutes explaining the whole story. I left nothing out.

"And where is the locker?"

"I don't know. Philomena, did Grandpa tell you where the locker is located?"

Philomena shook her head.

"And do you have any idea who might have wanted those paintings, Mrs. Hansen?"

"If you had asked me a month ago, I would have said my grandmother. But she died recently."

Officer Jensen spoke in short bursts and with no emotion, like one of those automated-response systems that companies install to save manpower. Each time I answered a question, he scribbled in his notebook, a tight messy scrawl. The wall clock signaled each passing second with a soft click.

"So it's not your grandmother. Who else knew about the paintings?"

"As far as I know, only Pierre Auffret, and I just told him the details on Saturday. Oh, and I mentioned it to Ben Portelli, a longtime friend of my grandparents."

Back in the waiting room, Jensen spent a few minutes talking to Pierre, then took down all my contact information, including the address of Grandmama's apartment and my office phone number.

"And your husband's phone number?"

"We're divorced."

Jensen's pen remained poised above the notebook. He stared at me, eyebrows raised slightly. I rattled off Jim's home and work numbers and gave him Ben's phone number as well.

"Thank you. We'll be in touch."

After delivering Philomena and her sister to Charmaine's apartment, Pierre and I drove back to Maplewood.

"Now what?" I said, negotiating a lane change in order to pass a school bus. "The key's gone. Philomena has no idea where the locker is, and neither of my grandfather's letters mentions the locker location. I've solved one puzzle only to find another one. I feel worse than I did when I left your house because now you know what my grandfather did, and you still don't have your family's paintings."

"Based on what I know about your grandfather, I'm sure he left you another clue. He was a very thorough man."

"But where? I already looked through every file he kept."

Pierre rubbed his chin. "It's not that simple. Whoever took the key has a motive. And he might be dangerous. You have no idea what kind of thugs are involved in art theft. Mobsters, small-time criminals, art collectors, artists, drug gangs. Believe me, I have heard incredible stories."

"Maybe the man who took the key doesn't know where the locker is either. And if that's the case, we need to find the location before he does."

"Do you have any ideas where else to look?"

"I'll have to comb through my grandfather's files again. That's where I found the second letter. Maybe he hid the information there, and I missed it."

Pierre looked at his watch. "What about work?"

"Damn. I forgot all about work."

Since the credenza and filing cabinets were in transit from Grandmama's apartment to Maplewood, we were unable to search through them until Tuesday evening, at which point we started with file folders I hadn't examined on the weekend. Pierre and I each took a large pile and checked page after page until almost midnight, both that night and the one that followed. We found nothing. Absolutely nothing.

"Did he leave anything else?" Pierre said as we sat in the family room sipping scotch.

"Only a box with a few war mementos. They're in my bedroom. I'll show them to you when we go upstairs."

Over coffee the following morning, we debated what to do.

"What if the man who stole the key knew where the locker was and has already taken the paintings?" he said.

"I don't want to believe that."

Pierre held up his hand. "Hear me out. You may not want to believe that, but if it is true, the paintings could already be on the market. Let me make a few inquiries. I will call some people I know in Paris and my acquisitions director. He's connected to some unusual characters. If I call now, it will be early afternoon in France."

"And if they're on the market?"

"We can negotiate for them."

"Do you mean buy them back?"

Pierre nodded.

I said nothing, contemplating the notion of buying paintings from a thief and feeling my life spinning more and more out of control. Who could possibly be responsible? For a wild moment, when Officer Jensen had asked for Jim's phone numbers, I had even thought my ex-husband might be responsible given the timing of our divorce and how solicitous he had been since Grandmama's death. *Think, Grace, think.*

"All right. You call your colleagues. The phone is in the kitchen. Paper and pen right next to it. Meanwhile, I need a break from Grandpa's files. But give me a kiss first." I put my arms around him. "Please."

Before leaving for work, I popped my head into the kitchen to see if Pierre was still on the phone.

"Well, I've put things in motion," he said. "Lucien is going to investigate."

"And now we wait," I said.

"Yes, and now we wait."

CHAPTER 44

September 1991

I'm not a patient woman and was never a patient child. Grandpa used to say, "Good things come to those who wait," but as far as the paintings were concerned, I was definitely out of patience. When I returned home after work, Pierre and Michael were tossing a football in the front yard. Clearly, Paul was maintaining his distance as he was nowhere in sight, and I debated the wisdom of asking him to be more polite but decided to let the matter rest for a day or two.

"What's for dinner, Mom?" Michael said as he threw another pass to Pierre, the ball arcing gracefully through the air.

These days, Michael was always hungry. With feet already the size of Paul's, he was destined to be tall like his father and was in one of his growth spurts. Watching Pierre with Michael reminded me of Jim and what the boys were missing now that their father lived elsewhere.

I cleared my throat before speaking. "I bought lasagna on the way home. And crusty bread to go with it."

Inside, Paul was slumped in front of the TV, sound blaring from a *Star Trek* rerun.

"How was school?" I asked as I began to organize dinner.

"Okay."

"Anything interesting going on?"

"Nope."

Paul was not in a mood to talk; however, his attitude improved during dinner when he discovered Pierre had spent a summer on a submarine researching underwater species and was an experienced scuba diver.

"Why didn't you make that your career?" Paul asked.

"My father thought a business career would be more suitable. I tried business for several years, and now I work at a museum."

"Pierre's being modest," I said. "In fact, he runs the museum in a city called Amiens. It's wonderful, full of paintings and sculptures and antiques from that part of France."

"Museums are stuffy places," Michael said.

Pierre answered before I could reprimand my son for his rudeness. "Well, they can be stuffy, but we work hard to make ours interesting for people of all ages."

"All right, you two," I said when dinner was over, "it's your turn for the dishes. I'm sure you don't have much homework yet. Pierre and I are going for a walk."

"We are?"

"Oui, monsieur."

Since coming home from work, I'd been waiting for an opportunity to tell Pierre my news, and we hadn't gone very far before I blurted it out. "I resigned from my job today."

"You did? *Mon Dieu.* What are you thinking?"

"It's partly your fault."

Pierre stopped and held both my arms so we were facing one another. "Please be serious. Leaving your job cannot possibly be my fault. You must explain yourself." His French accent was more pronounced than usual, and I wondered if I had triggered something from his past.

"I'm sorry, Pierre. I shouldn't have phrased it like that. But I remember when you spoke of wanting a career with more soul, and that notion has been on my mind ever since. And now with Grandmama's death and my trip to France and Grandpa's secret, I've been seeing things from a new perspective. I want to do something completely different." I took a deep breath. "And with the size of Grandmama's estate, I can afford to. I'm going to buy my grandfather's gallery back."

Throughout dinner, I'd wondered how Pierre would react to my decision. My boss had been annoyed, which was understandable given all the time I'd taken off to visit France and look after Grandmama. Promising to work a full six months before leaving had mollified Rick somewhat, and he had even smiled, although a little begrudgingly, when I spoke about my plans for the gallery. "If you were going to another insurance company, I would have been really pissed off," Rick had said.

"Your grandfather's gallery?" Pierre said. "What do you know about running a gallery?"

"What did you know about running a museum?"

"Touché," he said. "But I did spend a few years on the acquisition side before becoming executive director."

Hands loosely clasped, we continued walking, the still, humid air carrying the scent of camellias and the buzz of cicadas. Pierre kicked a pebble toward the side of the road.

"Your decision has caught me by surprise. I don't think I said the right thing."

"That's all right. My changing jobs isn't the only thing bothering you, is it?" Instinct suggested he had other things on his mind than whether I had the skills to run a gallery.

"How did you know?"

I shrugged and said nothing.

"Well, you're right. I live in France. You live here. And if you become the gallery owner, your time will be more than fully committed."

"And that's a problem because . . ."

"I want you in my life."

We stopped walking and looked at one another. I stroked his cheek and chin. *He wants me in his life. He wants me. Me.*

"You do?"

"*Absolument.* I know we only met in June, but I have never felt like this before. Do you know what I've been doing the past few days?"

I shook my head.

"I have been trying to determine which American museums might be interested in my experience."

"You have?" I stepped closer. "I've never felt like this before either."

"So . . ."

"So . . . we'll find a way. I need to talk to Paul and Michael. Paul isn't exactly thrilled that you're here. He's smart enough to know you're not just a friend. Michael is much more easygoing. And then there's—" Pierre put a finger on my lips, and I stopped speaking.

"I am falling in love with you, Grace. When I first saw you at the hotel, I imagined a little diversion with a good-looking American, but within days, you captivated me. You are so different from the women I've known. Curious, adventurous, down-to-earth. From that first dinner together, I felt as though we could talk about anything. Love doesn't always come at a perfect time, you know."

"Love?" I repeated the word to feel its soft echo curl against my tongue.

"Yes, and I want to find a way to be together permanently."

Tears welled up and slid down my cheeks. "Permanently," I said.

"*Oui, tout le temps.* Always and forever."

"*Oui,*" I echoed. "I'm falling in love with you too."

Pierre's declaration should have filled me with euphoria; instead, I was on edge the rest of the evening. When we went upstairs for the night, he followed me into my room and closed the door.

"I think you need a hug," he said.

"Yes, please."

He held me tight, strong and comforting. "Tell me what's wrong."

"I'm stressed out, or maybe a better word is *overwhelmed* by everything that's happened. Grandmama's death. Settling her estate. Finding Grandpa's note followed by what happened to Philomena. Quitting my job. Having you here with me—that's been wonderful, but it has made me very emotional. Life feels like a roller coaster running out of control."

"You don't have to do everything yourself, you know. I can help."

"I guess I've done everything myself for so long I don't even think to ask for help."

"What did I tell you earlier tonight?"

"That you're falling in love with me."

"And . . ." Pierre tipped my chin up and held my gaze.

"That you want to be in my life permanently."

"Permanently means we share things. I am a patient man. For now, let me worry about who has the paintings. All right?"

I hesitated. Returning the paintings to Pierre's family was my responsibility. Grandpa had entrusted me with the task. Honoring his trust these past few months had made me feel his presence again. Pierre's eyes held mine.

"We'll do it together," I said.

He nodded. "Together, then. I spoke to Lucien today."

"Did he have any news?"

"No. He's checked with all his usual sources, and no one has heard of them."

"So what does that mean?"

"He is going to check further, but that will take time."

I didn't know whether to be pleased or disappointed that the paintings were not on the market. If they were on the market, we at least had a chance to buy them back. If they weren't on the market, where were they? And did the man who stole the key know where to find them?

"What do we do now?"

"We wait."

"Patience is not my strong suit."

Pierre held me close. "I know. And to make things worse, I have to return to Amiens."

"When?"

"I booked a flight for Sunday night."

I nodded. Four weeks in France plus a week in Maplewood. For a moment, I wanted to cling to him, tell him not to leave, that the situation was too difficult without him.

"Will you make love to me?" I whispered, and lifted my lips to his.

I woke during the night and watched moonlight play on his face. He mumbled a little, but in French, and I had no idea what he said. *How has this man enchanted me so deeply that I am already prepared to spend the rest of my life with him?* His presence gave me no sense of disquiet, only the certainty that we belonged together.

CHAPTER 45

September 1991

The house felt empty without Pierre. I wandered through the kitchen and family room, re-creating moments together, then went outside where we had watched the stars on garden chairs pulled close so we could hold hands. The guest room was pristine, the bedspread neat and smooth, pillows plumped, Pierre's book and travel alarm clock no longer on the bedside table. For a moment, I wondered if I had imagined his visit, the warmth of his embraces, his Gallic shrug and penetrating gaze.

"What are you doing, Mom?" Paul poked his head out of his bedroom.

"You startled me," I said. "I'm just checking to make sure Pierre didn't forget anything. Are you doing homework?" *Silly goose, you're acting like a teenager.* Silly goose was Grandmama's phrase.

"When's he coming back?" Paul slouched against the doorjamb.

"He lives in France and has a demanding job." Technically, this was correct, but not a response to Paul's question.

"Mom, I'm not a child. I can tell you like each other."

"You can? Well, you're right, we do like each other."

"Good."

"Good? I thought you didn't approve of Pierre."

"He's okay. And he makes you happy. But I don't need another father."

"Right."

I thought it best to leave the conversation there. Any more questions on my part and Paul would retreat into grumpy teenager mode, a mode he seemed to be perfecting these days. Any reassurances about his father, and I ran the risk of revealing more than I wanted.

"Are you really leaving Colonial?" Paul said. "Don't we need the money? You know Dad can't afford to pay any more alimony."

"You told him? I didn't give you permission to tell your father."

"No, of course not, but I've heard him talk about that sort of stuff."

My anger beast stirred. Jim should never talk about our arrangements in front of Paul and Michael. What kind of idiot would do that? I inhaled deeply and held my breath for a moment to calm down.

"Why don't you come into my room, and I'll tell you what's happening." Paul gave me one of his what's-Mom-up-to-now looks, but followed me in, then flopped on my bed and propped his head on one arm. "This is for your ears, not your brother's. Is that understood?" He nodded.

"Grandmama left almost her entire estate to me. There's a provision for my mother and something for Philomena, but everything else is mine." *Now for the tricky part,* I thought. *Exactly how much should I disclose?* "With part ownership in the gallery, the Manhattan apartment, and so many pieces of fine art, your great-grandmother was a wealthy woman, which means we will be more than fine if I quit my job. More than fine. So you don't need to worry, sweetie."

Paul's eyes widened as I spoke. "But I can't imagine you without a job. You love working, don't you?"

"I do, and I'll let you in on another little secret. I'm negotiating to buy back Grandpa's gallery."

When Paul and Michael were younger, I had taken them to the gallery on many occasions, trying to impart some of what I'd learned from my grandfather about the beauty of art. Jim had shown little interest, so these forays were often time spent alone with my sons. Unfortunately, art could not compete with Jim's passion for sports, and I couldn't remember the last time I'd taken them.

"That would be cool, Mom. I always liked the gallery."

"You did?"

"Yeah, but I couldn't admit that to Dad."

I smiled and nodded, although the voice inside my head muttered more nasty comments about my ex-husband. "I've had a meeting with the majority owners, and I'm seeing Ben this week to ask his advice. Now isn't it time for bed?"

Paul grinned. "I knew that was coming."

As he rolled off the bed and stretched, I considered his broadening shoulders and lanky frame, both on the verge of manhood. Girls would soon be interested, if they weren't already, and he would draw away from me, setting aside his mother for other interests. Inevitable transitions that all parents face.

Sleep proved elusive that night, and at four a.m., with nothing but distraction in mind, I went to the basement and began to organize Grandpa's files in categories that made sense to me: family, gallery business, art purchases, household, World War I, important documents, major purchases, miscellaneous. I imagined finding useful information to share with Ben as I prepared for the next meeting with the gallery's majority owners. In the process, I discovered that my grandfather was not only astute, he was also a very thorough man who kept detailed records of every significant transaction from when the gallery first opened in 1922.

The mechanics of examining each folder to decide where it belonged were soothing, requiring enough of my mind to keep it occupied without demanding so much that new worries took over, and I was happily ensconced when I came across a file labeled *BP*.

Papers inside this folder, as with all of Grandpa's files, were organized by earliest date, and the first document was a letter from Grandpa to Ben, offering him a job at the gallery. Inconsequential items followed: letters concerning Ben's salary increases, vacation authorizations, a letter to the bank confirming Ben's income for a mortgage application, a photo of Ben alongside Grandpa when the gallery expanded its premises, Ben's resignation letter, full of gratitude for my grandfather's support and friendship.

I read the next document twice before its contents sank in, for it was a bail bond my grandfather had signed in 1972. The accusation was fraud.

Sitting on an old rocking chair, I stared into the distance, images of Grandpa and Uncle Ben twitching like an old movie reel. Back and forth, back and forth, the rocker creaking from years of neglect. Fraud. Uncle Ben. I could not believe it. More pieces of paper were in the file. A copy of a check from Uncle Ben to repay the cost of his bail, a small newspaper article describing Ben's participation as an intermediary in an art forgery scam targeting small museums, and an article in *Gallery News & Views* announcing the opening of Ben's business two years later. The final item in the file folder was a pink slip of paper with a telephone number, dated a few days before Grandpa died.

Discovering that someone you love is not who you thought them to be is difficult; discovering within one year that three individuals— husband, grandfather, and close family friend—had secret selves was staggering. Even Grandmama was not who I believed her to be.

But surely a fraud conviction from almost twenty years ago was no longer significant. My grandparents had never mentioned it. Uncle Ben made an unfortunate mistake, that's all. I looked at the pink slip of paper again and wondered why my grandfather had kept it.

Puzzle upon puzzle upon puzzle. I picked up the phone to call Pierre.

"*'Allo?*" He answered after three rings.

"It's me," I said in a voice that felt thin and adrift from reality.

"Are you all right? You sound strange."

Pierre listened as I related the story of sorting Grandpa's files and the bombshell contained in the one for Ben. He didn't interrupt until I had finished.

"*C'est bizarre,*" he said.

"Pierre?" I wanted to ask him a question I kept pushing away, the possibility of further betrayal too much to contemplate.

"Yes."

"Do you . . . do you think Ben knew about the paintings all along?"

"Hmmm. That is an excellent question. It is possible. But based on the difficult puzzle your grandfather set for you, he would not have been the one to tell Ben. Perhaps your grandmother did."

"Perhaps. So what should I do? I'm supposed to meet him on Tuesday to talk about the gallery again."

"Well, you have no proof of anything, just a few unexpected papers in your grandfather's files, so there is no reason not to meet with him as long as you act as you normally would. Can you do that?"

"I think so. Do you think I should call the telephone number Grandpa left in his files?"

"It might help to know who the number belongs to."

CHAPTER 46

September 1991

In between meetings on Monday morning, I placed the small slip of pink paper on my desk and bit my lower lip. Ever since I'd read Grandpa's diaries, life had been spiraling out of control into a surreal world of mysterious events, from the man who had followed me to the person who broke into my room to the theft at Philomena's apartment and now the revelation of Uncle Ben's fraud. My hand shook as I punched in the number.

After six rings, someone answered.

"Sterling here." A sharp voice. A no-nonsense voice.

"May I ask who I'm speaking to?"

"Lady, if you don't know who you're speaking to, why did you call?"

I'm not sure what I was expecting, but certainly not rudeness. After a long, garbled explanation about my grandfather's files and the pink slip of paper, during which the man grunted occasionally and once called out "I'm coming," I said, "And that's why I called this number."

"Well, lady, you've reached the NYPD. I'm Detective Sterling, but I have no idea who had this phone number ten years ago." He laughed, a short barking sound. "No telling how many people have had this phone number since then."

"Can you think of any reason someone would have called my grandfather from this number?"

"Investigating a crime, I imagine. That's what the police do, you know."

Despite his obvious irritation, I persisted. "What kind of crime?"

"Could be theft. Could be fraud. That's our unit. It was probably solved a long time ago. I wouldn't worry about it."

"But it's important to me, Detective Sterling." I put on the voice Jim used to say would melt butter. "Is there any way you could help? Perhaps I could talk to the detective who had your office before you."

During the few minutes we'd been talking, phones rang in the background, voices hollered back and forth, a door slammed, and every once in a while there was a loud squeak like a chair that needed oiling. Clearly, the NYPD was busy.

"This is a bullpen, ma'am. You gotta be more senior than me to have an office. I really don't have time for your question, but I'll make a call to the officer who had this job before me. If he knows something, you might hear from him. Otherwise, you should consider the case closed."

Sterling's impatience was clear. Continuing to push would be a mistake. "Thank you, Detective Sterling. You've been very kind. Perhaps you could tell the other officer it might have something to do with stolen paintings. Oh, and my grandfather's name was Martin Devlin."

Of course, I had no idea whether stolen paintings were involved, but I thought the notion would suggest a more serious matter, and

Sterling might actually fulfill his promise. The likelihood of hearing from whomever my grandfather intended to call was remote at best.

Although I tried to concentrate on my work, the thought that hovered at the edge of every activity was the possibility Ben might have something to do with Pierre's paintings. When we met for lunch the following day, I felt sure he would notice my anxiety; however, the conversation flowed easily as I showed him some of Grandpa's files on the gallery. According to Ben, Grandpa had always been a stickler for detail, often sending financial materials back for further clarification or questioning the classifications Ben had assigned.

"He made sure I knew the business inside and out," Ben said with a twist of his mouth that was part smile and part grimace.

"I bet it helped when you started your own business."

"That it did, Gracie. That it did."

As we discussed questions to ask Ian Whittaker and Brian Smiley along with a strategy for negotiating a reasonable price, Ben was his usual self, occasional bluster mixed with charm, nothing that would give the slightest indication of past transgressions or conflicts with my grandfather. The bail bond was real enough, though. *Proof of something,* I thought.

"What are you planning this weekend?" Ben asked after he settled the bill and stuffed his credit card back into a wallet that bore the ragged edges of long use.

"I'm not sure, but I have the weekend to myself since the boys are with Jim."

"How's that working out?"

"Fairly well and easier than I first imagined. Michael loves going to his father's place. Paul is a little less enthusiastic. However, they always come home with stories."

"You're a survivor, Gracie. Besides, having time on your own can be rather enjoyable."

"You might even say liberating," I added. "Thanks for lunch. I should have been the one who picked up the bill since you've given me so many ideas."

"Guess I'm an old-fashioned guy. If I'm out with a woman, I'm the one who pays."

When I arrived home, I called Pierre and relayed the conversations with Detective Sterling and Ben. "What do you think?" I asked.

"Was Ben helpful?"

"Very helpful. He had all sorts of suggestions for improving the gallery. And he's very enthusiastic. It makes me wonder why he didn't stay on with my grandfather. I'm sure Grandpa would have invited him to become a partner."

"Didn't you say they had a falling-out?"

"I'm not sure I would call it that. *Disagreement* might be a better word. Ben told me once they had different ideas about business."

And if memory served me correctly, Ben hadn't looked very pleased when he disclosed that bit of information. Did his displeasure go deeper than I had assumed? His demeanor at lunch had been encouraging and thoughtful, and we'd laughed many times as he reminisced about my grandfather. Nevertheless, the question nagged: Was the man I called my uncle really a friend?

"You know, *chérie*, Ben probably just made a mistake. And he paid for it. It is not surprising your grandparents kept his conviction a secret. You were young at the time, and your grandfather felt you did not need to know. From what you have said, Ben has always been good to you, so there is no reason to assume he's involved with the paintings. What about the detective? Do you think he will find anything?" Pierre asked.

"He seemed dismissive. I suppose I can't blame him. After all, the phone message in Grandpa's file is from years ago. It's likely he promised to look into it just to get rid of me. I don't really expect to hear from him. Has Lucien found anything?"

"No. Nothing at all. But he said to be patient."

"It's maddening. After I found Grandpa's second letter, I was sure the paintings would be in our hands within a few days. And now it's nothing but dead end after dead end. I'm beginning to think we'll never find them."

"Don't give up, *chérie*. And I have some good news: I'm flying in to New York on Saturday because I have to be in Chicago next week. I should be there between five and six."

CHAPTER 47

September 1991

Shortly after eleven the following morning, Detective Sterling called.

"I was wrong," he said without any preamble. "The case was never solved. The officer in charge had been checking known frauds involving works of art and came across Ben Portelli's conviction. Since your grandfather had signed his bail bond, the detective thought he might know something. At the time, there were rumors about Portelli suggesting he was participating in some shady dealings. According to the file, he was also linked to a multimillion-dollar art forgery scheme in Italy."

"Oh my God," I said.

"Nothing proved in either case. How did you know paintings were involved?"

"What do you mean?"

"When we spoke last time, you said the case might involve stolen paintings. How did you know?"

"My grandfather owned an art gallery, and Ben had worked for him, so I thought paintings might be involved." I chose not to mention the ones Pierre and I were looking for. "Ben still works in the art world, brokering deals between buyers and sellers. He has quite the clientele."

"Interesting. Probably a lot of money involved." Papers rustled in the background. "Do you still have any of your grandfather's files?"

"Some of them, although I assume he left a lot of files at the gallery when the new shareholders took over."

"And who are they? The new shareholders."

"Ian Whittaker and Brian Smiley. I'm the other shareholder. My grandmother left her share of the gallery to me." The detective didn't need to know I was trying to buy back the gallery.

"Just a minute," Sterling said.

As he spoke to someone—a grumbling of indistinct words—I checked my watch. I was late for a meeting, and Rick would be annoyed, but I had to hear what else the detective had to say.

"I want to send an officer over to look through those files. Will that be all right? Is someone at your house?"

"You can certainly send someone over, but no one is there right now. I should be home around six."

"Okay. Expect Sergeant Calarco. I'll brief him on what to look for."

They say time moves slowly but passes quickly. An apt expression for the days that followed. The sergeant whom Detective Sterling sent over found nothing in Grandpa's files related to a ten-year-old fraud despite staying until almost midnight. When I crawled into bed after he left, I couldn't sleep but instead rode the merry-go-round of all that had happened in the past eight months. At three a.m., I took half a sleeping pill and woke up groggy and sluggish.

Pierre called on Thursday and said Lucien still had nothing to report. And Philomena called the same day to tell me she was planning to move in with her sister. On Friday, Jim called to ask if we could switch weekends with the boys, and Joan called to cancel dinner with me at the last moment. Detective Sterling did not call.

CHAPTER 48

September 1991

Rain arrived Saturday morning, and the sky had a brooding look, suggesting a day cooped up indoors. Gardening was not going to happen, so I puttered around after breakfast waiting for Paul and Michael to emerge.

"What are you going to do today?" I asked Michael when he came into the kitchen a little after ten.

"It sucks that we're not at Dad's this weekend. He promised to buy me new Nikes, the kind Michael Jordan wears."

"I see. Well, I'm sure he'll take you next weekend instead."

"Yeah, but it still sucks."

"Do you want pancakes for breakfast?"

"Sure. Dad doesn't make them like you do. His are too thick."

"Is your brother getting up?" Michael shrugged. "Can you go and ask? Tell him I'm making pancakes."

Michael did as I requested, slouching out of the kitchen and shouting Paul's name as he stomped up the stairs.

After a lazy morning, I agreed to drive my sons to a movie with the proviso that they would walk home on their own. With a bit of predictable grumbling, they took jackets in case it was still raining when the movie ended. *Nothing wrong with getting a little wet,* I thought.

I hadn't really minded when Jim asked to switch weekends. He had been so cooperative about my trip to France and unexpectedly supportive when Grandmama died. Being flexible was the least I could do in return. I had yet to tell him about Pierre, though I suspected the boys had said something, and I didn't feel the least bit guilty; in fact, I took pleasure in the notion that Jim might be curious or even a bit jealous that someone was interested in me. More than interested.

When the front doorbell rang, I was downstairs looking through Grandmama's letters. A clap of thunder sounded just as I opened the door.

"Ben! What are you doing here? Come in out of the rain," I said.

"I had some more ideas about the gallery, so I decided to stop by. You said you were on your own this weekend, and I figured we could talk some more."

"Oh," I said. "You didn't need to come all this way. We could have met in town next week or talked on the phone. Turns out the boys are here after all. Jim had a change of plans."

"Paul and Michael are here?"

"Well, actually they're at a movie. Something called *Hot Shots!* Teenage boys are fascinated with action movies and ridiculous comedies. I read the summary, and it sounds unbelievably dumb to me, but then I'm just a mother. Did you like that kind of thing when you were a boy?"

I was babbling and a bit on edge. Ben had never just shown up. He was too old-school for that. So why was he here? Another clap of thunder sounded as Ben closed the door before wiping his feet on the front hall carpet.

"Would you like some coffee?" I asked.

"No, thanks." Ben had a jacket on, and his hair glistened with rain. "I thought we might go through your grandfather's filing cabinet."

"Oh. That's not necessary. I've been through it twice already, and in fact the police were here looking through the files as well in connection with . . . with the robbery at Philomena's. But you said you had some other ideas about the gallery. Why don't we sit in the family room? I'll go upstairs and get my notebook."

"I don't think so, Gracie."

"Pardon?" Ben's tone was off. Jittery instead of jocular, and he stared at me as though I reminded him of something he wanted to forget.

"I want you where I can see you. We're going to have a nice little chat."

"A nice little chat. What are you talking about?"

"Where are Martin's filing cabinets?"

"They're . . ." This was wrong. All wrong. Menacing. My brain scrambled for coherence. "I think you should leave, Ben. You don't seem to be yourself."

"I ain't gonna leave, Gracie."

"What's got into you? I've asked you to leave, now leave before . . . before I . . ."

"Before you what? We're going to do this my way, Gracie. I need something from you, and I need it now. Do yourself a favor and cooperate. Sit down over there by the window."

Ben pointed to a chair in the far corner of the living room. What on earth was happening? Such behavior made me wonder if he had suddenly lost all contact with reality. I thought about leaving the house and running to one of my neighbors, but Ben's bulk blocked my path to the front door. The side door could only be reached by passing through the dining room and the kitchen. He was sure to calm down if I went along with his request.

"All right, but you need to explain what's going on. You don't seem to be yourself at all right now." I sat down on the edge of the chair. Ben remained standing.

"I'll tell you what's going on. You think Martin and I were close. Well, we were once. I idolized him. But even with all the money he had, he wouldn't invest in my venture. I could have made a fortune, but your grandfather stood in the way. So I ended up as a middleman in art deals. You can't make money that way. Not big money like I'd planned. He took that away from me.

"And now I want something of his. The paintings he stole during the war. Did you know I was blackmailing your grandmother? Been blackmailing her for years. Every month, she sent me money. Every month. Just so I wouldn't expose her saintly husband. But she didn't know where they were. I kept asking myself who else would know. I thought it might be you, but when you told me about going to France with his diaries, I knew you had no idea about the paintings. I never thought you were smart enough to figure it out, but just in case, I sent someone along to follow you. Bloody idiot got himself killed.

"Back to square one. The last time I saw Cynthia, she said you'd figured it out. You knew about the paintings and were determined to find them. Then I overheard Philomena say something at the funeral that tipped me off. A lucky break, although all she had was the key. At lunch the other day, you mentioned some missing paintings, so I knew you hadn't found them. I have the key and now I need to know where they're stored, and you're going to help me." He laughed again.

"No, I'm not," I said. "If you don't leave right now, I'm going to call the police."

"Not smart, Gracie. I thought we could do this the friendly way, but I can tell you're going to make it difficult."

I gasped as he pulled a pistol from the waistband of his pants, one with a snub nose that fit easily into his hand. Ben waved the gun at me again. "Show me where the filing cabinets are."

My body froze. Ben had a gun. That gun was pointed at me. He wanted the paintings. A long-ago art fraud was nothing in comparison to what was unfolding in my own home. I was sure that if I took a single step, I would shatter into a million pieces.

"Now!" he shouted.

"They're in the basement." My voice quavered. Ben waved his gun, and I took a step toward the basement door. "Ben, you don't want to do this. I'll give you money instead. I just want the paintings. Please."

"No way. I've always admired you, Gracie. We have a lot of history together. But I need a lot of money, and I need it now. You have no idea how much they're worth, and besides, I already have a buyer. You can't charm your way out of this." He pushed me forward, and I stumbled. The phone rang, and I turned my head. "Don't even think about it."

The phone rang again. I walked through the kitchen and flicked the basement light switch and began descending the stairs, my head starting to clear. *Think, Grace, think. He's armed. You're alone. Pierre's not due until after five, and the boys won't be back for at least two hours. You have to get him out of here before they get home.*

At the bottom of the stairs, I took a deep breath and then another, exhaling slowly after each one.

"The files are over there, but I've been through them already. And believe me, I found nothing."

"Well. We'll just have another look now, won't we? And don't do anything stupid. Pull each file out one at a time."

"That could take hours."

"Then you'll have to be quick, won't you?"

A thought occurred to me. "Do you want to see the file he kept on you? The one with information about your fraud conviction?" I knew I'd surprised him by the openmouthed look that came over his face. "Yeah, I know about that, and I was still dumb enough to trust you. I guess you really are a criminal." I pulled out the file and opened it. "See that pink slip of paper? Do you know what that phone number is?" I didn't wait for him to respond. "It's the police. I called them last week, and they called me back after checking their files on you. Another art fraud, only this one was never solved. The detective said you were a suspect in that crime, and apparently you're also wanted in Italy. He's been through Grandpa's files, so he knows all about you. As long as you leave now, I won't tell him about today."

"Huh. That's really rich. You think I'll buy that story? Well, you're wrong. There isn't any detective. We're going to do this my way, Gracie. Start with the files in the top drawer."

"But you won't find anything."

"Quit stalling. You don't want me to be here when Paul and Michael come home, do you?"

I shook my head. I had no choice and began to extract each folder one by one, flipping through the contents so Ben could see them. He didn't know I had removed the folder labeled *AUFFRET* a few weeks ago. After a while, I checked my watch. An hour had passed, and there was still one drawer to go through.

Ben poked me again with his pistol. "Quit stalling."

Forty-five minutes later, I had shown him every folder. The only one that interested Ben was the folder labeled *BP*, which he took.

"What else did Martin leave for you?"

"Nothing."

"Don't give me that. He must have left something else."

"No. All the information was in the diaries."

"Then show me the diaries."

"They're in my bedroom."

"All right. We'll go upstairs. You can show them to me there."

Could I run up the stairs fast enough to get away? Would Ben really fire his pistol? If he did, a neighbor might hear the sound and call the police. Thunder cracked again, loud and furious. No, neighbors would merely assume any such noise was caused by the storm.

"Don't try anything stupid," Ben said, grabbing my left arm.

I had two choices: cooperate fully or risk my sons arriving home while Ben was still here.

"Let's be quick, then. The boys might come home any minute."

Once we were in my bedroom, I grabbed the diaries, the folder marked *AUFFRET*, and the tackle box. Paul and Michael would be home very soon, and Ben had already made it clear he would threaten them as well. I was out of time.

"What's all this?"

"If there's a clue, it's in one of these items. Grandpa left me his diaries, but he also left this tackle box full of items from the war and a file on the Auffret family. The family who owned the paintings. I'll help solve the puzzle if you leave the house with me right now."

"So you let me waste a lot of time going through the filing cabinet? That's not very smart, Gracie. How do I know I can trust you?"

I laughed, a harsh, scraping sound. "That's ironic. The man with a gun is asking if he can trust me. I guess you'll just have to take that chance, won't you?" I grabbed a jacket from my closet. "I need to leave a note for Paul and Michael. I'll tell them I've gone out for a while and they should have pizza for dinner."

Ben hesitated for a moment, then nodded.

"All right," he said.

CHAPTER 49

September 1991

Ben sat in the passenger seat giving directions to a location in Willets Point, full of one- and two-story industrial buildings, mainly brown and drab. Some were boarded up; others had broken windows and doors padlocked with thick, rusty chains. A movie studio could have used the location for a gritty crime scene.

"Turn left here," Ben said.

I obeyed, driving slowly down a back alley, nerves jangling and a headache surging against the back of my neck.

"Park there." He gestured with his pistol at the space next to a stack of weathered pallets.

I pulled in. "Now what?"

"We'll go inside and you can work on solving our little problem."

Ben took me to an office at the rear of an open space, where rusty filing cabinets lined one wall and a wooden swivel chair that had seen better days was tucked beneath a metal desk. He flipped a switch, and fluorescent lighting revealed a phone, stapler, and three-hole punch on top of the desk.

"Your office?" I said in a mocking tone. "Guess you really weren't doing well."

The slap came out of nowhere, snapping my head to the left, leaving my ears ringing and tears in my eyes from the pain. My mouth dropped open as I touched the cheek Ben had hit.

"You bastard."

"Watch your mouth, or I'll hit you again."

Shaking and in pain, I closed my eyes and tried to pull myself together. "You win. Let's get this done."

Ben dumped the tackle box, folder, and diaries on the desk. "Be my guest."

"I'm sure there's nothing else in the diaries. Grandpa used them to leave me a coded letter about the paintings." I gave the letter to Ben, and he spent a few minutes reading what Grandpa had written. "The folder also contains information about the Auffret family and a second letter telling me that Philomena had the key." I showed that letter to Ben as well. "I don't think there's anything else of significance. The only things I haven't examined closely are those in the tackle box." As I said this, I was thinking how stupid I had been. Grandpa would not have left the tackle box for me without some purpose.

I extracted the items one by one: the belt, the buttons, the letters from Jane and the one from Alan Butler, the bullets, and the magazine.

"Those are from a German uniform," Ben said, pointing to the belt and buttons. "The cartridges look like they might be from a British Lee-Enfield rifle. What about the letters?" His tone was less threatening, which I took as an encouraging sign.

"Jane was Grandpa's sister," I said. "She died in 1918 while nursing in France. Alan Butler was his captain until April 1917. He committed suicide after being discharged from a military hospital in London."

I looked more closely at the letters to see if Grandpa had marked them with dots as he had done with his diaries. Nothing.

"The magazine is in French," I said, "and I don't read French."

"Just go through the pages slowly."

Ben leaned close as I turned page after page, pausing to examine each one. "What's that?" he said, pointing to a small article on page fifty-three where someone had underlined a sentence.

La succession de Philippe Auffret contenait beaucoup de tableaux importants.

"I don't know. Auffret is the family who owned the paintings. *Beaucoup* means many, and I think *tableaux* means works of art. But I have no idea what *succession* means in this context."

For the moment, fear had disappeared, replaced by curiosity and an inkling that the solution was at hand. I peered at the sentence, wondering if Grandpa had placed dots beneath the letters. Nothing there. *What scheme did you use, Grandpa?*

"Keep turning the pages."

"But . . ."

"Do what I say."

I turned the remaining pages one by one, but there was no other mark.

"Flip to the back cover."

I followed Ben's instruction, and there it was. Grandpa had written *95* in one corner.

"Locker ninety-five," Ben said. "What the hell use is that if we don't know the location? Go back to that other page."

I found page fifty-three again.

"All right, Gracie. That's the puzzle. You solve it."

"But that could take a long time, assuming I can figure it out. There are millions of coding schemes."

"But you're smart. So get busy. We haven't got all day."

My watch said five thirty. Paul and Michael would be home, and perhaps Pierre would be there as well. Maybe he would think to contact Detective Sterling. He would certainly know my absence was unusual, and he knew I was worried about Ben. Would he put two and two together?

"I need a piece of paper," I said to Ben.

He opened a file cabinet and tossed me a pad of lined paper.

Grandpa had loved puzzles, the more complex the better, and as I grew older he had explained coding techniques used in espionage. The most common involve letter substitution. Sometimes numbers were used, but the text in this case was all letters, so I ruled that out. He might have used the letter shift method, which involved shifting the letters of the alphabet by a certain number; for example, a letter shift of three would replace *A* with *D*, *B* with *E*, and so on. Some people use keyboard-based patterns, shifting letters according to the QWERTY keyboard layout. To crack Grandpa's code, I needed to be calm and patient and I was anything but.

I began by writing the French text on a single sheet of paper. After trying various schemes, I was still baffled.

"Nothing's working," I said to Ben. "And I need to use the bathroom."

The bathroom was an excuse. I wanted to see what else the building contained and if there might be a way to escape. The windows on two sides were chest height, the floor concrete, the space mostly empty except for a long counter against one wall and stacks of leftover floor tiles. The bathroom itself was the size of a broom closet and not the slightest bit clean. Ben followed me and waited outside the door.

Seated once more at Ben's desk, I asked, "What used to be here?"

"A small construction company." He offered no further information. "Get on with it, Grace. Find me the locker location. Or do I go back to your house and bring the boys here for incentive?"

"You wouldn't dare."

"Just try me."

"What happened to you, Ben? You used to be my friend—not just my friend, my honorary uncle. I thought of you as family."

His face softened for a moment. "I'm broke. Worse than that, I owe a lot of money to the wrong people."

"Why didn't you ask Grandmama for help?"

"Your grandmother refused to help. She was very righteous when it came to money. Ironic since she's the one who convinced Martin to keep the paintings. So I blackmailed her instead. And now she's dead." Ben leaned close. "Get back to work," he said. "And remember what I said about the boys."

Returning to the pad of paper and the magazine, I tried to imagine Grandpa building the puzzle for me: the diaries and tackle box, a second letter stored in his filing cabinet, a key left with Philomena. The clue that unlocked the diaries was the date, or what I thought was a date, which turned out to be a sequence of numbers. A frisson of excitement ran through me. *Perhaps Grandpa used numbers to unlock the French sentence.*

I began by selecting every fifth letter from the sentence: *cippfcnepbxrs*. Not enough vowels. I selected every fourth letter: *usnhpuenaeyteirt*. Lots of vowels. In fact, probably too many. I crossed out every duplicate letter: *usnhpeatir*. The word *paint* leapt out, leaving *huser*. I switched a few letters around: usher. Paint, usher.

"What's that?" Ben said, startling me so much I jumped.

"Just two words I found. They probably mean nothing."

"*Paint* is one of the words. That can't be a coincidence." There was a hint of excitement in Ben's voice, and for a moment, I felt it too until I considered the consequences. I had actually hoped not to solve the puzzle. That way, Ben had no choice but to take me home. At least that was what I told myself, to keep from falling apart when we left the house and then again later, when he slapped me so hard my cheek still ached.

"Don't move."

Ben opened the filing cabinet and extracted a phone book so thick it reminded me of pressing leaves when I was young. He thumped it on the desk, releasing a cloud of dust. I sneezed.

"Look up *Usher* and see what's there."

Beginning at the back, I flipped quickly until reaching names starting with *U*, turning tissue-thin pages with care, *Ulster . . . Uptown . . . Urban . . . Usher.* An entire column of businesses starting with *Usher. Usher Clothing . . . Usher Electronics . . . Usher Services . . .*

"There it is," Ben said, reaching over my shoulder to tear out the page. "Usher Storage."

CHAPTER 50

September 1991

Shit, shit, shit, I thought. *Pierre will never get the paintings back now.*

Ben pushed me toward his car, the gun occasionally prodding my back. *Perhaps I could run away now. He had what he came for as well as the key. Why did he need me anymore? And if he didn't need me, why would he keep me alive?*

Dusk had almost given way to darkness with nothing but a filthy streetlight to illuminate the surroundings. To my left, the alley continued about fifty yards before joining the street; to my right, the alley turned ninety degrees just past the building next to Ben's office. I clenched my fists and took a deep breath.

"Don't even think of running away," he said. "I'm a good shot. You're going to drive me to the storage place, and if the paintings are there, I'll let you go for old times' sake." A grating laugh followed.

"What happens after you have the paintings? You can't stay in New York."

"Can't tell you that, Gracie. But don't worry. I have a plan, and I'll let you go as promised. For old times' sake."

Driving along Northern Boulevard through Jackson Heights, I paid little attention to buildings or pedestrians, my mind buzzing. If Ben let me go, could I call the police quickly enough for them to take action? Had Pierre arrived and figured out the message I left for him? Were my sons all right?

Ben had watched as I wrote a message to Paul and Michael before leaving the house. *Had to go out. Back later. There's pizza in the freezer. If Pierre calls, tell him I prefer sterling silver. Hope you had fun at the movie.*

"Who's Pierre?" Ben had asked.

"Just a man I met in France."

"What's this bit about sterling silver?"

"I think he likes me. He wants to send me a little gift, and he asked whether I prefer gold or silver."

Ben grunted. "So you had a little fling over there? Good for you, Gracie." He had laughed and pushed me out the door.

We used the Midtown Tunnel and after going through Gramercy Park turned south on Seventh Avenue. Traffic slowed then sped up in unpredictable patterns. After crossing Houston, Ben told me to slow down as he checked each street sign.

"Spring Street," he said. "Turn left. Usher Storage should be here somewhere. Go slow." I crept along, occasionally glancing at the rear-view mirror. Ben looked at the piece of paper he'd torn from the telephone book and had been clutching in his hand ever since. "There it is." He pointed to a nondescript building on the left. "Park over there."

As we got out of the car, Ben was so intent on the building across the road he didn't notice I left the parking lights on.

Usher Storage promised twenty-four-hour access, and sure enough, a man buzzed us through the front door when we pressed the bell. Ben tucked the pistol into his jacket pocket.

"Locker ninety-five," Ben said.

"Sign here," the security guard instructed. "And I need to see your identification."

"You should sign, Grace." Ben's voice exuded charm.

The guard took my driver's license and started keying into his computer, a slow hunt-and-peck operation. I clenched my fists and tried to breathe slowly.

"Right. Found your name, Mrs. Hansen. Second hallway on the left. Then up the stairs at the end. Should be easy to find from there."

I had expected something derelict, but instead decorative wall sconces illuminated the hallways, and the floors were carpeted in a serviceable but pleasing fashion. The lockers looked more like the kind of closets you would find in a well-to-do home, each door bearing a bronze plaque with an embossed number. We climbed the stairs as instructed.

"This way," Ben said, pointing to an arrow marked *75–100*. We made our way along another hallway, and suddenly, there it was.

Excitement combined with fear. Ben took a key from his pants pocket and slid it into the lock. As he turned the key, the bolt mechanism slid back with a thunk, and when he turned the handle and pulled the door open, a light came on, illuminating four paintings hung in elaborate gold frames. On a hook at the back was a tubular leather case.

"Bingo," Ben said, moving into the locker for a closer look.

I took my chance, slamming the locker door, quickly turning the key in the lock. Ben heaved his weight at the door as I ran. I heard shouting followed by the sound of gunfire. Then more shouts, the words muffled and undecipherable. I ran back along the hallway and down the stairs.

"Call the police!" I yelled at the security guard. "He has a gun!"

The guard stared at me for a moment or two before grabbing the phone, punching a series of buttons just as the unexpected sound of sirens wailed outside. Police appeared at the entrance, and the guard buzzed them in.

"How did you get here so fast?" the guard said with a puzzled look on his face.

Detective Sterling pushed his way through. "Mrs. Hansen, are you all right?" I nodded. "Where's Portelli?"

"Second floor. I'll show you."

"No, you won't. Your friend Pierre is waiting outside. You know, this whole episode needn't have happened if you'd been straight with me."

I nodded again. "I'm sorry. Be careful, he's armed. Locker number ninety-five."

"Okay. Come on, fellas. We have work to do."

Pierre was pacing back and forth outside. When he saw me come through the door, he rushed over and pulled me into his arms. "You have no idea how worried I've been. When Paul showed me your note, I knew immediately you were in trouble, but it took forever to find Detective Sterling and convince him to help."

"How did you ever find this place?"

"Sterling put out a bulletin for Portelli's license plate, and an officer saw the car driving down Seventh Avenue and notified us. We drove up and down the side streets until noticing his car with its lights on."

"I left them on hoping the battery would die."

"Are you all right? Did he hurt you?"

"He had a gun, Pierre. I thought if I cooperated, he wouldn't use it, then . . ."

"Then what?"

"Then he smacked me across the face, and I knew he would do whatever was necessary."

Pierre kissed my forehead and held me close. "Paul and Michael are very worried."

"What did you tell them?"

"The truth."

With Pierre's arm around me, we stood on the sidewalk about fifty yards from Usher Storage. I leaned against him, more grateful than I could have imagined for his solid warmth and strength. Blue lights atop three squad cars swirled round and round. It wasn't long before Sterling led a group of policemen from the building, Ben's arms gripped tightly on both sides by burly officers, his face cut and bruised.

"All secure now," Detective Sterling said when he reached my side. "The paintings are still in the locker."

"Thank you, Detective. I'm so glad you listened to Pierre."

"I might not have if the French National Police hadn't called. Turns out the man who was following you in France had a criminal record involving a string of art thefts and forgeries and God knows what else. They dug deeper and discovered a longtime connection with Portelli. Turns out he's made a lot of dough duping art collectors. Been involved in several major thefts. The French figured all that out.

"Detective Boudin ended up speaking to me since I'm the only detective specializing in this kind of crime. Good thing you'd also called me, otherwise I wouldn't have connected Portelli with you. Are you aware how stupid you've been? He might have killed you." Sterling shook his head. "Portelli is also wanted in Italy and Morocco for art theft."

I was shaking more than I wanted to admit, my head woozy. "Art theft," I repeated. "And fraud. And he was blackmailing my grandmother. I think I need to sit down."

CHAPTER 51

June 1981

Martin crouched down and, reaching to the back of the credenza, extracted the tackle box he'd stored there a few years ago. He checked the contents: two brass buttons and a belt from a German uniform he'd kept to remember all the soldiers he'd killed; the picture taken with Bill, Pete, and Michel right before they shipped out to France; the map showing the location where he had almost beaten a man to death; letters from Jane; the last letter he'd received from Alan Butler; the bullets remaining in his rifle after killing two unarmed German soldiers; and his war diaries, four pocket-sized notebooks recording the war. He knew what he had to do.

He'd been planning for months. As soon as he'd seen the article marking Philippe Auffret's passing, he knew he had to do something. But he was too old now to take the paintings to France, and too old to trace the descendants of the man who'd once owned them. Cynthia would make it impossible anyway, that and the cancer the doctor had diagnosed. Six months, maybe a year, the doctor said.

So Martin planned to ask Grace, but not in a way that would cause a rift with Cynthia. Instead, he had devised a puzzle for her to solve, one he thought would be too difficult for anyone else. On Saturday he and Cynthia were having dinner with Grace and her family. He would give the box to her then. Whether she solved the puzzle immediately or in a few years' time was up to fate.

Martin placed his letter to Grace on the desk and parsed the words into groups of four. Picking up the notebook in which he'd written his name and battalion and the date February 1915, he found a word with the letter *d* on the first page and marked it with a small dot.

Originally he had intended the diaries as a record of the war. Gradually they'd become a place to vent his anger and express the outrage he felt. At times he had wondered if the act of writing had been the only thing separating him from insanity. Martin hoped Grace would understand.

He worked all morning, stopping from time to time to read what he'd written so long ago, emotions tumbling forth as memories surfaced—fear and uncertainty, anger and pain, and the infinite sadness of so many lives lost. Bits of his own humanity left behind with each passing week.

Everyone was gone now. Michel died in 1970 and his wife, Marie, had called to let Martin know. They'd kept in touch after the war and on a few occasions Martin had visited Michel in person, but they weren't as close as they once had been. And Nully, the one who was at his side until the war ended, had passed away in 1951 at age seventy-two. As fine a man as Martin had ever known.

At one p.m. he made a sandwich, carrying it back to the library so he could continue to work. But he reminisced instead, thinking of Cynthia and the joys and sorrows they'd had. The paintings had secured a comfortable living and a degree of success he'd never expected.

"Stolen paintings," Martin muttered out loud.

For years he had resisted that word, but now that his time was almost over, he used it frequently. Although he was pleased with much of his life—especially the love he and Cynthia shared—he could never forgive himself for that act, nor could he forget the many lives he had taken.

What would things have been like without the war, he thought now.

Of course, he would never have met Cynthia, nor would he have likely left Toronto. Jane would have lived and perhaps he and whoever became his wife would have been friends with Jane and her husband, sharing vacations and Sunday dinners, looking after their parents as they aged. Instead, he and Cynthia had lived in Toronto until Lucas was six months old, then moved to New York City. He could still remember his mother's anguished tears at the train station. He sighed. *Such a very long time ago,* he thought.

Martin knew he had disappointed his parents, not just because they lived in different cities but also because they saw so little of Lily, the only grandchild who had lived beyond the age of two. He was glad they never knew of Lily's sorrow.

At three thirty he finished placing dots throughout the diaries. Cynthia would soon arrive home and he needed to hurry. Martin turned the pages of the magazine to the article about Philippe Auffret and underlined one sentence, then wrote the number *95* on the magazine's back cover. Locker ninety-five at Usher Storage. A smile of satisfaction.

Grace will solve it, he thought. *And Philomena has the key.*

With an unsteady hand, Martin took a small piece of paper and wrote,

> *4/3/12*
> *To my dearest Grace, read carefully. I never should have taken them.*
> *Love always, Grandpa.*

He placed it in the first notebook, tied a ribbon around the diaries, and returned everything to the tackle box, which he put back in the credenza.

A few minutes later, he heard the front door open.

"Martin? Are you here, dear?"

"Yes, sweetheart. I'm in the library," he said.

CHAPTER 52

February 1992

From the living room window, I gazed down at pedestrians hurrying along, encased in heavy coats and thick scarves. Beyond the streetscape, the sky was bedding down for the night, stars twinkling here and there and a full moon hovering against the horizon. Cold and crystal clear.

Why hadn't I realized New York was the right place for me to live? Not Maplewood with its sleepy feel and uniformity of people and opinions, its pristine gardens and white picket fences and marching bands. Maplewood had been Jim's choice, and as with many of the decisions we made in our marriage, it had been easier to go along than to argue. If there was one thing I had learned in the past year, it was that I was no longer prepared to go along.

My grandparents' apartment had turned out to be just the right size. Both boys had their own bedroom, and I took over the master suite. Grandpa's library had been converted into a place where we could all watch TV. Now redecorated in a more contemporary style with lighter fabrics and fewer drapes, the living and dining rooms felt spacious and welcoming. Most of the artwork remained in their original positions.

Jim had not been pleased with my decision. He wanted his sons close by; however, I held my ground, and our Maplewood house was now for sale. Paul was excited to live in the city, and Michael was beginning to adjust.

"There you are," said Pierre, walking across the room toward me. "You look beautiful."

Pierre's compliment brought a blush to my face. My dress had a black velvet top and black silk skirt shot with silver streaks to match the silver piping edging both bodice and cuffs. As for jewelry, I'd tried on many options before selecting my grandmother's pearl necklace and drop earrings. While I wasn't used to being called beautiful, I had been pleased when I looked in the mirror.

"What are you doing in here?" Pierre said. "Don't we have to leave soon?"

"Just looking at my city. And yes, we do need to leave soon. I wish . . ."

"What do you wish, *chérie*?"

"I wish I could do some things over again. Like working in the gallery with Grandpa and being closer to Grandmama as she aged. She was lonely, Pierre. She had no close family except me, and I was too busy raising my children and resenting the way she behaved. You should read some of the letters she saved. They've given me a new perspective on her life."

"Cherish wisdom as a means of traveling from youth to old age."

"Is that a quote?"

Pierre nodded. "And the rest of it says something about wisdom being more lasting than any other possession."

"Well, maybe I've gained a little wisdom this year. Do you know if the boys are ready?"

"They're waiting in the TV room. A dreadful concept, if you ask me, to have a whole room dedicated to the television."

I just smiled. After almost eight months, I was becoming accustomed to the many cultural differences between our countries. Some were amusing while others made me stop and think. So far, none had sparked major disagreement. Since the end of September, we had been spending two weeks together each month: one in Amiens and one in New York. Pierre was in open discussions with three museums close enough for us to live in Manhattan, and we both expected he would soon move here permanently to be with the boys and me.

The event that evening was the reopening of the gallery. Negotiations had taken longer than anticipated, but by the end of November, the gallery was eighty percent mine, and with the help of the previous owners and an event-planning firm, I had organized a launch party, inviting major collectors, well-known artists, various socialites, a few celebrities, and several politicians, including Mayor Dinkins, although I doubted he would attend. Pierre had flown in two days ago.

"Did you practice your speech?" he said.

"Many times. And I incorporated some of your suggestions. I know I'll be emotional, so I've kept it short."

As soon as we arrived at the gallery, Pierre and I, along with Paul and Michael, went to see the Luras paintings, positioned as a group on the west wall with plenty of space for viewing. Tonight marked their debut showing, and publicity about the event had featured their discovery. I would tell the full story in my speech.

"They're truly stunning, Pierre," I said.

Like the paintings hanging in Pierre's museum, Luras had used color and composition to create harmony between these four landscapes, replicating sharp blues, muted yellows, and deep reds through various objects. My favorite was a seascape that made me think of Honfleur. It conveyed energy and mystery through the use of small sailboats racing along the sea while a strikingly dressed couple, whose faces could not be seen, watched from the shore.

"Seeing them featured like this makes me very proud. I forgot to tell you I spoke to my father today, and he has finally promised to donate the paintings to the museum, although he wants to hang them in his home for a while. During that time, I'm sure he will bask in notoriety. But for once, everyone else in the family has sided with me, and we have prevailed on him to do what I believe my grandfather would have wanted."

I placed my hand on Pierre's arm. "They deserve to be hung with the others you've collected. I want to be there when that happens."

"You will be if I have anything to say about the matter," he said, putting an arm around my waist.

By six thirty, the gallery was buzzing with conversation and filled with people mingling around the pieces on display. Waiters circulated with hors d'oeuvres and wine, and Madison Gold, the event planner, kept a watchful eye from a small platform set near Pierre's paintings. We had kept the décor simple in order to feature the artwork hanging throughout the gallery, a mixture of modern and traditional pieces by artists who had long been associated with Grandpa's business, plus a few newcomers to the New York art scene.

Ian Whittaker and Brian Smiley had helped select the artists to feature. Although I was now the majority shareholder, both retained a ten percent interest, and Ian, the younger of the two, had committed to remaining active for a minimum of five years. I suspected Brian's involvement would be limited as he had initially been resistant to my offer and had been the one who had delayed the deal. I had a lot to learn.

Madison waved at me. She and I had agreed to wait until the room was decently full before commencing the formal portion of the evening.

"I'm going to the lectern," I whispered to Pierre, who had been talking to a small group of dark-suited men. He excused himself and followed me.

"Ladies and gentlemen," I said, then waited as the room gradually grew quiet, glad that my dress was long enough to hide my shaking knees.

"Ladies and gentlemen, thank you for coming tonight to the relaunch of this gallery space under the new name of Gallery Devlin. The name honors my grandparents, Cynthia and Martin Devlin, who founded the original gallery in 1922. I won't bore you with a lot of family history; however, some of you will know that my grandparents raised me from the age of five. During the past year, I've discovered many new details of their lives, and these have enriched my understanding of what it meant to serve during World War One, as my grandfather did, and what it meant to live in England during that time, as my grandmother did. I've also gained new insight into the challenges they faced as a young couple moving to a new country and the talents required to build a successful gallery.

"With the assistance of Ian Whittaker and Brian Smiley, who have run the gallery with great skill and dedication since my grandfather's retirement, I plan to continue the strategy of offering new and traditional forms of art at Gallery Devlin.

"Tonight I also have the distinct pleasure and honor of showing four paintings by the well-known nineteenth-century landscape artist Sebastian Luras. I hope you will indulge me as I tell you about the history of these paintings." I looked at Pierre before continuing. "Standing beside me is Pierre Auffret, whose grandfather owned these paintings at the outbreak of World War One."

Whispers flew around the room as I continued the story, and guests murmured to one another. Several shifted closer to the lectern, and a cameraman twisted the dial of his zoom lens in my direction. I paused, glancing at my two sons.

"As you might imagine, discovering this secret has been difficult for me and my family. However, recently I found a letter my grandfather left, asking me to return the paintings to the Auffret family, and in that letter, he expressed his deep, lifelong regret for taking the paintings, so I am doubly pleased that Pierre Auffret is with us tonight to take them home to France."

I stepped aside to let Pierre take the microphone.

"Thank you, Grace. And thank you to everyone here this evening. On behalf of my entire family, I am delighted to be returning these paintings to France. My grandfather's personal collection featured many French artists; however, his favorite was always Luras, and he spent many years trying to find these paintings. I am also delighted to announce that they will hang in the Amiens Museum, where I work. The French public deserves to experience their beauty, but for the next few weeks, they will charm those who visit Gallery Devlin."

The rest of the evening was a blur as I mingled with the guests, trying to speak to as many as possible, seeking new connections and reestablishing old ones. People shared stories about my grandparents, and those who mentioned the stolen paintings were quick to add a word of appreciation for my grandfather's reputation. Beyond publicity, the event was also a commercial success, with six works sold and several others on hold for potential buyers.

"I suppose it's time to go," I said, watching the caterers clear the last dishes and Madison gather up leftover brochures and information sheets.

"I have a taxi waiting for us outside," Pierre said. "Is everyone ready?"

"Why doesn't your family keep the paintings, Pierre?" Paul asked as the taxi took us home.

"A good question. My father thinks we should, but I feel that after such a long absence, they aren't really ours anymore. I have considered the matter carefully, and I think my grandfather would approve."

"Maybe you should give some of Nana's paintings away, Mom."

"Maybe I should."

In the morning, local newspapers featured the opening and the Luras paintings with eye-catching headlines:

STOLEN PAINTINGS REVEALED. GALLERY OWNER DISCLOSES LONG-HELD SECRET. FRENCH FAMILY REUNITED WITH MASTER-PIECES.

Pierre and I read every one.

"How do you feel about the publicity?" he asked.

"I'm glad to get it over with. Although the headlines are sensational, the articles themselves are fairly balanced. Maybe readers will be able to identify with a soldier's long-ago actions. But," I said briskly, "it needed to be done."

"And now you can get on with running the gallery."

"Speaking of which, I promised Ian that I'd be there by eleven this morning. Do you want to come along?"

"No," he said. "I have a few errands to do."

Sitting in the backseat of a taxi on the way to the gallery, I thought of my grandmother. In the weeks after her funeral, I read all the letters she kept. That process revealed much more of her heartbreak at the time of her son's death and the difficulties she experienced when my mother's mental health deteriorated. It also revealed a months-long depression after the doctors confirmed her inability to have more children. That she had chosen not to tell me about these parts of her life filled me with sorrow and made me wonder at the kind of relationship we might otherwise have had.

I did know she loved me. Letters from my great-aunts referred to me as Grandmama's "unexpected joy" and the third child she never had, commenting on the everyday details of my childhood she must have shared in her own letters home. Her boxes of mementos also made it clear how much my grandparents loved one another: photos, Valentine's cards, pressed flowers, letters, a broken watch kept in an envelope marked *Martin's wedding gift to me* in Grandmama's back-slanted writing.

Regret wove a cloud of *if only* and *what if*, which I tried to dispel. Grandpa had lived his life with regret, and now I knew that Grandmama had her own regrets. Such negative emotion, whether for what one has done or for what one hasn't done, keeps a person trapped in the past, holding him or her back from taking chances, festering over time like an untreated wound, and spawning pain—or worse.

Regret is part of life. I regretted my failed marriage and difficult relationship with my grandmother; I regretted staying too long at Colonial Insurance, and, for that matter, failing to join my grandfather at his beloved gallery after college. I wanted to learn from these mistakes and live my life looking forward, not backward. I could not change the past, but I could change the way I lived my future.

Running the gallery would make the bond with my grandfather even stronger. Living in the apartment marked a new beginning and would be a tribute to my grandmother. Finding Pierre was more than a new beginning—being together was itself magical.

Time would determine the rest.

AFTERWORD

First and foremost, thank you for reading *Time and Regret.* My greatest joy is to know that others have chosen to read the stories I tell.

A few years ago, my husband and I traveled to northern France to visit the battlefields, monuments, cemeteries, and museums dedicated to World War I. That trip was an amazing opportunity to see firsthand the areas where Grace traveled and where Martin experienced such wrenching horror and devastating losses. Ian and I went to Bailleul, Lille, Amiens, Ypres, Mont St. Eloi, and other towns and villages, and to memorials at Vimy, Courcelette, Thiepval, and Passchendaele. We visited the museum in Peronne just as Grace and Pierre did. We stayed at a hotel on which Chateau Noyelle has been modeled and dined at its next-door restaurant. Those places and the landscape of the region engaged every sense and, along with the hundreds of pictures taken, have fueled descriptions of meadows, villages, windows, tastes, gardens, restaurants, and other parts of the story.

Of most significance to *Time and Regret* is the night we spent at a café in the small town of Honfleur. Shortly after the waiter poured our first glass of red wine, I wrote a few words in a small notebook.

"What are you writing?" Ian said.

"An idea for a story," I replied.

Refusing to be put off by my cryptic response, Ian persisted. "What's the idea?"

"Nothing much. Just thought it might make a good story to have a granddaughter follow the path her grandfather took during World War One in order to find out more about him."

Ian took on a pensive look and no doubt had another sip of wine. "You could include a mystery," he said.

Now, you should know that mysteries are my husband's favorite genre. Indeed, I suspect mysteries represent at least eighty percent of his reading. So I played along.

"What kind of mystery?"

And that, dear reader, was the birth of *Time and Regret*, as ideas tumbled out and the plot took shape. Needless to say, the bottle of wine was soon empty.

Time and Regret is my third novel set during World War I, and the casualties and appalling conditions of that war continue to haunt me. Three emotions dominate—anger at the incredible ineptitude and callousness of military and political leaders; sorrow for what soldiers were forced to endure; and bewilderment centered on fundamental questions of humanity. Why did soldiers put up with unspeakable conditions for so long? What kind of leader would choose to use such catastrophic measures as poison gas? How could citizens live through nightly bombardments knowing that at any moment they might be hit? How could officers send their men "over the top" time after time? As of this moment, I ask the same questions of countries like Syria.

Writing Grace's point of view in first person was a liberating experience, and I enjoyed contrasting her voice with that of Martin's as a young, disillusioned soldier. I gave Martin a role in the 19th Battalion of the 4th Brigade of the 2nd Canadian army based on a real World War I account. To make his experiences as authentic as possible, I read that battalion's diaries, available on a Canadian government website, for each day of the war as well as other reports of the 4th Brigade's battle experiences. Since I had already researched World War I extensively for *Unravelled* and *Lies Told in Silence*, two earlier novels, I was able to draw on those materials as well. Battles and campaigns mentioned are as accurately depicted as I could make them.

Chumley Park is fictional; however, facilities of this nature did exist during the war and dealt with much more harrowing conditions than Martin's using what we might now call barbaric treatments. The artist Sebastian Luras is also fictional.

Small details make historical fiction come alive and I've sprinkled many throughout this novel. For example, RMS *Royal Edward* was a troop transport ship; soldiers carried something called a "housewife" containing items such as thimble, needles, thread, and buttons; "Keep the Home Fires Burning" was a popular World War I song; in the days preceding the battle for Vimy Ridge, soldiers did indeed dig graves for those who were soon to die; the Daughters of the Empire Hospital existed; and there was a casualty clearing station at Longuenesse housed in a former chateau much as described.

Fiction is only complete when readers add their imagination, experience, and thoughts to the story, and I love hearing from those who've read my novels. All comments are welcome. You can reach me at mktod@bell.net.

M.K. (Mary) Tod—August 2016

ACKNOWLEDGMENTS

Time and Regret would not exist without my husband's creativity and critical eye for a good mystery. Nor would it have been published by the highly professional folks at Lake Union Publishing without the help of Jenny Quinlan, my freelance editor; Carol Bodensteiner, author of *Go Away Home*; and a great group of beta readers: author Margaret Evans Porter, Kris Holtan, Douglas Burcham, and Glenn Stephens. At Lake Union my thanks go to Jodi Warshaw, who took the initial plunge to acquire the novel; Amara Holstein, whose insights and sensitively crafted suggestions enhanced the story; and Miriam Juskowicz, who managed the novel through to production. I am also grateful for the very professional Lake Union production team.

Encouragement is the Holy Grail for authors, and I've been blessed to find it in many places. My family has cheered me on, offered feedback, and listened when I needed an ear. Friends have enthusiastically purchased my two previous novels and asked that wonderful question: "When is your next one coming out?" Readers have sent heartwarming emails and posted reviews. Beyond these sources is the generous community of historical fiction authors who have responded to questions or sent along suggestions on social media and shared and tweeted my posts and promotions.

Grateful thanks to each and every one of you.

ABOUT THE AUTHOR

Time and Regret is M.K. Tod's third novel. She began writing in 2005 while living as an expat in Hong Kong. What started as an interest in her grandparents' lives turned into a full-time occupation writing historical fiction. Her novel *Unravelled* was awarded Indie Editor's Choice by the Historical Novel Society. In addition to writing historical novels, she blogs about reading and writing historical fiction at www.awriterofhistory.com, reviews books for the Historical Novel Society and the *Washington Independent Review of Books*, and has conducted three highly respected reader surveys. She lives in Toronto, Canada, with her husband and is the mother of two adult children.